The Pride of Central

David

B Mc

Copyright 2019

Joshua 1:9

2

This book is dedicated to my family:

My wife Shannon,

my son Joshua,

my father James,

my mother Earlene,

and my brother, Jeff.

For all the encouragement you gave me to write this story, and for all the help and time you gave me while writing it.

This book is also dedicated to my friends Dan and Laura, who made me believe I could accomplish one more impossible thing.

Central's Roster

Pete Roc, pitcher and center fielder, 19 years old
Andy Roc, catcher, 16 years old
James Thun, third baseman, 18 years old
John Thun, pitcher and first baseman, 16 years old
Jimmy Alphos, second baseman and shortstop, 16 years old
Matt Leander, left fielder, 17 years old
Nate Stoltzfus, right fielder, 18 years old
Tom Connor, second baseman, 17 years old
Sam Long, pitcher and center fielder, 18 years old
Phil Barr, shortstop and second baseman, 17 years old
Ted Biever, pitcher and outfielder, 18 years old
Jules Iscar, left fielder, 18 years old

Coaching staff

Nick Deem, head coach
Jerry Baptiste, assistant coach
Joe Arim, assistant coach

Home field
Central High School

Funded by
Harry Antes

Other teams in the Lebanon County Armed Services League
Vigortown (defending champion)
Lavernon
Nickelton
Meadville
Hemtown

6

Prologue

Even before sunrise, the old man knew exactly where he stood. He knew where everything was. When the rays of the dawn light hit the ground surrounding him, the old man smiled. This field was good.

He walked from the grass to the dirt, smelling the aroma from the field that had been mowed yesterday. Yes, this was good.

After a few steps, the old man stood with his foot on a white square. He left it and walked ninety feet to another white square. Ninety feet between the bases. That was good.

He gently strode onto another patch of grass until he reached a small hill of dirt and stood on top of it. The old man breathed deeply, not from weariness but appreciation. Then he stepped down and walked straight ahead. He stopped at the five-sided white plate that completed the diamond with the three bases. The plate was exactly sixty feet and six inches from the top of the pitcher's mound. This was good.

He stepped behind the plate and turned back towards the field. The old man took another breath. He simply enjoyed being on this field. Even with no one else here, it was beautiful. It was over three hundred feet from the plate to the outfield walls in front of him. It was fifteen feet to the wall and a mesh screen behind him. The stadium was filled with peace.

But the field was not for him to enjoy alone. He wanted to enjoy it with others.

As the old man walked to one gate in the fence, he took a minute to walk along the benches in the dugout. This dugout was for the nearby team from here in Vigortown. The bench on the opposite side of the field was for visiting teams. This was good.

The old man opened the gate, gently closed it, and walked up the bleachers behind home plate. There were smaller bleachers along the sides of the field he could have chosen. But whenever possible, the old man sat in the seats behind home plate in the topmost row. After going up the concrete steps, he turned around once he reached the last row. It was in front of the box for the

8

announcer and sportswriters. There was plenty of seating around the field for three-hundred spectators. This was good.

Yes, it was all very good here.

The old man sat in a seat. This was one of many baseball fields he would visit. Only a limited part of the story to unfold would happen here. He already knew that. This field and the team in Vigortown would have a part to play, but theirs were relatively small roles. More of the story would involve a team from another town, Central. In time, one character in the tale would be his son.

The old man loved his son deeply. But his son was not part of the story yet. It was best to relax now. Everything would take place as it should. Everything would happen at the right time.

The old man remained in his seat, waiting for the teams to arrive for the season opener. It would be several hours until the first pitch, but he didn't mind. He had all the time in the world.

Part I

The Pride of Central

Chapter 1

Baseball. No matter how much one understood the sport or how many plays a team executed correctly, sometimes no one knew how a game would turn out.

Take this season opener, Pete thought to himself. He did not expect it to be this close.

Maybe Pete had overrated Central's chances since he was the pitcher tonight. He had spent his freshman year of college pitching against men with years of collegiate experience. He thought he should mow down nearly every Vigortown batter he faced.

Mostly, Pete had been right. But in the bottom of the third inning, he had gotten lazy on his grip of a couple breaking balls. Those lapses had led to two runs for the defending Lebanon County champions. Pete, the only nineteen-year-old on Central's roster, knew he could not ease up like that.

Neither his head coach, Nick Deem, nor the assistant coaches, Jerry Baptiste or Joe Arim, said anything to Pete when allowed the two runs. When other players made mistakes, they received guidance. But they expected Pete would correct himself. Berating himself for the earlier mistakes, Pete retired nine Vigortown batters in a row in the next three innings.

Now in the visiting dugout of Wagner Memorial Stadium, Pete hoped that his teammates would get him back on the mound to close out the contest. Armed Services baseball only had seven innings, so this inning should be the last of the game. But Central trailed Vigortown 2-1, so a few batters had to hit under the stadium lights to keep the game going to the bottom of the seventh.

Pete watched the Vigortown pitcher's warmup tosses for the last inning and smiled. He saw that his opponent, unlike himself, was running out of arm strength as the night progressed. Pete walked over to where three of his teammates had grabbed their wooden bats. "He's lost some velocity," Pete said of the man on the mound. "Give it an extra fraction of a second."

His teammates heeded his advice. A few minutes later, John ripped a single to right-center field that scored James and Jules to put Central ahead 3-2.

Central did not score again, but Pete was confident he did not need more cushion. He ran out to the mound and threw his eight warmup tosses that the rules permitted before facing the Vigortown batters. He did not speak to his catcher before or after the warmups. There was no need to discuss strategy. The catcher was the person on the team who knew him best, his brother Andy. They had already planned how to approach each batter coming to the plate.

The first hitter had struggled to put his bat on the ball all game long. The muscles in his right arm still felt strong, and the June heat helped keep him loose while in the dugout, so Pete gave him nothing but fastballs. He put all of his six-foot, two-inch frame into each throw. One was fouled off, but the batter swung through the others for a strikeout.

It was his eighth strikeout, Pete thought. He was not certain, but it did not matter. The only statistic that mattered was getting one win tonight.

Pete and Andy realized that they could not put fastballs down the middle of the plate against the following two hitters. Andy gave the signal for curveballs, two fingers extended. Pete threw a curve low and outside, then another curve barely in the strike zone on the inside corner. He followed with a fastball well outside on purpose. That set up a low, inside curveball on the next pitch. The batter hit it on the ground to Pete's right.

Pete turned to see the third baseman, James, field the ball and make a perfect throw to first base. The fielder at first, John, made the routine catch as if he and the third baseman were brothers.

Which, of course, they were.

One more out to go. Pete was sure he could get this last batter to chase high pitches. Andy must have agreed since he was setting up his catcher's mitt almost at the height of the batter's eyes. He signaled for a changeup.

A changeup that high was dangerous. If the batter realized he was getting a slower pitch, it would give him time to get his bat around on it and send a fly ball deep. But Pete had confidence in his changeup and all his other pitches.

He was a better pitcher than any Vigortown player was a hitter. Likewise, Pete believed Central was a better team than Vigortown.

While keeping his motion the same as it was for a fastball, Pete threw a high changeup. The batter hit it, but the sound of the bat told Pete that it was not solid contact. The ball flew high but not deep into right field, where Nate snagged it.

With the game now over, Pete noticed the sounds from the stands again. About thirty fans cheered Central's one-run victory from the concrete bleachers behind home plate. About seventy others were quiet after Vigortown had started its county title defense with a loss.

It was not a large crowd, but Pete knew from his last three years of Armed Services ball that regular-season games seldom got large crowds. So be it. There were no bonus points for big attendance. Central had won its opening game.

Now it was time to turn winning into a habit.

* * *

Pete still felt like he was gambling with his life when he let Andy drive home from games. But his brother was still only sixteen, and the thrill of a new driver's license had not faded. Pete let the same person he trusted with calling pitches also be trusted with the steering wheel. Anyone from Central knew they were brothers, but he doubted any of the remaining Vigortown fans who saw them get into the car would have guessed. Pete was tall enough to feel cramped in the car, almost smashing his buzz-cut blonde hair against the roof. Meanwhile, the top of Andy's mid-length brown hair did not quite reach the top of the driver's seat headrest.

"Even Coach Deem seemed happy," Andy said as he started the engine.

"He's been waiting a long time for a team with enough talent to win the county," Pete said while unbuttoning his jersey. It was a blue top with "Central" in red script across it, the same one he had worn the last three summers. It also had an "Armed Services" badge on the right shoulder. Pete enjoyed playing in the Armed Services baseball league. He wished that more people understood that "Armed Services baseball", meant only that a local post of veterans sponsored a team of sixteen to nineteen-year old boys. He, Andy, and most of their teammates were not in military families.

"I almost told the Vigortown guys we've taken the county title away from them," Andy added as he drove the car out onto Route 22.

"You better not have," Pete said, with a slight edge. "Don't give anyone bulletin-board material. Or social-media material," he added, updating one of Coach Deem's old-fashioned phrases.

"Don't worry. I only thought about it. I didn't say it. But I am right, Vigortown is the one team that has a chance against us, and now we beat them."

It was a conversation they had been over several times. It felt a little different now to Pete since Central had won its season opener over Vigortown. That was all the more reason for everyone to be confident in Central's chances against anyone else in the league. Pete could not see the other four teams in the county finishing ahead of them in the standings. Hemtown, Nickelton, Meadville, and Lavernon City were not as good as Central. But in baseball, any opponent could be a threat in any game.

"Vigortown is the only threat to finish in first place," Pete agreed. "But we still have to play them two more times later this season. And that doesn't mean we can relax against the other teams. You realize Hemtown will be out to get us."

"Has a good baseball team ever come from Hemtown?" Andy said, glancing to his brother.

"Get your eyes on the road. And no, not that I can remember. But they are the only border rival we have in the county. We will have to be prepared, or they'll be ready to knock us back to one win and one loss."

"Look who's Gloomy Gary."

"That's not my nickname."

"So what does Sal call you?"

"That's a pet name, not a nickname. And it's private."

There was silence for a few moments, and Pete hoped it would last until they finished the twenty-minute trip home. He missed his girlfriend. Pete had spoken to Sal over the phone several times over the summer but had not seen her since the last day of spring semester at college. A little quiet would give him a few moments to think of Sal and about what he wanted to say when he called her tonight.

But he also wanted to visualize the next game. Central's next contest would be a game at Hemtown. Pete would not be pitching in it. Not enough time would have passed to rest his arm. Pete would most likely play in center field, meaning he would have to impact the game with his fielding and hitting.

But, before his mind drifted towards his girlfriend or the next game, Andy broke the silence. Pete was not surprised.

"If I had a cool nickname, more girls would like me."

Pete liked his brother, but sometimes he was just crazy. "You think girls would like you if you had a cool nickname?"

"I mean, we have an awesome last name. 'Roc.' The girls could call me 'solid' because I'm solid as a..."

"This is the stupidest idea you've ever come up with," Pete said, knowing this would not even make a top ten list. "You don't give yourself a nickname, other people do. And if you're awkward around girls, you won't be smooth because one of them calls you by a nickname. Besides, James and John have nicknames, and neither of them is seeing anyone."

Andy shrugged. "Thunder Boys. They earned that nickname."

Pete stifled a chuckle. John and James were known to get into shouting matches with each other. And with the last name Thun, the Thunder Boys nickname began early in middle school.

"At least they have the good sense not to shout at Coach Deem. Or Coaches Arim or Baptiste," Pete said, referring to the two assistant coaches for Central.

"Seriously," Andy asked, "Why are you the only guy on the team with a girlfriend? I mean a real, steady girlfriend."

"First, because I'm older and more mature. Second, I found a mature girlfriend at college, so we make the effort to keep a long-distance relationship working. And third, shut up and turn on the radio."

They had been over that conversation before too, and this time Andy kept his silence until they made it home.

Chapter 2

The ball skipped off the grass a little faster than James anticipated, but he was playing far enough behind the third-base bag to get his glove on it. The ball bounced to him like a rocket, so James had time to throw to first base to end the inning.

James walked over into the visiting dugout of Hemtown's field. He received compliments from both assistant coaches for the clean grab and throw. Coach Deem was saying something to Matt, the pitcher.

Matt was not the same caliber of pitcher that Pete was. Everyone on the team knew no one else could pitch like Pete. But Matt was doing well so far. In fact, everyone seemed to be doing well now, as Central held a 6-2 lead going into the fifth inning. James did not care what Coach Deem was telling Matt, but most likely he wanted to make sure his arm felt good enough to keep pitching today.

James relaxed on the bench, thinking he would not bat in this inning. John was hitting first. After taking two pitches, John hit a line drive down the first-base line that hit the ground in the outfield. James thought it should be a double, and it was. But for no reason that James could tell, John tiptoed to the bag instead of taking a long stride or sliding into the base.

James tried to remind himself of how much he loved his brother. He wanted to tell himself that John was the youngest player on the team and thus was likely to make mistakes. But it still boiled his blood to see John do those little things wrong, even when it did not hurt the team. It also riled him up that someone not paying attention might get confused which brother made a mistake. John was only a half-inch shorter and kept his hair a little longer. Otherwise, they would look almost the same from a distance in their baseball uniforms.

They never got mixed up with any of their ten teammates since James and John were the only two dark-skinned players on the squad. Though Phil tanned well, James knew he would never catch up in handsomeness.

When the next batter came up, James noticed that Pete had pulled Matt aside and was speaking to him a few seats down on the dugout bench. This time, he heard the conversation.

"I think you may be tipping off Hemtown," Pete was saying. "Every time you're going to throw a curveball, you nod your head right before the pitch."

"Huh. You're right. I never thought about it," Matt said, unhurt by the correction.

"That's why the last batter hit the ball so hard. He was waiting on the curveball. Try not to nod before any of your pitches, so you don't tip them off," Pete said. "Or, try to nod when you throw a fastball to confuse the hitters. But it's best to concentrate on the pitch and not do anything to signal them what you're about to do."

"I will. We don't need to fool these guys, anyway. I'll just keep my head steady."

James listened to the conversation between the two pitchers, realizing how he hoped to be like Pete. He did not wish to be a pitcher, rather the player who could impact the game when he was sitting in the dugout. Pete was not only the oldest member of the team, but he was also their leader. It may be an unofficial title, but it was still true. Pete's skill and a year of college baseball experience put him in that position. But gentle guidance of the other players defined Pete as a leader. At least, that was what made James respect him.

Then James noticed, on the other end of the bench, Coach Deem giving an approving nod with a slight smile across his wizened face. He must have listened to the discussion and held admiration for Pete as well.

The crack of a bat returned James's focus to the field. Little Jimmy, nicknamed because he was the shortest of Central's players and to distinguish him from James, singled to center field. John scored from second base on the hit.

John came into the dugout and received a few high-fives from the coaches and his teammates. But James wanted to scold him for his weak approach to second base on his double. It did not matter today, but in a closer game, those stutter steps could lead to a key out.

But before James got up from the bench, Pete walked by him and whispered, "I'll handle it."

James watched as Pete walked up to John and gave him another high-five. Then he whispered as he pointed to second base. John said nothing but nodded.

Two things crossed James's mind before the half-inning ended and he trotted back out to third base. First, Pete seemed to like the sound of his own voice, considering how often he gave out his solid advice. Second, there would be another chance to yell at John for a silly mistake.

Later, in the bottom of the seventh, James caught a foul pop-up that was the final out of game. After securing the ball in his glove, he looked at the Central fans that lined the third-base side of the field. He saw almost as many supporters as had attended the Vigortown game. When he was playing the game, James only heard the voice of his mother. He would like to ignore all the off-field noise, but there was no way to keep her cheers from reaching his ears and mind.

Both he and John could be loud, but they had inherited their tones from their mother. James had inherited his physique from his late father. He was the most muscular player on Central's roster. That was not bragging. It was stating a fact. He showed his strength in the spring when he was the only player to hit a home run for Central's high school team. John had a little muscle too, but he was leaner. But no matter how much they had grown, regardless of how much muscle they had built, their mother would cheer them on as if they were still six years old.

His mother's cheer for the last out reached James's ears, but what his eyes saw were the three girls from the softball team who were there too. Maggie, Jo, and Martha. Blonde hair, black hair, redhead. Tanned, dark-skinned, forever pale.

It was like an art museum of the prettiest female athletes in town. It was always nice to have them supporting him. James tried to pretend that they were celebrating him even if he knew they were applauding the whole team's victory.

James also saw that one old man, old even when compared to his coaches, on the top of bleachers. He never learned the man's name. James never saw him give a cheer or a jeer, or do anything besides watch. But he attended every game, in the highest seat from the field.

The old man and young girls were distracting James. Now, he had to line up with his teammates to shake hands with the Hemtown players. Then they listened to Coach Deem's post-game speech and cleared all the equipment out of the dugout. All those things were no inconvenience when Central had dominated its border rival. In fact, nothing felt like a problem when Central had started its season with two wins and no losses.

This year, James realized, Central should win the county championship. If my brother doesn't mess it up, he added to himself.

Chapter 3

In Armed Services baseball, there was little pomp for a team's opening home game. Still, Nick Deem could feel a bit of electricity as Central started its home opener.

That they had already played and won two games did not matter. It did not matter that the head coach had seen more season openers, season finales and games in between than he could ever hope to remember. It did not matter that the Central's home field had no special features to it. The field, near Central High School, was a standard grass-and-dirt field with brick dugouts and an outfield fence of average depth.

The first game of the year on your own turf always means something. It means more if you win it, though, Coach Deem thought to himself.

Victory was never in much doubt. John, the youngest of the players on the roster this year, was pitching his first Armed Services game. Coach Deem had figured that Nickelton was a good opponent for his sixteen-year old pitcher to face in his first turn on the mound. The team from the southern edge of Lebanon County was considered a light-hitting team. Nickelton was living up to that reputation.

Meanwhile, Central had scored three runs in the first inning and a couple more in the second. Coach Deem had to make sure his team stayed focused until the last out, but there were no signs of any comeback by the visitors.

While watching John retire another outmatched batter in the sixth inning, Coach Deem realized that everything had gone as he had hoped. Almost everything.

There were twelve good baseball players on Central's roster. There were no average players, nor were there good athletes at different sports who happened to play baseball to fill time between other seasons. These were a dozen good baseball players. A few of the younger ones lacked experience, and Pete's talent stood out over the others. Still, it was a formidable roster.

The only thing that did not work out for Coach Deem was he never got the eighteen good baseball players that he had hoped to suit up. Instead, the last six slots of the official Central roster were blank.

He wanted to have those additional six players for many reasons. It would give Central more pinch-hitters and relief pitchers available every game. That would help build up the program for future years. The daily practices and games might even help some boys in the community stay out of trouble.

But Coach Deem was a stickler for following the letter of the law. He knew it, and the athletes around Central knew it. If someone wanted to play for his baseball team, they had to attend every game and every practice. It might mean they could not work a job over the summer, or they would miss a family vacation, or they would disappoint a girlfriend. Deem did not want to hear about any of those excuses.

In his playing days, which were admittedly long ago, those were the rules. Those rules should never have been changed. The Central coach from five years ago was not so strict. Back then, Central would get seventeen or eighteen players to join the team, but the coach could depend on less than half to show up for a game.

Coach Deem would not tolerate any more of that. He would rather have twelve boys who loved the game than a full roster where half-hearted athletes. More reserves would give Central some things it lacked now. One left-handed hitter would help. But it was not worth the headache of wondering who would be there for game time.

And there were benefits to having the smaller roster. With fewer pitching arms, it was easier to give John a chance to throw in the third game of the season. Though the competition was not much of a challenge, the old coach noted as a Nickelton batter grounded out, John was not making any obvious mistakes either.

If John or anyone else were making any small blunders that escaped his notice, Coach Deem was sure that his assistants would tell him. Joe Arim held the same view on most issues, baseball or otherwise. Both Nick and Joe were retired senior citizens. They both had played baseball since their youth, and both were widowers with their children living in other states. Coach Deem was a few years older, and perhaps his face was more weathered than Coach Arim's. Otherwise, they looked the same, like two old men retired from everything except baseball.

There was little else to do with life for either of them other than going to the ball field, though Coach Deem missed his wife each time he returned to his empty home. But he could not complain about how much time he spent involved in the game to which he was dedicated. It seemed that Coach Arim felt the same way.

The other assistant, John Baptiste, was not cut from the same cloth. He was also a dedicated baseball man, but from a different generation. He was in his mid-thirties and struck Coach Deem as being a touch lenient about the rules. But Coach Baptiste's oddities stood out. His hair was longer than anyone else's on the team, standing out with a bushy mane while the other coaches had their conservative cuts. Even the players did not have hair as wild as Coach Baptiste's.

As for Coach Baptiste's diet, well, how many times had he seen the man eat honey-dipped grasshoppers? Coach Deem had never even understood the organic diet craze. Coach Baptiste's eating was beyond his ability to explain.

His peculiarities did not hinder Coach Baptiste's abilities to coach the players. He had less of an age gap to overcome with the boys and grabbed their attention a little more easily than Deem or Arim did.

The last Nickelton batter of the inning flew out to Jules, the left fielder. Cliches about games not being over until the final out aside, Coach Deem knew Central would win this game.

For the first time since taking over as head coach, he had a team that should win the Lebanon County championship and should advance to the Region D tournament. They might even win a few games at that tourney.

Less than an hour later, when Central had finished its 9-1 win over Nickelton, Coach Deem was even more convinced of the team's destiny. His post-game talk with the team, like usual, was brief. Most of what he had to say was said in practices and before the game. After victories in particular, he liked to keep it short.

"Guys, I like what you did today. Not just winning, but not making any mistakes. No errors today, no one was thrown out stealing, no one missing a sign from a coach. You can win at least half of your games just by doing your own job. John, excellent pitching, especially for your first game. Nate, Ted, Phil, good hitting. Everyone, good job today. Be here on time for tomorrow's practice, and the next game is..."

"Here, against Meadville, in two days," Coach Arim said.

"Then practice at five tomorrow and arrive even earlier the next day. Bring it in."

The team put hands together in the middle of their huddle. "Central!" the boys shouted. Then they worked on their post-game chores. Some players had to clear the dugout of equipment, some had to take bases off the field, and others had to rake the footprints out of the infield dirt.

Then all the players talked to their families and tried to flirt with the girls in the crowd.

Coach Deem chuckled at the youth and walked back to the dugout to get his clipboard and scorebook. He would call in the final score and statistics to the local papers that covered the Lebanon County League.

He silently corrected himself. They were not newspapers. They were media outlets, which happened to print papers. The printed word was a reminder of his own age.

There had been one thing he could have mentioned to his players, he realized, but he did not want to ruin the win in their first home game. There would be plenty of time to bring it up again in tomorrow's practice.

For five years now, neither Coach Deem nor his assistants could get these boys to put down a quality sacrifice bunt.

* * *

"Get that stuff out of here before someone sees us," Pete said, getting out of his car.

James looked up from where he sat on the sidewalk. "Just one more swig," he said.

"You too, John," Pete said, as his brother Andrew got out of the passenger seat.

John shook his head but threw his beer into a nearby trashcan. James also tossed his can, never getting off the cement. Even if he had stood up, James could not have stared down the taller Pete. Not that he wanted to challenge him. Pete had all his respect, so telling James not to drink while he was around was no big deal.

Pete sat between James and John on the sidewalk in front of the abandoned strip mall on the eastern edge of the Central school district. The place had become an empty parking lot for a series of empty shops that had not been occupied since the players had been in elementary school.

It was not the nicest hangout place, but it was one where James and John figured no one would see them drinking. So that's where they met up tonight after the team's practice, and after someone else had picked up the beer for them.

Pete was carrying a six-pack himself, but one that did little to excite James. The star pitcher pulled a can off and tossed it to James, then to John and Andrew. "Here. Have a drink that won't get us cited by the police."

"Oh, soda," James mocked. "Getting a little wild there with your vices, aren't you?"

"Next thing, he will offer us chocolate," John agreed.

"Hey, get off his case," Andrew said. "At home, when our parents aren't around, he pumps the volume on his music up to two."

Pete shook his head and smiled at the good-natured ribbing. The two sets of brothers were comfortable picking at each other. Pete's strictness had become their favorite subject ever since he received a baseball scholarship.

"You guys don't have to worry about losing a scholarship like I do," Pete said. "The fewer times I'm around anyone who is doing anything that could make me look bad, the better."

"Would they really revoke your scholarship over drinking beer?" John asked. "Or for being around other people drinking?"

Pete shrugged. "I doubt they would go that far, but there could be a suspension. Why take the chance? Where did you get the beer from, anyway?"

"Mr. Hellickson," James said. "I thought he was giving it to everyone on the team."

"You can always count on Mr. Hellickson to let you enjoy yourself," John added.

"Guys, this summer, we need to be enjoying ourselves on the baseball field," Pete said, cracking open a soda can. "We've got a big opportunity this year. You guys don't want to lose games for getting caught drinking."

James wondered about that. Getting suspended for underage drinking might be a bad thing for him and the team, but mostly he thought it would upset his mother. It would doubly hurt her if both he and John were caught. The last thing James wanted to do was disappoint his mother after all she had been through in the five years since his father died. But she must suspect they were drinking occasionally. His mother was a teenager once too. At least she said so.

"Doesn't Mr. Hellickson offer you a beer or two?" John asked, pulling James out of his thoughts.

"He does, but I'm just not interested," Pete said. "I told him I couldn't take the chance. He gets frustrated with me when I say no. But I'm serious about my scholarship. I'm not taking any chances. And besides, Sal doesn't drink either. I don't think she would be happy if someone caught me drinking."

"Show me a picture of Sal," James asked.

Pete pulled out his phone, tapped it a few times, then handed it to James, who became jealous right away. He wished he hadn't asked.

"Yep, if avoiding beer keeps her happy, then I agree. Don't drink," James said, handing the phone back.

"As beautiful as she is, she's even sweeter when we're together," Pete said, only to have James groan while Andy and John waved him away.

"Once you guys have a real girlfriend, you'll feel the same way," Pete replied, sliding the phone into his pocket. "I don't mean one of your two-week flings. I'm talking about something serious."

James thought about that for a moment. He had dated a couple of girls. The relationships lasted longer than the two weeks Pete had said, but never more than two months. He knew he was not ready for a serious commitment. There were several girls at the baseball games, and it felt good to have a pretty girl cheer for him when he came to bat. James especially appreciated the three who attended every Armed Services game: Maggie, Martha, and Jo. But as a steady girlfriend, James thought none of them were right for him.

He had allowed himself to be distracted by thoughts of those girls anyway, James realized. He refocused on the conversation that the other three boys were having.

"We need to take advantage of this season," Pete was saying. "I'll be too old for Armed Services baseball next year, so this is the last time we're all going to play together. It's about time we won something. No, it's long overdue that we actually win something."

"You're sounding like Coach Deem," John said. "Next you'll tell us about all the virtues of sacrifice bunts."

"I won't do that," Pete answered. "Giving the other team an out does not help us. It also won't help you if a college scout is in the stands. If you get the signal to make a sacrifice bunt, either pretend you never saw the sign or intentionally miss the next pitch. Then swing away."

"It would thrill Coach Deem to hear his coach on the field talk like this," Andy said. "But I agree."

"He would be more than happy with me getting you guys, and the others, to realize we've got to play better overall. This has to be the year for big things, bigger goals, bigger accomplishments."

"Our win over Nickelton yesterday put us at three wins and no losses, you know," James said. He said it half to point out that fact, but also to cover for zoning out of the conversation for a minute. "That's got to count for something."

"A little, but not as much as we'd like," Pete said. He took his can of soda and chugged it. A moment later, he let out a huge belch. "There, that's about what three wins should be worth to us after all the years we've been playing together."

"This will be our best season," John said. "Better than any year we've had in Armed Services, high school, any other league. If you had still been pitching for us during this high school season, we would have won our division. We might have even won in the district playoffs."

"But what did you actually do?" Pete asked.

"Um, third place in the regular season. Good enough to get in districts, but we lost in the first round."

"That's exactly my point," Pete said, standing up. "We're not just average ballplayers. We should have won titles of some kind. Sports fans should be talking about Central baseball as one of the best teams in this region. Newspapers and websites should have big stories about us. You know, we might be as talented as that team over in Berks County...what's their name?"

"Puraton," Andy answered. "They've won more Pennsylvania state titles than any other team."

"We can't help that someone has a better history than we do. But today, we should be on Puraton's level. We're not, because we're always finishing as a runner-up in the regular season and losing in the playoffs."

"That's not entirely true," Andy said. "We won one district playoff game in high school last year, your senior year."

"Yeah, you pitched a shutout against Middleburg," James agreed.

"Yes, I did," Pete answered. "Why haven't there been more games like that since last spring? We lost in the second round of districts. Then last summer we got swept two games to none in the playoff semifinals. Over this spring, you guys didn't win a playoff game, and my college team only won a third of its games."

There was silence for a moment. James wondered if Pete was trying to inspire them or depress them. "Where are you going with this?" he asked.

"We're better than that," Pete said. "A first-round playoff win should be routine for us. That should've already happened three times, not once. This summer is our last chance to do it together, to win championships, to string several playoff wins together."

"We will," John said. "We're the best team in the county, and we're already the only team without a loss. In part, because I pitched well," he added, turning to James and hitting him on the shoulder.

"You still can't make silly little mistakes," James answered. "No more little ballerina steps while running to bases. If we're going to win, we need more than your arm."

"James is right," Pete said. "We can't have any distractions if we're going to live up to our potential. I'm not saying we have to go undefeated, but we shouldn't have any games where we make it easy on the other team. We should win Lebanon County and the Region D tournament. But we can't afford any extra problems along the way." Pete gestured to the trash can. "So no getting caught with beer."

"Enough," James said. "So, is our season a success only if we make it to the national tournament?"

Pete laughed. "I hadn't thought about that yet. To go to nationals, we need to go through the county, Region D, the state and Mid-Atlantic tournaments. Still, that should be our ultimate goal, no matter how hard it would be to get there."

James considered that. "Those bigger tournaments, reporters from other states cover them, right?"

"Sure," Pete said.

"So, not just that guy from the Lavernon paper?" Andy asked. "Lucas whats-his-name? Not that he shows up at many of our games, anyway."

"But if we made it to the Mid-Atlantic or national tournament, the scores of our games would appear in other states, right?" James asked.

"Some places would show our box scores and have stories and videos from our games just because they were national tournament games."

The sudden excitement for James must have been showing on his face. Pete was smiling and gesturing in front of him to get him to calm down. "We may be good enough to get there," Pete said. "But we have to earn it. That means a lot of work, and playing by the rules on and off the field."

James heard him but it only barely registered in his mind. He knew how long the Armed Services baseball playoffs were. They started in local county tourneys but ended in a national tournament. However, this was the first time he considered what it would mean to play in it. The notoriety that could come from having "Central" in headlines around the country seemed immeasurable.

"Yeah," James said aloud to the others but no one in particular, "Let's have them read about us in California and Texas."

Chapter 4

Pete meant for the pitch to be on the inside corner of the plate, but instead, it was past the outside corner. Pete grunted. Too many throws were getting away from him today. Not that it was affecting the game. In the fourth inning, Central was still beating Meadville 5-0. Pete had contributed to the offense with a double and had scored a run afterward on James's hit. Andy had helped too, with a single that scored both Matt and Jules.

Central was hitting, but Pete was not pitching his best. His brother-catcher knew it too.

"Does anything hurt?" Andy asked as he walked out to the mound to hand the ball back to Pete after the Meadville batter took his base on balls.

Pete shook his head. He could not blame Andy for asking. That was the fifth walk Pete had allowed already, which was more than he usually gave up in an entire game. Fortunately, Meadville had only one hit, which was why the visiting team had not scored.

Andy walked back behind the plate and bent down into his crouch. As Pete got into the stretch for his first pitch to the next batter, there was no fear about losing control of the game. He knew Central would win. But Pete also knew he could not finish the game as the pitcher.

He threw a strike right down the middle of the plate, which the right-handed hitter watched. On the next pitch, Pete added a little strength to the fastball, and the batter swung a little late. It turned into a lazy fly ball to right field, which Nate caught without breaking into a run.

That was how it had been all game. If Meadville batters had to swing at Pete's pitches, they either missed or hit them weakly. But too often Pete had let them reach base without swinging the bat. That meant that Pete had already worked too hard.

The fly ball was the last out of the inning, so Pete walked into the dugout. When he sat down, he heard Coach Deem call out, "Ted, warm up."

That's what Pete suspected. He had thrown too many pitches to keep him on the mound. There were two reasons behind the coach's decision. First, there were pitch-count rules in Armed Services baseball. Those rules dictated how many pitches one person could throw in one day, and how many days that person would have to wait before pitching again. Pete had not reached the limit of one-hundred twenty pitches in one day yet. If he did, though, he would have to stay off the mound for four days. There was no reason to risk that in a regular-season game with a big lead.

But there was something else. Coach Deem did not want to have any trouble with Pete's college coach if Pete hurt his arm from overuse. Though the college team and Armed Services team held no authority over each other, they did not want to cause problems.

Coach Deem had not yet come over to tell Pete he was out of the game, so he stayed focused. He processed through all the possibilities in his mind for the next set of batters he could face in the fifth inning.

Meanwhile, Nate led off the bottom of the fourth and hit a ball that flew over the left-field fence for a solo home run. That was the first home run of the season for Central. Pete and his teammates walked out around home plate to give Nate high-fives and slap his batting helmet after he finished circling the bases.

After congratulating Nate in the dugout, Coach Deem walked over to Pete, who was back in his spot on the bench. "We're going to bring Ted in to pitch now. I just wanted us to get one more insurance run."

Pete nodded. Given a chance, he would pitch every inning of every game, but neither rules nor physics allowed for that. "Okay, coach."

There must have been disappointment in his tone since Coach Deem patted him on the shoulder. "There are bigger games ahead."

Pete did not go out to center field, as the coaches let him rest for the final innings of the game. Ted took his place on the mound. Though he allowed two runs, the victory was assured.

Later, after Central had beaten Meadville 7-2, Pete was calculating in his mind when he might retake the mound. According to the pitching rules, he could not throw against Lavernon in the next game. It would be unwise to pitch in the following contest against Hemtown even if it were within the rules. Maybe the game after that.

"Did you notice he was here again?" Andy asked.

Pete came out of his thoughts and then resumed putting his equipment in his bag. "Who?"

"That old man," Andy said. "I didn't notice him during the game, but I saw him walking back to the parking lot."

"No, I didn't notice," Pete answered. "When I'm pitching, I never notice anything in the crowd. Besides, I think he's been to every game all four years I've played here."

"Yeah, he always shows up," Coach Arim said. He was walking back into the dugout to pick up his notebook. That was where he kept his notes on pitch counts and other notes on each pitcher. "I don't know anything about the man, even his name. I just know he attends every game, at home or on the road, and he always takes the highest seat in the bleachers. That's surprising for a guy who looks that old. You'd think he'd want to save his legs."

"Do you think he's a scout for a college?" Andy asked.

"No. The old man would be taking notes, and he wouldn't always be coming to our games. A scout has to watch lots of teams if he's trying to keep a college team competitive."

"He could be one of those baseball lifers, like you and Coach Deem," Pete said, hauling his bag over his shoulder. He gestured to Andy to make his way to their car.

"He's more than that," said another voice. Pete turned and saw Coach Baptiste had strolled to them. "It's true, he's been here since the beginning. But that old man has a son, a son who knows so much about this game, I wouldn't even deserve to carry his cleats."

"Oh, I didn't know that," Coach Arim said. "So, you've met his boy?"

Coach Baptiste smiled. "I'm pretty sure we will all see him soon."

Pete was now bored with the conversation and walked away, Andy behind him. Having fans in the stands was nice, but beyond his family, it did not matter to him who was watching. In the back of his mind, he wondered what Coach Baptiste meant when he said the old man had been here since the beginning. The beginning of what?

As he and Andy got to their car in the emptying parking lot, something caught his eye. Nate, one hero of the win with his home run, was talking to Maggie, one of prettiest of Central's fans. She was standing by her car, and Nate was leaning on it. They were not touching, but they were close together, and at ease with each other.

There was nothing specific that caught Pete's attention. But there was a subtle hint to the upturn of Maggie's smile, the way she swayed at the hips. Likewise, he saw how Nate was just a little too close to her without Maggie acting at all uncomfortable. That made it easy to see a building attraction.

"Think something's happening there?" Andy asked.

"Not sure," Pete said. It was none of his business, anyway. He did not like other people prying into his relationship with Sal, and he had no intention of finding out about anyone else's relationships. "Maggie played outfield for the softball team. She's probably reminding Nate to take a couple extra steps to his left when a left-handed batter is hitting."

"Or Nate is reminding her he is single again," Andy quipped.

Pete got in the car, deciding he would drive this time. He thought about how Maggie was acting like Sal had when things started to click between them. He smiled. He needed to call her again tonight.

* * *

Maggie finished the can of beer. "Oh, that's a good buzz."

Nate pulled another can off of the six-pack's ring. "Want another?"

She gave him a smile but shook her head. "No, buzzed's enough. I can't seem drunk when I get home to my blarents."

"Blarents?" Nate laughed. "I don't think you're fooling anyone."

Maggie giggled uncontrollably. Nate opened another can for himself.

Finally, she calmed. Maggie had only one beer, but it was enough to loosen her up, which was another reason she did not drink a second. She needed caution with a boy around, even a boy as good as Nate.

"I can't have a hangover tomorrow, either," she said. "I work the opening shift at the grocery store."

"I'll drink this one in your honor," Nate said, chugging his.

They were at a small playground near the Central pool. Though there were people in the pool after dark, no one was at the playground other than the two of them. Maggie remembered when their mothers would take them here to play together when they were small children. She recalled dozens of moments like that throughout the years. Their families lived only a block apart in town, so they had seen each other often since they were toddlers. They were each other's first friend.

Though they never dated, Maggie and Nate's friendship grew each passing season. Mud pies, hide and seek, tag, toys, video games, picnics, bonfires, first cars, first jobs, and lastly graduation earlier this month. Every childhood and teenage event, they were always there for each other.

But Maggie suspected that Nate's invitation tonight might be about more than enjoying some beer together as friends. When he talked to her after Central's win over Meadville yesterday, she thought there might be a hidden message in his words. She should be able to trust him like she had when they were children.

She trusted him. And Maggie was certain what was coming next.

"How'd you get the beer this time?" she asked. "Your parents will figure out you stole six cans."

"Mr. Hellickson got them for me. He didn't even ask me to pay." Nate downed more of his second beer. "But you're right, can't go home stumbling drunk. I'll save the other three for next time."

"You can always count on Mr. Hellickson to let you enjoy yourself," Maggie said.

Nate leaned back against the jungle gym, and Maggie sat down at the bottom of a slide. Even in darkness, she could see Nate's smooth baby face. It made him the cutest of all the players on the team. He had been her friend for years, but that face, the blonde, spiked hair, the soft brown eyes – he had always been her favorite.

But more than seeing Nate's face, she could see the question brewing behind his eyes. Did she want to answer? She could stall a moment longer.

"You should take a couple extra steps to your left when a left-handed hitter up," Maggie said. "You don't always have to wait for the coaches to yell it to you."

"I prefer to wait until I'm told to move. It helps to know where I'm supposed to be and what I'm supposed to do, but it's best to know what the coaches want me to do." Nate set down his beer can. "Do you think we'll win the county this year?"

It was not an idle question from Nate. Maggie knew he respected her opinion on baseball. Softball and baseball were so similar that she understood the game from experience. She also watched enough of Central's games to realize what the team was going through.

"Yes, I believe you will. You might even do more than that. You'll probably win every game that Pete pitches, and you all hit well enough you can win most of the other games. I just wish you had one or two lefties in the lineup."

"It would help, but none came out for the team," Nate said. "So, you going to keep stalling, or are we going to talk?"

Here it comes. Nate is my friend, and I'll tell him the truth, Maggie thought. Maggie had let it slip out the last time she and Nate were talking alone. She was not sure if she meant to say it or not, so she tried to make it sound like a joke. But she could not fool Nate.

"Be serious with me. You've never been with a boy?"

Maggie shook her head. "Never. Surprised?"

36

"A little. You were dating the same guy through our whole senior year."

"Well, that was not a hot romance. I think I may have been with him so I could say I had a boyfriend. That may have been the reason he was with me."

"I'm sorry."

"For what?"

"That you were with someone that long and it fizzled out."

"It happens. We didn't have a big fight, and nobody cheated, so I can't be outraged. But that's not the reason we didn't give in."

"Oh?" Nate asked, raising his eyebrows.

"My mother made me promise. I gave my word I'd wait until after I graduated high school."

"Why? I mean, why was graduating the difference to your mother?"

"I was born during my mother's senior year of high school. Dad had graduated the year before, and it all worked out in the long run. But Mom didn't want me to have to face any extra burdens until I at least had a diploma." Maggie hesitated, not quite willing to admit her fear that, no matter how cautious she might have been, she would have gotten pregnant in high school if she had taken even the smallest chance. Then she continued, "So I gave her my word, and I kept it."

Nate stood up and moved towards her. "And now that you've graduated?"

"I can decide as my own woman now."

Nate sat next to her on the slide. "Are you telling me all this, um?" He seemed unable to finish the question.

"I'm torn," Maggie answered anyway. "We're never going to be in love, and we both know it. We've been friends for too long for that to happen now. But I've known you longer than anyone, and I trust you more than anyone. And I'm not sure I want to, er, keep waiting." Maggie was too nervous to say any more.

An awkward silence fell over them. Maggie felt a deep emotion toward Nate. It was not romantic love. It was a love that only the best of friends share. There could never be a real romance between them. Still, if it was going to happen this summer, Maggie thought Nate should be the one.

He put his arm around her. The evening was already hot, yet his touch made her feel a new warmth. "You and me? I would, but, well, we need to be sure we want to do this. Not kind-of sure. We need to be one-hundred percent certain that this is what we want."

Maggie knew Nate was right. It was one reason she trusted Nate more than the other boys in town. Nate had a degree of caution. If this did happen between them, it would need to be at the right time and place.

She picked up her empty beer can. "I don't want it to happen when I've been drinking, even a little. In fact, I don't want to decide for certain if we are going to do this unless I'm sober."

"That's fair. Next time we can be alone, we won't bring any drinks. We will decide responsibly."

Maggie just nodded and laid her head against his shoulder. He tightened his grip around her but did not become more amorous than that. She felt safe.

But she only felt seventy percent sure she wanted this to happen between Nate and herself. More than anything, she needed more time to decide.

Chapter 5

Occasionally, James wondered just how high some of these pop-ups soared into the air.

He was not wondering that now. There was no time to wonder with Central one out away from winning its fifth straight game and the said pop-up coming into his area around third base.

James listened for Phil's voice. Wait, had Little Jimmy come in to play shortstop for him earlier? Whoever the shortstop was, he was the general of the infield. If he called for it, the pop-up was the responsibility of the shortstop.

Since there was no other voice, James yelled "Mine, I've got it," The ball made its long descent into his glove. He secured it with his other hand and heard one umpire call, "Out, that's ballgame."

The final score was 11-2, Central beating Lavernon. Failure to catch the pop-up would have no impact the outcome. Nevertheless, James was nervous about dropping one of those easy catches in front of everyone. He had done it a couple times back in Little League, and John never let him forget it.

But today he made that catch and soaked in the applause from the home crowd. It was mild since the result was never in much doubt. Everyone realized that Central had its best team in years while Lavernon had not had a good team since anyone could remember. This victory was fine for the players and the fans, but a win over Lavernon did not generate much excitement for anyone.

It seemed to James, though, that the crowd grew larger game by game. Good. Before he got into the line to shake hands with Lavernon's team, he looked to the bleachers. Maggie, Jo, and Martha were there, as usual, but no other teenage girls were there.

Dang.

There was another quick post-game speech from Coach Deem. The coach gave the briefest hint of displeasure that Central was not getting sacrifice bunts down, but James ignored that. He grabbed his equipment and walked back to his car. Only when he got there did he remember that today was John's turn to rake around home plate and cover that area of the field with a tarp. Their mother had already gone home as she often did after a game. Many of their post-game conversations were at their house.

So James had to stay here until John was done. He put his equipment bag into the back of the car and was about to hang out with the other players. Then he heard someone call his name.

Turning around, he saw a man who appeared exactly how James hoped he would look like in twenty years. He had perfect hair, a muscular physique, and stylish sunglasses. Devon Hellickson looked like the classic definition of worldly success. James never quite understood what he did for a living, but whatever his profession was, Mr. Hellickson seemed to have a dream life.

James also did not care what Mr. Hellickson did professionally. He came to several of Central's games, so he considered him a fan and a supporter of Central's team. When he had his bag with him, James knew what was being delivered. It was his way of supporting the team, and except for Pete, all the players appreciated it.

"Go out and celebrate," Mr. Hellickson said with a smile. "Most teams never win five in a row to start a season."

James took the bag and hid it under the equipment bag and other items that filled the trunk of the car.

"Don't worry," Mr. Hellickson said. "No one is looking. Even if they did, no one knows what I gave you."

"My teammates could guess."

"And they'd want to make sure you save a can or two for them. Have a good time. Spend some time with one of those pretty girls who are always watching."

"They're not interested in me."

"Get away from him," another voice joined the conversation. But this one was not suave like Mr. Hellickson's. There was gruff anger to each word. James glanced over his shoulder, and there stood Coach Baptiste, continuing to growl. "Stop pestering our players."

James had a moment of panic that Coach Baptiste might have noticed the bag. If he did, he might guess there were beer cans in there. But the coach was staring at Mr. Hellickson, who laughed in response. "I will leave because James here doesn't want anything else from me. At least, not today. But you have no right to send me away. I will return whenever I want and how often I want."

Mr. Hellickson turned around and walked to his sports car. He must have bought a new one since the last time I saw him, James noted. The older car was blue, this one was red. James turned his attention back to Coach Baptiste. If the coach knew what was in the bag James had just taken, he did nothing to show it.

"Be careful with that man," Coach Baptiste said. "You, your brother, your teammates, everyone. He cannot be trusted."

"Sure will, coach," James lied.

"Unbelievable," the coach continued, and James thought Coach Baptiste was talking to himself. "We are having a great season, and half the time I can't enjoy it. I'm always worrying about what Devon and Harry might do to it."

James let him wander away, but pondered the words. This was not the first time that Coach Baptiste had warned James or other players about Mr. Devon Hellickson. Though he understood that the underage drinking was illegal, James had a hard time believing that enjoying a little beer was wrong. He felt Coach Baptiste was a little too harsh about it.

It would be a shame to disappoint him, James thought, if he ever found out that several of us were drinking whenever Mr. Hellickson delivered the beer for free. It seemed like a nice gesture to James. He did not know Mr. Hellickson well enough to trust him completely, but he had no reason to distrust him either.

John was finally making his way off the field and towards the car. As his brother walked to him, James considered the other portion of the Coach Baptiste's parting statement: Mr. Harry Antes.

Yes, James understood why no one trusted that man. He also realized why there was nothing Central's players or coaches could do about him.

Chapter 6

John's fastball whizzed by the batter, who the umpire called out looking.

He's pitching well today, Coach Deem thought to himself. This is about as well as he has thrown all year.

There was one out in the top of the seventh inning, and Central was ahead of Hemtown 7-1. John was two outs away from pitching a complete game. He might have had a shutout if a bloop single by Hemtown had stayed up in the air a half-second longer earlier in the game. So be it, the old coach thought. There were no rewards for winning by extra runs. Regardless of what the scoreboard showed, Coach Deem knew John had pitched well enough to shut down the other team completely.

He was more encouraged about how the season was going now than he had been on opening day, and he already felt good about it then. He was beginning to think the team was the favorite, not just in Lebanon County, but in all of Region D. He would not speak that out loud because he did not want to add extra pressure for his players. But he could say it if he wanted.

The next batter did not hit one of John's changeups as much as he tipped it with the bat. Sam, playing first base while John pitched, fielded the weak ground ball for the second out.

"What's his pitch count now?" Nick asked aloud.

"Seventy-nine," Coach Baptiste answered. "And he doesn't look tired."

That shouldn't matter, Nick knew. He just wanted to make sure John was working as efficiently as he thought. The sun was not low in the evening sky yet. The fast pace of the game was mostly because of John's quick pitching.

A pop-up to Little Jimmy behind second base ended the game. The Central players gathered near the mound to give each other high-fives before getting in a line to shake hands with the Hemtown players. Coach Deem was at the end of the line. As he shook hands with the other team, he had a nagging suspicion that the first loss of the season was coming. Things had gone a little too well in these early games. Even a good team was due for a few struggles by now.

Not that a loss or two in a fifteen-game regular season was a big problem. The top four of the six teams in the league would play in the playoffs. That was probably too many, Coach Deem thought. It was not like the old days when earning postseason berths was a challenge. But he had to coach Central in today's Lebanon County League, not the league from his youth. If there were weaknesses in Central's team, it was better to find and fix them now when they could afford a misstep or two. When the playoffs started, they would always be one or two losses from elimination.

The players gathered around Coach Deem in front of their third-base side dugout. Sometimes, even short post-game talks were hard, if a coach wanted to put any meaning in them. This was an excellent chance to remind players on what they had to focus on, individually and as a team. But there were no mistakes all evening, which made it difficult to tell the players there was more work to do. There had been no fielding errors, no baserunning blunders, and no poor decisions anywhere on the field in all seven innings. What was there to tell them they needed to improve on?

The team still struggled with putting any heart into sacrifice bunts. But there were no situations tonight for a sacrifice bunt, so there was no reason to mention it now. Coach Deem was happy with everything that happened in this game. Still, he knew Central needed encouragement to be better, or else other teams would catch up to their level.

"It was a good game all-around boys," Nick started. "John, that was a great pitching performance. Jules, Phil, solid hitting in the early innings. Those two-out, run-scoring hits made the rest of the game a lot easier on all of us.

"Now, the one thing I want to make sure you're all aware of is that it's not always going to be like this. Vigortown pushed us in the first game of the year. Since then, we've had it easy. But we won't always be ahead. Eventually, we're all going to have a test in front of us, and we will all have to respond."

Coach Deem was going to continue but saw that Mr. Antes was walking over to the team huddle. "Hold on boys. It looks like our sponsor has something to tell us."

"Sorry, coach," Mr. Antes said as everyone turned their attention to the rotund man. "I just got news from the league president. He has postponed the game at Lavernon tomorrow. So it's up to your coaches to either have you practice or have an off day."

"What happened?" Coach Arim asked. "Weren't they able to get nine of their players to commit for tomorrow?"

"The president said the fire in Lavernon affected three players' homes," Mr. Antes said, flicking ashes from his cigar. "I asked if we could get a forfeit win, but he said the league by-laws make exceptions for tragedies." His message delivered, Mr. Antes turned abruptly and walked away, what remained of his hair falling to the sides of his head.

Coach Deem remembered hearing about a fire in Lavernon city on the radio around noon, but recalled no details. Only then did he realize that the sponsor of his own team sounded like he was only concerned with getting a win out of the tragedy, and not about the families who had lost homes to the fire.

"Do we know when the game will be rescheduled?" Matt asked.

"I'll talk to Lavernon's coach when I can," Nick said, not happy that his players also seemed to be thinking more of the game than anyone affected by the fire. "For now, let's prepare the field and head home. Come back tomorrow at five for a light practice."

Coach Deem stood where he was and watched some of his players do the post-game field work. Most of the others walked over to their families. A couple visited the girls who always were at the games. A few others walked straight to their cars. But his two assistant coaches also stayed in place.

"Was I the only one who noticed that our sponsor reacted to that fire like it's all about us?" Coach Arim asked.

"No, you were not," Coach Deem answered. "I'm glad he's provided the money to the veterans to keep the program stable, but sometime's he's a...,"

"It's still daylight," Coach Baptiste interrupted. "We could go over into Lavernon and check out what happened. We could see if anyone needs help."

Coach Deem considered it but decided against traveling. "If you want to, go ahead. Details will be on the internet tonight and in the newspapers by tomorrow. We should probably say something to the team during tomorrow's practice. I want them focused more on baseball than on getting tans or their girlfriends...,"

"Or their girlfriends' tans...," coach Coach Arim added.

"But I don't like seeing them completely miss the significance of families being put in danger. Those are baseball players who don't live that far away. You'd think a few of our guys would know their players, at least a little."

Coach Baptiste walked over to the team bench and picked up his folders with his notes on the pitchers. "I'll see what happened. When I hear about things like that, I can't forget about it. I feel like being there shows a little support."

Coach Deem and Coach Arim gathered their items and gave a quick look over to make sure the players taking care of the field. Satisfied, Nick made his way to his car and drove home. He wondered how to use this as a teaching moment for the players.

Coach Deem wished that he could teach them how not to become like Harry Antes. He was the most obnoxious man Coach Deem had ever met, but he was the man who funded the team. All Armed Services baseball teams were sponsored by a local headquarters. That headquarters was run by retired Armed Service veterans and their families. But those headquarters could use their funds to sponsor several causes. A few years ago, when money got tight, the Central headquarters almost cut off the baseball program.

Enter Harry Antes, who donated money to the local headquarters with the understanding that it supported only to the baseball team, and no other causes. Mr. Antes had never served in the military, but the sponsorship gave him something to brag about to anyone who would listen. He was a wealthy man who liked for everyone else to know he was wealthy. When the team won, Mr. Antes would never be shy about reminding people that the only reason the squad still existed was because of him.

Coach Deem shook his head. There was nothing he could do about the team's sponsor. All he could do was guide players. He drove home, figuring out how to best use the extra day of practice.

* * *

It was one of the longest days of the year, so there was still plenty of sunlight as Coach Baptiste drove by the Lavernon Mall. He turned north onto Twelfth Street to search for the buildings that burned in Lavernon that morning. A few more turns and he saw where it had happened.

Though the homes were still roped off with yellow caution tape, Coach Baptiste was free to park wherever he wanted on the road. Getting out of his car, he got his first up-close look at the damage. There were five blackened row homes, looking like a skeleton of infrastructure. Two more houses, one on either end, appeared to have received some damage as well. Coach Baptiste guessed emergency crews arrived here in time to prevent the blaze from spreading any farther than that.

Coach Baptiste never knew anyone who had a home fire, but looking at what remained from the devastation gave him chills. Knowing a few of these homes had been for growing families made it more painful to look. He could not even imagine how painful it was to experience.

"Was your family living here?" a voice beside Coach Baptiste asked.

Coach Baptiste turned and saw an older, bearded man whom he did not recognize. "No," he answered. "I heard about this earlier today, wanted to see it now."

The other gentleman looked toward Coach Baptiste's chest. "Oh, now I see. You're from Central."

Coach Baptiste had forgotten that he was still in his coaching uniform. He answered, "Technically, I live in Hemtown, but yes, I'm an assistant coach for Central."

"That's who my nephew's team would have played tomorrow," the stranger answered. "Poor boy, he was so excited to pitch tomorrow."

"Was his family in one of these homes?"

The man nodded. "His family is staying in my brother's house right now. I think the inn on the west side of town will put them up starting tomorrow night."

"And the other families?"

"Don't know. But we will hear soon from two of the others. They were teammates of my nephew."

"What's your nephew's name? And his teammates'?"

The man answered with three names familiar to Coach Baptiste, but none were people whom he knew personally.

"Everyone survive?" Coach Baptiste asked.

"So far as I know. Two people went to the hospital for breathing in smoke. Those weren't my relatives, so I haven't heard for sure, but I think they've been released."

"At least that's good news. I hope all the victims land on their feet soon. When you see your nephew or any of his teammates, pass along our team's...," Coach Baptiste struggled for the right words. "Sympathies and best wishes."

Driving back home soon after, Coach Baptiste felt a hole in his gut. There ought to be something Central could do for Lavernon's players. Not just the Lavernon players, he realized. There were three baseball players involved, but at least five homes. They should help those families beyond rescheduling their next baseball game.

Based on the lack of a reaction the news of the fire received from the Central players, Baptiste feared that he would be fighting a lonely battle. The team's laser-like focus on the baseball season was usually a good thing. In this case, it would make getting any of the players to help the victims of the fire a challenging task. The players were not merely focused on baseball. They were also self-centered. Problems that didn't happen to themselves did not seem to matter to anyone on Central.

Something had to change that.

Chapter 7

Almost everyone who has ever stepped foot on a baseball field knows about one of *those* games.

Sooner or later, even the best teams play in that game where nothing goes right. Every time the team hits a nice line drive, it flies right at a fielder. Yet when the opposing team bats, every weak grounder sneaks between fielders for singles.

Against Meadville, Central was having one of those games. Not only that, it was happening in front of its home crowd, too. James realized it was happening shortly after the game started.

In the top of the first inning, two Meadville batters hit weak dribblers to him. Neither time was James playing in close to the hitter. He was at his regular position a few steps behind the third base bag. James could not get either of those slow-moving grounders in time, so they resulted in infield singles. James knew he had done nothing wrong, but it was still frustrating.

It was even more frustrating when both runners scored to put Central down 2-0 early.

But that was merely the setup for James's disappointing day. In the bottom of the second inning, the Meadville pitcher threw a snail-like pitch right down the middle of the plate. It must have been a breaking ball that never curved. Instead, it stayed straight and did nothing to deceive James.

But it was so slow James could time it precisely, and he put the right part of the bat on it. He used all of his muscles in that swing. He could feel the ball soar over everyone's heads. James ran to first base, but was getting ready to slow into a home-run trot. But after rounding the bag, he saw the fly ball settle into the glove of Meadville's center fielder, who had his back against the outfield fence.

Sometimes, even a good team has a game that gets away from them early. After James's near home run fell short, Meadville scored three more runs in the top of the third. None of the balls seemed well-hit to James. But the goal of the game is not to hit solid line drives or deep fly balls, he remembered. Those usually helped, but the goal was to run around the bases. Meadville did that, and Central did not.

Sitting in the dugout while his teammates batted in the bottom of the fourth inning, James noted the mood. Neither his teammates nor coaches were too downcast even though they had fallen behind 5-0. It seemed like everyone understood that this game would not go their way, but no one would let it define the season.

An undefeated season was never the goal. Coach Deem had never mentioned that. Neither had Coaches Arim or Baptiste. Even Pete, for all his preaching that this should be a championship year, never desired perfection.

Central would recover and still win Lebanon County. James was sure of that.

* * *

"They must be so ticked," Maggie said as Meadville scored two more runs in the top of the fifth to build a seven-run lead.

"I'm not sure they even care anymore," Martha replied. "Sometimes you've got to let go."

"There's no clock in baseball," Jo reminded her two softball teammates. "Or softball. Remember the game against Sweetsville?"

The girls paused in their talking, all taken back to the greatest highlight of their softball season. They had been down by six runs with two outs in the last inning. The Sweetsville players had been so upset by the loss they forgot to shake hands with the Central High School players.

"That was a great game," Martha said, breaking the silence.

"But you know what I've noticed?" Maggie said. "Once they fell behind, the guys tried to pull everything. Even the breaking balls."

"Yeah, it's better to be patient and hit them to the opposite field," Jo answered. "But they're boys. They think they can make an entire comeback with one huge swing."

"Shouldn't their coaches be setting them straight?" Martha asked.

"They probably are, but we should tell them anyway," Maggie said. "If they'll listen. After all, they are boys."

"They should listen to you," Martha answered. "You were the best at hitting the ball to the opposite field. I don't care if it was softball, it's still the same idea. Don't over-swing and try to hit a home run, or else you'll get under the ball and pop out. Wait on it and hit it evenly...,"

As Martha's voice trailed off, Maggie and Jo realized that they had unwanted attention. An older, overweight man was walking in front of them back to his seat from the concession stand.

"Yeah, we understand the game," Maggie said to the balding gawker. "We're athletes, not models."

The man shook his head, stuffed a cigar in his mouth, mumbled something about "softball players know nothing," and walked away to his own lawn chair. He set himself between a woman much younger than him and another woman who was younger still. Maggie did not care where Mr. Antes sat. She was just glad he was now out of earshot.

"Can't stand that man," Maggie said.

"Watch it," Jo said. "I know there are rumors that Mr. Antes has done some nasty things, but he has enough money to...,"

"His money doesn't impress for me," Maggie interrupted. "I hate the way he looks at us."

"He still is the only reason the local Armed Services post can afford to sponsor the team for Central," Martha reminded her.

"He won't punish them to get at me for talking back," Maggie said. "The team is an extension of his ego, nothing more."

All three girls looked at the rather unpleasant man, who was red in the face and on his bald head.

"He seems to be taking this game poorly," Martha agreed.

Jo, perhaps unwilling to keep talking about one of the most annoying people in town, changed the subject away from both the game and way from Mr. Antes. "So, Martha, which of the boys are you trying to snag with that outfit? Maybe Maggie thinks you're not a model, but I can't remember you ever showing off so much of your legs."

"I hate when you talk about boys when the game is going on," Martha responded, shaking her head. Her smile showed that she was annoyed but not offended.

"You're just waiting to see which of the players comes over first, needing a hug after the first loss of the year...," Jo continued.

"Shut up," Martha said, though again smiling. "I'm not looking for a boyfriend."

"My mother says that's when you always find one. The perfect guy always appears when you aren't looking," Jo said.

"Then I guess you won't find one, because you are obviously looking," Martha charged.

Jo made an innocent, "who, me?" gesture, but now Maggie could not resist getting into the conversation. Maggie, like Martha, would not talk about boys while the game was being played. It always upset her when she was playing a softball game, and she could overhear boys talking about her and her teammates. Well, she did not mind if they were talking about them as athletes during the games. What upset her was when they would talk about which player was hottest.

But for Jo to accuse Maggie of trying to reel in a boy and then act like she did not have one in her sights was just wrong. The game in front of her felt lost anyway, so why not have a little fun with Jo's infatuation?

"You have been staring at Phil since the game started," Maggie said. "Actually, since May."

"You've been worse about it since June," Martha added. "Ever since that tan came in really nice."

Jo somehow kept the blood from going to her cheeks, but her eyes showed the truth. Maggie or Martha didn't need the clue. They had both suspected Jo was interested in Phil for a long time, and they were close enough with her to feel Jo's embarrassment when they said it.

"He's cute, but not any cuter than the other boys on the team," Jo defended herself.

Maggie and Martha stared at her. Maggie knew the pressure would get Jo to speak again.

"I want everyone to do well. Central is our team."

The staring continued.

"Phil too, but not only him."

Stares.

"He's sweet and all, but that doesn't mean we'd be a match."

Jo looked right at Martha, and left at Maggie. "Leave me alone!"

Maggie burst out laughing, and Martha did too.

They sat through the rest of the game, which resulted in a blowout loss. As usual, the three girls talked with the players afterward. Maggie spoke with Nate for a few moments, saying nothing about their romantic plans. They did not have the chance to be alone, and after Central's first loss, Nate did not seem to be in the best of moods, anyway. She just gave him a quick wink before she drove home.

Maggie was glad she was hiding her growing interest in Nate better than Jo was with Phil.

Chapter 8

Doubleheader. The word made Pete happy.

Two games in one day versus the same opponent. Today, that opponent was Lavernon, on the field north of Lavernon city. It would be a whole afternoon and evening of baseball. What better way was there to spend a summer day?

It helped that Pete was the pitcher for Central in the first game. Lavernon was a struggling team, which would not be one of the four teams to get to the county playoffs. If he kept his focus and kept the ball near the strike zone, this had the potential to be a good day for Pete.

Unlike the last game he was on the mound, Pete looked like the college-level pitcher he was. He struck out nine Lavernon batters. Only one hitter reached base on a hit and one other on a walk. Throughout the game, it seemed to Pete that the Lavernon players were not interested in the contest. It was not just that they had trouble against his pitching. When Central was batting, Lavernon's fielders were a step slow to get to the ball and a second late to decide where to throw it.

In the back of his mind, Pete remembered why this was a doubleheader. A fire had affected three of the Lavernon players' families. Maybe the team had never recovered from that. Pete knew the blaze was unfortunate and more important than any baseball game. But it was also none of his concern, nor was it the concern of anyone else on Central's team. They still had to play their best on each pitch.

For the last pitch of this game, Pete put a curveball on the inside corner that a Lavernon batter swung through for the final out. Before giving high-fives to his teammates, Pete took just a moment to glance at the scoreboard that showed Central's 8-0 victory. He could not remember the last time he had pitched a complete-game shutout.

Pete and his teammates got into the handshake line with the Lavernon players. It was when he was up close to the competition that he saw a glazed-over look in his opponents' eyes. Maybe it was the continuing issues after the fire, or because they were the last-place team in the league standings. Either way, Lavernon looked disinterested in being at the ballpark.

Central's players entered the third-base dugout and sat down, but did not stay there long. "I don't have much to say," Coach Deem said to them. "I'll save the post-game speech for after game two. The lineup will be ready in fifteen minutes, and the next game starts in about an hour."

That seemed to be a long break to Pete, who expected about thirty minutes to rest. But he felt that would help him refocus for the next game, in which he expected to be playing center field. But as most of his teammates scattered among the families and friends who had made the trip for the road game, Coach Deem walked over to him.

"I'm going to have you sit for game two," the coach said. "It's not about you, it's about the other players."

"How do mean that, coach?"

Coach Deem lowered his voice, probably to make sure no words carried in the air. Lavernon's players and scant few fans sat on the other side of the field but were close enough to hear a regular conversation. "We are playing against the worst team in the county, a team distracted by off-field issues. Your teammates need to win this game. They need to play well with no help from you."

Pete was disappointed that he would not get to be in the second game, but he could not argue with his coach's logic. When the county playoffs came around, the experience would help everyone.

Still, he asked, "Any chance I get in as a pinch-hitter?"

Coach Deem smiled and patted Pete on the shoulder. "If the opportunity comes. But you've done your work today. Good pitching, Pete."

Taking the news in stride, Pete was just about to find his parents. Then he thought to ask Coach Deem if Andy would play in the later game or not. If he wasn't, his mom and dad would not want to stay for the nightcap. For Pete, two baseball games made for a fun afternoon. For his parents, a game in which neither son was playing made for long, dull afternoons.

But before Pete said anything, Phil hurried over. "Coach Deem, may I leave between games?"

Coach Deem twisted his face. "I don't care for that, but does your family know you're heading out?"

"Yeah, and I'll be back in time," Phil said.

Pete glanced over his shoulder, to see if Jo was at the game. She was there, sitting with Martha and Maggie, as usual. He thought Phil might sneak off to spend time with the girl that everyone knew was interested in him. But that was not the case.

Coach Deem nodded though a frown showed his annoyance. "Sure, but if you're late, you're out of this game and the next."

Pete could barely hear the "Thanks, coach," by Phil before he rushed to the parking lot.

On the edge of the parking lot, Pete saw the concession stand. He forgot about asking Coach Deem whether or not Andy would play in the next game, and instead walked to the snack bar. Pete had not been sure how much he wanted to eat when he still expected to start in both games. Now that Pete knew he was not playing in the nightcap, he felt much hungrier than he had five minutes ago.

But when he got to the front of the stand, he saw the window was boarded up with a paper reading "closed" on it. That seemed absurd to Pete. They had fans who would be at the field all day, and Lavernon's sponsors could not sell drinks and food to them. As he walked back, past the visitors' dugout and to his family and fans, he took closer note of the field itself. During games he pitched, Pete paid attention to the mound and the area around home plate. The condition of those two spots dictated how well he could pitch, and how easily Andy could catch if one of Pete's low pitches hit the dirt.

Now he analyzed the entire grounds as he would in the games where he was playing in the outfield. When he played in center field, Pete's concerns would be different. He would note slick spots that might change the trajectory of the ball or any inclines or declines that might affect his ability to chase down a fly ball. But what stood out was the grass was not cut. Most fields, whether cared for by volunteers or coaches, were mowed regularly. The Lavernon field, though not ignored, was not being given the detailed attention it should get.

Then Pete realized that no one was tending to the field between games. In other doubleheaders Pete had played in, the infield dirt would be dragged with a net on the back of a riding mower. After that, someone watered it down to keep any dust from flying during the game. That happened before the first game, but it was not happening now.

Pete remembered the dazed look on the players of Lavernon and their less-than-inspired mood during the game. He began to think the players were not the only ones who had stopped giving their best effort. Lavernon's whole team was a mess, not only the players but all the volunteers involved with the club.

It was all because of the fire. There were plenty of bad baseball teams that still brought their best effort every game. Almost every team took good care of their home fields. But being a bad team and then having something terrible happen away from the sport seemed to have stolen Lavernon's heart.

Not our problem, Pete reminded himself. It was something to turn into an advantage. The most important thing Central could do was exploit this weakened opponent and stay tied with Vigortown for first place.

When he walked over to his family, who were watching from the third-base side of the field, Pete noticed that most of the spectators had food. They were all munching on sandwiches.

"I don't care if everyone else is eating them. These sandwiches are lame, mom," James said off in the distance.

"And gross," John added.

Pete looked and saw the Thun brothers, this time arguing with their mother instead of each other. Whatever food Mrs. Thun had brought to the field and was sharing was not the meal they had wanted.

"Here you go, Pete," his mother said as she handed him a sandwich. "Mrs. Thun wanted to make sure you got one too when she found out the food stand wouldn't be open today."

Pete thanked his mother and realized what the food was. Everyone was eating fish sandwiches, with fried filets between the slices of bread. That would be an odd choice at most baseball games, but Pete would accept any food right now. Before he took a bite, the argument farther down the line continued.

"It's summer! Baseball! You're embarrassing us with this weird food," James said.

"It's time for hot dogs!" John added.

"Burgers!"

"Barbeque!"

"Even steak would make more sense!"

"Shut up!" Mrs. Thun silenced them.

Thunder Boys, Pete thought.

Pete shook his head and turned away, disregarding any more shouting in the Thun family. He couldn't quite get the attitude. There had been times when his parents and his brother had embarrassed him by words or actions. But even at his angriest, he saved any yelling for when they were back at home. Family deserved respect. During any shouting matches that might take place at home, Pete would remember he was talking to his own family.

The same carried over to Sal's parents. He had seen them a handful of times during the spring semester back at college. He felt it was never too soon to give them the respect he should show to in-laws. Just in case.

He bit into his fish sandwich, which was tasty despite being cooled off in the Thuns' cooler. Pete hoped to relax since his services were not needed in the second game. He agreed with Coach Deem. The other players should be able to win against Lavernon without his help.

Pete's parents and Andy said little, so for a few minutes, he could let his guard down and enjoy a summer day. It was a pleasant warmth, but not a sweltering afternoon. His family was together here between two games, and Pete was sure that both games would be wins. Their silence was peaceful instead of awkward.

It was easier to relax when the baseball season was successful.

But the breath of fresh air was cut short. Mr. Antes walked over from the parking lot, a cigar in his mouth, his wife in one arm and step-daughter in the other. They were walking right by the "This field is smoke-free" sign. He said nothing yet, but Pete sensed a confrontation was coming.

At first, Pete ignored the sponsor of Central's team. He turned his back to Antes, who was still farther up the line and conversing with Tom. Pete thought now would be a good time to talk with his family. Then he would be less likely to hear anything when the blowup came. Pete knew it would.

When he turned, he saw Coach Baptiste down by the team bench, eating his peculiar snack of grasshoppers dipped in honey. Yuck. But before Pete could even ponder the odd diet that his coach had, Coach Baptiste set his food down and stomped in Mr. Antes' direction. The coach was red in the face. Apparently, he would not turn away from whatever nonsense Mr. Antes was saying. Pete considered not turning back around and ignoring the upcoming argument. But since it was Coach Baptiste, he wanted to hear what the coach would say.

In truth, Pete admired Coach Baptiste for standing up to someone in authority over him. But he also feared it. Sports history was littered with teams who had promising seasons fall apart from off-field bickering.

"I don't want you giving advice to our players," Coach Baptiste shouted as he stomped in front of Antes.

"The only reason they play for you at all is that I paid for everything the team needed this year," Mr. Antes answered. His tone was strong, but his pose became a little defensive, pulling his wife and step-daughter closer to himself. "I paid for it all the last five years. Equipment. Uniforms. Rental fees for your field. I'll tell them what I please."

"You may watch the games, but you're no baseball man," Baptiste answered, his anger not cooling. His face had changed from red to crimson.

"I wasn't talking baseball anyway," Mr. Antes said. "I was encouraging Tim here."

Pete nearly let out a laugh, but he did not want to draw attention to himself. Mr. Antes had been talking to Tom. Though to be fair, Tom had a twin brother named Tim. But Pete doubted that was the reason for the mistake. Mr. Antes was a know-it-all who knew all too little.

"I heard your words of 'encouragement'," Baptiste said, and for a moment Pete thought he might strangle Antes. "That is no way to encourage a young man, or any man, how to live. Neither your words nor your actions are those of a mentor."

Andy turned to Pete and whispered, "What did Mr. Antes say to Tom?"

Pete shrugged and looked off to the edge of his vision. Coaches Deem and Arim were both back on the team bench, nervously watching the encounter. They did nothing to get their fellow coach out of this argument.

"If I asked to have you removed, it would happen," Mr. Antes threatened. "You should apologize to my family and me for speaking this way."

"In public, too," Mrs. Antes said.

Coach Baptiste glared at the woman. He softened his tone, but Pete could still hear. "Do you think I don't know who you are? I know which family you really belong to."

Now Mrs. Antes turned red, though it seemed from her tightened mouth to be as much about embarrassment as anger. Pete wondered if the rumors about the Antes household were true.

"Fire him now," Mrs. Antes said, and the words could not have been hotter had fire come from her mouth.

"Easy, dear," Mr. Antes said before turning back to Coach Baptiste. "You have offended my family, but you have the respect of the players, and that counts for something. I can see they all lean in each time you speak even if you are speaking poorly of me. So, for now, I'll let you continue coaching. But no more of this!" He turned around, his wife and step-daughter walking along with him, and hurried back to the parking lot.

Before they reached their car, Coach Baptiste shouted at them. "You embarrass this team, and you make a mockery the veterans whose headquarters they represent! Someone will soon show you the truth, and you cannot send him away!"

When the Antes family had left, all the Central players and some parents gathered around Coach Baptiste. "What was that all about?" Pete asked before anyone else spoke.

"Tom," the coach said. "What did that man say to you?"

"Well, the part you're angry about, he told me I could get a different girl every weekend if I would hit the ball over the fence."

Among the things that the coaches preached to the players was never to swing for a home run. It was best to try for a line drive or a hard ground ball, and with those swings, the occasional deep fly ball would come. But Pete knew lousy baseball advice never would have caused the last confrontation.

"That attitude towards women turns young men like you into scoundrels like him," Coach Baptiste said. "You do not want to take his word or his example as something to follow."

"So, you know what's really happening in his family?" John asked. "There are rumors. I mean, there are a lot of rumors."

"Some of those rumors about them are false, but this much is true. That woman is indeed Mrs. Antes, but she never married the Mr. Antes you know. She is married to his brother."

"They're not divorced?" James asked.

"No. And her daughter is from a relationship before that, so she is neither Mr. Antes' daughter nor niece." Coach Baptiste took a deep breath and exhaled long and loud. Composed, he continued. "I'm acting foolish now. There's no reason to dwell on the man now that he's gone. Don't worry so much about how he treats women. Instead, make sure you don't make the same mistakes. A woman's love is a gift to be treasured, not a trophy to be bought."

Coach Baptiste clapped his hands. "Sorry, I didn't mean to distract you so much between games. Sometimes when I preach I forget to stop. You better warm up for the evening game."

Most of the players walked back over to the visitors' dugout, but Pete and John stayed next to Coach Baptiste. "Do you think he will fire you?"

"Remove. I'm a volunteer," Coach Baptiste reminded them. "But yes. I am sure I won't be coaching here for long. Don't worry about that. Before I'm gone, someone else will come to give you much better instructions. He will guide you on the baseball field and away from it. And he will teach you better than I ever could."

"Who?" Pete asked.

Coach Baptiste turned away for a moment, then looked back to Pete and John. "When he arrives, I will tell you."

Pete and John walked back to the dugout with Coach Baptiste. Pete noted the direction that the coach had looked towards and glanced that way himself. He saw that old man, the one who seemed to attend all the games, on top of one bleacher. Though he had not noticed the old man earlier, Pete was not surprised that he was there. Was Coach Baptiste's glance to him a coincidence? Did the old man have something to do with this person that the coach said was coming? Would the old man himself speak to the team someday? Pete had never heard his voice.

Why couldn't Coach Baptiste have said the name of whoever was coming? That would have been a lot easier.

Just before the second game started, Phil finally returned. Pete had forgotten that Phil had left, with the shouting that was going on between games. Phil was bright red in the face when he got back into the dugout, though he was not as irate as Coach Baptiste and Mr. Antes were earlier.

Pete never came in as a pinch-hitter in the later game. He watched from the dugout and was pleased to see his teammates score fourteen runs in an easy victory. The path to a Lebanon County championship was looking more comfortable. Under normal circumstances, he would have taken more note of Phil's aggressive play. It seemed like he wanted to tear the ball apart with his bat each time he came up to the plate.

But Pete was continuing to analyze the argument between Mr. Antes and Coach Baptiste. Pete sensed that more distractions were coming. Though Pete agreed with Coach Baptiste that Mr. Antes was no role model, he wished everyone would just stay quiet and let Central play ball.

Chapter 9

Rain delay. The words made James depressed.

Central had a 5-1 lead in the third inning on Nickelton's field, which was now damp with the steady rain. It was not a mud pit, but the umpires decided the field was bad enough for the game had to stop. A heavy tarp covered the pitching mound and the dirt around home plate, but the rest of the field continued to get soaked.

This was an afternoon game, so plenty of time remained to resume the contest if the sun ever broke through the clouds. James hoped it did, and soon. Rain delays might depress him, but postponements were much worse. Everything would have to be replayed from the beginning. That would feel almost like a loss, at least to James.

Rain delays were often somber for James, different from the breaks between games at doubleheaders or tournaments. Players rarely got to converse with their families or friends at the game during the delay. Central and Nickelton sat in their dugouts and waited out the weather. Some of his teammates seemed to enjoy the time, though. Matt and Tom were having a seed-spitting contest. They were aiming for progressively smaller and smaller targets from farther and farther away. Other players laughed along as they tried to hit their goals, only to have the seeds hit their teammates instead.

Even Pete, as serious-minded as he was, seemed to let his guard down during the delay. He was building a tower of paper cups at the end of the dugout. So far he had raised it up to eight levels, each one narrower than the one beneath. The coaches were also more relaxed, and seemed in light conversation about, well, whatever old men talked about to pass the time. James paid no attention to them, but they were not in a serious discussion about the game or the season.

James remained silent on the bench. Central needed this win. Victory would not be a surprise. Central already had the lead today, and Nickelton was not even going to be one of the top four teams in the league to qualify for the playoffs. Even so, if they wanted to be the best team in the county, they needed to get every win they could. To be in the best position possible in those playoffs, they needed to take advantage of every opportunity. Finishing first in the regular season would help set up good scenarios for the postseason. It would be easier to end up in first if Central had a margin for error when they played their remaining two games against Vigortown.

Vigortown. No, James caught himself. The opponent today is Nickelton. It was time to focus on them.

The only other player who was not relaxing during the break was Phil. In fact, Phil had not been himself since the middle of the doubleheader at Lavernon. No one seemed to know why. If Phil had shared the reason behind his change in emotion, James had not heard it. All James knew was Phil burned over something, and he seemed mad during each at-bat. In the second game against Lavernon, this anger led to wild swinging during each plate appearance. His swings were more under control today, but he approached each plate appearance as a frustrated hitter.

If it had been his brother, James would have told John to get over whatever was distracting him. But for his other teammates, James chose to give space so they could fume. Maybe Phil's anger was about something serious, like a relative's illness. He could not be sure, so James remained silent.

It was then that James realized the rain was now a drizzle or even a mist. He saw the umpires walk around the field. They signaled for the Nickelton coaches and a handful of volunteer field staff to put sandy drying agents on the dirt around the infield. The game would resume soon.

That lifted James's spirit. He got up, pulled a sunflower seed out of Matt's bag, and spit the shell on top of Pete's cup tower. It did not knock the tower over, but it earned James applause from his teammates.

After allowing both teams a little time to throw and jog to warm back up, the umpires resumed the game. With the restart in the top of the fourth inning, James was batting with Phil on first base and no outs. James looked to Coach Arim in the third-base coaches' box and saw the signal he and all his teammates dreaded.

A touch of the cap, a pat on the right arm, another pat on the left ear. Those were the signs for a sacrifice bunt.

It was the opposite of everything James believed in as a ballplayer. Yes, it would move Phil to second base and slightly improve Central's chances of scoring another run. But sacrificing would also mean that James would most likely get thrown out at first base. Wouldn't it increase Central's chances more if James took a full swing and got a hit himself? If any scouts were at a game or looking at his stats, wouldn't they be more impressed if he were adding singles instead of bunts to his numbers? Wouldn't the girls at the game, all of whom had stayed through the rain delay, be more impressed with a hit?

James had pondered all those issues over his years of playing baseball. None of that crossed his mind in the batter's box on Nickelton's field. He had been through it all before whenever he or teammates saw the bunt signal. There were two ways they responded. Sometimes, they acted like they did not see the sign and took a full swing. That would work here or there, but the coaches would never believe the whole team never recognized the signal.

But the coaches might believe the whole team, despite its talent, was terrible at bunting. That was true anyway, considering they never tried.

So James squared up to bunt, and as everyone could see, was nowhere near making contact. But while anyone could tell that James made a poor bunt attempt only his teammates knew he missed on purpose.

Coach Arim gave the same signal for the second pitch, but this pitch was so high that James would neither swing nor bunt at it. On the third pitch, James received the same signal, and again, bunted and missed.

James was not as good at this faking as some of the other players. Jules, for example, could bunt the ball foul whenever he wanted. That would give him a chance to swing away later but might convince his coaches he was trying with an honest effort.

Down in the count one ball and two strikes, James now saw the signal to swing away. As far as he could remember, his coaches had never signaled for a sacrifice bunt with two strikes. A foul on a bunt, unlike a foul on a full swing, would count as a third strike and a strikeout. There was no sense in risking it.

James swung hard and hit a foul ball on the next pitch. But the following three pitches were outside the strike zone and James walked, forcing Phil to second base. James did not know how many scouts or girls he impressed with a walk as opposed to a sacrifice bunt. But it was better for the team on the whole and made James feel better too.

Andy was batting now, and James looked over to see the signal from Coach Arim. Coach Arim usually called for any bunts, steals or hit-and-runs himself. In crucial situations, Coach Deem would send those signals in from the dugout.

There was no special signal this time, so the coaches were allowing Andy to swing away. James heard Coach Baptiste, in the first-base coach's box, say, "Make sure the pitcher pitches to home, and don't let the fielders tag you on a ground ball." James had heard this every time he was on first base since his first summer of Armed Services ball.

And as he did every time, James took a lead off first base by two long steps. He kept a close eye on the pitcher, to make sure the pitch would go to home plate. Once he knew there would not be a pickoff throw back to first, James took another couple of strides towards second.

But, from the edge of his vision, James noticed a movement he was not expecting. Phil was sprinting from second base and trying to steal third, even though no coach had called for that play.

Andy did not swing at the pitch, and the Nickelton catcher threw the ball to third. It looked like it would be a close play to James. He realized too late he should already be running toward second base, but he had not known Phil would try to steal. If he ran now, he would be out by ten feet. Nickelton's third baseman would have a chance to throw to second base and get James out if he moved, so James stayed at first base.

But it turned out Nickelton's third baseman had no opportunity to throw the ball. He could not do much of anything at all. When Phil slid, the third baseman tagged him well before he touched the base. But while Phil never got his feet to the bag, he stabbed his left cleat into the third baseman's thigh.

It was not a cry of pain, but more of a grunt that came from the third baseman. But James recognized when another athlete was trying to act tough in front of others, and this was one of those times. Blood was soaking into the uniform now.

James wondered if the umpires would eject Phil from the game. They did not, but Coach Deem took care of that himself. He replaced Phil with Little Jimmy at shortstop when Central took the field in the bottom half of the inning.

After the 7-2 victory, Coach Deem informed everyone that Phil would not be playing in the next game. The suspension would have been longer if the coach knew for sure that Phil had premeditated his spiking the Nickelton player. However, since it was unclear if it had been an accident, Coach Deem limited his discipline.

James was happy that the incident had made everyone forget about his failed bunt attempts. He had gotten away with deliberate misses again. How could he show off his muscles while bunting?

Most of the players were leaving the field and getting ready to drive the length of Lebanon County back home. James and John, though, walked over to Phil's car to ask him what had happened. It turned out that Pete was already there for the same reason. That was no surprise. Pete was the leader on the team and finding out what was going on was part of his job.

James and John missed the beginning of the conversation, but they had no trouble hearing Phil's explanation. "I had my reasons. But it won't happen again. It won't need to."

Phil drove away after that, leaving Pete shaking his head. James and John got into their mother's car. James was so distracted by his thoughts on Phil's behavior he did not race with his brother to ride shotgun. He did not even pay much attention to the inevitable but pointless argument John was trying to goad him into on the drive home.

James was trying to figure out Phil's motivation. He would not pry, so he would never know for sure unless Phil came clean later in the season. He guessed somewhere along the line that Nickelton player had spiked Phil in a game. Since it was already clear that Central would win today, Phil chose now to get his revenge. Phil had played shortstop as long as James had known him, and shortstop was a position where fielders suffered spikings every so often. Sometimes those incidents were accidental. Sometimes they were not.

Whatever the reasons, Phil would not be a part of the next game. But Central could win the next game without him, James thought to himself. Then he corrected himself. Central would win the next game. After all, it would only be against Hemtown.

Chapter 10

This batter can't stay off of the high pitch, Pete thought to himself. Andy must have noticed the same thing, since he signaled with his index finger and putting his catcher's mitt up above the strike zone.

Pete delivered a fastball directly over the plate, but around the level of the Hemtown batter's neck. As he expected, the hitter swung through it, unable to get his bat around fast enough for such an elevated fastball. The strike ended the at-bat and the inning.

The top of the fifth inning was over, and once again Central was winning with ease. Pete had forgotten the exact score, but he looked over the outfield fence to the scoreboard and saw it was 11-2 in the home team's favor.

Pete was not excited by that score, even though it was lopsided for Central. He should not be giving up two runs to Hemtown. Hemtown was not the worst team in the league. They could finish the season in fourth place and get the last Lebanon County playoff spot. But they had nowhere near the talent of Central or Vigortown.

To be honest, Pete could not figure out why he was pitching today, anyway. The next game would be against Vigortown, who was one game behind Central for first place. He had expected to throw in that game. Maybe Coach Deem thought that contest might be too long after his last start, making him a little rusty. But the head coach never said that. Coach Deem told Pete after the game at Nickelton that he would pitch against Hemtown, and nothing else was said.

When Pete disagreed with his coaches, he only argued if something morally unacceptable was happening. Pete might be the leader of the team among players, but the coaches were in charge.

Pete put the next game out of his mind. As he sat down, he thought about the next three Hemtown batters he would face. Pete had made the last out of the bottom of the fourth inning and was unlikely to bat in this frame. It was natural for him to focus on how he wanted to pitch when he took his place back out to the mound.

Nate batted in the bottom of the fifth and came to the plate with one out and Little Jimmy on first. Pete had already decided how to approach his pitching by then, so he refocused on his teammates on the field.

His first thought was how well Little Jimmy had played so far in Phil's absence. Phil actually stood there in the dugout and in uniform, but Coach Deem had repeated that Phil would not play. But there was no drop off at shortstop. So far, Little Jimmy had fielded all three balls that had been hit to him, and now he had reached base for the second time.

It was still odd not to see Phil at shortstop, no matter how well Little Jimmy performed. Phil always seemed to be there, to the side of second base. Different players might play at second base, but the shortstop area was the most demanding spot on the infield. Phil could always be depended on at the position.

Even as Pete considered this, he knew if he were in charge, he would have suspended Phil for two games instead of one. He felt it was intentional when Phil had spiked the Nickelton player, so one game out of the lineup did not seem like enough. But again, Pete was only a leader among the players. The coaches alone could issue discipline.

Nate took a swing and fouled a pitch into the protective backstop behind home plate. The sound of the foul ball was odd, and it seemed to Pete that Nate must have broken his bat. Nate glanced over the bat and kept it instead of heading to the dugout for another.

Nate appeared to make solid contact on the next pitch, but nothing else about the play was perfect. His textbook swing resulted in a weakly blooped ball into left field, and the bat split in two. Though the hit was not ideal, it was still effective. The ball fell in front of the left fielder for a single.

John, the on-deck batter, ran out to grab both halves of the bat and bring them back to the dugout before he took his turn at the plate. Coach Deem took them, but Pete got up to look at the wood. The bat did not split smoothly but instead had a point in the middle like a pencil. Based on that and on the swing, Pete and Coach

Deem both knew the bat must have cracked on the foul ball, and then snapped on the hit.

The game continued, and Pete retired the last six Hemtown batters he faced as Central won 13-2. For all the runs and hits that the team accumulated, Nate's broken-bat single was the subject of much of the post-game talk.

"You've got to take a closer look," Coach Arim said. "Or take it more seriously if you see a chip or crack in your bat."

"Yeah, but it was Hemtown," Nate said, loud enough for his teammates to hear, but not loud enough to drift to Hemtown's players.

"We should be able to defeat them with broken bats all game," Andy added.

"Isn't it amazing that Central and Hemtown can be so close to each other, and all the good players are west of the town line?" Matt asked.

The players laughed. Even Pete chuckled though he knew some of this happiness was more about Hemtown being Central's geographic rival. Based on the actual talent levels of each team, this win was no big deal. Central had a better team, period. But Pete's teammates exaggerated Hemtown's ineffectiveness.

Coach Arim did not laugh, but he smiled. "I guess we come from better stock here."

"Watch it," Coach Baptiste said. "Never believe you're born better."

Pete turned to him, and so did the other players. They all knew the mocking was all half-jokes, but Coach Baptiste seemed upset.

"You could build a great baseball player from stones if you wanted," Coach Baptiste continued, but then his tone softened. "But where is your heart? That is what will matter most."

The players stayed silent for a moment, but Pete hoped they all got the message. Talent mattered. But the will to win, to play hard on each pitch, to dedicate oneself to the team, those were the intangibles that would allow Central to finish in first place.

Pete turned to Nate to say something else to him about the broken bat, but Nate had already walked over to the girls and was talking to Maggie. Nate did not speak about Maggie to the other players much, but Pete knew something was developing there. Still, he noticed there was no touching, no hugs, no holding hands. There was nothing that even a couple starting out would do. He could not tell for certain if they dated in private or were still just best friends. It was possible that Nate was trying to make the jump from friends to a couple. Though Pete would never ask, other players did, and they always got the same response. Nate enjoyed being around Maggie, and that was all he would tell.

Oh, well. No reason to dwell on another boy's girl, whether the relationship was real or Pete imagined it. It was time to head home, hope his mother had made a nice dinner, and then call Sal.

After that, one day of practice and another home game the following day.

Vigortown would be the next challenge.

Chapter 11

Coach Deem walked to home plate with Phil by his side. Phil was holding Central's starting lineup card, with copies for the umpires and Vigortown. Pete performed this duty before most games, but tonight was different. Besides sitting out the previous game, Phil had to join the pre-game meeting with the umpires and the other team's head coach to get back on the field.

The teams exchanged lineups. Before returning to the dugout, Coach Deem asked the home plate umpire to clarify the rules about interfering with fielders. When the umpire explained in detail, Phil looked embarrassed.

Good, Coach Deem thought. He had to make sure that his starting shortstop never made the same mistake again.

After that, the teams lined up on the baselines for the playing of the national anthem over the speakers. Everyone, including the fans, stood. A few Armed Services baseball teams could get a singer for each game, but Central always played a recording. After the song was over, Coach Deem turned back to the dugout while the players gathered in a huddle before taking the field.

He noticed that the crowd had twice the number of people he was used to at Central's home games. The families of the players, the three girls from the softball team, and a handful of other regulars were there as usual. But now there were other fans who Coach Deem did not recognize watching from up the third-base line. New faces were in the bleachers near the infield or in their own folding chairs out by left field. And Vigortown had at least twice as many fans travel to Central as the other teams who had visited here.

When Coach Deem sat in his customary spot at the end of the bench, he could still hear Pete giving his pregame speech to the team. The nine players who were starting took their places in the field while the three reserves sat on the bench. John took the mound and warmed up to pitch the first inning.

Pete, now in center field, had never questioned the choice to pitch John today. Coach Deem knew Pete must have wondered how he came to his decision. He was too much of a competitor to not want to be on the mound for this game. The reasons would become clear in time, so Coach Deem decided not to explain it yet. He wanted to see when Pete would discern the logic behind the decision.

Though today's game against Vigortown was vital, they would meet again in the last game of the season. By pitching Pete against Hemtown two days ago, he had Pete's resting schedule perfectly lined up to throw in that contest.

Coach Deem had full confidence in John. He was excelling this year as much as any of his teammates. In the top of the first inning, it appeared that John would succeed again. The young pitcher retired all three Vigortown batters with little effort.

After that, though, the evening turned into palatable frustration for Coach Deem.

In the bottom of the first, Pete came up with a runner on first base and no outs. Coach Deem figured this to be a low-scoring game against Vigortown's top pitcher. It would be best to play for one run here. He signaled to Coach Arim at third base for a sacrifice bunt. But Pete missed the first bunt and then fouled off the second. With two strikes, the coaches took off the bunt sign, and Pete popped out on the third pitch. Central did not score in the first inning.

In the third, again, Central's first batter got on base. This time John was batting and given the bunt sign. He missed twice, and when allowed to swing away, John struck out.

Refusing to believe his team could mess up the fundamentals three times, Coach Deem called for another sacrifice again in the fifth inning. Then there was a runner on first with no outs and Nate batting. Nate fouled the ball off twice, and on the third try, he grounded into a double play. What made their inability to move base runners up with a bunt even more upsetting was that John was pitching well. After five innings, the game was still scoreless.

In the top of the sixth, Vigortown hit two doubles, allowing the visitors to score the game's first run. Coach Deem knew they were facing tough odds once they trailed and Vigortown's best pitcher was still in the game. Those three lead-off runners they never moved up were the only hits that Central had in the whole contest. They needed to get some hits together now.

But they never did. In both the sixth and seventh inning, Central was put down in order. Vigortown won the game 1-0 and Coach Deem could see the league standings shifting in his mind.

There was now a tie for first place between Vigortown and Central, with ten wins and two losses apiece.

After shaking hands and trying to ignore how happy Vigortown was on Central's field, Coach Deem spoke to his players afterward in front of the dugout. "You can win a decent number of games on talent. You'll win a few more by knowing most of your fundamentals. But it's hard to win a county title when everyone struggles with one of those fundamentals. We need to get better at bunting. Successful teams can't always wait for a three-run double. We can't always string three or four singles in a row. If we can't get better at sacrificing ourselves, we won't live up to our potential. Tomorrow's practice, we are working at least an extra fifteen minutes on bunts correctly."

The players did not seem to be receptive, probably because they were still coping on the loss. At least that was what Coach Deem hoped. He had to believe they would work on this one flaw the team had. He had to hope they would learn how important sacrificing was.

Chapter 12

James felt a strange tension from all his teammates the moment he arrived at Meadville's field. He recognized that sensation because he felt the same way himself. So did John, which may have been why there were no arguments between the two brothers today.

While their mother set up her lawn chair along the right-field line, James and John joined their teammates. The team hurried through their infield-outfield warmups on the field which was a baseball diamond in the middle of a small grassland. James could sense it. There was building anxiety.

Meadville was not as good as Vigortown, but Meadville was the third-best team in the league. They had beaten both Central and Vigortown once each. There was little question that Meadville would join the two more dominating teams in the county playoffs. But it was not Meadville that James and the rest of Central players feared.

Their confidence against Meadville this time around was justified. Central scored in the top of the first inning when James singled in Pete. In the top of the third, they added another run on a triple by Nate. Andy scored on a wild pitch in the fourth.

Meadville scratched out a run in the bottom of the fourth, but James was still optimistic about the game itself as they moved to the fifth. After Pete walked to lead off the inning, James looked to Coach Arim in the third-base coach's box for his signal.

A runner on first with no outs was the perfect situation for the coaches to signal for a sacrifice bunt.

The team had spent yesterday's practice putting extra work in on sacrifice bunts. A few players discovered that they did not have to pretend to be poor bunters. Others, like James, found that they could bunt to move a runner to the next base if they wanted. But just because they were able to bunt did not mean they desired to make sacrifices. If he could swing away, maybe he would hit a double into the outfield and drive in a run. The last thing he wanted was to give his coaches the thought James should allow himself to be out and set up someone else for the big hit.

No one had said it at Meadville's field, but several players had mentioned it or texted it to each other after yesterday's practice. Coach Arim or Coach Deem would call for a sacrifice or two, even when it was unnecessary. They wanted to prove a point.

With a lead, but not a large one, James suspected that now would be the time. The coaches would force him to put down a bunt. Or he would at least have to put a better effort to make the sacrifice. He could pretend to bunt again and tell the coaches it was harder to do against the other team's pitcher than it was in practice. That would at least be true.

But to his relief, a different signal came in: swing away.

James did and got under the first pitch. He popped it up to the shortstop.

Walking back to the dugout, James punched his right fist into his left hand in frustration. He had let himself get so focused on being allowed to swing away he hit a pitch that was too high. He never should have moved the bat.

Central did not score, and Meadville did not score in the bottom of the fifth either. But when Matt led off the sixth with a single, everyone on the Central bench knew what was coming. Sure enough, the signal started from Coach Deem to Coach Arim, then from Coach Arim to Jules in the batter's box: sacrifice.

Jules, like James, had shown some ability to put down a bunt. But like all Central players, Jules had no desire to get thrown out at first base on purpose. James noticed that Jules looked over to Coach Baptiste in the first-base coach's box. The coach nodded, confirming the signal.

On the first pitch, Jules shortened up to bunt, but let the pitch go by for a ball. The sacrifice-bunt signal came through again. Jules held the bat and appeared to measure the fastball coming in, and this time he made contact with the ball.

But James noticed something about the way Jules bunted the pitch. The purpose of a sacrifice bunt was to goad the other team into throwing the batter out at first and allow the runners on base to move. The bunt should roll where it would to be fielded by the third baseman or the pitcher, but in a bad spot for any fielder to throw anywhere except first base.

That was not how Jules bunted. He gave the bat an extra push as it contacted the ball, and it flew out in the air farther than a sacrifice bunt should. It still fell to the ground untouched, and Jules turned his "sacrifice" bunt into a bunt single.

Later in the inning, Tom hit a two-run single that scored both Matt and Jules. Central had a 5-1 lead, and no one doubted that victory was in hand.

As Jules came back into the dugout after scoring, he gave high-fives to all his teammates. But once he got to the teammates on the far end of the bench where Coach Deem would not hear, Jules said, "Never sacrifice yourself."

James couldn't agree more.

Chapter 13

Maggie sprinted from her car to the bleachers. She was behind schedule after visiting several stores for college shopping, finding new school supplies, clothes, and other items for her dorm room this fall. But it was midway through summer, and that meant each game Central played became more and more critical.

She hurried toward Jo and Martha in the front row of the third-base bleachers and sat down between them. The first pitch of the game was being thrown. She had missed the national anthem, which was only odd because she was usually there before her friends.

"Well, look who's Latey McLate Late," Jo said.

"This ain't chemistry class, this game is important," Martha added.

"Oh, shut up," Maggie answered, sitting down and taking in the game. She glanced out to right field. There was Nate. Good old patient Nate. It had been weeks since they had first talked about getting together. Though they had spoken many times since, both here at the field and other places around town, she had not brought up the subject again. Nate was still interested. That was why he always made a bee-line right to Maggie the moment the post-game team huddle was done. But he never brought it up when anyone was around to hear. Between ballgames and Maggie's job, they had not spoken alone since that evening at the playground almost a month ago.

That would change after this game. Nate deserved an answer now.

Maggie tried to remove all the thoughts about Nate out of her mind, as much as she could, anyway. She did not want to give anything away to Jo and Martha. They must have figured out something was going on between them. They were always right there when Maggie and Nate were talking after every game. Maggie was almost afraid her friends would read her mind.

Both Jo and Martha seemed intent on watching this game. There were fewer jokes and more focus on each play and pitch than there had been in games earlier this summer. Maggie could not blame them. There were only two games left in the season. If Central beat Nickelton now and Vigortown tomorrow, they would win the regular-season county title.

Central should beat Nickelton today. That was by far the easier of the two tasks. But the stakes made the game feel more intense, especially early in the game.

"Isn't this the team they were playing when that Phil spiked a guy?" Martha asked in the second inning.

Maggie had forgotten about that incident. Now she remembered that Nickelton was the opponent that game.

"That may be why Phil's not playing today," Jo said. "Or at least why he's not starting."

"I bet that third baseman must have said something nasty about you," Maggie teased. "He was defending your honor."

"No jokes," Jo said. "Baseball."

Jo's rebuff did not seem rude, but she did not seem embarrassed when Maggie brought up her obvious crush on Phil, either. She and Martha were so intent on the game they did not want to talk about much else.

In one sense, it was refreshing. Maggie never liked it when she was playing a softball game, and she heard fans talking about which movie they wanted to watch that night. She and her teammates, including the two she was sitting between, worked hard to play their best and deserved the attention of their fans.

Nevertheless, Jo and Maggie could afford to turn down the intensity a bit. Central was in good shape with a 3-0 lead after the first two innings.

In the bottom of the third, Nate led off the inning, and Maggie could feel a slight jump inside her. For this one at-bat, she focused only on the game.

Was she really falling?

No, she was not, not yet anyway. Maggie was sure. If she truly loved Nate, making him happy would be her priority, and it was not. She wanted him to be happy, but this relationship was about proving her own value.

But she cared about him. She trusted him. But the timing was a factor.

Maggie realized she was not as focused as she thought. The crack of Nate's bat brought her back to the real world and out of her thoughts. He hit a line drive between the right and center fielders and ran to second for a double. Maggie jumped up and clapped, yelling as Nate made his way to the base.

He made eye contact with her for a moment, and Maggie thought she saw the slightest smile from Nate. There was something different from love there, she knew. Whatever it was, she was ready to explore it with him.

Nate did not score, but Nickelton never did either. Central had a comfortable 5-0 lead heading into the top of the seventh. Jo and Martha were letting their guard down a little, no longer leaning forward in their seats but reclining back into the bleachers. They had stopped talking about the game going on now. Instead, they were already talking about the game coming up tomorrow.

"Can you make it?" Jo asked.

"Of course," Martha said.

Maggie just nodded.

"Okay, I'll drive," Jo said. "I'll pick you up, and then we stop to get burgers on the way."

"Vigortown has a concession stand."

"Oh, yeah, that will be cheaper. But we have to make sure we get there early so we can get our seats. I know there will be a big crowd there."

"I'll be ready by four."

Maggie could not concentrate on the talk. She knew in a few minutes, she would tell Nate her decision, and she was unsure of his response. But she could not talk to him about it with Jo and Martha close enough to hear.

"I'll text you tomorrow," Maggie said. "Then I'll let you know when you can pick me up from my home. I have to go. My parents expect me. I have to organize the college things I got. Soon." The excuse sounded terrible coming out of her mouth, so she doubted Jo or Martha believed the lie. Still, Maggie got up and walked towards the parking lot. When she knew her friends weren't looking, she cut over to the first-base side of the field and hid behind the Nickelton dugout. The back wall of the dugout was a solid brick, so no one on the Central side of the field would spot her.

She peeked out from the edge of the wall to watch the last play, a fly ball to right field. Nate got under it and tried to catch it with only his glove. The ball popped out for a moment before he used his bare hand to snag it for the final out of the game.

Maggie waited behind the dugout for a few minutes as many fans started to leave. She snuck another look. The post-game team speech must be over, as Nate was packing his equipment bag. He looked over to where Jo and Martha were, but he did not walk that way. He shrugged his shoulders and turned to make his way to the parking lot.

Before going to intercept him by his car, Maggie noticed that Jo was waving down Phil, who jogged over to talk to her. He had not done that after the other games. Maggie wondered for a second if Phil was caving towards Jo or if he was only being nice.

Or, what if Phil had his eyes on Martha?

Who could tell what a boy was thinking? Or a girl, for that matter. Which was the reason Maggie needed to get to Nate now.

"On the softball team, we're told to use both hands," Maggie said as she caught up to Nate. He turned with surprise all over his face. But Nate steadied himself and gave that baby-face smile that Maggie adored.

"You're only the eighth person to tell me that," Nate answered, though his smile told her she had not offended him. "And the game only ended five minutes ago."

Maggie got into step next to him. She took a glance over her shoulder. Her friends were still talking to Phil, and no one else was within earshot. They would have to keep their voices low, but this was her chance. Still, she would take her time to get to the heart of the matter. That was one of the many prerogatives of being a woman.

"So, if you win tomorrow, you win the county championship, right?" she asked.

"Yes," Nate answered, opening the back of his car to toss his bag in the trunk. "At least, the regular-season championship. But it's the playoff champion that goes to the Region D tournament, so it's not a disaster if we don't win tomorrow night."

"But you're going to win, right?"

Nate smiled. "Of course. We're better than Vigortown. We never should have lost the last time we played them."

Maggie smiled and tried to make the smirk mysterious. But without a mirror, she was not sure if she looked like she would burst in giggles or tears. "You know, we haven't had many chances to talk alone. And I didn't want to text you about something like this."

Nate looked around the parking lot. "You never know if someone's looking over your shoulder when you're looking at your phone, or if someone in the next row is listening at the movie theater. But it looks like we're safe now. Are we finally going to finish up what we talked about at the playground?"

"Yes. You've been patient while waiting for me to make up my mind. I said things to you I wasn't sure I should have. But now, with some time, I've decided."

Maggie hesitated for a moment, not because she was unsure what to say next, but because she wanted to see the anticipation in his soft brown eyes. Those eyes widened. Nate's fingers clenched.

"But my decision is not a simple yes or no. It's not yet."

"You need a little more time?" Nate asked, though his smile told Maggie he was not hurt that she was holding out a little longer. "I can respect that. I want you to be ready."

"Two weeks," Maggie blurted out. "It's just, I'm ninety percent ready. I just need to be, you know, completely ready." She felt embarrassed. She had pictured herself telling all this to Nate with authority. Now she was stumbling over her words.

But Nate hugged her, and she embraced him in return. "I understand," he whispered. "If that's the time you need, I'll give you all the time you need."

Maggie felt safe in Nate's embrace. She did not care anymore who saw them or who would misunderstand the relationship between her and her best friend. She trusted Nate, and that was all that mattered.

Nate pulled back, and Maggie could tell from his sideways look he was trying to figure out something. "What is it?" she asked.

"You know, we will win the game tomorrow," Nate said.

"Of course," Maggie replied, unsure of the sudden change in subject.

"And we will win the playoff title next week. And we will win Region D the following week."

Nate did not lack any confidence, Maggie saw. But all the boys on the team thought that way. She decided to puff up his ego. "I bet you don't just win the county and the region. I bet you don't lose a game in either tournament."

"My point is, the region finals are two weeks from now," Nate explained. "After we win the Region D title, you and I could, celebrate, privately."

Maggie smiled, both at Nate's idea and that he was the one stumbling over his words now. "Even more of a night to remember."

"But," Nate said, "since you are making me wait, may I choose where?"

That caught Maggie off guard. Who and when were vital to her. Where, she had never decided. So she nodded, curious where Nate had chosen.

He whispered in her ear, and what he said sounded like a bad idea. But Nate's smile was beyond mischievous now. She had known him too long to misunderstand his jokes. This was serious.

It was wrong. It was risky. It was exciting.

At first, Maggie was stunned at the request. Now she was surprised at how much it appealed to her. "Deal." She gave him the lightest kiss on the lips.

Maggie chose the time. Nate chose the place. It would be fair. And it would be perfect.

Chapter 14

After Central defeated Meadville, Pete figured out all the possible scenarios for how the regular season could end. Hemtown, somehow, had clinched the fourth-place spot and would be in the playoffs. So would third-place Meadville. Central and Vigortown would be the top two. The only question remaining was which of those two would be the regular-season champion.

That champion would be the team that won the last game of the regular season tonight.

On the drive to Vigortown's Wagner Field, Pete and Andy talked about how tonight's game might not be as important as it seemed. Both teams would be in those playoffs no matter what happened. But the brothers also agreed that if their goal was to be the best and to make up for several years of mediocre baseball, success had to start now.

This win would put Central on top of something. The team might only be on top of a list of six teams in the Lebanon County League, but it would be a start. Then the county playoffs, Region D playoffs and so on would build on that.

Both teams may have already earned their berths in the postseason, but this game mattered. And it did not matter to only Pete and Andy, or just to the players. It must have been important to Coach Deem. Now Pete understood why he had not pitched the last time Central played against Vigortown. Coach Deem had given Central a chance to win against Lavernon without Pete playing in the game once. He also tried to give them a chance to beat Vigortown without Pete pitching.

It had not worked in that last game against Vigortown even though John had pitched well that day. But there was no fooling around now. This was the biggest game of the season so far, and Pete had to be on the mound.

All those things were in Pete's mind in the hours leading up to the night game under the Wagner Field lights. But they were not in his thoughts now. Pete stood on the mound in the bottom of the first to face the first batter in Vigortown's lineup. Central did not score in the top of the first, and Pete himself struck out in his first at-bat. Even that was not present in his mind.

He had a job to do: keep any Vigortown player from ever touching home plate.

Pete and Andy were familiar with the tendencies of the Vigortown batters, which was one benefit of having played against the team twice this season. At the same time, Vigortown's hitters had seen Pete's pitches before, in the season opener. But there was a difference. Pete's game, refined by age and a year of college experience, was a half-step ahead of even Vigortown's best hitters.

The first inning would be crucial. No signs of weakness would be allowed. Just keeping Vigortown from scoring was not enough. Pete needed to make the opponent believe they had no hope of scoring the whole game.

Pete looked in for Andy's signals, but he knew what he would see for most of the time. The brothers had already decided how they would approach each batter. Against the leadoff man, Pete started with a slider which the hitter took for a strike. A curveball dropped into the zone for another strike. Then he swung through a high fastball for a three-pitch strikeout.

The second batter was the key in Pete's mind. This hitter shouldn't be able to catch up to his fastest pitch. Three top-notch fastballs, right in the middle of the strike zone, proved Pete right.

Then the third hitter in Vigortown's lineup, who was the most talented batter on the team, stepped up to the plate. He would have caught up to Pete's fastball, if Pete threw it to him. Not that Pete was afraid of letting a hitter make contact. He believed in the fielders behind him. But Pete wanted to send a message to Vigortown and to his own teammates.

There was no way Vigortown could score today. The best pitcher in Lebanon County would pitch his best game.

Pete started the at-bat with a changeup. After seeing the second hitter get only fastballs, the third batter swung too soon. The second pitch was a curveball that made a sharp break downward, and the hitter swung over it. The third pitch was a slider that started high, then broke down at the last millisecond through the strike zone for a called third strike.

Nine pitches. Nine strikes. Three strikeouts.

Pete did not hear the one hundred or more Central fans cheer, nor did he notice the quick silence of the Vigortown fans. But he heard the hollering from his teammates in the field. That would generally be an inappropriate response to a game that was scoreless after only one inning.

But they knew Central had already won this game. And Pete hoped that Vigortown already knew it too.

* * *

James punched his fist into his glove and let out a celebratory yell as Pete struck out the third batter. He sprinted back into the dugout, knowing he would bat in the top of the second. More than that, he knew he would be on the winning side.

The two batters before him both made outs but that did not faze him. James strode up to the plate with confidence. Maybe he would not get a hit in this plate appearance, but he was convinced that Central would be victorious regardless of what he did.

Vigortown's pitcher was not the same hurler that had shut out Central the last time the two teams met. James knew Vigortown's top pitcher had enough rest by the Armed Services pitching rules to throw again. James had to assume he was not physically ready.

Whatever the reason, James was now batting against a pitcher he did not remember ever facing before tonight. But he and the coaches noticed that everything he threw was either fastballs or changeups. No pitches ever changed directions. They only altered speeds. The locations of most of the throws were not far off from each other either. It had been effective so far, but if a batter guessed correctly about which pitch was coming, he had a chance to rope a ball deep into the outfield.

James took the first pitch for a strike. It was a fastball. Guessing that a changeup was coming, he made a late swing at the next pitch and missed a fastball.

With two strikes, James looked for a fastball. He figured that if he was wrong, and the pitch was a changeup, he at least had a fraction of a second to adjust. The other way around, it would be too late to alter his swing again.

He guessed fastball, and a fastball he saw. It was right down the middle.

James's swing made perfect contact with the ball. It felt effortless to him. The connection did not feel at all like the one deep fly ball that was within inches of being a home run against Nickelton earlier in the season. It was almost like he took a hard practice swing that never even hit a ball or anything else.

But he knew he had hit it when he heard the perfect crack of the bat. He took off running towards first base, looking at Coach Baptiste to see if he should continue going to second or hold up there. But the coach was staring out to left field. As James reached the bag, the coach held out one hand.

Coach Baptiste was offering a high-five. Only then did James become aware of the cheers and see the base umpire circling a hand in the air. It was a home run.

James could not believe it. He had hit one home run in the spring during the high school season, but that homer was against a bad pitcher on a lousy team. This one was against the best opponent in the county. After giving Coach Baptiste a high-five, he sped around the bases, slapping hands with Coach Arim at third base. He finally crossed home plate for the game's first run.

The home-plate umpire was telling his Central teammates to stay back in the first-base dugout. They stayed off the field but were all cramming by the entrance to greet him, yelling like James had not heard all season. When he got to them, they were hugging him, knocking his batting helmet off and rubbing their hands through his hair.

"Home-run derby champ right here!" Andy said.

"Have you been saving that power on us all year?" Matt asked.

"Feel those muscles!" Nate shouted.

James had to catch his breath from racing around the bases and then enduring the celebration. "How far did it go?"

"Over the scoreboard in left field," Pete said. "I'm guessing four-hundred feet. You crushed it."

"It almost hit one of the cars parked past the outfield," John added.

The next batter made the last out of the inning, so James put his glove back on and started to run out to third base. But then, Coach Deem stopped him for a moment. He put out his hand to James. James took it and gave a firm shake. There would be no weak handshakes with the head coach.

"Good hit," Coach Deem said. "Perfect timing. Nice, level swing. Now forget it ever happened and play good defense."

James smiled and ran out onto the field. He looked over to the scoreboard and realized that the ball must have sailed over it. It was not four hundred feet away from home plate, but it must have been over three hundred and fifty feet.

Though he remained focused throughout the game, everything else after his home run seemed like a blur when James tried to remember it later. Several strikeouts by Pete were mixed in with the two singles that Vigortown hit. One of them was followed by a double-play ground ball. James started that double play himself when he snared a hard ground ball to his right. The other Vigortown batter to get a hit was thrown out by Andy while trying to steal second, with Tom making the tag.

When Central batted, hits were still scarce. But Central made the most of the hits they did earn. John singled in Jules for one run, and Andy doubled to knock in Little Jimmy for another. James could not recall which innings those runs scored in, and he did not care. With the way Pete was pitching, the extra runs never mattered. One run would have been plenty.

In the bottom of the seventh, with two outs, Central had a 3-0 lead. The batter for Vigortown had two strikes on him, and James sensed another strikeout coming. But the hitter was able to make contact, and the ball flew into shallow right field. James kept his eye on it and saw that John had taken a few steps backward from first base and caught the ball.

All the Central players converged on the mound, and there were so many hugs and high-fives going on that James did not always know who he was facing. The twelve teammates were all yelling as they congratulated each other and themselves as well.

Coach Deem got their attention with a whistle. He reminded them they still had to get into a line to shake hands with the Vigortown players, which they did in a hurry. Then they continued their yelling as they trotted back to the dugout. They could not wait to see their family and friends.

There was still the post-game talk from Coach Deem, but James could not listen. They had done it! After being stuck in mediocrity for years, Central baseball had finished in first place.

When the post-game speech from the coach had ended, the team huddled up again. Pete was telling everyone how proud he was of them and reminding them that there would be a playoff title to win next week. The players yelled out "champions!" and broke the huddle.

A man walked up to James and asked if he could talk to him. James did not recognize him right away but said yes. The man held a recorder up to him and asked him about what type of pitch he hit for the home run. James answered and realized this was the sportswriter from the Lebanon County newspaper. Lucas something or other. James could not remember. It did not matter who the reporter was. He was happy to think about having his name in the story about the biggest game of the year.

So far.

* * *

The celebration continued on the field, now with fewer hugs but more jovial laughter and high-fives.

The old man observed from his seat in the top row of Wagner Field's bleachers behind home plate. He was happy for Central's team and its players, but not in any way surprised. He knew this championship was coming even before he walked onto this field on the morning of opening day.

It was no surprise to him either that things were not going as smoothly as the players believed. Central was a good baseball team and would win the Lebanon County playoffs. But if things remained unchanged, they would go no further.

That was only a slight concern to the old man. He stood up and continued to watch as players continued to joke with each other, still in the afterglow of their biggest win. A few of the boys were now meeting with parents and relatives, or with the girls who always attended the games.

But also making his way to almost all the players was Devon Hellickson. Tonight, Devon was not saying or doing anything that would arouse suspicion. But the old man knew Devon much better than anyone else there did. He would work in the open when he could and then work in the shadows when he needed.

There was the real problem. Central's players did not realize that Devon made them something less than they should have been, both on the baseball field and away from it. He had torn down many other teams before he came to Central. But no one had both the power and will to make Devon go away. And even if someone forced the deceiver away, it would take someone of wisdom and compassion to undo the work he had already done.

The old man could do it, but no one on the ground below was ready yet to deal with his face and voice up close. The difference between generations would be too much, not from his point of view, but from theirs.

He took one more moment to look upon the players, both the winners from Central and the losers from Vigortown. With love in his eyes, the old man reached for the phone he kept in his pocket.

He dialed, and in a second, the call was answered. The old man needed to speak just one sentence.

"Son, it is time."

Part II

Hometown Fans

Chapter 15

Pete's right arm felt strong as he did a few soft tosses with his brother. Part of him wished Central did not have these days off between the last regular-season game and the first playoff contest. He wanted to start the postseason as soon as possible since Central was playing so well. But that was how the Lebanon County League scheduled the tournament. The positive was that the extra time allowed Pete to pitch again in the playoff opener tomorrow at Hemtown.

Pete was excited to face Central's next-door neighbor in the semifinal series. His enthusiasm was because playoff baseball was more fun than the regular season, but also because he was sure Hemtown would not hit well against him. Pete had little doubt that Central would win the best-of-three semifinal series. Then they would most likely get to take on the more dangerous Vigortown team in the championship series.

Pete caught himself in mid-thought. He was getting ahead of himself. Focus on Hemtown for now. Central was the better team by a significant margin. But any playoff game required his full focus and the concentration of his teammates.

"That's enough, Pete," Coach Deem called from the infield, where he was doing fielding practice with the rest of the team. "You've done plenty for today. And we're done over here."

The head coach turned back towards the other players but still called out loud enough for Pete to hear. "Be here at least an hour before the first pitch."

"Or else you won't be able to park with all the fans we'll have here," John interrupted.

That got a good a chuckle from most of the players, even Coach Deem. "We might get a few more than usual. But we need to get a lot deeper into the postseason to draw giant crowds. And don't worry yourselves over that. Trophies and banners don't grow larger if fifty or five hundred people are here."

After making sure that no players had any questions, Coach Deem and Coach Arim allowed the boys to go home, which the two coaches also did themselves. Coach Baptiste hung around with a handful of players who took their time getting to their cars in the Central High School parking lot.

Pete tossed his glove in his car and was waiting for Andy to do the same, but his brother was looking back towards the field. So were James, John, and Phil.

"Why are you all still waiting here?" Pete asked.

"Mr. Hellickson said he'd be coming over today after practice." Phil's voice trailed off as he remembered Coach Baptiste was still in earshot.

The coach had already heard enough, though. "I keep telling you that shouldn't trust that man. Is that him walking over here?"

Pete also turned toward the field, and indeed a man was walking toward them. After a moment, though, it was clear this was not Mr. Hellickson. This individual was shorter by an inch even though he seemed to walk erect and not slouched. His dark hair was wavy and down to his shoulders in a neat cut.

"He, he's here," Coach Baptiste said.

"No, that's not Mr. Hell...," James started.

"I know it's not him. This is the man I've waited a long time to see again."

Pete did not understand what was happening. Coach Baptiste seemed in awe of this stranger as he stared with a glazed expression.

As the man came up to them by their cars, Coach Baptiste seemed to snap out of his trance. He smiled and embraced the mystery man. Both men roared with laughter.

Andy elbowed Pete. "Do you know who this guy is?"

"No idea," Pete answered, and a glance at James, John and Phil told him that his teammates were as confused as he was.

Coach Baptiste turned towards the players but kept one arm around the newcomer. "Let me introduce you. This is Jonas Davis. He is a distant relative of mine. We grew up in the same neighborhood and were always together until we were, uh, how old were we, Jonas?"

"Twelve," Jonas answered, speaking for the first time. His voice was a deep baritone, reminding Pete of his grandfather. It was not a threatening tone as a principal or dean might sometimes use. In its depth, Pete found comfort in his speech.

"The last time we were together was when our families took that trip to Washington, D.C.," Jonas continued. "The time my mother thought I was lost in the city."

Coach Baptiste laughed again. "Oh, yes, I remember. My family moved that same summer." The coach turned back to the players. "But we've been in touch ever since then. And I'm telling you, if you want to succeed, you'll listen to him."

"So, are you here to be a new coach for us?" John asked.

"Not in the way Jerry here is," Jonas said, patting Coach Baptiste on the back. "But I have much to teach you. Tell your teammates. We will meet several times. Sometimes it will be at the field, sometimes other places, before or after games. In the end, my purpose in being here is to get you to your ultimate goal."

Ultimate goal? Did he mean the national tournament? Fifteen minutes ago, Pete was telling himself not to look ahead. Now someone is telling him about the final tourney in the Armed Services playoff system. The national tournament would be after the county, Region D, state, and Mid-Atlantic tournaments.

But this was a man who they had never met before today. How could they be sure that this Jonas knew anything about baseball?

Pete made eye contact with Coach Baptiste, who seemed to understand the dilemma in Pete's mind.

"I vouch for this man," the coach said. "You need to listen to him. I will speak with the other coaches and with your parents if I need to explain anything. But there is much you will learn from Jonas. He knows so much that you need to understand."

"Oh, now I get it," James said. "You called him here to help us."

"Actually, I didn't," Coach Baptiste said. Turning to Jonas, he continued, "I figured you would come to us, but I wasn't sure when. How did you wind up here? Did you read something on the internet?"

"No," Jonas answered. "My father called me, so of course I came right away."

"Of course," Coach Baptiste answered.

"Jerry, could I ask a favor of you? I ran out of water while walking on the way here. Do you have anything I could use to wash my face?"

Coach Baptiste walked back to his car and soon came back with two bottles of water. As Jonas opened the first bottle and drank from it, Phil asked, "Does your dad come to our games? Maybe we know him."

Jonas did not answer right away. He opened the second bottle and handed it to Coach Baptiste. For a moment, the coach did nothing. Then, after Jonas nodded, Coach Baptiste poured the water over Jonas's head, cleaning off dirt that Pete had not realized was there.

From the baseball field, a voice crackled over the public address system and made the players jump. "He is my son. I love my boy, and you would be wise to listen to him."

The players looked over towards the second floor of the press box behind home plate. Pete knew the only place with a microphone was at the top level. There was a man up there, but they were too distant to tell who it was right away through the window. But when the individual walked out of the press box, they saw it was the old man that always found his way to the games.

"That man is your father?" James asked.

"Yes, though you won't be seeing him at your games anymore," Jonas said, wiping the water away from his eyes.

"Oh, it's just, um," James stopped. "I'll ask another time."

Pete looked back to where the old man had been, but he seemed to have disappeared. In his place, though, another car was driving on the road behind the field towards them. Pete recognized it as Mr. Hellickson's red sports car.

It seemed that Jonas also recognized the vehicle, for his face narrowed into clear displeasure. "Excuse me. Stay here a little while longer. I have more to talk to you about, but I must deal with this now."

Jonas walked towards the car which parked thirty yards away from the players. Pete was not sure if he was violating anyone's privacy, but sensed something memorable was about to happen. It was possible that a fight was brewing. He inched closer to see if he could listen to what Jonas and Mr. Hellickson would say. Coach Baptiste came up from behind and put a hand on his shoulder.

"I think it's fine to listen," the coach said. "But don't get involved. Jonas will handle this alone."

Pete strained to listen as Mr. Hellickson stepped out of his car. Jonas was staring back at him. They started speaking, Mr. Hellickson with anger, Jonas with sternness and composure. Their faces made it seem like each one was keen on bettering the other, but only a smattering of words reached Pete's ears.

"They won't listen to you. I can fulfill their desires," Mr. Hellickson said.

More words followed that Pete could not make out. Then from Jonas, "I don't need to do something amazing to prove myself. Doing what my father said is enough."

For a moment, Pete thought the conversation ended and had turned into a stare-down. Then Mr. Hellickson replied in a dark tone, "We'd both be more successful if you worked for me."

"Go away from here!" Jonas answered. Those were the only words spoken loud enough for the others in the parking lot to hear. Pete thought he heard Jonas add, "I work for my father, and my father only," but he was not sure.

Mr. Hellickson was back in his car so fast that Pete could barely follow the movement. The car sped out of the school parking lot, leaving tire marks over the asphalt. Jonas, meanwhile, walked back to Pete and the other players.

"One of your teammates will see him again," Jonas said. "But the five of you here will not."

Pete was not certain that one heated conversation would keep Mr. Hellickson away, though he would be glad if that was the case. He was never comfortable when he was around that slick gentleman. But Pete could see the disappointment in the eyes of his teammates.

Jonas must have seen it too. "You are disappointed. But it's better for you to be disappointed and not get what he was carrying in that car."

"And, you know what he had in the car?" John asked.

"Better than you do," Jonas said. "Besides what you were hoping for, he had several kinds of drugs in there. He intended on giving you a few for free, then charge you when you came back to him."

"Wait, illegal drugs?" Coach Baptiste asked. "I didn't think he went that far."

"Yeah," James said. "I thought all he was about was, you know."

"James is trying to say, 'beer'," Phil said.

"And it may not have seemed like a big deal to you, but there is no limit to Devon Hellickson's corruption," Jonas said. "He offers people whatever they think is not too bad. For you, a team of teenage boys, it was easy for him to work his way in with free alcohol. It's not that drinking itself is so bad, in moderation and when you are old enough for it. But Devon's real goal was to get you in the habit of breaking the rules. He wanted you to feel like getting away with something was enough reason to do it. The drugs were the next step in a never-ending downward spiral into a pit. And even if you refused the alcohol or the drugs, he would have eventually returned with new temptations of different kinds."

"Stop," Pete said. He had had enough. "How do you know what Mr. Hellickson said to us?"

"Pete," Jonas answered. "You must accept that I already know what people have tried to keep hidden. My father watched you more closely than you realize."

His father was always distant from us, Pete thought. He may have been at all the games, but in the farthest seat from the field. Had the old man been at any of the practices when many of their encounters with Mr. Hellickson had taken place? Pete could not remember for sure.

The old man must have snuck into the press box a little while ago without no one noticing. Soon after that, he left without a trace. Maybe there was something to it. Still, it struck Pete as a little creepy now.

But Coach Baptiste was saying to trust Jonas, and Coach Baptiste was as dependable a person as Pete had ever met. So Pete felt he could wait a little while until he decided if he could trust this newcomer. Jonas might be trustworthy, so Pete felt compelled to give him the benefit of the doubt.

For now.

While Pete was processing all that, James was speaking. "I don't mean to be rude, but I have a question about your father."

"Certainly. Ask what you want. There's much more to my father than you can imagine."

"Well, do you mean he is your birth father, or are you adopted?"

"That is rude!" Phil said before Jonas to respond.

"No, it's not. At least not to me," Jonas said. "Why do you ask?"

"Um, he's black," James said.

Pete had seen but not taken note of Jonas's olive skin, almost the same tone as Coach Baptiste's. This man, who Pete was now guessing was in his early thirties, was not of African descent. But he was not of European descent either.

"Hold on," Phil said. "His father is white. Although, that still doesn't explain everything," Phil stopped, obviously embarrassed to bring up such a touchy subject.

Jonas laughed again and Coach Baptiste joined him. "Both of you think you've seen my father up close when you haven't. Many people think they know him when they don't. You never had a good look at him and assumed that he has the same skin color as you. Suffice to say he is my father, and he wants me to help you get to your ultimate goal."

All the players stared at Jonas. His hair was as dark as Coach Baptiste's, but not as long. Jonas was not as tall as Pete, but Jonas noted his shoes were thin sandals, so he might be losing an inch to his footwear. Though he might stand out because of his height, Jonas's outfit did nothing to call attention to himself. Just a plain white shirt and a pair of jean shorts.

Could this man be that important in getting them through the Armed Services baseball playoffs? In changing them from a good team to a national contender? He spoke like a madman. It was not his delivery, which was still comforting to Pete. But Jonas did not give much in the way of answers to their questions. What had taken place between him and Hellickson? Why did his father care about getting them to the national tournament? If Jonas could do that, why hadn't he come years ago?

"I'll send texts out myself, but you all should talk to the other guys," Coach Baptiste said. "We can all meet for lunch tomorrow, well before the game. I'll pay, so don't worry about that. Jonas, you always liked the cafe at the end of town, right?"

"Been a while since I've eaten there, but I'll happily meet with all your teammates then," Jonas said, walking with Coach Baptiste to the coach's car. "In fact, I'll be looking forward to any food at all. I haven't eaten in days."

While driving his brother home after the surprising encounter with Jonas, Pete realized something. Coach Baptiste had never told Jonas which players were which. No one even said which players were still in the parking lot when Jonas arrived and which ones had left. They weren't in their uniforms, so Jonas could not have seen a jersey number.

Yet Jonas had called him by name.

Had Jonas seen his picture in a newspaper or on a computer? He had said nothing about watching any of Central's games. All Jonas said was that his father sent him. In fact, most of what he said kept going back to his father.

Who is this man? Was he a genius with great perception? A shady character hiding something? A lunatic?

Pete hoped that the lunch tomorrow would make it clearer, one way or the other.

Chapter 16

Pete parked his car at the end of the strip mall at the eastern side of the town of Central, outside the cafe. This was not his favorite place to go, since he only half-heartedly enjoyed coffee. But this is where Coach Baptiste had invited them, so they would eat lunch here now. If nothing else, a free meal is a free meal, Pete reminded himself.

Along with bringing his brother Andy, Pete had picked up John and James. They were walking up to the door of the restaurant when they saw Coach Baptiste pulling up with Jonas in the passenger's seat. When they had parked, the coach opened his door and called out, "It's good that you're early. We need to talk about several things."

Jonas came out of the car and walked over to them, giving Pete another chance to look at him. What stood out on this second view of the man was the calmness behind eyes. It was not sleepiness, but peace.

"It's good to see you all again," Jonas said. Pete held the door open for him. "Thank you."

The six of them put two tables together in the cafe and sat down in the wooden chairs. "Will the rest of the team be here? We'll need more seats," Coach Baptiste said.

"Phil is coming," James said.

"We texted the others," Pete said. "They'll all make it sooner or later. But a few of the guys don't get up until noon, so it may be a while."

Coach Baptiste laughed. "The wonders of being young in the summertime. Well, order whatever you want. I cleared it with Coach Deem, and we're using the team account for lunch. Wonder how Harry Antes would feel about it. I don't care. I just wonder."

The men and boys ordered shortly after sitting. Pete, who never was a fan of coffee anyway, ordered an iced tea and a flatbread sandwich. Then his focus returned to Jonas.

"Before the others get here, could you give us a hint about how you'll get us to the national tournament?" Pete asked.

"Did I say I would?" Jonas asked back, smiling.

"Well, you said you wanted to help us to our ultimate goal," James said.

"And it felt like you said it to us as a team, not any one of us," John added. "So I took it to mean our goal as a team, not like my goal to attend Harvard."

"You don't want to go to Harvard," James replied.

"I meant it as an example, not literally. And neither of us has any business going to Harvard."

Jonas sat up straight in his chair. "I'm not talking about Harvard either. If you want to reach your goal, this has to start with you." His gaze fixed on Pete.

"Are you saying I need to play better now because it's the playoffs?" Pete was not hurt by the implication. It was only common sense that athletes had to pick up their games in the postseason. That would be the case if they made it to the Region D tournament and had to play other county champions.

"It wouldn't hurt," Jonas said. "But it doesn't stop there. Your coaches never named any players as official captains, but you must be the leader. Until now, you have won games but have done so as individuals. You possess more talent than the other teams in Lebanon County, so you can still win even though you are fractured as a team."

"But we all get along," Andy said.

"Get along with each other? Yes. But that's not the same as playing as a team. Suppose the coach gives you signal that you can, but do not have to, steal a base. Do any of you think about if your running helps or hurts the batter? Or when you are batting, and the coach signals you to lay down a sacrifice bunt, what happens then? Don't all of you either try to put down a bunt for a hit instead or intentionally miss the bunt until the coach lets you swing away again?"

Pete glanced over at Coach Baptiste, wondering if he had been telling his friend about the players' distaste for sacrifices. But the coach was drinking his black Guatemalan coffee and gave no sign of whether he was telling the team's secrets or not.

"How do you know about that?" Pete asked, looking back to Jonas.

"My father saw it," Jonas answered.

"It's true, we haven't played the best team baseball we are capable of, especially when we're supposed to sacrifice," Pete said. "I think we will still win the Lebanon County tournament playing this way, but we might run into trouble at Region D if we don't refine our game. But what does that have to do with me, in particular?"

"You're the oldest," Andy said. "I mean, I don't care. You're just my older brother that can set me up with a college girl sometime." Pete turned to Andy and sneered at him, but his younger brother continued. "You have more experience at this. You're playing college ball on a scholarship. The other guys respect what you say and do."

"Your brother is partially right," Jonas said. "You are the oldest and most experienced. But I am telling this to you because my father chose you."

"Chose me for what?"

"The time is coming when you and your teammates will have many greater tasks in front of you than trying to win Lebanon County. When that time comes, you need to be a real team, not a team in name only. And that team will need leadership. Though anyone could lead for a short period, that burden will ultimately fall on you."

Pete leaned back in his chair. His tea was on the table now. He paused to sip it and consider what Jonas had said. "Coach Baptiste, do you agree with what Mr. Davis is saying?"

"Call me Jonas, please."

"Sorry. Do you agree with what Jonas is saying?"

Coach Baptiste nodded. "Yes. And I realize what I'm about to say is going against everything every coach has told you since you first starting playing baseball. But even though Jonas is not a coach, you need to realize that what he tells you is more important that what I tell you."

Pete could not remember any coaches ever telling him to take anyone's baseball advice more seriously than their own. But, since Jonas was elevating Pete's own role on the team, it was easy to take this new instruction. Maybe it would be nice to have Jonas around as a consultant to Central.

But apparently, the other players still wondered. "So you know each other that well?" Andy asked Coach Baptiste.

"Yes. We are cousins."

"Wait, you're related to that old man? Sorry, to his father?"

Coach Baptiste shook his head as he set his coffee cup on the table. "No. I am related to Jonas through our mothers' side of the family."

"How much do you know about our team?" James asked, returning everyone's focus back to Jonas. "Was your father at every single game to give you a scouting report on us?"

"A 'scouting report' doesn't do it justice," Jonas answered. "Trust me when I tell you, nothing about Central's team has been hidden from me. I am aware of everything about you as a unit and as individuals."

"So you've heard about all our strengths and weaknesses, in the field and at bat?" Andy asked. Pete could tell that his brother did not even try to keep the doubt out of his voice.

"More than that. I know each play, each pitch from this season," Jonas answered, not offended by Andrew's suspicion. "And I have more knowledge than that. For example, I know that Pete helped Matt to not tip off his curves during the second game of the year at Hemtown. That showed wisdom on your part."

Pete thought back. He had forgotten about it, but the second game had been at Hemtown. During that game, he had talked to Matt about the way he was giving a slight nod before he pitched a curveball.

"Also," Jonas continued, "in that same game, Pete pulled you aside, John. He saw you had made a baserunning mistake while running towards second. The coaches had missed it but Pete, you saw it. You corrected it with gentleness."

"I took my strides around the base all wrong," John said. "I knew I messed it up and didn't need anyone to point it out to me. But, Pete, he's right, isn't he? It was you who talked to me about it."

"Yes, both of those things happened, and both at the same game in Hemtown," Pete said. "But this has me confused: Neither of those conversations happened on the field. They were in the dugout. And I wasn't yelling at Matt or John, so how could your father in the stands hear us?"

"Were you at that game?" Coach Baptiste asked. "Hemtown was where you first lived, wasn't it?"

"Almost. It was where my family moved to when I was two years old," Jonas answered. "But I was not at that game. Only my father, who told me all he knew from all the games you've played."

Jonas's gaze left the others at the table, and he looked over them. His voice remained strong, but he seemed to address someone else.

"For instance, I know that Phil had to leave between games of the doubleheader you played this year at Lavernon," Jonas said.

"We all remember that," James said. "He nearly missed the second game."

"Yes, but I understand why," Jonas said, still looking past the players at the table. "Should I tell them?"

Pete turned around and saw that Phil was standing behind them. He wondered if he had been there listening for a while or had just come in the cafe. Through the windows of the cafe, Pete could see that the rest of his teammates were arriving.

"Um, sure, why not," Phil was answering. "It doesn't make much difference now."

"Courageous of you," Jonas said. "Not everyone would want a story like this told. Phil had a girlfriend who lived ten minutes from Lavernon's field. He was going to spend part of the day with her. But when the game was rescheduled into a doubleheader, he knew he would have to sneak out to see her between the games. So, once he got Coach Deem's permission, he drove over to see her. To be kind, I will ask again. Are you alright if I tell them?"

Pete glanced back to Phil again. His jaw was hanging open. Pete could guess why. Phil had never mentioned a girlfriend. He must have been keeping it a secret from everyone. Phil, dumbfounded, nodded to Jonas for him to continue.

"When he got there, she was in her front yard, kissing another young man," Jonas said. "You all should remember this other fellow. He was the third baseman from Nickelton, the same one Phil spiked in the next game."

"Phil, why didn't you tell us we had a soap opera going on?" John asked, laughing. "This would have made the season much more entertaining."

"Stop it," James said. "But my brother is right. If you would have told us, we could have helped take care of that Nickelton guy."

Pete said nothing. His teammates had gotten distracted by the story of Phil's relationship and breakup and missed the most important thing. There was no way Jonas should know about any of this. To be aware of Central's success and their habits on the field was unlikely, but still possible. His father may have been putting together a scouting report, and Jonas may have memorized it. Baseball people did those sorts of things.

But how could Jonas remember what conversations were going on in the dugout during a game he was never at in the first place? Pete would have forgotten about those talks had Jonas not mentioned them. How could Jonas tell a story about a bad breakup in a relationship that was a secret? Based on Phil's reaction, it seemed that Jonas had again been correct in that retelling.

Phil was almost pale, which Pete read as more shock than embarrassment. Phil turned to the door of the cafe. Pete thought he might run off, so he ran over to calm him. This was all odd, but it was probably nothing to fear. Jonas was perceptive, and maybe had inside information he had not revealed. But he was not behaving threateningly. If anything, Jonas seemed to be happy just to share the stories.

But as Pete caught up to Phil, he realized that his teammate was not running out of the restaurant. He was intercepting the rest of the team coming in the door.

"You need to hear this man," Phil was saying to them. "He's telling us everything, everything we've done this year. Conversations we've had. A girlfriend I hid from you guys, how we broke up, why I spiked Nickelton's third baseman. He knows all about it."

"Is this about the same guy that Coach Baptiste said would lead us to the nationals?" Nate asked.

"Yes. He's right over there, sitting next to Coach Baptiste. He's the man drinking his tea right now," Phil said, rushing his words together.

"I'm more curious how you ever got a girlfriend," Jules said, walking by Phil and over to the table.

"This is serious," Phil said. "I don't understand how this stranger has learned so much about us. But Coach Baptiste said this Jonas Davis originally came from Hemtown and that we need him in order to succeed as a team. Now he's there telling us every little detail about us."

"Slow down, Phil. Catch your breath," Nate said. "A baseball genius who knows everything that happens everywhere? Has anything that good ever come out of Hemtown?"

"Come and see."

"Phil's right," Pete said. "He knows about private conversations I've had. And Coach Baptiste has listened to all this too. He's told us we need to listen to Jonas even more than we listen to our coaches. Sit with us and hear what he has to say."

Nate shrugged and walked with them toward Jonas. The other boys, now taking up half of the cafe, were sitting around four tables. They squeezed in and listened to Jonas. He was telling another tale, this one about the last-inning win at Vigortown.

But Jonas stopped mid-sentence. He looked at Nate as he found a seat. "Now here's a player who's not afraid to tell people what he thinks. I hope you slept well last night, what with the playoffs starting today. You need to have your energy."

"And why wouldn't I have slept well?" Nate asked.

"Because you weren't sleeping at your own house last night," Jonas answered.

The cafe's music was drowned out by the hooting and catcalls that came from most of the Central players. Pete thought they might get kicked out and yelled at everyone to be quiet.

Besides, they did not need to embarrass Nate. His teammates listened and became silent.

I'm already filling out this leadership role quite nicely, Pete thought to himself. But even as he got his teammates to calm down, he was wondering if Jonas was aware of how Nate had been flirting with Maggie.

"Oh, you teenagers," Jonas said. "Your mind always goes to just one subject. It was just that the air conditioning at Nate's house blew a fuse last night, so he had to sleep at his grandparents' house."

Nate looked down as if he were ashamed. Pete felt a little embarrassed that he had assumed that Nate had spent the night at a girl's home. He should not have assumed that. But Nate's embarrassment had a different source.

"I apologize," Nate said, then he looked up and straight at Jonas. "I thought Phil was exaggerating. I'm not sure what your trick is, but no one could have known that. My parents picked me up this morning and brought me home. That was before the guys got me to come here. I hope you're as great a baseball mind as you are a mind-reader."

"He is," Coach Baptiste said. "Trust me on that. But more importantly, trust Jonas. Don't just listen for facts. Listen for guidance."

"And if I'm reading anything, I'm reading your hearts, not your minds," Jonas said. "As for baseball, in the future, get a new bat at once after chipping it on a foul ball."

Nate smiled. "I got a hit that at-bat, so it was not too bad."

"Yes, but that's no reason to wait to fix the mistake." Then Jonas addressed everyone. "Not for your own sake, but for your team's sake. A mistake like that can hinder everyone, while correcting it right away can help everyone. I will have more to tell you, but they are about to take our meal orders now."

"Please, one more thing," Pete said. "One more inexplicable insight you can share."

"Certainly," Jonas relented. "Nate, you can verify this for me. Your cousin, Lydia, will be here by the end of the county playoffs."

"Lydia!" several of Pete's teammates shouted.

Nate nodded.

"Why didn't you say something?" Ted asked.

"Because I'm embarrassed by how you guys react to her, ogling her all the time."

"The way we do? The way everyone does, you mean," Jules said.

Pete knew how they felt. He had not seen Lydia since last summer when she had visited to see a handful of games. Nate's cousin was in her late twenties, a huge baseball fan, and was by far the prettiest woman Pete had ever seen. That included Sal and any other woman he had seen in college. When Lydia was around, it was hard to take his eyes off of her. That she followed the sport that these boys played only made her more popular.

"Perhaps I should give you all one more bit of insight into Lydia," Jonas said.

The team, except for Nate, all turned to Jonas and were listening even closer than earlier. Even Pete, committed and faithful to Sal, couldn't stop himself from wondering what secret he might learn about this beauty.

"She's into older guys, not younger," Jonas said with a smile.

Everyone turned to Nate, who was laughing and nodding.

* * *

Their lunch had started with confusion and wonder over Jonas's ability to recall events he had never seen. But the Central gathering at the cafe turned to a happy time. All the players shared favorite stories from throughout the season. They also talked about their goals for the first playoff game coming up this evening against Hemtown. There were a few comments about Phil's ex-girlfriend, who they had only learned about minutes ago. But most of the conversations centered on what happened on the field. Some of it was about well-executed plays that highlighted the season, and some of it was about the fun time they were having in such a successful year. But the main link was that they had a passion for baseball.

No, James corrected himself. They had a passion for winning at baseball. So far, their talent had allowed the twelve of them to beat teams with eighteen players. James knew they could win the Lebanon County playoffs with no extra help. But when they faced teams with similar talent and deeper benches in the Region D tournament, any advantage would be welcome. Maybe Jonas was it.

But if they were going to trust Jonas, they should know what his approach to the game was. It was best to find out now what kinds of instructions they would get from him.

"Jonas," James said after the waitress dropped off their bill and the conversation lulled, "what is your, um, philosophy of baseball?"

"Philosophy?" Jonas asked back.

"Well, your strategy. What matters the most to you if you are trying to make a winning team?"

Jonas paused. Then he placed his right hand over his chest. "Your heart must be right before anything you do on the field matters."

"I don't think that's quite what my brother meant," John said. "What is the most important aspect of the game? If you were an official coach, what would you be emphasizing?"

"Ah," Coach Baptiste said. "They mean how I value batters who can hit for average over ones who hit for power. Or how Coaches Deem and Arim try to build a team around two or three good starting pitchers first."

"That is closer to what I meant," James said. "I guess everyone would say any of these things help. But what is most important to you? The pitching, or the hitting?"

"Or the fielding?" John asked.

"Are the power hitters more important?" Jules asked.

"Or is it the guys who can draw a walk and steal second?" Matt added.

"Would you rather have one great starting pitcher or a few good but not great guys to throw a couple of innings each?" Pete asked.

Jonas waved his hands as all the players spoke over each other. "Everything you're saying matters, but none of them is the most important. I can show you what is most important if you give me a few minutes. Meet us at the pool, the one next to the high school, and I will show you there."

"I didn't bring swim trunks," James said.

"Don't go into the pool, just park there. It will be clear then."

While Coach Baptiste and Jonas took care of the bill, James got into Pete's car, along with John and Andy. Pete drove them over to the pool.

"Are we all together on this, guys?" Pete asked during the drive. "Jonas's is different. Odd. But everything he's said so far is correct, and we can trust him because Coach Baptiste says he trusts him. Right?"

"Definitely," John said. "And since he's not a coach, we can always stop listening to him if we're wrong."

"But why is he sending us to the pool to teach us what he thinks is important for a baseball team?" Andy asked.

"There are two small baseball fields next to the pool," James said. "I bet he wants us to do something on them, like a team-building exercise."

"If it's that falling-backwards-and-let-your-teammate-catch-you thing, I'll let someone else catch me," John said.

"I'd catch you," James said. "Then I'd drop you. Step on you too."

Pete parked at the pool, which was busy on another hot summer day, at the same time as the other players. "So what do you guys think is going on?" Tom asked as the team stood together.

"I think Jonas wants us on the kids' fields for a team-building exercise," Pete answered.

"Don't think we can," Matt said, pointing. "Several children are running around on both fields."

"If we have to, we can go to our home field," Phil said. "It's just on the other side of the school. No one will prepare it for the game for a few more hours. I don't think anyone would object."

"That's not what I was asking," Tom said. "Could Jonas's father, that old man, really have told him all about us? Or has he been stalking us somehow?"

"I'll grant it's hard to believe Jonas could know so much about us," James said. "But I was there yesterday when the old man told us that Jonas is his son. And Coach Baptiste has spoken up for him more than once."

"And I will continue to, as long as I have the chance," Coach Baptiste said, walking up behind the team. He had parked and walked over with Jonas without the team noticing. "Jonas, teach. I will stay here and out of the way."

Jonas smiled and patted Coach Baptiste on the shoulder. Then he gestured to the players. "Come, over to the fields."

They followed him, though Pete said out loud, "We can't use either field. Too many little kids are playing."

"Watch them," Jonas said, stopping between the third-base line of the one field and the first-base line of the other.

James looked back and forth between the two fields. There were several boys and girls on each field. They were all playing baseball or at least a game that looked like baseball. The playing areas themselves were smaller than what Central used. There were only sixty feet between bases instead of ninety. Also, the kids were not always hitting the ball to get on base. Sometimes, the catcher would roll the ball back out onto the field to give a smaller child a chance to run to first. After a moment, James also realized they were not keeping track of outs. They did not seem to even have teams. They were giving everyone a turn at bat and running out to play in the field after they were out or scored a run.

It was refreshing to see in some ways. There was not much pickup baseball any more. Many kids played the sport, but most of them participated in organized leagues. Here children were playing while their parents were either in their nearby homes or relaxing in the pool.

James's teammates watched for a few minutes before Pete spoke again. "I don't see anything. Well, nothing that tells me what is most important. They are all hitting, running, and fielding. But no one is using strategy. It's just a silly pickup game to them."

"Listen," Jonas said.

Silence. No, not silence, James realized. The Central players were silent, but the kids were not.

"They're laughing," James said. "Is that what you wanted us to hear?"

"The children have joy," Jonas said. "They are all happy just to be playing the game. If you do not have joy while playing the game, you won't find what you are looking for in it."

"We do enjoy the game," Pete said.

"Did you enjoy the two games you've lost this year?" Jonas asked.

"Wait, are you saying we should enjoy losing?" Jules asked.

"No, I am saying you can have joy whether you win or lose. There is nothing wrong with trying to win, but enjoy the game itself. If you win or lose, if you win a championship or finish as a runner-up, if your season ends or continues, have joy in the game. Have the joy that a child does."

Jonas tilted his head to bring their attention to the field on their left. A boy, taller than the other players there, was batting. He swung through three straight pitches. The catcher rolled the ball onto the field, pretending as if the last of those pitches had been a hit, just like they had been doing for the smaller kids. Even then, the tall boy was thrown out at first base by two steps. He did not seem upset by his poor performance. Instead, he was laughing, and even gave a high-five to the first baseman after being out.

"That child is the tallest and oldest one here," Jonas said. "He tried to hit the ball. He tried to reach first. In both those things, he failed. You might expect him to succeed against the younger children and be disappointed when he didn't. But being out did not take away his joy. In the same way, you need to have the children's joy in playing both when you win or lose."

Jonas turned and walked away from the field. "Whoever has the joy of a child when playing the game are the ones who are the most important on my team."

James and the other players looked at each other and followed Jonas back to the pool parking lot. This was not at all what James was expecting. There was nothing wrong with the reminder to enjoy the game like a kid, but he had hoped for more strategic insight.

Jonas walked back to Coach Baptiste. "I will be at your opening playoff game tonight, but I won't teach you any more until tomorrow. I will speak with you again after the second game of the series with Hemtown. The days are long enough now I can speak with you after evening games. Make sure your parents know I will be speaking to you. No secrets. No lies."

Jonas and Coach Baptiste got in the car. As the coach started the engine, Matt ran up to the open window on the passenger's side.

"Do you think we will win both games before you talk to us again?" he asked.

Jonas smiled. "I shouldn't be giving everything away."

James could hear Coach Baptiste laughing as the car pulled away.

"He's kind of strange," Pete said. "But I got his point. Enjoy the game. Since this is my last Armed Services season, I guess I should take the season seriously and enjoy it at the same time."

"I wonder if he was telling us about baseball, or about life in general," John said.

"Forget that," Tom said. "How did he know there would be kids playing baseball in those fields right now? And did he know the one boy would strike out and laugh about it?"

James's head hurt. There seemed to be wisdom in what Jonas told them, but it was counter-intuitive that he could know all the things he did. "Let's wait until after these two games against Hemtown and see what he says after that. If he starts contradicting himself, keep our distance. But if he can keep building on what he says, maybe he could help us win."

"Maybe he can help us get to the Armed Services national tournament," Pete finished.

* * *

Lucas plugged in his computer and set up his papers in the Central baseball press box. He decided to cover this game between Central and Hemtown in the playoffs, and not the Meadville-versus-Vigortown game. Tomorrow, he would staff the second game of that other series.

The sportswriter guessed that both series would need only two games. Meadville was decent while Hemtown was average at best. Central and Vigortown should be able to sweep them in two games, making the third game in each series unnecessary.

Lucas pulled a baseball scorebook out of his bag and wrote the starting lineups. As expected, Pete Roc was pitching for Central today. That was another reason Lucas was here.

Central's success in the Armed Services baseball season had caught Lucas a little off-guard. He had been covering Armed Services baseball for the Lebanon County newspaper for several years. Well, now it was more of a website than a paper, but that was an issue Lucas did not want to think about now. No matter whether he was writing for print or online media, he had seen his fair share of teams through the years. Lucas was usually right about how the local baseball clubs would do in a given season.

Lucas thought Central would be slightly above average, like Meadville. They might be unbeatable when Pete pitched, but mediocre on other days. Central surprised him with their consistency. His editor did not allow Lucas to go out and cover any regular-season games until the finale. That saved travel money, in case a local team made it into the tournaments later in the season. The last regular-season game was the first time Lucas had seen Central.

When he wrote the story of that contest, Lucas felt it close to impossible to convey how dominant Central was against Vigortown. Vigortown was the team was the team Lucas had expected to win the county until now. From what he could gather,

Central was the best Armed Services baseball team from Lebanon County in recent memory. They were undoubtedly the best squad in the twelve years since he graduated college and moved here.

After the national anthem, Lucas sat at his keyboard. He was ready to send out social medal updates and to write notes for his story. He would record highlights on his phone, too.

One thing he would not do was make small talk with people in the little press box. Lucas glanced over at the announcer, the scoreboard operator, and the sound system controller. He felt comfortable interviewing people, but he was shyer around people who had no connection to his job. Lucas could talk to his editors and photographers from the newspaper. He could also have conversations with Marcus, the writer from Harrisburg, if they happened to be covering the same event.

But connecting with other people, Lucas was starting to find, was getting harder and harder. Lucas did not know why. He knew he would enjoy watching this game and writing about it afterward. But once he finished his work, all he had to look forward to was an empty apartment that night.

Sipping from a water bottle and taking a bite out of a cheeseburger from the concession stand, Lucas made his notes in the scorebook and notepad. He marked dots in the boxes for walks and strikeouts. Lucas drew lines in different directions to show what area of the field a batter hit the ball. He scratched in numbers, some to indicate the position of the player who recorded the out, other times to show the number of runs a batter's hit scored.

To those unfamiliar to a baseball scorebook, it looked like gibberish. For anyone familiar with traditional baseball notation, it showed that John Thun had two run-scoring singles and that his brother James drove in a run. Pete had seven dots next to his name for strikeouts, but none for walks, and three for hits.

When the game was over, Lucas jotted the final score of the game on the top of the scorebook page. Central six, Hemtown zero.

As he walked down the steps to conduct his interviews, Lucas realized that he would write about Central many more times.

Chapter 17

Pete stood in the outfield, throwing soft tosses and fielding practice fly balls from Coach Deem's swings. Despite pitching seven innings yesterday, his arm somehow still felt strong enough for him to take the mound again today.

The pitching restrictions, which would keep him off of the mound for a few days, made Pete angry. He wondered what the headlines would have been if he pitched shutouts against Hemtown in both games of the playoff series. People across the state, at least, would talk about him as the best pitcher in Pennsylvania. His college coach might take Coach Deem to court, though.

In the next moment, Pete knew he was being unreasonable. No one would pitch fourteen innings in two days. But given the chance, he suspected that he would keep Hemtown off the scoreboard again. Hemtown had qualified for the playoffs, but it felt like they were the best of the bad teams, allowed to join the three good teams in the postseason.

Pete knew Vigortown had won their game against Meadville yesterday. If the same results happened again, it would be a Central-Vigortown final. He was hoping for it. Winning the title would be more meaningful against Vigortown.

But first, Central had to take care of business. Pete expected no problems with that, but they still had to get this win before making any other plans.

As he jogged from the outfield to the dugout when warmups ended, he remembered that Jonas had come from Hemtown. He would have played in a different era, decades ago. But it still seemed like an odd place for a baseball savant to call home.

Pete and the other players had not spoken with Jonas after the opening playoff game yesterday, though they saw him there. Unlike his father, Jonas did not sit in the highest place available. Instead, he took a seat near the field of play, close to the action at home plate. Pete glanced over before entering the dugout and saw Jonas once again. Like before, he was dressed in a plain white shirt and jean shorts. He was sitting in the first row of the bleachers, just like yesterday's contest.

Not that there were that many seats here. Central's bleachers seated one-hundred spectators at most, so many people watched from their lawn chairs. Here at Hemtown, there was only half as much seating, so almost everyone was in lawn chairs or standing. There were dozens of people around the field. In a playoff game that was a ten-minute drive, there were as many Central fans here today as there were for the home game yesterday. Pete guessed around one-hundred fifty people were here to support Central.

When he got into the dugout, Pete set his glove down on the bench. He would bat in the top of the first inning before he took the field, anyway. He saw Coach Baptiste, who had come in from hitting the infield-practice ground balls. "Hey, coach," Pete said. "Is that Jonas guy going to be talking to us? I mean, with real instructions about the game."

Coach Baptiste nodded back and forth. "He certainly will, starting after tonight's game."

"Why after the game? Why not before when it can help us?"

Matt snuck up from behind Pete. "He must know we don't need the help against Hemtown."

"Stop it," Coach Baptiste warned. "Take every opponent seriously. But there's always a reason behind everything Jonas does and says. Sometimes, it will take wisdom and discernment to understand. And often it doesn't make much sense until after the fact."

Pete put Jonas out of his mind over the following two hours, focusing his own wisdom and discernment on the game. He fixated on Hemtown's pitcher. Phil was the leadoff batter in the first inning, and Pete stood in the batters' box trying to time his practice swings with the pitchers' rhythm.

There were three pitches in Phil's at-bat, and Pete thought all three were meant to be fastballs. They lacked the "fast" part, though. Phil hit the third pitch right back past the mound, over second base and into center field for a single.

Pete decided to take the first two pitches thrown to him, regardless of where they were. They were both right down the middle for strikes, but all the same speed as the pitches Phil faced. Pete focused on the pitcher's hand, hoping to catch what grip was being used. In that fraction of a second, Pete recognized the fastball grip. The earlier pitches had already told him that this thrower did not have the arm strength to give a fastball a steady velocity.

Pete hit a low line drive down the right-field line. He could see the ball go into the right-field corner as he ran to first. If he hurried, he could get to third base. While hearing his teammates cheer Phil on his way to the plate for the game's first run, Pete saw Coach Arim wave him into third base. He did not even need to slide.

Then he heard one umpires yell, "Dead ball, runner moves up a base."

Though Pete had not seen it, he knew Hemtown's throw back into the infield must have sailed over the fence and out of play. Pete trotted the last ninety feet to home plate. It was not quite a home run, but rather a triple and an error. Regardless, Central had a 2-0 lead, and it was clear that Hemtown had no quality pitchers left for this game.

The rest of the contest played out as everyone had expected. Pete batted four times, and he hit the ball as hard the last three times as he did in his first at-bat. Even though Hemtown tried a few different pitchers, they were all the same. They were not pitchers so much as throwers. All their not-quite fastballs reached the plate at about the same speed.

Pete had another single and scored that time on a single by John. His other two well-struck swings resulted in outs, one on a deep fly ball and the other on a line out to the first baseman. But his teammates, mostly, found their measure against the Hemtown pitchers as well. The result of the game was never in doubt.

From center field in the defensive half of the innings, Pete could tell that John was not at his best. The curves were not breaking as sharply as they should. But it was more than enough in

118

this game. Hemtown scrapped out two runs with a few luckily placed soft hits, but the victory was in hand.

Pete had a few plays to make in center field though none were challenging. He had a clear view when Sam, filling in at first base while John pitched, caught a pop-up to end the game. Central had earned a 9-2 victory.

It was no surprise to sweep two games from Hemtown and advance to the finals. Even winning all five times they played Hemtown this season was no big deal to Pete. But this was a win in the postseason. It was a sweep of a semifinal series. That mattered a lot.

* * *

James looked behind himself to be sure that the other players were coming. Sure enough, all eleven of his teammates were carrying their equipment bags behind the backstop to where Jonas sat. This time, Coach Baptiste had already headed home and would not be with them. However, several of the parents of the players were coming over now. James and John had told their mother about Jonas. She was both concerned and intrigued at how this stranger had learned so much information about her sons. She started out yelling about her concerns, then managed to argue herself into being intrigued.

Jonas was smiling, sitting on the ground now instead of the bleachers. James remembered him seated on one bleacher earlier, but he must have moved around the crowd during the game. James noticed that the parents were standing around, forming a semi-circle around the players, close enough to hear.

"Well done, my friends," Jonas said. "It's been a long time since a Central team won a playoff series. I hope you're all appreciating the moment."

"It feels good to sweep a team," Pete said, sitting across from James. "Even if it was just Hemtown. But the real prize comes if we win the finals."

"Has anyone heard if Vigortown won their game?" Matt asked.

"I saw something on my phone," one father answered. "That game was tied in the sixth inning."

"If they win, we play the first game of the championship series tomorrow," John said. "But if Meadville wins, they have to play again tomorrow, and we get a day off."

"Do not worry about what you need to do tomorrow," Jonas said.

James and the others returned their gazes to him. That calm, yet authoritative, voice pulled all them in closer. "Focus on the day you are in now," Jonas continued. "Even if now, this evening, all that means is to get home and to rest well tonight, then focus on that. Do not concern yourself with a game you may or not play tomorrow until tomorrow comes. Each day has enough problems, and each game has enough challenges, without rushing into the next one."

"Sir," one parent said. James turned and saw it was Phil's father. "The boys told us about you, and about how you seem to know a lot about them. Some of us are a little worried. The boys say Coach Baptiste speaks well of you, but he seems to have already left the field. So could you tell us, what is your interest here?"

"What are you trying to teach our sons in these little meetings you want to have with them?" James's own mother asked.

James wished that his mother would have kept quiet. At home, it was comforting to have a mother that wanted to protect him. But there was nothing more embarrassing than her protecting him in public.

Jonas, though, was not offended by the suspicion. "I wish to teach them, and anyone else who will listen, this: that the winning team is more than the team that scores more runs. Winning players are players who admit they need instruction from others to improve. They regret the mistakes they make and accept correction with humility. Successful teams play within the rules even when the umpire is not looking, and who do not try to make the other team look bad. Winners play for the joy of being in the game. They do not seek to harm the other side and are willing to be mocked for playing to a higher standard by those who do not understand."

There was silence for a moment. That was quite the list, James thought. He lost track of some things Jonas said, almost like he had trouble following some stories in his English classes during the school year. But what he could follow all sounded positive, including the ending about a "higher standard." If they were meant to win Lebanon County and have a chance at a Region D title, maybe they needed to set their standards higher.

"And that's all?" James's mother asked. "That's the essence of these meetings?"

Please be quiet, James thought to himself.

"Anything I teach them will connect to those concepts, yes," Jonas said. "But there will be more depth to them as the season continues. And anyone is included in these meetings if they will listen. If you wish to listen to what I am saying to them, join us. There is much for all to learn. In fact, I invite all the fans of Central's team to these discussions. That includes the handful of girls who seem to be your biggest fans."

Parents? The girls? While a few of the parents giggled at the boys over their "biggest fans," James felt the words push against his pride. James hoped Jonas's instructions would be for the Central players only, a reward for those in red uniforms with blue lettering. While his openness with everyone implied that Jonas could be trusted, James also found himself a touch disappointed.

James looked over to the parking lot next to the field. He saw the girls leaving just then. "It looks like our 'biggest fans' didn't want to wait for us," he said.

"Don't worry, they'll join us tomorrow after you beat Vigortown," Jonas said.

"I thought we didn't know if Vigortown had finished their semifinal series yet," Jules said. "And that we aren't supposed to worry about it."

"You can know about something without worrying about it," Jonas said. "And trust me. Anyway, the sun is low in the sky, and I have no more to teach you today."

"Did you teach anything, to begin with?" one father asked, with a hint of derision that James noticed.

"'Each day has enough problems, and each game has enough challenges, without rushing into the next one,'" Matt said, reading from a paper. Matt was taking notes. Oh, yeah, notes. Not taking notes was part of the reason James struggled with those English class stories.

Everyone left, except for a few parents who came up and talked with Jonas in private. James's mother was one of the stragglers, so he and John waited. They wanted to find out what she thought of this whole situation.

"She could have let other people ask those questions," John whispered.

"Oh, yeah," James answered.

There were few people left at the field by now, waiting near Jonas, but James saw there were about six adults he did not recognize. There was also a girl from Hemtown that James did not know by name, but knew by reputation. She was not the kind of girl he would want his mother to see him with. Come to think of it, she was not the type of girl James wanted to be with.

The girl who seemed to be eavesdropping wandered off, but the adults stayed. Then Jonas waved James and John back to him. They stood, one on each side of their mother. "Listen," Jonas told them. "I think you will have more to learn from this."

Jonas turned around to the adults who had been waiting behind him. "I know you have something to say."

"We know who you are," one man said. "You going to try to convince the Central team you're something special?"

"I came to teach those who will listen," Jonas answered. "I wish Hemtown's team had listened to my words, but they did not. So I turned to the team that would listen."

"You turned your back on your hometown team to help their rival," another man said. "I have to assume that you will stab Central in the back sometime."

"I do not turn anyone away," Jonas said. "You, your sons, and the coaches of your sons refused to accept what I had to say. All the teams, here and elsewhere, have an ultimate goal. Central's road there will be long, but they will get there and Hemtown will not."

The first man who had spoken spit on the ground in front of Jonas, who did not flinch.

"Your own hometown should come first," he said and wandered away from Jonas. The others followed.

James, John, their mother, and Jonas were the only ones left on the field. A handful of people were in the parking lot, so soon they would be alone there.

"That was one angry baseball father," James's mother said.

"Jonas, why did we need to see that?" John asked. "Why were they so rude to you?"

Jonas opened his mouth, but James spoke first.

"I understand. Earlier, I was thinking to myself that I wanted Jonas to be teaching us and us alone. You would speak with just the players on the team. Not our parents. Not the girls who came to the game. We were special. Apparently, that's what the people in Hemtown felt the same way."

"Exactly," Jonas said. "Through me, you will get to your ultimate destination. But my words to you are not to be secrets. Whether someone was born in my hometown or across the world, I want to share these teachings with them. But these people from my hometown could not understand when I first tried to reach them three years ago. They still do not understand now."

There was a buzzing sound. John pulled out his phone. "It's a message from Pete. Vigortown won. Game one of the finals is at home tomorrow evening."

Chapter 18

This was precisely what Pete had been waiting for ever since the college baseball season ended. The county championship series against the only team that could beat Central in a best-of-three contest: Vigortown.

Pete wanted to win, but he also hoped that Vigortown would be up to the challenge. It mattered to him that Central played well to win the series. If they only won because Vigortown made mistakes, it would cheapen the victory.

And through five innings, the opponent did not disappoint him. Neither did his own teammates. There were no errors, no wild pitches, and no silly mistakes. The score was tied at one run apiece.

The only thing missing was that Pete was not on the mound. He wished that he could have been, but he was still out of the rotation due to the pitch count and rest rules. Any disappointment at that was being washed away by Ted's pitching effort, which Pete had an excellent view of from center field. Vigortown put a few singles together in the top of the fourth inning when their hitters were getting a second up-close look at his pitches. That was when the visitors scored their run.

Vigortown's pitcher was throwing effectively as well. In the bottom of the first, he got Pete to miss a two-strike curveball that looked like a strike until dropping to the ground at the last moment. Pete made contact his second time up, but his pop-up was caught in the infield for the final out of the third inning.

Fortunately, Ted proved himself with the bat in the fourth. He hit a single that scored Phil for Central's first run.

Now Ted was trying to get through the top of the sixth without giving up the lead again. Vigortown had runners on first and second base with two outs. Pete knew Coach Deem would like to warm up another pitcher now and replace Ted before the next batter. But neither Pete nor John were allowed to pitch today due to the resting rules, and Sam had to wait for tomorrow's second game of the series.

Pete remembered the last time this batter for Vigortown came to the plate. He drove in their one run by hitting the ball into the left-center field gap. Though no instructions came from the dugout, Pete took four extra steps in that direction. Sure enough, the hitter smacked the ball into that area. This time, Pete's positioning got him to the ball for an easy catch and the final out.

Though relieved that the score remained tied, Pete felt that Central's turn at bat in the sixth needed to produce a run. They might need to score two or more. Ted was running out of strength, and they could not be sure that Vigortown would be held at bay again in the seventh.

We need to score now, Pete thought to himself. He hoped that someone would get on base before his turn at bat. Pete would bat third in the inning. He did not want the temptation of swinging for the fences for a home run. Everything would be easier if there were runners on ahead of him.

Almost as if he wished it into existence, Little Jimmy and Phil walked to start the inning. Pete stepped to the plate, just looking for a ball he could drive for a single. But he had to wait. Vigortown's coach came out of his dugout to replace the pitcher. Pete took some practice cuts with his bat while the reliever threw his eight warmup pitches and wondered why the coach made the change now. Pete had done so little when he batted against the starter all day.

It must have been the two walks, he realized. They did not want to walk Pete and load the bases with no outs. That meant this reliever would most likely throw in the strike zone. If Pete recognized the pitch as the pitcher released it, he had an excellent chance to drive in Little Jimmy from second base.

It only took one pitch.

The first pitch was a changeup, but the reliever's slow motion gave away the reduced speed. Pete waited on it, and the ball came into strike zone where he had guessed. The moment he made contact, Pete knew he had elevated the ball, and hoped he had kept it away from the outfielders.

Coach Baptiste's enthusiastic reaction at first base, which included an emphatic "go" signal, told Pete that he succeeded. He ran past first and slid into second base. When he stood up again, he saw that both Little Jimmy and Phil had scored.

John came up to bat next, and he hit a grounder up the middle, almost right to where Pete had been standing. He was not there anymore. When Pete rounded third, he turned his head to first base, where John had beaten out the throw for an infield single.

Then it was James's turn. After a few pitches, he hit the ball down the third-base foul line. Pete, like anyone who has played the game more than a brief time, was standing in foul territory while taking his lead off third. If a fair ball hit a runner, even a runner that was standing on a base, he was out. But a foul ball hitting a runner was only a strike on the batter. So Pete was in no danger of getting hit as the ball skipped along one foot into fair territory. He realized that there was no risk of being out at home when the ball got by the diving third baseman on the fair side of the line.

After Pete crossed the plate, he saw that John was hustling around the bases and Coach Arim was waving him home. Pete stepped away from the home plate area to make sure he would not interfere with the play, but also made sure he was where John would see him. The relay throw to home would make this a close play.

"Slide!" Pete yelled, but there was enough crowd noise that John could not hear him. Pete kneeled down and hit his hands against the grass to make his instruction clearer.

John made a foot-first slide to the infield side of home plate, while Vigortown's catcher caught the throw on the foul side. The catcher turned to tag John, but John's right foot had already hit the plate. Pete saw that and had to hope the home-plate umpire saw it too. But when the umpire put his hands wide in a "safe" signal, Pete knew Central was now winning 5-1.

He also knew Central was about to lead the championship series one game to zero.

* * *

She had only seen a few baseball games in person, but even Sammi could tell that this game was probably decided. "It's never over until it's over," one of her exes used to say. But usually, a team with a big lead late would win.

Sammi opened her water bottle and took a large gulp from it. It did not matter to her what Central did. But she had been at last evening's game at Hemtown and saw Central win that contest. She knew Central was playing here tonight in the championship round and decided to spend an evening at the game.

The reason Sammi was here at all was that she was curious about the man who had attracted so much attention after yesterday's game. She stayed a little distant, but she listened to him teaching the Central players and their parents too. After that, many adults from Hemtown seemed so angry when confronting him. Some of those adults were the same ones who did not want her around the ballpark or even around town. Maybe that was why she found this man so compelling. Enemy of her enemy, or something like that.

Sammi was sitting in the front row of the one bleacher on the third-base side, and the man who she was looking for was at the other end. But her curiosity did not help her overcome her fear of speaking out loud. She took a drink of her water and thought again of how to approach the stranger. There was no one between her and the man, but she had no idea how to speak to him. What could she say? What did she want to ask? To be honest, Sammi herself was not sure.

But she did not want to stay much longer. In the next bleacher over to her left, she could hear comments by the girls. Between the loud cheers for the Central team and the laughter at more appropriate jokes, she still picked up the whispered jeers at her. It was not surprising. In her hometown or here, her reputation was the same. She was a dirty joke, especially to the "good" teenage girls. She knew that for sure, since she would have mocked a woman like herself too, four years ago when she was still in school.

Sammi was thinking about going home now. One of her other exes would have considered that unthinkable, to leave a baseball game before the last out. But her thoughts about the younger girls' taunts had distracted her. Somehow, the man in whom she was curious was now sitting right next to her.

"Pardon me," he said. "Could I have some water? I have no money with me to buy any."

It was Sammi's first up-close look at him. He looked to be about thirty years old, with olive skin and robust features. He reminded her a little of the more athletic boys she had been with, though he was a touch older than they were. The stranger had longer hair too. But she felt no physical or romantic pull towards him. The attraction was hard to define. Psychological? Spiritual? Sammi wasn't sure what had brought her to this point.

All she said was, "I'm sorry, I've already drunk out of this bottle. I don't think you'd want to drink out of the same one."

The man smiled. It put Sammi at ease. The baseball game and the scornful girls, no farther away than before, seemed to disappear. "If you knew who I was and why I am speaking to you, you would ask me for water. Water that would fill your desires for life."

From another voice, this might have sounded like a complicated pickup line. But Sammi had heard and fallen for enough of those to recognize that this was different. This voice spoke of compassion.

"Where can I find that water?" Sammi asked. "Where is there water that is not just to keep me from being thirsty, but to allow me to follow the dreams I ignored?"

"Go home, and bring your boyfriend back with you," the man said.

Sammi took a deep breath, a little of her unease returning. "There's no reason for me to do that. The man I live with, we're together, but not...," She lowered her voice. "I can't even call him a boyfriend."

"True," the man said, but he also kept his voice low. "You have had seven boyfriends, and the man you live with now is not even a friend at all. You have been very honest with me."

Something shook inside Sammi's chest. She had lived with seven boyfriends. That was seven whom she actually dated, not counting the man she was with now. How could someone she had never spoken to before describe it down to that detail?

Her fight-or-flight response turned on in her mind. For a moment she thought to lash out at the stranger, saying he did not know her. Or she might leave now and forget any of this had happened. But a second later, she calmed. While there was nothing in the man's voice or face that implied he approved of the choices she had made, she felt no judgment or threat. With no one in her life she trusted, she decided to trust him.

"What is your name?" she asked.

"Jonas Davis. And you are Sammi."

Well, if he knew about her past, it was no surprise he remembered her name. "The people in Central seem to trust you as a kind of teacher. But the people in Hemtown treated you like a fraud yesterday. Who are you that you are making so many people react like this?"

"I am leading people to their ultimate goal, even though many do not understand what their goal actually is," Jonas said. He looked toward the baseball field. "Some people are perplexed. But I can teach and guide the confused. It is only for the unwilling that I can do nothing."

"I am willing," Sammi found the words spilling out of her mouth. "I don't want to be like this anymore. A few years ago, I was like those girls over there." She gestured with her head towards the young fans in the other bleachers. "When I was in high school, I still dreamed of running a business. I thought I would find the right man, one who would respect me, and I would respect him."

"The man you are with now, leave him," Jonas said. "It will be difficult, being on your own. But follow those dreams. Work for a living. Wait to find a husband. And in time, you will even teach your own children the lessons you learned here."

Could he really be sure that going out on her own would work out so well? How could a stranger be sure she would have children one day? Her heart told her he knew it all, but her brain was not convinced yet. But her heart and mind agreed on one issue: Things would not get better if she stayed where she was.

"I will gather the few things I have tonight, and move out tomorrow," Sammi said. "He is not a violent man, the man I'm with now. He won't hurt or threaten me. Won't help me either, but there's no other way. And I will find you tomorrow, I guess, at Vigortown?"

"For you, talking with me today here is enough," Jonas said. "You don't need to seek me here again."

"But you are teaching these Central players several times, right?"

"Yes. But the circumstances are different from what you face. After today, you will not hear my voice again, but you will hear theirs instead."

Sammi stood up, her water bottle forgotten, along with the game and many of the trials she had been through in the last few years. Without knowing how she understood it, she was convinced life was about to get better. Not perfect, but better.

"Thank you. Thank you. If I do not get to see you again, thank you a thousand times now."

Jonas smiled and nodded his head. But now standing and turned towards the bleachers, Sammi saw those high school-aged girls again, girls like her four years ago. Her eyes darted back and forth between Jonas and the girls.

Sammi realized what she had to do.

* * *

What is Hemtown's bad girl babbling about, Maggie wondered to herself. She was trying to watch the end of the game, but the talk was distracting.

The young woman was pointing to the man sitting on the other set of bleachers on the third-base line. She kept saying that Maggie and her friends had to go over there.

What do we care what you think, Maggie thought to herself. But she stayed quiet.

"He told me everything I ever did," the woman said. Maggie thought her name might be Sammi. "And then he told me what I need to do next."

"Hooray for you," Jo said. "Could you get out of the way? There're just a couple more outs until the game is finished."

Sammi did not move away. Instead, she put her hands on her hips. "I used to be where you are. I wish I had listened to someone like Jonas when I was your age." She glared at Maggie and the others, then walked away.

Jonas. Maggie looked over again at the man on the other bleachers. It was the man that the Central players had started talking to. Or they were taking lessons from him. Or they were doing something else with him. It was not clear to Maggie what was going on there. Nate had said something about the team having meetings with Jonas before or after games. He seemed to think this stranger would give them an edge over their opponents. Maggie decided she should talk with this Jonas to see what company Nate would be keeping.

Maggie got up and walked to the other bleacher. "What are you doing?" Martha asked.

"I'm going to have a friendly conversation," Maggie said.

She sat down next to Jonas, who smiled at her and greeted her. "Hello, Maggie. I'm glad you're here. Your friends will join us soon."

"I'm curious why a woman like that was telling me I had to speak to you," Maggie said. "This should make for an interesting story."

If Jonas was flustered by that, he did not show it.

"Sammi needed to hear the truth, just as you do, and your friends and the baseball players," Jonas said. His eyes were not on Maggie but on the field. Maybe he was looking at Nate. "The truths that Sammi already knew from her hard life are different from the ones you know. But none of you have the whole truth."

"Truth?" Maggie asked. "Truth about what?"

"That you want to know the truth, but you do not understand where to look for it."

This conversation was getting circular, but Maggie continued anyway. "Here's what I want to know. What would be the best major for me in college? Should I work during the semester or wait until next summer break? How to find the right boy, no, the right man for my life?"

"That is a shadow of the truth you truly want," Jonas said, turning his head to the side, looking at and around Maggie. "And you, and you."

Maggie realized that Jo and Martha had come over, standing by her. "Um," Martha started. "To be honest, Maggie just said something about boys, so we were interested."

"They're worse than I am about boys," Maggie said.

Jonas smiled, and the smile did not seem to be an amused grin. It was like an invitation to Maggie, a chance to go deeper into whatever truth he was speaking.

"While it's true that each of you wants to succeed in college, get jobs, and marry, all of that is a part of a greater truth," Jonas said. "You need to know you have value. You want to be certain you matter."

"Of course we matter," Jo said. "Everyone matters."

"Does Sammi matter?" Jonas asked.

Maggie said nothing and noticed that Jo hesitated before answering. "Well, yes. Why wouldn't she?"

"As much as, say, the shortstop out there?"

Maggie had to glance to the field and saw that Phil was at shortstop. Maggie and Martha knew Jo was interested in Phil. But they had known her for years and sat with her during every game this season. Was it a coincidence that Jonas picked him?

Jo, blushing, looked down sheepishly. "What's the point?"

Maggie answered before Jonas did. "We think everyone matters to us, but in our hearts, we don't feel that way. Phil, and all the players, they do something we enjoy, so we decide they matter. Sammi's been with a lot of guys, so we act like we can dismiss her."

Jonas nodded. "You're starting to understand."

"But, if we're right about that woman, she's wrong to be doing that," Martha said. "Choices make a difference."

"They always do," Jonas said. "Her decisions hurt her. They hurt the men she's seeing. They hurt the people in the families of those men even if they are not aware of what is happening. Sammi's life needs correction, as all your lives do. But no decision, right or wrong, changes your value. Your worth does not vary. It is constant."

"And is that the truth you meant?" Maggie asked. "How did you say it? That we did not understand where to find it?"

"Yes. How many times have you allowed the clothes you wear, the car you drive, even the school you attend determine your worth? Many people feel that their value, or the value of others, varies. It changes with age, with wealth, with prestige or with a job title. You cannot imagine the number of people I have seen doing the same thing with their romances. But no boyfriend or husband will ever give you your worth. It would be better for you to find a husband who recognizes your value and understands that it does not change."

Maggie knew Jonas was right. Her parents always told her how important she was.They would always love her, and she would always be valuable to them. But this was more extreme. What her parents said was their opinion of her. Jonas was saying she had worth all the time, in any circumstance, no matter if others thought she had value or not. And he made it clear to her in their first conversation.

Jo and Martha now seemed to be enthralled by Jonas's words. "Is this what you're teaching the players?" Martha asked. "Are we allowed to be there when you're teaching?"

Jonas stood, and Maggie stood next to him. "You may always hear my teaching. There may be times when I speak to the team when you won't be able to join them. But all these lessons are connected. They are all part of even larger truths I still must teach."

"I don't understand all this," Maggie said. "But I want to learn more."

"That is good," Jonas said. "I'll be there in Vigortown tomorrow for the second game of the championship series. I will see you during that game. But for now, I must speak with the Central players again. Feel free to join us, though this time you will find it repetitive."

Maggie looked to the field again. She saw a Vigortown batter hit a ball into right field, where Nate caught it for the final out. The Central players all jogged to the middle of the field and had a mild celebration for the win. Maggie was not surprised that they were only slightly happy, since they had made it clear for a month they expected to win the county title. They still needed one more win for that.

"Are you going to tell them what you told us?" Martha asked. "About everyone having value, no matter what happens?"

"Truth does not change," Jonas said. "I'll have to phrase it in a different way. I'll talk about how a player on the winning team who does not get a hit is still a winner."

"Because boys only think about sports," Jo said.

Jonas smiled. "For these boys, that is often the case," he agreed. "Tomorrow, I will talk with you and the team again. You during the game, and to each of the players one by one after they receive their trophy and medals."

He walked away, out onto the field where the players were clearing their equipment from the dugout. Maggie wondered if Jonas was optimistic about Central's chances to sweep the championship series, or if he somehow knew.

Maggie was sure of one thing. Now that she had heard Jonas for herself, she knew this man was an exceptional teacher. She looked forward to hearing from him again.

Chapter 19

James leaped as high as his legs would allow, but the line drive still soared over his glove. By the time his feet came back down, he already heard the Vigortown runner from second base running by him. That meant the runner would score right after the runner who had been at third. This was not turning into a good first inning.

When the game started, James had allowed the surroundings to distract him. One thing that Vigortown had over Central was the most beautiful baseball stadium in the county. The field itself was always in top-notch condition. The concrete bleachers behind home plate were full even for unimportant games. There were also a few fans on the metal bleachers along the side. And all of it was for a game under the lights.

Though winning the county title at home would be nice, there also seemed something appropriate about winning it here too. But now, that was looking a little unlikely. Central was ahead in the series 1-0 and needed one more win to take the trophy. But Vigortown was already winning this game 2-0, so the series might come down to a winner-take-all contest.

So far, this game had little to do with James. He had not batted for Central in the top of the first, and no eighteen-year old would catch that line drive that flew over his glove. Still, he blamed himself for not being focused. Now he had to get back into a competitive mindset, and the game would not wait for him to do it.

The game would also not wait for Sam to get control of his pitching. He walked the next batter and Vigortown had runners at first and second base with one out. The deficit could get out of hand early.

Three pitches into the following batter, a scalding one-hopper bounced near James. He had to dive to his left to grab the ball, but he snagged it. Though he was on the ground, his momentum was still carrying him towards second base. He made an accurate throw to Phil, who threw a perfect strike to John at first.

The inning ended with that double play. But it already seemed to James like Central was barely staying in the game. He did not feel much better when he struck out on three pitches in the second inning. Central did not score.

In the bottom of the second and third innings, Sam pitched well enough that Vigortown did not increase its lead. But both times, runners got on base. Sam could not dominate a game against a good opponent like Pete or John could.

James corrected himself. Like Pete would, and John might.

Still down 2-0 in the top of the fourth, James batted again with two runners on base and one out. For a moment, he remembered hitting a home run here in the last game of the regular season. James knew better than to swing for a home run. No matter how strong he was, that approach always failed. But the memory encouraged him. He might succeed here in the biggest game of the year.

A fastball a bit inside seemed like a good pitch to James, and he hoped to put a ground ball through the infield with it. He did hit a ground ball, but he saw it hop right to the third baseman. James feared that he had hit into a rally-killing double play like the one he had turned back in the first inning. But the Vigortown third baseman threw to first base for the second out of the inning.

James shook his head on his way back to the dugout. His teammates still gave him high-fives and encouraging words for moving Phil to third base and Pete to second. He did not have time to wonder if they were being kind to him or if they meant it. Sam, the next batter, hit a single to center field.

Along with his teammates, James was yelling at the two base runners to get to home plate as fast as they could. Phil scored easily. Pete was being waved home by Coach Arim, but when he got within five feet of home plate, the catcher already had the ball to tag him out.

When James took his position at third base for the bottom of the fourth, he knew Central was now closer. Yet the game felt no more competitive. The out at home took the air out of everyone.

Well, it deflated everyone on Central's side. The players in the Vigortown dugout seemed happy.

They seemed happier when Sam's next pitch wound up twenty feet over the left-field fence. James put his head down and refused to look at the batter making his home run trot. He knew this game would not end Central's season. Vigortown would have to beat them today and then again tomorrow to take the series.

James was still disgusted. This was not how it was supposed to be.

* * *

Lucas noted the last out of the fourth inning in his scorebook. He wondered if he would have to cover a game tomorrow now. Coming into this game, he wished for a day off.

It would not be a day off the way most people thought of them. Journalists rarely have true days off, and that included sports journalists. But he would have less to do tomorrow if Central clinched the county title today.

He was not rooting for Central. He took the duty of a writer to be neutral in such things seriously. It was fine to hope for a big story, but not to create one that did not exist. He could be a slight homer if a local team played an out-of-area opponent, but even then he had to report the game fairly.

But both Central and Vigortown were in the area Lucas's newspaper covered. It was supposed to be like having two of your own children playing against each other. Not that Lucas ever expected to experience having children.

One other thing Lucas could hope for was that the games he covered would be a big event. That had happened. There was hardly an empty seat in Wagner Field, and many people stood past the bleachers. From the press box atop the home-plate bleachers, Lucas saw out past the center-field fence. Out there fans set up lawn chairs to watch from the grassy hill beyond the outfield wall.

There was no official attendance taken, but Lucas knew there were well over three hundred people here. That did not include the teams themselves, the volunteers at the field, or the handful of people with him in the press box.

Vigortown's pitcher walked the first Central batter in the top of the fifth, and that brought the coach out of the dugout to talk to the hurler. There would not be a pitching change now, Lucas was sure, but the meeting held up the game a few moments. The scoreboard operator and announcer were talking to each other, and no other reporter was there. There was no one for Lucas to engage in conversation.

He had hoped that Marcus, the writer from Harrisburg, might be there. But from what Lucas saw on social media, he was at the Dauphin County championship game. Oh, well, Lucas thought. I can catch up with him at the Region D Tournament when one of these teams would still be playing.

Lucas looked over the crowd for a moment again, impressed by its size. It was a larger crowd than he had ever seen for an Armed Services game, and he tried to remember the last time a high school game...

Wow.

Lucas was stunned, both by the woman who came into his sights and by his adolescent reaction to her. He hoped he had not spoken what appeared in his mind, but since no one looked at him, Lucas figured he had remained quiet.

The gorgeous woman walked in front of the bleachers. She was not at the game earlier. Lucas would have noticed. From this angle, Lucas only saw clearly above her neck. Dark brown hair rested on her shoulders. Blue eyes highlighted a face that seemed to come to a natural rest in a half smile. She had beautiful lips though from here Lucas could not tell if she wore lipstick or not.

She looked up into the bleachers, glancing around as if trying to spot someone. Lucas would give up two months pay to have her looking for him.

What has gotten into me, Lucas thought. Sure, he had encountered attractive women through the years while on the job. Several softball and field hockey coaches were cute. But Lucas' mind was not put to distraction over them. Now this stranger put him off balance, and he had not heard her voice or even seen below her neck yet.

The woman waved and walked up the steps, inadvertently giving Lucas an unobstructed view. She wore a loose-fitting purple top and a mid-length skirt. Since he was a sportswriter, Lucas' thoughts did not turn to her figure right away. His first thought was he could not tell which team this woman supported. Neither Central nor Vigortown had purple in their team colors.

Then he appreciated her figure, and immediately felt guilty. Yes, it was a natural reaction, but still, she was a stranger. He should not be ogling her, especially while working.

Lucas took quick note of who she joined. They were Central fans. He gave a closer look and realized it was the family of the right fielder, Nate Stoltzfus. Maybe she was related.

The game had already resumed, and Lucas got back to his notes. Work still had to come first, with no unnecessary distractions. He might never see this woman again after tonight, but he had a responsibility to report on this game.

He told that to himself several times over the rest of the game, unable to go more than two pitches without sneaking a glance at this new beauty.

* * *

Somehow, Central was still only down 3-1 heading into the seventh and final inning. Sam was still allowing hits, but Vigortown had stranded runners at third base in its last two at-bats. That meant there was a realistic chance that Central would win this game.

Even though they could win the series tomorrow, that thought gave James no comfort. It would be easier to finish this now.

But after the first two batters in the top of the seventh were out on a pair of ground balls, even James doubted. Now Phil was coming up to bat with two outs. Watching from the dugout, a bat in his hands, James knew they needed to get Phil on before there was even a chance of tying the game.

He saw the Vigortown half of the crowd stand up and cheer on their team. It was almost as if the stadium itself knew the series was about to be tied.

James had his heart in his throat on each pitch to Phil, knowing each one could be the last pitch of the game. Maybe this was why he did not want to play a third and deciding game tomorrow. The stress of a game like that must be unbelievable.

There were several pitches to endure, but Phil walked. Pete walked up to the plate, and James took his spot on the on-deck circle. He hoped that Pete would hit a home run and tie the game. James's legs were weak. He wanted someone else to be batting with only one out to go.

Pete did not swing at either of the first two pitches, but Phil stole both second and third base. Since he was not the tying run, Vigortown ignored him.

Then Pete took a swing and put a ground ball through the left side of the infield to score Phil. Central was now within one run, but it was not the ideal situation for James.

It seemed like an eternity getting to the batter's box. The bat often felt like an extension of James's own body, but now it was dense and unmanageable. Crowd noises he usually could ignore out by mere concentration vibrated all around him. The voice of his mother cheering was drowned out by the sounds of the Vigortown fans encouraging their pitcher.

James's lack of playoff baseball experience seemed to overwhelm him. The two games against Hemtown and the first game against Vigortown had never come this close to being a loss. James felt unprepared, like a child in his first at-bat in front of a crowd.

The pitcher threw to home. James never saw the ball come out of his hands and felt unable to swing, anyway.

At the last moment, he jumped away from the plate and something stung his bicep. The pitch had hit him. Sure that he was the most relieved man on the field, James trotted to first base and watched Pete make his way to second.

Though the drama of the game still hung over everyone, James's anxiety melted away. There was still pressure on him as the potential go-ahead run. But running the bases was easy compared to getting on them.

As he took his lead off first base, it occurred to him that now John might be the hero. Unbelievable. Well, the dummy had better do it. Better to have him bragging about a big hit than to lose the game.

Seconds after those thoughts, James found himself running as John's fly ball hit the ground in the gap in right-center field. Having already seen where the outfielders were before the pitch, he knew he would get to third base and that Pete would score the tying run. But as he made his way towards third, he saw a frantic Coach Arim waving him home.

Again, James heard the crowd, those on his side and those with the opponent. But this time it did not distract him. It inspired him. Friend and foe were watching him, and this time, he did not have to worry about hitting a little ball. He only had to beat that ball to home plate.

James came around third and made as straight a path as possible for the plate. Pete was there and James was waiting for a signal from him to slide. But Pete instead put both of his hands up above his head. There would be no play at the plate. James could score standing.

That's not dramatic enough, James thought to himself, and he took a head-first slide over the plate.

* * *

Pete wanted to be on the mound for this inning. Not because Sam could not get Vigortown out, but because this was the moment he had been waiting for over the years. At least he was on the field for it.

He hoped for the Vigortown players to hit the ball to center field. It could be right at him, off to either side to make a running catch, or anywhere. This was the inning where Central would finally be the champion of something, and he wanted to be in the middle of it when it happened.

Yes, Central had finished in first place in the regular season. But the victor in the playoffs was the official Lebanon County champion and qualified for the Region D tournament. Winning both validated the team's quality. But of the two, this championship series mattered the most.

The first batter hit a ground ball to first base which John fielded before touching the bag for the first out. The second batter hit a pop-up into foul ground behind home plate that Andy caught.

My turn, Pete hoped.

He tried not to lose himself in anticipation of the final out. Central still led by only one run. One error in the field and the game would become tenser. But this was the goal. It was not the ultimate goal, but one of the essential goals along the way.

The Vigortown batter hit a fly ball. Pete ran to his left but soon realized that it was out of his area. But Nate was already in position for it and made a routine catch to end the game.

Pete kept right on running towards Nate, but Nate ran towards the mound where the rest of the team jumped on top of each other to celebrate. Pete and Nate were the last to arrive, and they leaped on top of the pile of yelling players. After a few moments, when everyone had regained their feet, Pete heard the Central fans cheering. There were Lebanon County Armed Services baseball officials coming out onto the field.

"Let's not forget ourselves, boys," Coach Deem called out from somewhere. Pete knew what that meant. He got in front of the line and led Central in shaking hands with dejected opponent.

Still, Pete was glad that Vigortown had been the opponent. They had proven to be a challenge, and that only made the championship more meaningful. He doubted that half the teams in the Region D tourney were as good as Vigortown.

Region D. No, not going to think about that now, he decided. Appreciate the moment.

The Central players lined up on the first-base line and received small medals for their Lebanon County championship. The medallions were handed from the league president to Coach Deem and then put over each player's neck. Pete looked at his medal, and though his eyes told him it was only the size of a silver dollar, it was Olympic in scale to him.

There was also a trophy which would become the property of the Central Armed Services headquarters. Pete hoped that it would not be taken by Harry Antes, but instead stay with the veterans who ran the headquarters. But that was something else he would not think about tonight.

The players and coaches posed for pictures with the trophy out in left field, beneath the scoreboard that still showed the 4-3 final score. The image would be in newspapers, websites, social media feeds and the Region D program. Pete thought it was perfect. They all were getting what they deserved.

After the photos were taken, Pete looked for his parents, and also desperately wanted to call Sal. He wanted to share this moment not only with his teammates, but with those who had supported him through all the years of his baseball journey.

The first person he saw was Mrs. Thun, who charged onto the field the moment they opened the left-field gate to allow some Central fans to join the team. She grabbed John and James in a bear hug and was a ball of tears, though those tears were from joy. The brothers hugged her back. Pete doubted he would get them to admit it, but they hugged each other as well.

More Central fans were coming in through the gate though most still stayed out by the bleachers. Pete was still trying to find his parents, then thought to turn back and find Andy. Maybe they were with him. But first, he noticed Jonas Davis approaching to him.

"Congratulations, Pete," Jonas said, and as the words reached his ears, a calmness come over him again. He still had the happiness and satisfaction from the win, but he now felt at rest at the same time.

"Thank you, Mr Davis. Sorry. Thank you, Jonas," Pete said. He pulled up the medal from around his neck and showed it to Jonas. "I'll hang this on the fireplace, above all our family pictures."

Jonas held the medal between his thumb and forefinger and seemed to examine it. "It is a nice medal. And it was earned, not given. But don't put too much value into something that could be lost."

Then Jonas handed the medal back, patted Pete on the shoulder, and walked away to speak to some of his teammates.

Odd thing to say, Pete thought. Did he mean the value in the championship isn't the medal but the experience of winning? Or that the important thing was the feeling of victory, more so than the win itself?

Pete had plenty of both right now. And though he tried not to think of the future, he was sure that Central still had more victories ahead.

Chapter 20

Martha and Jo were already out of the car before Maggie could put it in park. She had volunteered to drive in her parents' new car back and forth from Vigortown for the playoff game and had somehow lived through all the screaming. Her friends were at least as excited as the actual Central players. They were yelling more than Maggie ever remembered after any of their high school softball wins. Though their softball team won its share of individual games, it had never won anything beyond that. No one ever handed them a trophy.

On the drive back to Central, though, Jo received a text from Phil that the team was going an ice cream shop in town for free food. There was no question the girls would join the boys for that.

As she pulled up to the ice-cream store on the main drive in town, Maggie wondered why it was even still open. It was now after ten, which was when it usually closed on a summer weeknight. Jo and Martha ran out to hug the players, with Jo running to Phil first. As her friends embraced the boys, Maggie figured out why the stand was open and how the food was free.

Mr. Antes was there, trying to make himself the center of attention. He was making exaggerated gestures at the window, making a point of how much the total cost of the celebration was growing. There was a fair number of people there. All the players, all three coaches, and most of their relatives were all either in line or gathered around the ice-cream stand. Everyone was talking, and several people were already eating ice-cream cones or dishes.

Mr. Antes was not only using his wallet to make this evening about him instead of the team. He was there with his...wife? Knowing what she did now, what should Maggie call that woman? His step-daughter, or whatever she was, was there too. Somehow, Maggie doubted that either of those women was an actual baseball fan. Though they were usually around when Mr. Antes was, they rarely cheered or applauded. They seemed to be a couple of trophies he liked to carry with him.

Oh, well, Maggie thought. Free food is free food.

But then as she stepped up to get in line, Mr. Antes yelled, "Everyone celebrate. For my birthday, everyone eats for free!"

That almost got Maggie to walk away. No one was celebrating because of his birthday. But she remembered that she had driven Jo and Martha here, so she had to stay. Anyway, at that moment, a voice spoke from right behind her. "He's been like that ever since we got here. You'd think he won the game by himself."

Maggie turned around and saw Nate. She hugged him as she had at the field. Nate smiled and returned the embrace. As they released the hug, a woman who Maggie vaguely recognized walked up from behind and joined them in line.

"Maggie, this is my cousin, Lydia," Nate said. "Lydia, Maggie."

Maggie put on a smile and realized from looking at Lydia that good looks ran in Nate's family. Unlike Nate, though, Lydia seemed to have a sense of fashion.

"Hello," she said, admiring Lydia's mixture of violets. "Nice top."

"Thank you. Wearing fashionable clothes all the time is one demands of my profession."

"Are you a fashion designer?" Maggie asked, hoping the answer would be yes. She wasn't going to college for fashion design, but that had been a fantasy job for her at one time.

"I have to do little of everything," Lydia said before Nate interrupted.

"Lydia owns a small clothing manufacturer in Virginia."

"Medium-sized," Lydia emphasized. "Clothing and accessories."

Nate silently mouthed "small" to Maggie.

"I try to take time off each summer to get up here for Nate's Armed Services games. This year I was too overwhelmed with special orders," Lydia stopped and turned to Nate, "because we are growing. But anyway, tonight was the first game I could get to. I have a couple weeks off now, so I'll be able to catch the Region D games coming up next week."

"It has been fun watching," Maggie said. "It's been a years since a team around here made it to regionals. I'm excited for Nate and everyone on the team."

"So how long have you two been a couple?"

Maggie froze, but Nate took it in stride. "We're just friends, nothing more."

"I'm eight years older than you. I know how 'just friends' works. And you're holding hands."

Maggie had not even realized it, but her right hand was interlocked with Nate's. She could not remember touching him, but it felt natural and comfortable. They had risked one or two public displays of affection in the last week, but this was different. They started holding hands without even knowing they had.

Maggie did not know what to call their relationship anymore. Were they going too far to be best friends? Could they ever be a real couple?

"Sorry, I've embarrassed both of you. I just wanted to get back at Nate for mocking the hard work I put in at the business," Lydia said. "Sorry, Maggie. I remember what it's like to be a teenager. But I'll stop talking about it if you guys point out where that Lucas guy is."

"Lucas?" Maggie asked, glad the conversation was turning.

"The sports writer from the Lebanon paper," Nate explained. "She spotted him interviewing Sam and John after the game."

"Nice-looking fellow. I'm curious."

"But he's old," Maggie said, with a smirk that filled in the "like you" she didn't need to say. That will get back at her for calling us out, Maggie thought.

Lydia mirrored the smirk. No harm. All good fun. Maggie figured she would like Lydia.

"Anyway," Nate said, "he must be back at the newspaper office or someplace writing the story. But he's not here."

"That's a shame," Lydia said. "I'm sure I'll see him at the regional tournament. And you'll play games and stuff," she added with a dismissive wave. Nate batted her hand back.

The interplay between Nate and his cousin seemed so funny to Maggie. She had no siblings, and she rarely saw the few cousins she had. The fun between them impressed her, and made Nate seem even more appealing.

No, don't get that attached, she warned herself. Trust Nate, but don't commit to him long term.

"The reporter didn't talk to me," Nate said. "He should have. I caught the last out."

"Hooray, let's have a parade for you," Lydia said.

Nate ignored her. "But Jonas did. I think he wound up talking to everyone."

"Who's Jonas?"

"He's kind of a life coach and baseball coach all in one. I'll explain later. He didn't talk to all of us at once this time, but he came up to each of us after the game. I guess that's why he's not here."

"To congratulate you?" Maggie asked.

"Yes, but also to tell us not to value something that can be taken away or something like that," Nate answered. "I think he meant the medals or the trophy, but I'm not sure."

"He talked to me a bit during the game," Maggie said. "He was telling me a story. It didn't seem to have anything to do with the game. Something about a coach running a softball summer clinic for one-hundred girls. One girl gets lost during the clinic, and the coach leaves the other ninety-nine players behind to find that one. It was a nice tale, but I didn't quite understand why he was telling this to me."

They had drifted to the front of the line. Maggie ordered a vanilla cone and Nate chose a twist. Lydia took chocolate in a dish, and then drifted away to mingle with the other fans.

After they got their ice cream, Mr. Antes came up to the window and paid for their food. Maggie noticed that he pulled out a pair of hundred-dollar bills where the people nearby could see them.

There's nothing this man won't show off, Maggie thought to herself. She wished that the baseball team was not dependent on him for the funds they needed to play. It felt creepy.

"Dance for everyone," Mr. Antes shouted.

At first, Maggie thought he was calling out to her. She spun around to look at him, but Mr. Antes was instead looking at his step-daughter. Maggie saw through the girl's coy look. She was planning something. Maybe the whole Antes family had a plan.

"I'm not sure I want to," the girl replied. The voice might have fooled some listeners, but not Maggie.

"Remember my promise," Mr. Antes said. "You dance as a gift for my birthday, I give a gift back to you. Whatever you want."

The stepdaughter smiled back with a grin that any girl would recognize. It was a sign she needed to hear the promise one more time before going forward. She pulled out her phone and played a dance track that Maggie recognized. The people around gave her space.

It occurred to Maggie that Mr. Antes asked her to dance for his birthday, not to celebrate Central's win. What a self-centered jerk.

The girl set the phone on the ground nearby and started her performance. At first, Maggie found the dance entertaining. Whoever this young woman Mr. Antes dragged around was, she clearly knew how to dance. For a moment, Maggie admitted that the girl had a real talent.

In fact, she seemed to be quite athletic. The girl might not be a baseball fan, but the way she balanced on a few toes and stretch her limbs proved that she had an athletic background. To her own surprise, Maggie found that she respected the girl now. She must have put hours of work into the routine.

And yet, this dance also unnerved Maggie. It was not because the boys, including Nate, were suddenly enthralled with this other woman. Boys like beautiful women, especially when they dance. She could deal with that.

What she could not deal with was why this dance was happening at all. Mr. Antes seemed to be the villain yet again. He bribed his step-daughter so he could show her off.

Almost as if Nate read her mind, Nate pulled her close and whispered in her ear, "I'll never show you off just for my ego's sake."

Whatever the reason for the dance, it continued to impress. The song that was playing was an extended mix of the dance track. But the girl persevered through her performance for more than five minutes. Drenched in sweat by the end, she finished in front of Mr. Antes. After catching her breath, the girl spoke. "May I have my gift now?"

Mr. Antes reached over and pulled the dancing girl close to him. "Of course. I gave you my word. If it's something I can give now, it's yours."

"It is." Now the girl raised her voice for all to hear. "Fire that man." Her finger pointed out towards where the coaches were standing together. Anyone who remembered the argument between the Antes family and Coach Baptiste needed no explanation which man she meant.

Mr. Antes turned back to the girl and whispered something to her, something that Maggie was too far away to hear. But his wife shouted, "How long are you going to let his slandering of us go unpunished?"

Only then did Maggie realize that they were serious. They wanted Coach Baptiste gone from the team on the same night Central won the Lebanon County championship. His only crime had been telling the truth.

Mr. Antes took a deep breath. Maggie doubted that he wanted to go through with it. The man was so arrogant that he took the team's success as his own. Mr. Antes did not want to do anything to upset their progress with even bigger tournaments coming soon.

But the promise he made in front of everyone meant more to his ego. Mr. Antes pushed through the people and walked up to Coach Baptiste at the edge of the crowd. The two men stared each other down as everyone else kept silent. Maggie had no guess what Mr. Antes would say, but Coach Baptiste spoke first.

"Do what you will," he said. "I have already done my part. There are plans in motion bigger than what you can imagine."

Maggie shook her head but stayed as silent as everyone else. Even Coach Deem and Arim did not act. What could they do?

Would Antes fire them too? Could he leave the team without coaches?

Mr. Antes reached out for Baptiste's neck. No, Maggie realized, not the neck, but the collar of his uniform. Then he pulled and tore at the shirt, making the buttons down the middle of the jersey pop off.

"You will not be at Ammonville, or anywhere else this team plays, again."

Part III

Going the Distance

Chapter 21

Lucas slowed to a stop at the traffic light and set his left turn signal. He was half an hour away from Ammonville High School, the site for the Region D Armed Services baseball tournament. Lucas still did not quite feel like he fully woke up this morning, despite driving for fifteen minutes already. He sipped his coffee while he had the chance, hoping for extra energy to face his work.

At least Central would play in the second game of the day. They were scheduled to start at noon against Sweetsville in the first round of the double-elimination tournament. Two other teams had already started the opening game of the tourney, and Lucas was glad he would not have to be there early enough for that.

By the time the day ended, Lucas would be wishing he had been covering the earliest game possible so he would have more time to himself afterward. Not that he had any plans. Apart from his work, he had little to do.

Being a sportswriter was enjoyable, at least to Lucas. His old friends from high school and college might not have agreed, but watching and writing about games energized him. Even if his coffee failed to wake him, Lucas knew he would get a burst of strength by being at the ballpark. He had never been much of an athlete. Whether in baseball or another sport, Lucas did not advance past junior high. But he appreciated and understood most sports. That understanding along with a bachelor's degree was enough to get him this job for the last fifteen years.

The drawback was the odd schedule he worked as a local sportswriter made building connections with others difficult. The games he would write about always happened during the time other people would have off from their jobs. This Saturday afternoon game he was driving to was a perfect example. He drifted apart from old friends because he often worked when they were hanging out. Apart from other people in the media, it was difficult to find times to go anywhere with anyone. And while he

liked his co-workers, the times he saw them in the office were
enough.

Lucas was not lonely, since he had plenty of time to talk
with those coworkers when he worked in the office. But sometimes
it got to him when he was alone in his apartment with another
weekend passing. Lucas had not given up on the chance he could
have a better social life someday, but he did not see a way for it to
happen now. Nor had he given up on the possibility of having a
woman in his life again. There had been no steady girlfriends since
shortly after college. His last date was two years ago.

But after seeing that gorgeous woman at the last game of
the Lebanon County championship series, he had hope. The
thought of her, that nameless beauty, woke Lucas up at the wheel.
He drove east on 322, approaching the county line into Lancaster
County. It would take twenty more minutes. He checked the clock.
He would be there well before the opening lineups to Central's
game were announced.

For a second, he thought he was being foolish for being so
enamored over a woman he never spoke to and never saw before
that most recent game. He usually felt awkward when he allowed
himself to be distracted by a pretty face in the stands while he was
supposed to be taking notes on a game. But this time, the
embarrassment passed. He knew beauty did not prove that this
woman possessed any other virtues. But that being said, this
stranger was so attractive that there was no avoiding these feelings.
If she was the same place as Lucas, he would be pleasantly
distracted.

She might not come to this game. She could be taken. She
probably had no interest in dating a sportswriter. But if she was at
the Region D tournament without a boyfriend on her arm, Lucas
would take a shot.

With that decided, Lucas forced his mind back to the
regional itself as he drove through Ammonville. Region D was the
first of many double-elimination tourneys. The best-of-three series
format, like the one used at the Lebanon County tourney, would
not be used again. Tournaments from this point forward would
have eight teams. In this case, there were six county champions

with one runner-up and the host team. The event would last five days, at least for the teams that won enough to make it to the end.

Lucas only concerned himself with the games that Central played. Since one loss was not a fatal blow for a team, he knew he would make this drive to Ammonville at least twice. He suspected that it would be more often than that. Lebanon County teams had struggled in recent years during the Region D tourney, but Central seemed to be better than those past squads. At the least, he guessed Central would win its opener today with Pete Roc as the starting pitcher. Sweetsville, Central's opponent today, was the Dauphin County champion.

Lucas did not know much about those other teams. But Lucas was impressed with Central in the few games he saw during the Lebanon County playoffs. He had heard about some drama with the team after their county championship. People said that one coach had been removed from Central. Lucas made phone calls to find out exactly what happened, but no one would say anything on record.

Well, an assistant coach couldn't make that much difference. Central still had all its players, and they had a chance in any game of the regional tournament. That would mean five trips to Ammonville, which might mean five opportunities to introduce himself to the nameless beauty.

Dang, he thought as he reached his destination. I've got it bad.

* * *

"Central!"

The team broke up the pre-game huddle and made its way into the third-base dugout at War Remembrance Field. Coach Deem felt the instinct to go in with them and sit at his customary spot at the end of the bench closest to home plate. But he had to break with tradition today. Today, he had to walk over to the first-base coach's box.

Coach Baptiste should be here, Coach Deem thought to himself. But he was not here, and Central would have to face the Region D tournament without him.

Not that Coach Deem believed Coach Baptiste's absence was likely to affect any results. Even after his "firing," Coach Baptiste had told Coach Deem that the team did not need him anymore.

The thing that stuck in Coach Deem's craw was that Coach Baptiste was not getting a chance to see this. He had no opportunity to watch Central play against these other county champions. It had been a long time since Central had won a county championship and been a part of the Region D tourney. This afternoon's opening-round game, under a cloudless blue sky, was a reward in itself. The outcome mattered, but win or lose, just being here was tremendous progress for the team. Coach Baptiste had put the work in over the years and should have been allowed to see his players in this tournament. He should have been able to look around the field and see two hundred members of the community make their way down to Ammonville to support the team.

Coach Deem and Coach Arim had both wished to stand up to Mr. Antes after the way he had demeaned Coach Baptiste in front of the team. But the truth was there was nothing to stop the man from removing all the coaches. Maybe he would have tried to coach the team himself. Perhaps he would request that Central forfeit its postseason games. He could have even pulled the funding for the team for next season. There was no telling with him.

Well, all twelve of Central's players were here, Coach Deem thought. His job was to coach for them. That was the whole point of taking this position. His knowledge about Sweetsville was limited, but experience told him that Central should be at least an even matchup for anyone here.

The top of the first inning began with Phil striking out, but Pete followed with a walk. "You remember what Baptiste always told you?" Coach Deem asked him as he stood on first.

"'Make sure the pitcher throws to the plate, don't let anyone tag you,'" Pete repeated, in the same cadence Coach Baptiste always had.

Coach Deem nodded and said nothing more. Half of a first-base coach's duties was reminding the players of what they already knew.

After the top half of the first, in which Central did not score, Coach Deem walked back to the dugout. He strolled towards his usual seat. When Coach Deem did though, he took noted the artificial turf on War Remembrance Field. Curious, he thought to himself. As an old-timer, Coach Deem preferred the natural grass and dirt. Still, he understood why certain teams liked to play on this drainable field. The artificial surface let even the hardest downpour dry off in about fifteen minutes. A nasty thunderstorm might delay the tournament, but it would not wipe out a whole day of games.

But the turf also made ground balls hop faster and farther out than average, so Coach Deem made sure that his infielders knew how to play on the different surface. He instructed his fielders to play deeper by an extra step or two. He had also heard, though not yet experienced himself, that the turf made it hotter than usual for the players. That did not apply today. It was mild for a July afternoon, for which Coach Deem was relieved. He did not want his best pitcher getting overheated in the first game of the tournament.

In the bottom of the first inning, Pete showed no danger of wearing out at all. In just six pitches, he retired three Sweetsville batters. Coach Deem hardly had time to get comfortable on the bench before he had to trot back out to first base.

In the second inning, Central did not get a run, but again Pete turned Sweetsville away with shocking quickness. It appeared to Coach Deem that Sweetsville's strategy was to swing at the first or second pitch every at-bat. Though they were putting the ball in play, any contact they made so far was weak.

If that kept up, and if Central could score, this would be a distinct advantage for Central. The fewer pitches Pete threw, the more likely he could return for the championship game on

Wednesday. That was looking a little far ahead. But it would be nice to have the choice of letting Pete pitch again.

Coach Deem could remember when the postseason meant an increase to nine innings per game. Back then, having a handful of quality pitchers was a necessity to survive any tournament more than a few days. Then the rules changed, and playoff games were scaled back to the same seven innings the regular season had. Coach Deem preferred having the longer games to decide the most deserving winner. It rewarded depth. Champions usually had several good pitchers instead of one great hurler.

But with a roster of only twelve players and only four whom he wanted pitching at all, the shorter games were in Coach Deem's favor this year.

In the third inning, Pete batted with Matt on third base and two outs. Coach Deem made no signals. For today at least, he was leaving any strategic decisions up to Coach Arim at third base. Pete hit the third pitch to deep left field, where the most extensive set of bleachers stood beyond the fence. The ball did not quite get that far, but it was over the outfielder's head. Coach Deem waved Pete to second base, but Pete did not even need to look at him to make his way to a double.

This first-base coaching stuff is pretty easy, Coach Deem decided.

As the game progressed, Central tacked on two more runs. More importantly, Pete was still getting outs with few pitches. Sweetsville rarely varied from its strategy of swinging early in each at-bat, and Pete did not give them much of a choice. Almost every pitch was a strike, so the few batters who were patient found themselves in two-strike situations.

With a 3-0 lead in the bottom of the seventh, Coach Deem knew there was a good chance that Central would win. There was almost as good of a chance that Pete would stay under the pitch limit so he could return to the mound by the last day of the tournament.

The first batter swung at the first pitch and flew out to right field. The next batter took a strike and then grounded out to Phil at shortstop. Finally, the next batter also took one pitch, again a strike, before hitting an infield pop-up that James caught at third base.

With the final out, Coach Deem snapped his thoughts away from pitch counts to what Central had just done. They had a win in the Region D tournament. There was no celebration on the field beyond some high-fives. The applause from the crowd was warm but not ecstatic. With four more days to go in the tournament, no one was getting too excited today.

But it was a win in a regional tournament. Coach Deem took a moment to process that, thinking it through as the teams lined up to shake hands. He called the team together for a quick talk before they had to clear out the benches for the following game.

"Guys, that was what you have to do to win a playoff game, a playoff game against another county champion," Coach Deem added. "No errors, no big mistakes, near-perfect pitching. Not every game will go like this, but we know we've got the potential. Pete, great game. John, you get the ball tomorrow. We're in the night game, so be ready to be under the lights. Try to be here early."

Coach Deem backed up as the players crowded in for another huddle. Pete was saying something to them that the coach could not hear, but then it ended with all twelve players yelling, "Central!"

Coach Deem grabbed his clipboards and walked off the field and towards the third-base bleachers. He shouted a reminder to the players to take their equipment with them. A couple of fans congratulated him and shook his hand. Most of the people were there for the players, and that was as it should be. The boys received hugs from their mothers and accolades from their fathers. There were cheers from strangers and pleasant glances from the regular trio of girls.

Off in the distance, under a tent reserved for Armed Services officials and media, Coach Deem saw Lucas. The writer would want an interview, he knew. Then the coach noticed that Marcus, the writer from the Harrisburg paper, was there as well.

He was covering the Sweetsville team, but he might want an interview too.

Coach Deem did not mind being interviewed, even though he was not one to seek the spotlight. He hoped the two writers talked to him at the same time. He was not looking forward to answering the same questions twice. Coach Deem would be happy to enjoy and reflect on the win in peace.

But before he spoke with anyone, or pondered how much of the next game he wanted to scout, John tapped him on the shoulder. Coach Deem turned back to him.

"Coach, Jonas wants to speak with the team," John said, looking sheepish. "Is that all right?"

The victory had made Coach Deem forget about Coach Baptiste's friend. Coach Deem still did not know much about the man beyond Baptiste's endorsement of him. But the game was over now. The players could do as they wished.

For an instant, though, he wondered what Mr. Antes thought of Jonas. What did Jonas think of Mr. Antes? Were the two men aware of each other at all? Mr. Antes had banished Coach Baptiste just a few days ago, and this Jonas was a friend of his. Coach Deem had heard they might be distant relatives.

It was best not to endorse Jonas, Coach Deem thought. But he was not the players' boss after the game ended, either.

"What you do with your time is your own business," Coach Deem said. "If he gives you some good insights into the game, fine. Just remember that Coach Arim and I are in charge once the game starts."

That seemed to be enough for John. He smiled, nodded and walked towards the refreshment stand, where Jonas Davis was already standing.

Coach Deem had a sense that something important was happening, but he could not quite tell what.

Chapter 22

Pete's right arm felt so strong he believed he could have thrown another inning. He was not sure if that was adrenaline or if he had that much energy left in him. But whatever it was, he was confident he could pitch at full strength towards the end of the Region D tournament if Central stayed in it.

He patted Andy on the back as his brother took off the last of his catcher's equipment. "Good job, man," Pete said. No more words were necessary for his batterymate. Andy had called the pitches and then caught them perfectly through the entire game against Sweetsville. Pete needed to make sure he acknowledged his brother's effort.

Andy gave him a quick smile and nod in reply but then pointed. "Do you think Jonas has advice on how to play five games in five days?"

Pete turned around and saw Jonas by the fence behind the dugout. A few of his teammates and the girls were with him. "Let's not get ahead of ourselves. Focus on tomorrow."

"Yeah, well, you aren't pitching tomorrow. You'll get a break," Andy said. "I may catch thirty-five innings. I've never seen you get into a catcher's stance once, tough guy."

"And I've never seen you with a girlfriend," Pete answered. "Are you seeing why I chose to be a pitcher now?"

Andy shoved Pete away, but Pete knew it was no different from any other brotherly response over the years. "Speaking of girlfriends, is Sal going to be here at all?"

The first negative thought of the day crept across Pete's mind. "No," he answered. "We talked last night, and she told me she couldn't get off from her summer job. She lives too far away to get here between shifts."

Pete thought about the girls who had been following Central since the first game of the year. The other guys got to play in front of them. He did not want his teammates worrying over girls while they were out on the field, but it helped to have the support of someone interested in you. Sal had been at every home baseball game of his freshman year of college. Even if they only got to talk for five minutes after the game because of classes, those five minutes inspired him until the next time he saw her.

But his college team had only had a mediocre season. Central had already won a county title, and after this opening-round win, they had a realistic shot at a regional title. With the way Jonas was building them up, they might even go farther than that. Maybe they could get to the national tournament. The truth was that they were playing much better ever since Jonas had started giving his lessons to them.

Sal was the only missing piece. If he could share this success with her, it would feel twice as good. He was envious of Nate, who obviously wanted to be with Maggie. Pete suspected they were seeing each other in private. That relationship was none of his business, but he knew the game meant a little more when your girlfriend was watching.

Pete, Andy, and the other players gathered around Jonas by the War Remembrance Field concession stand. Jonas was once again in a white shirt, jean shorts, and sandals. He motioned out to left field. "I won't have much to say this time. But anyone who wants to listen, meet up with me over there, in the outfield bleachers."

Jonas walked that way, and Pete followed along next to him. Most of the players were right behind, though a couple stopped at the concession stand for a postgame snack before following them. The three girls were there too. Pete also noticed Lydia, Nate's cousin, walking along the macadam path. That was a surprise.

Pete and Jonas passed the wall dedicated to the residents of Ammonville who had died in combat. That was the Remembrance for which the stadium was named. It caught Pete's attention for a moment, but not for long. He had a question he needed to ask.

"Jonas, do we have to come out here? Couldn't you have told us what you have to say back by the dugout?"

"In a hurry to get into the shade?" Jonas asked back with a smirk.

"I'm just wondering if there is there a reason you can't talk to us in front of everyone else today?"

They were up to the step of the left-field bleachers, which were empty and in the direct sunlight in the afternoon. The seats were intended for high school football games in autumn when the outfield was part of the gridiron. Baseball fans sometimes sat out here, but usually, everyone was around the infield.

"Are you afraid of Mr. Antes hearing you?" Jules asked. "He did get rid of your friend."

"A friend and a relative," Jonas reminded them. "Of all the baseball coaches you have ever known, none were better than John Baptiste. But what Mr. Antes did to him has nothing to do with speaking to you now."

"So, is this our little secret out here?" Matt asked, pulling a small notepad out of his bag.

"What I have to teach you is something I invite anyone to listen to," Jonas said as he stood at the front row. "Or write down, in your case, Matt. But though any are welcome, only those who choose to follow will hear it. If you're paying attention, someone new is joining us."

Pete wasn't sure if Lydia wanted any extra attention as she sat by the steps apart from the rest of the listeners. He made the slightest jerk of his head towards her to show he knew who Jonas meant.

Jonas nodded. "She has a part to play in this too."

The other players, including the ones carrying hot dogs and barbeque sandwiches, now sat around Jonas. The girls were mixed in between. Pete noted that Maggie was next to Nate. He wished Sal was next to him.

Pete could also see that Borderville and Steamsburg were warming up for their opening-round game. Central's next opponent would not be coming from that contest. Tomorrow, they would play the winner of the evening game between Ammonville and Boatsville. He was not concerned with the current action on the field.

"Victory is a shared experience," Jonas started. "So is defeat, but defeat was not the theme of today, was it? Today, I want to talk to you about victory."

"Hey, these guys already know all about that," Jo said. She gave a smile towards Phil. Great, now there's another couple for me to be jealous of, Pete thought. He was determined to call Sal before getting out of the bleachers.

"You are winning on the field," Jonas said. "Eighteen wins in twenty games this summer. And we all know you're not done. But do you actually understand it?"

"What's there to understand?" Tom asked. "We score more runs than the other guys. We win."

"I'm guessing he means something deeper than that," Jules answered.

"Yes, but Tom is close to my point," Jonas said. "You don't need many speeches on commitment. None of you are worried about your batting averages or who gets the most runs batted in, right?"

A chorus of yeses followed.

"What about laying down sacrifice bunts?"

That brought an awkward silence. Pete was glad that none of the coaches were there to hear about the one skill that no one on Central was interested in developing.

"Thought so," Jonas said, unsurprised. "This hasn't changed since I first met you. But that is a discussion for another time. The point is, each of you knows if the team succeeds, you have your individual success."

Jonas held out his hand, drawing everyone's attention back to the field behind him. "But even though you understand that there," he pointed back behind them, "you don't understand it there."

"Where?" Phil asked.

"Are you pointing back home?" John asked. "I'm terrible at directions."

"Actually, I'm pointing anywhere that isn't a baseball field," Jonas said. "You may not worry about going through a whole game without a hit if the team wins, but you trouble yourselves over other smaller things. You don't take the time to consider what will truly matter."

"What kind of things that matter?" Maggie asked. "Do you mean like, helping poor people? Curing cancer?"

"Or like stopping wars?" Ted asked, pointing to the Remembrance Wall. "So our names never wind up on anything like that one over there."

"All these are good examples," Jonas said. "But so is the condition of your own families, or places where you work, or your hometown. Most of you have siblings, and each one of you wants to have a car of your own before your brothers or sisters do. No matter who gets the car first, doesn't having an extra car in the family help everyone? Doesn't it allow more people to go where they want? But ask yourself, do you even bother to think about how the whole family is affected? Or do you only focus on having the car for yourself?"

Pete saw his own life in that example. He was already in college while Andy had only recently gotten his drivers' license. It made sense that Pete had a car before his younger brother. But Jonas's next words hit him harder.

"Consider your relationships," Jonas said. "Consider them from different points of view. Those of you who are dating someone, aren't you always looking for a fun time for yourself?"

"What's wrong with having a fun time?" Jo asked. "As long as you're not doing something illegal."

"Fun, in and of itself, is no crime. Just like owning a car or getting four hits in the game is good in itself. But when you focus on having a good time yourself, you can blind yourself to how your boyfriend or girlfriend feels. If each date is about you enjoying yourself, are you building a strong relationship? Aren't you hitting a home run in a game you lose? Wouldn't it be better to do things your partner likes so you are stronger together? Shouldn't you try to gain more joy by making your partner happy rather than yourself?"

In an instant, Pete saw the past several months with Sal differently. Yes, it had been special to him that she was at all those home baseball games during the college season. But he could not remember being at any events that mattered to her. They spent time together in the dorms, at pizza shops and anywhere on campus. He had always assumed it was enough that they enjoyed being together. But if he was serious about being with Sal, shouldn't they have spent time somewhere that she wanted to be? Why were they never at an event that connected to only her interests?

Jonas continued speaking. "In all these things, seek the right thing to do, then you will have all the things you need. By helping your team to win, you will have your own personal success by being part of that winner. By helping your family, you will have security by being a member of that family. By considering your partner's desires, you will have a stronger bond."

That was a lot to digest for Pete. Jonas seemed to know that. He smiled at Pete and walked out of the bleachers, leaving Pete and the players in their silent thoughts.

Words. There was wisdom in Jonas's words that Pete only partially understood. But could words be the difference for Central when their next game started?

Chapter 23

Jonas was back in the left-field bleachers again, as he had been when he had taught the Central players after yesterday's win. Today, it would be a pregame lesson which meant any of the players who wanted to be there had to get to the field extra early. Jonas would have to speak to them not only before the game, but also before pregame warmups.

Eight of the twelve players were already there when James and John arrived. At least they did not show up last, James told himself.

James and John knew they wanted to hear Jonas again. Not that Jonas's earlier talks were lacking, but what he said after the win over Sweetsville resonated with both of them. On the drive home and afterward, they had talked about how to put aside personal concerns could help bring more meaningful results. Some of it was about baseball, like when John mentioned letting himself get thrown out between bases if it allowed another runner to score. Some of it was about life away from the field, like when James brought up putting a few dollars aside into a fund for a weekend party.

Their mother overheard parts of the conversation. For the first time, she encouraged James and John to go to hear Jonas again. That was almost enough to make James question going, but the pull of Jonas and his teaching was too much to resist.

As the brothers made their way up to the bleachers, they saw that none of the girls were there, but this would have been early for any of the fans to make it. The game before Central's, a winners' bracket contest between Maroon Town and Borderville, had just started.

James hoped that Jonas's talk would be as meaningful as the ones before, but he also hoped it would be short. If Central beat Ammonville in the night game, they would play the winner of the contest going on now. It would be nice to get a little time to scout both teams.

On the other hand, a loss tonight would mean a game against Wood Grove in a losers' bracket game tomorrow. But James did not want to think about the losers' bracket or anything to do with losing right now.

"Keep an eye on the game, gentlemen," Jonas said. "I don't have anything to say yet. And scouting your next opponent will do you good."

It was amazing how many times Jonas seemed to know what was going on in James's mind. Not just that he wanted to watch this game to get a feel for the next opponent, but that Jonas was also focusing on Central winning tonight. If Jonas doubted that Central would beat Ammonville, would he have made it sound like a certainty they would face the winner of this game? Jonas must not expect them to fall into the losers' bracket.

He sat next to his brother and Pete. They were watching the starting pitchers for Maroon Town and Borderville. James remembered that neither Pete nor John would likely pitch again tomorrow. But mostly he wondered how much Jonas knew about what was coming. Did Jonas have a positive attitude all the time, or could he sense when wins were coming? Did Jonas know how much success was ahead for Central? Were his vague comments about getting to their "ultimate goal" about reaching the national tournament?

Soon after, Matt and Jules, the last two players, arrived. With all twelve players there, James expected Jonas to speak, but he kept his eyes on the field. All the boys were in their shirts with the sleeves torn off and not in their game jerseys yet. They looked like random guys taking in a baseball contest. But if Jonas wants to turn this into an instructional time, he could not wait too long, James thought. The coaches will get here soon. Around the fifth inning of this game, they will expect us to gather around them to start stretching. We won't be able to stay here.

Unless Jonas does not have much to say this time. Maybe some days he only wants to be with the team. James had not thought of it before, but it was not clear what Jonas's life was like when he was away from baseball. Jonas had a father, but that father stopped coming to Central's games when Jonas showed up.

That seemed odd. The only other friend Jonas even mentioned was Coach Baptiste. Former Coach Baptiste. Since Mr. Antes had dismissed him, Baptiste had not been around the games. Had Jonas seen him since then?

Did Jonas have anyone else he hung out with when the games ended? What was he doing on days when there were no games? How did he spend his time in the offseason? Was this all of his social life? Was there a woman somewhere in the picture, or who used to be? How was he even getting to these games in Ammonville? Coach Baptiste had always driven him before Mr. Antes fired him.

Jonas's advice, both in baseball and life, seemed wise. Central had been playing better ever since he started giving these instructions. But was Jonas here mostly because he was lonely? Did he take a bus or hitchhike down into Lancaster County and stay in a motel?

"This play," Jonas said out loud, drawing James out of his thoughts. "Watch closely. This will show you why I want to talk to you today."

That's odd, James thought. There's nothing unusual happening. It was the top of the fourth inning, Borderville was winning 2-0, and Maroon Town's first hitter was batting. There was a leadoff batter every inning of a game. What was unusual about this one?

Whoever it was hit the first pitch into right-center field. The ball split the outfielders but came down well short of the fence. The hitter was being waved to second base by the first-base coach, but James could see he would never make it for a double. His turn around first base was much too wide.

The batter did not stop. He was well out of the base path on his way to second base. That was not against the rules on a hit to the outfield, but it meant he was taking far too many extra steps. By the time he arrived at second base, the shortstop had the ball on a throw from the center fielder, and he was out by at least five feet.

Jonas stood up and turned to the team, speaking from the same spot he had yesterday. "Before I start, does anyone know what I am about to tell you?"

"Not to be too aggressive," Pete said. "Not to take unnecessary risks."

"Although there is a time to be cautious, there is also a time to be assertive," Jonas said. "No, there's something else I want you to learn from that play."

"Don't always listen to your coaches," Sam said.

That got a good laugh from everyone, including Jonas. "Though it is true that your coaches are not perfect, you are wise to follow them. That batter was not out at second because of his coach telling him to keep running. He should have made it. Why didn't he?"

"He took too big of a turn around first," James said. "He looked like he had decent speed, but he made it take too long to get to second."

"Exactly," Jonas said, smiling to James. "And what did you learn in geometry about two points?"

James hated geometry, so he kept his mouth shut. His brother answered instead. "The shortest distance between two points is a straight line."

"Our coaches have told us about this," Tom said. "Always try to stay in control as much as you can running the bases, no matter where the ball is. Smaller turns around each base make it easier to advance and score."

"And you have learned that lesson well," Jonas answered. "You've been a good baserunning team, especially since the playoffs started. But that's not the lesson I'm here to teach you today. I want to teach you what John just said."

"That the shortest distance between two points is a straight line?" John repeated himself. "What do we need to know that for?"

"Because the shortest distance between where you are now and your ultimate goal is a straight line," Jonas said. "Try to understand this. The road you must travel is straight, and it is narrow."

He said nothing more, and none of James's teammates spoke either. The game progressed, with Borderville batting now. But no one paid attention to the field. James could not figure out what Jonas was trying to convey to them. He could not mean a literal road, so what was he referring to?

"Oh, I get it," Pete said. "You mean it's important to stay in the winners' bracket in these tournaments. If you fall into the losers' bracket, you have to win more games. It wears out your pitching and gives you less room for mistakes before you're eliminated."

"States is double-elimination, too," Matt said. "I think Mid-Atlantics also is double-elimination. It would be hard to keep winning these tournaments if we lost in the first couple of days each time."

Jonas waved his hands from side to side and shook his head. "You're not looking at the greater lesson here. There is only one way to score a run. You must touch each base in order, then home. You cannot go backward, skip one, nor can you run too widely around any base. One way or another, you will be out before you get home. In the same way, if you stray from the one path, the one straight and narrow path, you will never get to your ultimate goal."

"But what path is that?" James asked.

"A simple one, that you will find to be impossible," Jonas said. "Trust in me and follow my teachings."

Again, silence. All the players were so quiet that the umpire's strike call from more than three-hundred feet away could be heard.

"Is that all?" Pete said. "Just listen to you?"

"Not listen. Trust and follow."

"And that will get us to the national tournament?" Andy asked.

"It will get you to your ultimate goal," Jonas said. He glanced above them to the scoreboard. "It is nearly midway through this game. Your coaches will be here soon, so get ready to stretch. But continue to keep your eyes on this game going on right now."

Jonas started to walk away, but Jules asked, "Are we watching for another lesson about running straight?"

Jonas stopped and turned back to them. "No. You are scouting your next opponent. Because you will win tonight. Tomorrow you will play the winner of this game in the winners' bracket final. And it never hurts to scout the opponent." Jonas walked a bit farther, but before stepping out of the bleachers, he stopped and turned one more time. "Don't lose your focus on tonight's game against Ammonville. But just so you know, tomorrow's opponent will be Maroon Town."

Chapter 24

John Thun threw a pitch. Lucas marked it in his scorebook as a strike. Then, Lucas snuck a glance over at the woman who had caught his eye a week ago.

Pitch. Note. Glance, over and over. This was Lucas' rhythm through the early innings of the game. He was not so distracted that he did not know what was going on in the contest. Central was winning 1-0 in the second inning. John Thun was not getting batters out with as much ease as Pete Roc had yesterday, but he was stopping Ammonville from scoring runs.

But his mind was divided, and had been ever since the first pitch. This beautiful woman was sitting on the far end of the third-base bleachers. Unlike yesterday's games, this time she sat alone. Other people were nearby, but no one was next to her.

He wanted to go over to at least introduce himself. It could go poorly right from the start, and it would get her off his mind. Or perhaps it would go well.

Pitch. Note. Glance.

This time, she was already looking his way. She smiled and patted the seat next to her.

Lucas did not expect that. She had not looked at him yesterday. Despite how confident he had felt when driving to the field, Lucas had talked himself out of approaching her on the first day of the tournament. Now she seemed to be flirting.

He had a job to do, but how many chances like this would come his way? He wished that there was an appropriate way to put his work aside. He could just introduce himself between innings. It would be brief, but it would be a start.

"Go over there," a voice said.

Lucas snapped around to his other side. There was Marcus, the Harrisburg sports writer. "Don't just make googly eyes at her. I put up with it yesterday. I won't stand for it two days in a row. Walk over there and introduce yourself. Find out if she roots for Philly, Pittsburgh or Baltimore. You know, the important stuff."

Marcus had been writing longer than Lucas had. He understood sports journalism inside and out. Though Marcus only paid attention to Lebanon County teams if they got deep into the playoffs, he crossed paths with Lucas more than a few times a year. Marcus was a good man to talk to during games, either to ease the boredom of a dull game or to discuss the impact of an entertaining game.

But this was not about baseball.

"I have to do a full story on this game."

"You don't have to do anything," Marcus said. "I'll give you all the play-by-play and the notes when you're done talking with her. Take your time. I know what it's like to be too distracted by a lady to think about anything else."

"How'd it turn out for you?"

"It was twenty-two years ago at a concert in Sweetsville. I eyed her, she eyed me. I got up the nerve to talk with her. I took her on a date the next weekend. We got married the next year. One son, one dachshund and one rabbit later, we're still in love," Marcus winked. "It turned out fine."

Lucas stood up, swallowed the lump in his throat, and turned back to Marcus. "You're not going to tell my bosses I stopped watching?"

"Get over there," Marcus repeated. "Before she decides she wants to date a wrestling writer."

That made Lucas chuckle, but then the nerves returned. But he had to go through with this. Whoever this woman was, it was her he had seen when he closed his eyes at night for the last week.

Lucas walked in front of the third-base seats and towards the woman, who was still sitting on her own at the end. He could be a coward, wave and walk by and go get a hamburger from the snack stand. But then he would torture himself wondering what might have been.

It was the moment of truth. It was time to use the line that, back in Lucas's college days, worked the best.

"Hello."

The woman smiled, a smile that told him she really was interested in him. "Hello there," she said. "Want to join me?"

"Thank you," Lucas said, setting himself down next to her. He made sure not to sit too close. "I'm Lucas."

"Lydia. Thanks for joining me. Sorry that I'm taking you away from your work."

I'm not sorry, Lucas thought. But he said, "It's all right. I'll get everything I need later. So, are you a relative of one of the Central players?"

"Nate Stoltzfus is my cousin," Lydia said. "There're a few of us cousins. I'm the oldest, and he's the youngest. Everyone other than Nate has moved out of state, but I make it a point to come back to Pennsylvania each summer to see my aunt, uncle and him."

"Where do you live now?"

"Virginia."

Lucas experienced a moment of disappointment, but Lydia was here now. He may as well enjoy her company while he could.

"I saw you were at the last game of the county championships," Lucas said. "It seems like you picked a good time to come up here."

"I did. I'll be here long enough to watch Central in the state championships if they make it that far."

"It's possible," Lucas said. "So, do you only follow Central, or are you more of a baseball fan?"

"It's the only sport I spend time watching. I never played organized sports in school. I was more of an artist. But my dad always followed Washington's team, and I'm still always checking out the scores and highlights. I only sit down and watch when it's my cousin's games."

"Are you an artist now? I mean, is that your job?"

"It is a part of my job. I have to do a bit of everything. I own a small, I mean, a medium-sized clothing business. Clothing, apparel, and accessories." She picked up her purse and showed it to Lucas. "This is one of mine. I design and produce, with help, of course. But I picked the shade of lavender. The purples, the violets, those hues are my favorite."

Lucas remembered Lydia's striking appearance when he first saw her, and how she was wearing purple at the time. It was the right color for her. Someday he'd be able to say that to her, but not in their first conversation.

"What is it like being a sportswriter?" Lydia asked. "Journalism sounds interesting. I bet you find something to enjoy in any sport."

Lucas was not sure if she was just polite. But as he described his regular work days and responsibilities, Lydia asked questions with a smile. She listened with her eyes focused on him. There was even laughter when Lucas shared anecdotes of some odder characters he had to interview over the years.

She actually enjoys talking with me, Lucas realized. He did not know if she would be interested the second time around, but he would enjoy this evening with her whether or not there would be another.

"Maybe you'd like some inside info since you are a reporter," Lydia said after one of Lucas' stories. "You heard that a coach was fired, right?"

"Yeah, Baptiste. Why?"

"I was there. I didn't quite understand it, even after Nate explained some things. But apparently, Coach Baptiste had rubbed Mr. Antes the wrong way. That's Central's sponsor, Harry Antes. But Mr. Antes' wife and daughter were even angrier with him. It's an odd story, but they got Mr. Antes to fire Coach Baptiste at the celebration for the county championship."

"This Antes family sounds like a fun group."

"There was something else Nate told me, but I'm not sure if it's connected to the firing or not. A relative of Coach Baptiste is here and has been giving the team speeches."

"Speeches? Like, pregame inspiration?"

"No, that's not quite it. From the way Nate described it, it's a kind of mix between baseball insights and life coaching. I heard him after yesterday's game. It was deep, though this man speaks a little differently."

"Who? What's his name?"

"Jonas. Jonas Davis, I think. He talks like someone who knows things inside and out. But he's odd."

"Odd in what way? Threatening or creepy?" Lucas asked, wondering where this lead that Lydia offered might be heading.

"No, not like that. Jonas seems to read people well. He knows what you're thinking without you saying a word. And Jonas knows what will happen before it does. Or he's just great at predicting what play is going to happen next or who will win each game. At least, that's what Nate said. I don't want to judge by the few minutes I heard."

"Jonas Davis. I'll make a note of the name. I don't know if there's a story here or not, but thanks for being my source."

"I could be a lot of things," Lydia said, giving Lucas a sideways glance. Lucas just smiled in return.

The game played on, the sky got darker, and the couple laughed at each other's stories from their homes and jobs, from their memories and their dreams. Everything was better than Lucas could have hoped.

Lucas realized that the game was now in the seventh inning. Central was going to win, already being ahead 8-2. Lucas knew he would have to get back over to the media tent to get the notes from Marcus. Though Lucas could remember a few of the big plays, most of the game had not made a dent in his memory. He hoped that this first night talking with Lydia would stay with him for years.

I'm getting myself in deep quick, he thought. Lucas stood and told Lydia, "I need to get back and catch up on my notes, and then interview the coach."

"I understand." Lydia stood next to him. "I need to ask you something."

Lucas nodded, wondering what was coming next.

Lydia whispered, "You and I...we can't go out together now, right? As long as Nate is playing?"

"Unfortunately, no," Lucas whispered in kind. "It would look like favoritism to Central's team. Or favoritism to Nate if I wrote about what he did in a game and not his teammates."

"Can we see each other during games?"

Lucas smiled. "I may not be able to ignore the game like this again, but yes, we can watch together."

Lydia was blushing, and Lucas knew he was too. No matter how old get, this never feels natural, Lucas thought. Even though his desire to be with Lydia felt completely natural.

* * *

"It's hard to believe you played so well back-to-back games," Coach Deem said as the Central players gathered around him. The lights around the outfield were off already, but the infield was still lit, and Pete could see light in the old coach's eyes. Pete did not take his comment as a back-handed compliment. The coach appreciated how hard it was to get this far.

"You've beaten two county champions," Coach Deem continued, confirming Pete's thoughts. "A lot of good teams would have been knocked out by now. Actually, two teams already have been eliminated. To still be in the winners' bracket is an accomplishment in itself. But the longer you're there, the harder it is to stay."

Coach Deem looked back, and when he turned around to the team, he had a grimace on his face. His voice lost its enthusiasm. "Anyway, we are the late game again tomorrow. Maroon Town is the opponent. I watched a few of their hitters today, but I don't know anything about who they'll be pitching against us. Get here tomorrow at the same time you got here today. Sam, you'll be on the mound. See you all tomorrow."

Pete thought Coach Deem was done speaking anyway, but Mr. Antes shoved his way in front of him. Pete wondered to himself, how could it be that the more successful this season becomes, the more irritating this man gets?

But at least his first words were positive.

"Guys, I wanted to let you know you are playing the best baseball this team has played in years," Antes said, still understandable through his cigar. Pete was sure this was a non-smoking area. It was also Ammonville's pricey artificial-turf field. But no one ever seemed to stand up to Antes about anything now that Coach Baptiste was gone.

"I don't have files or records old enough to be sure what the farthest is that a Central has ever made it in the Armed Services playoffs," Antes continued. "But I believe there's only ever been one other team we've had win two games in the Region D playoffs. That team got into the finals and lost. So you've got at least the second-best team in our history here, and maybe the best if you keep playing like this. It's good for the Central Armed Services. Good for the community and for the school district. Good for everyone around, and you should be proud."

This was the longest stretch of positive words that Pete had ever heard from the team's primary sponsor. He wondered if the next word would be "but" or "however."

"Nevertheless," Antes said, and Pete cringed, "I am concerned with your behavior off the field. I've seen that all of you have been hanging around with that wanderer. I don't trust him. I don't like him putting ideas in your head. If you need to talk more about baseball, talk to your coaches. Spend extra time with them. But this Mr. Davis, he reminds me too much of Coach Baptiste."

Thanks for reminding everyone why we can't trust you, Pete thought. But he kept silent.

"I don't think that fellow is here anymore tonight," Mr. Antes said while allowing ashes from his cigar to fall to the turf. "And I can't stop him from coming to the games. But I am warning you, don't hang around with him. It will only lead to disappointment at best, and trouble at worst. Good luck against Maroon Town tomorrow night."

As Antes walked away, the team sat still and silent for a moment. The thrill of the win was still there, but it was tempered by the renewed memory of Coach Baptiste's firing. Coach Deem was rubbing his chin as if he was pondering the situation. Coach Arim stepped in front of the team.

"Gentlemen," he said, quietly so that the exiting Antes could not hear, "All we can do is ask you to do what you know is right."

There was the slightest hint of a smirk. Pete looked over to Coach Deem, who gave a slight nod with a smile himself. The coaches were telling them all, while they would not tell the players to listen to Jonas, they would not stop them either.

After waving good-bye to their parents as they pulled away in their car, Pete and Andy gathered their equipment bags and walked out to the parking lot. "It would be nice if we had someone to carry this stuff after a game," Pete said. "What do you think about what Mr. Antes said?"

"I can't imagine Mr. Antes doing anything to us anyway," Andy answered. "Our winning makes him look good. But our roster is thin. He doesn't want to kick any of us off the team."

"He doesn't have the authority to do that," Matt called from a few parking spaces away, tossing his bag into the back of his car. "It's somewhere in the bylaws. He can appoint and let go of coaches, but coaches make decisions involving the players."

"Antes won't do anything to Coach Deem or Coach Arim, either," Jules said, opening the passenger door. "He doesn't want to leave us with one coach or have to find a new coach for us now. It's all bluster."

"But many people can be influenced by a man's bluster," a voice from behind them called out. "Especially by a man with so much wealth."

Pete knew it must be Jonas, but even when he saw Jonas walking towards them in the nearly empty lot, he was surprised. "We thought you left," he said.

"I am aware of what Mr. Antes said about me, and how he feels about me," Jonas said, walking up next to Pete. "He is a clever fox in his own mind. But I will continue to work with you here, and work with you in Salem, and finish my work in Virginia. The question you all must answer is whether you will continue to listen to my words over this time."

Pete looked around him. All his teammates had gathered around, the ones who had been ready to leave having gotten out of their cars when Jonas showed himself. A few of the parents were still around, including John and James's mother, and he even saw Maggie, Jo, and Martha in the distance. But those others were distant from the Pete and the other players. This question was for the twelve who put on the team uniform. But the other eleven said nothing, so Pete would speak for them all.

Well, he hoped he was speaking for them all. He was the leader.

"Jonas, who else would we listen to?" Pete said. "Where else could we go for this much wisdom? Who else could not only teach us about baseball but also turn so much of the game into lessons about our lives? Other coaches talk about learning from sports, but you have given it to us in ways we can understand. You've described plays before they happened. You seem to know everyone's thoughts and desires. And we are playing better than we ever had before you arrived."

"We would follow you even if it meant being kicked off the team," Tom said from somewhere behind Pete. No one else spoke, but Pete felt relieved. He was sure the others agreed.

It was now dark. The lights over the field were off, and the street lights were too far away to brighten the parking lot. But Pete saw Jonas smile. "You can see now why I choose these twelve," he said aloud, the parents and friends able to listen. But then he mumbled something, and even Pete could not be sure what Jonas said. It sounded like, "It's a shame that one of you will turn away."

But before Pete could ask about that, Jonas raised his voice again. "Do not let the empty threats from Harry Antes discourage you. It is a time for joy. Few baseball teams get to enjoy what you are doing now. Be happy today with your win. Smile in the morning. And the next three days, you will celebrate victories again."

In hearing those words, it was as if the victories had already happened. Pete felt as if Central had already scored more runs than their opponents and recorded all twenty-one outs. Not knowing what else to do, he gave an aggressive high-five to Jonas and shouted. His teammates laughed, but Jonas just smiled.

Chapter 25

A smile crawled across Pete's lips as he walked towards the left-field bleachers at War Remembrance Field. He had made it a point to get to there early, both to listen to Jonas's next lesson and to watch the afternoon game. What pleased him was that all his teammates had beaten him and Andy there.

Not only were all the other ten Central players there, but the three girls who had been the most loyal of their fans were sitting among them. The guys were all in their same pregame, torn-sleeve shirts as always. Pete's teammates were nothing if not a touch superstitious. The girls were all in light-colored tank tops, also showing off their muscles from softball season.

He walked up the steps to sit down, choosing a spot between John and Nate. Pete noticed that Maggie was on the other side of Nate. They were touching, not holding each other's hand, but showing signs of greater comfort with each other. That said something in public, in front of Nate's teammates. Pete had noticed some hand-holding before, but it was never consistent. If they were trying to hide their growing affection, they were failing. Pete and everyone else knew there had already been a flicker between the two, one that needed time to turn into a flame.

Phil and Jo, meanwhile, were sitting on opposite sides of the group. Phil was next to Jules, while several yards away Jo and Martha were talking with John and James. But it only took Pete a couple moments to notice Phil was looking more at Jo than at the Borderville-Boatsville game on the field. He was doing scouting of a different kind.

Everyone finds their partner at their own pace, Pete's mother used to say to him. That was before he met Sal at college.

Pete was about to turn melancholy again at missing his girlfriend, but it was then he saw Jonas walking by the third-base bleachers. He was heading their way. Looking toward the field, he also took in what was happening in the game. Borderville was already leading Boatsville 6-0 in the fourth inning. It was an elimination game, so it looked like Borderville would still be around, and Boatsville would be out of the tournament.

"Anyone know what happened in the first game today?" Andy asked, sitting one row above the other players.

"Ammonville beat Wood Grove," James answered. "The score was something like 12-1. I think Ammonville took out all their frustrations from us crushing them last night."

"Or Wood Grove ran out of pitching," Pete said. "These five-day tournaments will do that to you."

"So who's left?" Maggie asked, and Pete could see she was now holding hands with Nate.

"If Borderville wins this one, it's them, Ammonville, Maroon Town and us," John answered. "And our game tonight is the winner's bracket final. We will keep playing tomorrow regardless, and so will Maroon Town."

"But the winner tonight is in much better shape, and gets to play under the lights one more time," Jules said. "That's the way to play. Makes me feel important."

"And you are important," Jonas said, only then strolling up the steps to the team's gathering. "Just remember that your opponents are important too. Even the ones who don't get to play at night."

Pete stood. "Jonas, as you can see, we are all here. Mr. Antes doesn't scare us."

"Your loyalty, courage, and faithfulness with all be rewarded," Jonas said. Then he put his hands on Pete's shoulders, and gave him a firm but friendly shake. "Pete, you will be the rock for all that this team accomplishes, in ways you haven't even imagined yet."

Jonas's arms felt so strong that Pete was sure he could have been a starting pitcher and a power hitter in the big leagues. But after Jonas let him go, Pete allowed the compliment to sink into his mind. The rock. Solid, dependable. "Thank you. But, aren't some of my teammates a rock too?"

"I'm not sure how to take that," John said.

"Calling a catcher a rock isn't so bad," Andy responded, patting himself on the chest.

"Except catchers have a reputation for having a rock in their heads," Pete answered to his brother.

Jonas, ignoring the barbs between the brothers, gestured for Pete to sit. "I call Pete the rock for a reason, but he is right. Though I would not call every one of you a rock, I know that all of you have a role to play in what this team does. And not just the twelve of you who put on the uniforms."

Pete looked back to Martha and Jo, then over his other shoulder to Maggie. He appreciated their support, but was Jonas saying they had a direct influence over Central's success?

"All of you have taken an important step," Jonas continued. "You have chosen to listen to me, despite your surprise at my arrival a two weeks ago, and despite criticism from others. That is good, but it won't be enough. And my example to you will happen right now."

Jonas pointed out to the field. As if the teams were actors and Jonas was the director for a movie, the pitcher threw toward home at that moment. The batter for Borderville hit a ground ball to Boatsville's shortstop, but the ball bounced through the fielder's legs.

"Phil," Jonas said. "What did the shortstop do wrong?"

Pete was not amazed Jonas foresaw the error. Even his teammates seemed to take the prediction in stride. The inexplicable had become commonplace.

"Well, he didn't get down in front of the ball," Jimmy said. "He stood up tall, but on a low bouncer like that, he should've been closer to the ground."

"Exactly," Jonas said. "Now, considering Boatsville must be a good team to be here, do you think their coaches already told the shortstop to do that? To get down on low grounders?"

"If they are anything at all like our coaches, they hear it several times each practice," Phil said. "And several times in a game if you forget and let one roll by you."

"But what good did it do that he heard the lesson?"

"None."

"It is the same with what I have taught you, and what I will teach you," Jonas said. "You must trust me first and then listen.

But if you wish to experience what I am offering, you must put my words into practice. The lessons must not be mere theories to you, but a part of your lives."

"And what lesson do you have for us today?" Pete asked. Jonas smiled. "Oh, for today, that was it."

"So, you're telling us we should do what you've already said we should do?"

"I am asking each of you to look into your own hearts, your own minds," Jonas said. "You have all listened. But how many of you have changed anything about what you do? Keep silent, just ponder it."

Pete considered it. Yesterday's lesson, about keeping to the narrow path, was the freshest in his memory. He understood it almost right away. But had he ever considered changing anything in his life because he comprehended the lesson? He sometimes cut corners in his college classes, for example. He could upload old essays and papers for his classes on any computer. There were easy chances to plagiarize and get a good grade. Pete was never so blatant, knowing cheating would jeopardize his scholarship. But sometimes he received help from other students who he knew had used those earlier reports. That wasn't any more honest. That was not the straight path Jonas taught.

Until now, it had not occurred to Pete to use these lessons for anything other than baseball. He had thought the knowledge of what was right and wrong was enough. But maybe it was not. Knowing it did not make him more likely to choose the right thing. He had to make a conscious choice.

"Some of you are feeling guilty," Jonas said, snapping Pete out of his thoughts. "But that is not my intent. I want to you get the most out of this opportunity, both on the field and off of it. But it won't happen just by listening. Follow my instructions."

"Will you tell us anything tonight, after the game?" James asked.

"Not this time," Jonas said. "No further lessons today, and no surprises in the parking lot tonight. Not for you, anyway. I will have someone else to talk to then."

Jonas walked away but continued speaking over his shoulder to them. "I will speak to you again, before your game tomorrow night."

Tomorrow night would be the game in which the Central-Maroon Town winner would play. Jonas was predicting a win again. Pete was ready to walk over to the tourney bracket by the concession stand and write Central's name into the winner's slot. But when he looked over there, he saw Mr. Antes, chomping yet another cigar, looking back at the team with disgust.

Tough, Pete thought. I cannot explain everything Jonas does, and his approach might be different from other teachers and mentors. But no one will pull him away from us.

"Come on, guys," Pete said, standing again. "Let's get out behind first base and throw. Our coaches will be here soon, and like what Jonas said, we have a game to win tonight."

"Sure, Pete," James said, grabbing his equipment bag. "But do you want us to call you Pete, captain or rock now?"

"Any of those will be fine. Just address me with the proper amount of reverence and awe."

Several of his teammates groaned, and Martha even booed him. From the top row, Pete could hear Andy say, "I've got other names I'd like to call you right now."

Chapter 26

James stood shoulder to shoulder with his teammates while he listened to the national anthem. He sang the lyrics to himself, but his mind was not on the words. He was locked in on the game.

That was nothing new. Though James could be a bit distracted before the first pitch, he usually had his focus when the action began. But this game felt big, for lack of a better word.

With a win today over Maroon Town, Central would be sure of at least two more games here at the Region D tournament. James had thought about reaching these levels before, and about the accolades that would follow these triumphs. But the fantasies never carried the intensity of actually standing on the field for the games themselves.

In this case, he stood on an artificial field. James still was not used to the rubbery substance beneath his feet. But he and his teammates had adjusted to playing bounces off this surface. With this being another evening game with the sun already low in the sky, there was not much heat coming off of the turf, either.

Everything was going Central's way. As James took his position at third base for the top of the first inning, he sensed that they would win again. Even though in sports no one knew the winner before the game, there was eerie energy around him. It was as if the game had already been decided.

Or I'm just overconfident, James thought. I have to guard against that.

Still, James thought Central had an advantage over Maroon Town and any other opponent. With only four teams left in the Region D tourney, any team still playing must have talented players and solid coaches.

But not everyone had Jonas. Extra coach? Team consultant? Loyal fan? Prophet? James was not sure what to call him, but Jonas helped James focus on the games. At the same time, he was assisting James to play such crucial contests without being overwhelmed by his emotions. Pete was right. There was nowhere else they could turn for such unique and powerful words. It was still bizarre how Jonas knew what people were thinking or would to happen, but James would accept the odd predictions in exchange for victory.

Still being in the winner's bracket helped his stress level, too. Even a loss tonight would not knock Central out, though it would make the next day's game much more stressful.

No looking ahead, James reminded himself. Sam threw the first pitch. It was a good thing that James snapped back to the present. The second pitch was hit right at him on a hop that did little to slow the ball. But James positioned himself perfectly for it. He grabbed the grounder at chest height and threw over to John at first base for the out.

It soon became clear to James and everyone that Sam was pitching the same way he had all summer. His performance was nothing that a college scout would salivate over, but it was decent. Maroon Town picked up a hit here and there, and two batters walked, but they never could get several hitters in a row on base.

The Maroon Town pitcher, presumably their third-best hurler, was not so fortunate. Maybe Maroon Town got this far on the strength of its top two pitchers, who had already pitched in the first two days of the tournament. Perhaps one of their pitchers was injured or sick.

When James saw a hanging slider on the first pitch of his first at-bat, he knew he it would be a good night. The pitch looked like a floating beach ball, and James felt like his swing cracked it into the ocean. Coach Deem's frantic waving at first base told him he could not get into a home-run trot, so James ran at full speed. As James rounded first base, he saw the ball land in right-center field, the deepest part of the park. It might have been a home run if he had hit it anywhere else, but James settled for a double.

He knew more hitting would come before this game ended.

* * *

As the players dispersed after the postgame speech, Coach Deem looked at the scorebook again.

There was a large "13" written on top of the page with Central's batters listed on it. There was a corresponding "4" over Maroon Town's lineup.

As impressive as beating the Cumberland County champions was, what made it more impressive to Coach Deem was that none of the runs were given away. There were no errors by either side. That was partially due to the clean bounces that the ball made off the artificial turf. Coach Deem still considered that an abomination.

But with Maroon Town making no mistakes, Central had to hit to get runs. And they had hit singles and doubles all over the field. Pete smashed a triple. There were three hits each by John and Nate.

And then there was James. Goodness, he had a game. He hit two doubles and two singles and also scored four runs. It was like everyone on the team was getting better as the games became more important.

Even having lived through it, Coach Deem could scarcely believe the number of hits and runs that Central had since the tourney started. Winning the games did not shock him. Though their opponents must have been good too, Coach Deem had suspected since the beginning of the season that Central could win the regional. The three wins in a row to open the tourney guaranteed them of placing no worse than second. Coach Deem did not know for sure that would happen back when the summer began, but it was no surprise, either.

It was the domination over other county champions that was not expected. Central had not trailed in any of the games and had not been threatened at all. Coach Deem expected to at least be in some late-inning drama somewhere along the line. But so far, no team had stayed close to them.

"What are you checking for?" Coach Arim asked, noticing Coach Deem still staring through the stats in the book.

"Just trying to digest how well we've done," Coach Deem answered.

"Tomorrow will be the toughest one to keep everyone focused," Coach Arim said. "Some people call it the throwaway game."

"I've heard that too," Coach Deem said. "But I agree more with the people who call it the driver's-seat game."

Both Coach Deem and Coach Arim had been around baseball long enough to understand the ins and outs of the double-elimination format. On the fourth day of the tourney, the last unbeaten team had one game to play against one of the remaining one-loss teams. That undefeated team would still play in the finals on the last day of the event. But if they won the "driver's-seat game" to stay unbeaten, they would get two chances to win the title. A loss on day four would mean that Central would get only one chance to win on day five.

"I think I agree with you," Arim said. "But that's still no reason to put Pete on the mound tomorrow. No matter what our situation is for the finals, he will be the one we want starting."

"True," Deem said. "I think I'll wait until morning to decide who should pitch tomorrow night. I've seen bits of Borderville's games each day, but nothing that tells me who of our non-regular pitchers will have the best chance against them. I'll call around noon to the guys who might throw and find out who got a good night's sleep. Whoever is well-rested can give us some innings."

"You think any of those boys will tell you they didn't sleep well? When they can pitch in a playoff game? Besides, none of them will sleep well. They'll all be awake until two in the morning playing video games or texting girls."

"That's why I'll call at noon, not nine in the morning."

Coach Deem put the scorebook in his bag, slung it over his shoulder and walked off the field. Some players and their families were still there, while others had left. Most of the lights were being turned off around the field, but the concession stand was still open. Deem considered grabbing something before it closed, but then noticed in the light from the snack bar that Jonas was still there. This time, though, he did not seem to be interested in calling the whole team together.

"Is Mr. Antes still here?" Coach Deem asked, taking a look around the field himself.

"No, pretty sure he left in the last inning," Coach Arim answered. "I haven't seen him since the game ended."

"Thanks. I'll see you here around five tomorrow."

Coach Deem walked towards the concession stand, but decided to take no chances. Coach Arim might be wrong. Mr. Antes could still be somewhere around, perhaps looking in from the parking lot to see if anyone would defy him and speak with Jonas. Coach Deem walked to a dark corner where he could not be seen from the lot and then tried to wave to Jonas.

He got Jonas's attention. The younger man walked over, staying in the light himself, But he was right next to Deem, who was still in the darkness. Jonas handed him a hamburger. "You look hungry," he said. "No need to pay me back."

"Thank you," Coach Deem said. "But I'll try to make it up to you at another game." Deem took a bite. Mustard and relish, and a hint of onion. There was no ketchup. "I suppose it's pointless for me to ask you how you know how I've liked hamburgers since I was a boy."

Jonas smiled. "I could have grabbed a hot dog for you, but they don't cook them as crisply here as you prefer."

Coach Deem hesitated before taking another bite. Perhaps Jonas had seen him prepare a hamburger after a game earlier in the season. Maybe he noticed that the Central concession stand made his hot dogs to order, black and crispy. But combined with all the other stories he had heard of the man, it was one more difficult thing to explain.

The players had been mentioning that Jonas had been able to predict the exact pitch when there would be a big hit or a critical error. He was using those moments as examples to his lessons. Deem had not seen these predictions himself, but the Central players had been talking about it too often for him to dismiss it.

The players had also been mentioning the lessons themselves, and the ethics behind each teaching as well. That was why Coach Deem was here now.

"There is a reason I wanted to speak to you," Coach Deem said, but now that he had time with Jonas alone, he was not sure how to phrase what he needed to say. "You have enemies. Harry and some players' parents don't trust you or want you out of the way. But you have friends. Coach Arim and I both know if you were not a good man, you would not be teaching the kinds of lessons you are. And if you were not effective, you could not convey the lessons so well that the boys keep talking about them."

Jonas looked into Coach Deem's eyes. He felt a shudder, yet the shaking was not in his body. It was a tremble in his own spirit. "I'm going to tell you the truth," Jonas said. "I am here to make those players and all those who will listen to me into new men. Or into new women as the case may be."

"Yes," Deem said. "You are making them into better people. Done right, even a few lessons can change someone's life."

"No, you misunderstand," Jonas interrupted "I'm not here to make people better. I want to make them into new people. Only new people will be able to do what my father wants of them."

Coach Deem did not know what Jonas's father had to do with this, but his mind was focused on a different issue.

"New? What do you mean by new? Can a person become someone else?"

"The old person seeks his or her own benefit. Sometimes in ways the world accepts, sometimes in ways it rejects, but the old person always seeks its own desires. I have come to make people new. The new creation does my father's will, and will place other's needs and desires ahead of its own."

"This is hard to follow. You're giving me a headache before I have to drive home."

Jonas gestured out to the baseball field, which now was almost entirely dark. "Out there, you understand all the signs. You perceive all the clues. If a third baseman takes two steps in, you know the defense is ready to field a bunted ball. If the outfielders take steps towards right field for a right-handed batter, you know the pitcher will throw to the outside of the plate. You recognize these things, but you do not understand what my purpose is here."

Coach Deem had no response to that, so he stalled by taking the last bite of his hamburger. Was Jonas calling him stupid in a roundabout way? Or was there symbolism between the baseball plays he described and the lessons he was teaching the team?

"Do not worry," Jonas said, turning back to Deem. "Though it seems complex now, you will see it clearly soon." Jonas turned back in the opposite direction. "I will be here again tomorrow. I'll be talking to the players and the girls again before your driver's seat game."

Well, at least he used the right term for the game. That means that Jonas also sees tomorrow's game as important, Coach Deem thought. But now he was more confused than ever about the man.

"Wait," Deem called out to Jonas as he was walking away, though Deem did not risk stepping into the light for fear of being spotted. "Could you at least tell me when this will become clear?"

Jonas stopped and turned back. "I will tell you where. First, in Lincoln. Then, in Lavernon. After that, you will understand." Jonas turned and walked by the bleachers to the exit.

Deem stayed in place, and the light from the concession stand was darkened. Before walking to the parking lot and his car, he considered the two places Jonas mentioned. Lincoln was the host site for the Mid-Atlantic Regional in Virginia. Central had to win Region D and then finish either first or second in the state tournament to even get that far. Wasn't that expecting a lot at this stage, no matter how well Central was playing?

But even more puzzling was him mentioning Lavernon. It was much closer to home, but Central had no more games there. There was no reason for him or the players to be there all at once.

What did Jonas know?

Chapter 27

Walking on air.

James always thought that phrase was meant only for love songs on the radio, but now he thought he understood those words. When he woke up late that morning, it finally hit him how far Central had come. The other teams from Lebanon County were long done with their seasons. Even half of the teams that had made it to Region D were finished.

But more than standing longer than other teams, it was how Central stood that really hit him. They had played three games in the tournament and had not been challenged yet. The other teams were not making many mistakes. There was an error here and there, but nothing out of the ordinary. The victories had been won easily by Central, not handed to them by sloppy or unprepared opponents.

Even if tonight's game against Borderville ended poorly, they would still have a chance to win the regional title the next day. With a win, Central would get two chances tomorrow. James would play in a regional championship game, one way or the other.

So would his brother, for whatever that was worth. James told John something to that effect on the drive to Ammonville and almost drove the car off the road when he tried to punch James back. Their mother, who would come later after work, would not have been happy if James had hit a nearby fire hydrant.

They arrived unharmed at War Remembrance Field as the other game of the day was starting. The loser between Ammonville and Maroon Town would be eliminated. The winner could be the opponent for Central on the last day of the tourney. But as James walked by the bleachers, he did not think hard on any future opponents. He looked over to the left-field bleachers, but no one was there.

"I'm not used to beating Jonas here," John said. "I told you we didn't have to leave so early."

"It can't hurt to watch a little of this game," James said. "Or the girls from Ammonville and Maroon Town," he added,

194

wondering when he'd find a girl who could make him feel like he was walking on air.

"Any girl from those towns would slap us for what we've already done to their teams," John said. "I think we will need to find girls who aren't baseball fans. Field hockey girls or something like that. Maybe not even sports fans at all."

"I'd be bored by a girl who has no interest in sports," James said, putting his equipment bag down and sitting in the bleachers behind home plate. "But if she were only interested in one, and it was baseball, that would be enough."

"I don't think you can afford to be picky. When a woman who likes painting butterflies and comparing prices in the grocery store starts flirting with you, you better go for it."

"Why would that interest me?"

"Because by then you'll be fifty-five years old and she'll be the last woman in the world not to give up on you."

James was about ready to return the punch John had delivered to him in the car, but when he spun around, he saw that Jonas was already at the game. He was not in his customary pregame spot. James pointed down the first-base side of the field, and John turned. There was Jonas with a handful of their Central teammates, standing well behind the fence in one of the open areas teams held their warmups.

"I guess I'll give you more dating advice later," John said, walking over towards the others.

James picked up his equipment bag and carried it over, walking in front of the Maroon Town fans in the first-base side bleachers. He set his bag down when he got to the warmup grounds, though no one was warming up yet. It would be too soon for that. James noticed, though, that Jonas was holding a bat. Through all these lessons about baseball, James could not recall Jonas carrying any baseball equipment. Was the visual aid a sign that Jonas had something particularly important to share?

Matt, also among the players who were there, seemed also to notice this difference. "Mr. Davis."

"Please, Matt, call me Jonas. I'm a friend who happens to teach you, not a teacher from school."

"Sorry. But, I don't remember you mentioning any stories from when you played. Were you ever part of a team that won the region? Or a district title in high school?"

"My playing days were so long ago it would be hard to describe them for you. But while winning a regional title may seem important now, you will realize other things that are more impressive."

"Today's lesson is about building bonds with teammates that last a lifetime, isn't it?" James asked. "Sounds like something the football coach at school likes to go on about for hours."

Jonas shook his head. "This isn't the lesson. But you should know, I saw a man who was one of the best to play this game. I did not play in any games with him, but I saw him hit the ball like few ever have. Had great speed, and he fielded his position well. He wasn't much of a power hitter, but got on base so much it didn't matter."

Jonas frowned. "For all he understood about the game on the field, he understood so little about living off of it. He was a violent man. He took out his aggression on opponents, teammates, and sometimes people in the stands watching the game. There was much prejudice in him." He took a deep breath. "I saw this man, the greatest player of his generation and one of the best of all time, humbled repeatedly in his sport's greatest event. He reached the championship round three times. His team lost all three times. He hit the ball only a third of the time that he did in the regular season."

James did not understand who Jonas meant. He guessed it was someone who played Armed Services or high school ball back in Jonas's youth. "Where did he play?" James asked.

"He wasn't from around here. He grew up in Georgia, but the team he played for was in Michigan."

"You must get around a lot to have seen someone playing out there," Phil said.

Jonas smiled again. "You have no idea. But my point is this. It is good you have the talent to play baseball at a high level, and good that you will be in the region final tomorrow. But these are not the things that should bring you joy. Be joyous over this:

My father chose each one of you to reach your ultimate goal. Find happiness in what he has given you."

It sounded a little circular to James. If Jonas's father sent him to Central to reach the national tournament, didn't that mean that his father had given them these championships?

He did not get the chance to find an answer. By now, all the other Central players were there, and Jonas took a smooth swing with the bat. "I'm glad to see you all made it so early. This will be one of the most important lessons I have for you."

Jonas took the bat, and this time took a full swing with it. "Taking a solid hack at the ball can become so commonplace you forget how much fun it is. But it seems like you guys don't have fun any other way."

"We've been fortunate," Pete said, standing towards the back of the team. "To be honest, I don't think any of us expected to score this many runs here."

"Well, you are good at it," Jonas said. "And I mean each one of you. Even players who are usually at the bottom of the lineup are hitting better than the average Armed Services player. I don't need to teach you anything about that."

Jonas slid his right hand up the bat, keeping his left hand towards the handle. Then he put the bat out parallel to the ground. "This is what I need to teach you."

"Bunting," Jules said with what sounded like a groan. "We decided from the beginning of the season we'd play better if we did not hand the other team outs."

"Before you got here, we occasionally bunted for hits," Phil said. "But when the coaches signal us for a sacrifice bunt, we either ignore it or intentionally miss until the change the signs." Phil hesitated before continuing. "What am I even talking for? You somehow know how we get around the bunt signals, don't you?"

Jonas smiled and nodded. "While it is true that you have some accomplishments from your approach, that will not get you to your ultimate goal. It won't be an issue today, but between now and the end of your journey, you will need to learn how to sacrifice."

"Actually, Jonas," Peter interrupted, "it's not that we don't know how. We may not have been putting down sacrifice bunts, so we're out of practice, but we have the knowledge. We felt it was holding us back."

"There was a coach, a professional coach I heard of, who said you can't give away any of the twenty-seven outs in a nine-inning game," John said. "In Armed Services ball, we only get twenty-one outs, but the logic still makes sense. We don't like to give away any outs for free."

"Are you all so concerned with giving up one of your twenty-one outs, or with giving up the opportunity you have in that one at-bat for yourself?"

There were no comments from the players this time. James was stung a little, being called out like that. A random fan saying that would have gotten a wise comment back from a few of the players, but Jonas had earned the right to say it.

"I'm not here to instruct you on anything about technique," Jonas said after the players had a moment or two to process his earlier question. "As Pete said, you all know what you have to do. You've allowed yourself to become rusty at putting down a sacrifice bunt in game action, but you know how to do it. What I want you to learn is what a perfect sacrifice is."

"Do you mean a suicide squeeze?" James asked.

"Not necessarily," Jonas said. "Though you could have a perfect sacrifice with a runner on third base. Is there anyone else wants to guess at what I mean?"

After a moment, Nate spoke. "The ball should land about twenty-five feet away from the plate, down one of the baselines. Too far out for the catcher to get it quickly, but not so far out that the pitcher or a corner infielder can reach it too fast."

"That could be a well-placed bunt," Jonas said. "But you are still thinking as if you are bunting for a hit."

"Oh, now I get it," Pete said. "A perfect sacrifice would mean making sure they throw to get you out at first and not get any of your teammates on base."

"You're catching on," Jonas said. "The goal of a sacrifice is not to reach first base or to gain opportunity or glory for yourself.

The goal is to give up yourself. Give up the out in the game. Give up the attention of the fans or the reporters. Let others benefit. The runners on base will get a better chance to score, and the batter coming up after you will have a better chance to get a run-scoring hit."

"So, you would deliberately bunt to the fielder who is most likely to throw you out, but less likely to throw out a runner?" Andy asked.

"Yes, but there is more to a perfect sacrifice than that. In a perfect sacrifice, your intent is critical. You bat without any thought of ever making it to first. Your entire goal is the safety and progress of the runners. You put the bunt down with the full intention to surrender yourself."

James nodded, seeing both the literal application of this lesson and the symbolic one. Jonas may want them to bunt more often, but he wanted them to be giving to others. Who those others were supposed to be, James wasn't sure, but the point was to give to them without thought of reward.

Jonas continued. "Then, at the end of a perfect sacrifice, you are safe anyway."

Again, there was an odd silence before anyone answered. Then Jules spoke slowly. "Didn't you, I don't know, completely contradict yourself? You said to set ourselves up to be out on these bunts."

"If you make a sacrifice and are out, but the runners move up safely, that is a good sacrifice. But not a perfect one. When a perfect sacrifice is made, the batter puts down the bunt with his focus solely on moving the runners up and succeeds in that. But even then he still is safe at first. In a perfect sacrifice, a person gives up his or her freedom so that friends may have freedom. Yet after the trials that follow that decision, that person still has his or her own freedom, along with the friends' freedom."

"I'm not sure I understand," Little Jimmy said. "Could you give us an example? Someone we know who has done this?"

"Yeah, I can think of people from history class who gave up something for others," Matt added. "But usually at a large personal cost."

"The one who makes a perfect sacrifice may still have a great cost along the way," Jonas said. "But I do not need to give you an example. You will see one soon."

James at once turned his head back to the game. Maroon Town was batting, and there was a runner on first base. James expected there would be a sacrifice bunt to underscore this lesson.

"No," Jonas said. "This time the game we are watching will not be the example. That hitter won't bunt. He should, though."

On the next pitch, the Maroon Town batter hit into an inning-ending double play. As ludicrous as it sounded in his mind, James was beginning to wonder if Jonas had a remote control that moved the baseball where he wanted.

"You will see perfect sacrifices soon enough," Jonas said. "Not tonight, not in the game against Borderville. Sacrifices won't be needed to win that game. But tomorrow against Ammonville in the finals, then you will see them. And again next week in Salem, you will see a more poignant example."

"Poignant?" John asked.

"Meaningful, dummy," James whispered.

Jonas looked past the team. "It appears your coaches are here now, so I will get out of the way. Oh, there will be no lesson tomorrow, but I will be here once the game begins. And I will be at your celebration afterward."

The players each said good-bye as Jonas walked away, and he waved back with a smile as he wandered over to the bleachers.

"We really are going to win this thing, aren't we?" Andy said.

"Well, we are the best team here," Pete said. "And we are the only unbeaten team left in the tournament, and Jonas said we are going to win. I've got to think we will."

James almost slung his equipment bag over his shoulder. Then he remembered that he was already where he was supposed to be for pregame stretching. James pondered Jonas's words. He felt he understood this lesson the first time. He still felt averse to laying down a sacrifice bunt, but Jonas had not yet led him astray. Maybe a perfect sacrifice would get Central to where it wanted to be.

"That was odd," John said, reaching in his bag for his batting gloves.

"We aren't used to being told to put down sacrifice bunts," James said. "Or being told to sacrifice anything else."

"Not that part. I mean before that when Jonas was talking about watching the great baseball player he saw that was nasty to everyone."

"What about it?"

"It sounded like a man I've read about that played in the early twentieth century. He's long dead. Anyone who ever saw him play is gone."

"He may have meant someone else who happened to be from the same places."

"Could be. I guess it doesn't matter that much."

"Get your gloves out," Coach Deem called out as he and Coach Arim walked over, apparently unaware of the conversation the team had just had with Jonas. "Time to warm up."

James reached into his bag for his glove, pushing thoughts of old players and sacrifice bunts out of his mind. He glanced at the scoreboard. Ammonville was winning the afternoon game 2-0, but it was early. Either way, the obstacle for today was Borderville. The time had come to focus on that.

Chapter 28

Though it was still warm, Lucas was glad he no longer felt stuck to his seat at the press table to the left of home plate.

During the sweltering afternoon heat, Ammonville had beaten Maroon Town in a losers'-bracket game to stay in the Region D tournament. Now Lucas sat next to Marcus, watching Central play against Borderville. They were ten feet away from home plate, behind the backstop and under the media tent. Since Central was still unbeaten in Region D games, a win today would be beneficial, but unnecessary. Borderville had one loss already and needed to win to make it to the last day of the tournament.

Under the circumstances, Lucas was not surprised that Central left their top pitcher, Pete Roc, on the bench this game. If Central knew it would play for the championship the next day, why tire out the best throwing arm on the team? But Borderville's best pitcher stood on the mound in its "do-or-die" contest.

When that Borderville pitcher started throwing in the top of the first, Lucas saw her. Lydia was sitting in the first-base bleachers with Nate Stoltzfus's family. She must have arrived at the same time that the game started. Lucas certainly would have noticed her if she had come in any earlier.

So by the time "Little" Jimmy Alphos pitched in the bottom of the first for Central, Lucas was already distracted. From the angle at which he watched the game, Lydia was on the edge of his vision. Except when she became the center of his view.

Then Lucas would remind himself that he needed to focus on the game and his job. He did not wander over to talk with Lydia during the game. Temptation pulled at him, especially when he caught her glancing back his way, giving him a sheepish yet inviting smile.

After talking through the game two days ago, Lucas and Lydia had both arrived early for yesterday's game and talked for two hours. They spoke about everything and nothing all at once. Lucas had become convinced that their attraction was no longer only a physical reaction. They discussed anything from serious political issues to their favorite meals that their mothers made for them when they were children. He felt so at ease with her, and Lydia seemed to feel the same way around him.

Unfortunately, scheduling his time around seeing Lydia caused Lucas to fall behind in his office work. He had to get caught up in the office earlier today and only made it to Ammonville minutes before the game started. That mean he had to rush to get the starting lineups copied down in his scorebook and to have his computer set to send out live updates. He was finally prepared when the national anthem was being sung.

That also meant he had not been able to speak to Lydia yet today. He had to talk to her after the game. Once his interviews with the coaches and players were finished, but before he wrote his story, he had to spend more time with her. After two weeks of seeing her at games, he still found her alluring. There were often pretty young women at sports events, but he never felt the need to approach them. Not so with Lydia. He could not stay away long.

It was no longer about her beauty. Talking with her made Lucas happy. Even more importantly, speaking with Lydia made her happy. When Lucas looked her way, his thoughts were more on how they connected than her appearance.

But against all this desire was a need for caution, since her cousin was one of the players he was covering right now. Once Armed Services baseball season finished, he could date Lydia, if she was willing. If they worked out a long-distance relationship, but Nate was still on the team, he would tell his editor he could not cover Central next summer.

Wow, I'm getting ahead of myself, Lucas thought.

Despite the pleasant distraction, Lucas could keep track of the game itself. When the contest had started, it was still daylight, but neither team scored until the sun set and the stadium lights brightened. Sam Long and Phil Barr each hit a run-scoring single for Central in the third inning. Borderville scored in the fourth to make the score 2-1.

Now in the top of the fifth, Central had runners on second and third with two outs. James Thun was batting. Lucas knew this was a key part of the game. If Central scored more runs here, it was difficult to believe Borderville could come back.

A moment later, James hit a line-drive single to right field. The two runners, John Thun and Nate Stoltzfus, both scored. The cheering from more than one hundred Central fans was loud, but there was an eruption of shouting from the dugout. It appeared to Lucas, even though the championship game would not be until tomorrow, the players knew already that they would win the title.

Ted Biever was batting next, and he hit a slow ground ball near third base. Lucas, with an almost perfect view of Ted's run to first base, saw he was going full-speed to beat the third baseman's throw. Even so, Lucas knew before the play finished that he would be out if it was a good throw.

The ball was in time and on target, and Ted was out. One fraction of a second later, though, Lucas felt like he would vomit.

In his rush to first base, Biever's left foot caught the bag and snapped his ankle. Or maybe it was the lower part of his fibula. From his distance, Lucas could not tell exactly where the break happened, but it was terrible. A human leg should not be able to form that kind of angle.

Ted, lying on the ground by the bag, screamed first, then cried out in one part pain, one part horror. Teen boys, as a general rule, held their emotions in check in public. The moment was excruciating for the young man.

Since he had watched sports for several years, Lucas had seen even more gruesome injuries at games. Though repulsed, he took a breath and recovered his nerves. This kind of injury is often treated and rehabilitated. Ted would be fine in the long run.

But while Lucas had experience viewing these injuries, he was reminded that most of the people in the stadium did not. Coach Arim ran across the field to Ted, who was prostrate by the first-base bag, Coach Deem kneeling next to him. He heard a players on both sides scream, and others cursed. After the first gasps in the crowd, there was open crying from some fans.

An athletic trainer, a volunteer for the tournament, was over by the injured player in moments. Soon after that, Ted's parents ran on to the field. For a while, nothing happened that Lucas could see.

The game would be delayed for a long time until a medical professional could move Ted safely.

An ambulance arrived some time later, though how long Ted had to wait for it, Lucas was not sure. There was an awkwardness in the stands as time passed. Many people, Lucas included, only glanced at Ted and those huddled around him. No one wanted to watch. The incident was too upsetting for anyone to go over to the concession stand or to have an idle conversation. Lucas did not even think of Lydia during the delay.

The EMTs splinted Ted's leg, put him on a stretcher, and rolled him to an ambulance that had pulled up by first base. The crowd, both the Central and Borderville fans, applauded as Ted was helped from the field. But what Lucas noticed was someone who was not clapping.

Jonas Davis, that odd man about whom Lydia had spoken two days ago, walked towards the ambulance. Lucas had seen Jonas sitting in the front row earlier, but paid him little mind until now. Jonas entered the ambulance as Ted was rolled into it. Ted's mother also stepped in, while his father jogged to the parking lot, presumably to get the family car.

Jonas's actions struck Lucas as odd. He knew about Jonas having these meetings with the Central players. Some people thought highly of him, and others thought little of him. When he had been talking with Lydia yesterday, he had seen Jonas speaking to the Central players gathered around him in the left-field bleachers. But Lucas didn't know Jonas had a personal connection with the Biever family. If he had a link to them. The man might be compelling, but he also was an oddity.

Lucas pulled out a new notebook, separate from any in which he kept his information on the baseball season. On the first page, he wrote "Jonas Davis," and some quick notes from the stories he had already heard. He suspected there was a story here.

* * *

The game lingered on after Ted Biever's injury. The teams played the last few innings without any heart. No one blamed the players. Even the older fans, who might have made a comment about the game not being played like it was in a bygone era, understood that this was different. No one could put their full effort into a game after watching what had happened to Ted.

Lucas suspected that Central would be in good shape for the championship game tomorrow. They needed to know Ted would be fine in the long run. The poor boy would not be playing any sports or even walking for a quite a while, but he would be okay. Add that with a night of sleep and the players would be refocused.

Central would be down to eleven total players, though. That meant only two reserves. There would not be much more room for any more injuries in the championship game. For now, Jules Iscar replaced Ted in the field, but what the strategy would be in upcoming games was unclear.

Each team got a couple of runners to first base in the late innings, but neither side threatened to score. The game ended as a 4-1 Central win. The fans applauded the team after the last out, but though the claps were well-meant, they seemed tepid. The players did not smile as they shook hands with Borderville, which appeared to be happy to be off the field now despite their elimination.

It seemed like such a shame to Lucas. This was the biggest win Central has had in years. It kept them unbeaten in the tournament and gave them two chances to win the title tomorrow. But no one could appreciate it.

Central gathered around Coach Deem to hear the postgame speech. Lucas grabbed his folder and recorder to walk over and do his interviews once the coach finished speaking. He asked Marcus if he was coming along, but the other writer was almost at his deadline and already typing his story.

Lucas walked to within earshot of the Central team. The coach said something about still not having heard anything from Ted's family about what was going on at the hospital. Coach Deem told the players when to arrive at War Remembrance Field for the championship and confirmed that Pete would pitch that contest.

Lucas had no intention of interviewing any of the players after a game like that. Talking to athletes after a disappointing game is one thing, but after watching a friend being hurt in such an upsetting way would be out of bounds. He made his way over to Coach Deem when he noticed the players had stood up and turned towards him. It seemed like they were surprised he was there. But after a few seconds, he realized that the boys weren't looking at Lucas. They were looking behind him.

Curious, Lucas turned around, and he saw what the Central players did. Ted stood on the field. He was not in a wheelchair. He had no crutches.

Ted walked towards his teammates, without so much as a limp.

John was the first to react. He ran up to Ted but stopped short of touching him. "What, wha? Are you all right?"

As the other players gathered around him, all looking amazed, Lucas found himself also walking closer. He had seen the injury. It should have taken months for Ted to recover fully.

"I'm not sure what happened," Ted started. "I thought my leg had snapped off, and the pain was terrible. Then when we were in the ambulance, he touched my leg and said I would walk before I went to bed tonight."

"Who?" Jules asked. "The EMT? A doctor?"

Ted turned his head, and Lucas saw several yards behind him was Jonas. The man stood under one of the lights around the infield. Jonas was not drawing any attention to himself, but it was obvious that was who Ted meant.

"Jonas didn't do anything else. He touched me, talked to me, and calmed my mother down," Ted said. "I think the EMTs told him not to touch my leg again, and he didn't. When we got the hospital, Jonas calmed down my father, too. They took me for x-rays and found no damage. The hospital staff didn't believe my parents or the EMTs when they said it had been broken."

Suddenly, Pete put his arms around Ted. He said nothing, but his tears showed the whole experience affected him. Then the entire team gathered around Ted, and it seemed as if the celebration that should have been right after the game was happening now.

Lucas looked at the scene for a moment. He appreciated seeing a team celebrate something more than a victory in a game, but rather the surprising healthy return of a teammate.

Then Lucas looked to Jonas. The story Ted told did not make any sense at all. His leg had been broken. There was nothing that Jonas could have done in that small space of time to heal it. There was nothing that the entire hospital staff could have done to heal it.

And yet, here Ted was.

Lucas did not see Lydia walk up next to him, but he felt her presence. As interested in her as he was, he had to keep his eyes on Jonas. Something was there, in that man, that he could not explain. Lucas suspected that Lydia had her eyes focused on Jonas.

"Do you know who this man is?" Lydia asked. "Can you explain any of this?"

She must have listened to Ted's story as well and could make as little sense of it as Lucas had.

"I don't know," Lucas said. "But if your cousin's team keeps playing long enough, I hope to find out."

Chapter 29

"If you've got one hundred and twenty pitches in that arm, I'll use you for every one of them."

Coach Deem's words gave Pete an extra boost of confidence, though his spirit was already filled with the certainty of victory. Still, it was good to know his coach was willing to use him for the maximum number of pitches allowed today.

This would be the biggest game in Central's history. Pete was not sure how long the history of Central Armed Services baseball was, but he knew they had never won the Region D championship. They had never played in the state tournament.

It was Pete's job to make sure that all changed this afternoon. It was everyone's job, but as the starting pitcher, more of the burden fell on Pete. He felt well-rested, with no lingering issues from the complete game he had pitched on the first day of the tournament. While warming up with Andy, he had full control of all his pitches: fastball, curveball, slider, changeup. Everything was going at the speeds he wanted and in the locations he wanted.

Pete did not allow himself to think about the possibility of Ammonville winning this afternoon game. That would turn the day into a double-header, with a winner-take-all game to be played in the evening. Central needed to do this the easy way by winning now. Besides, they had beaten Ammonville in the second day of the tournament with John pitching. John was a good pitcher, but Pete knew he was better. There was no reason for Central not to win today and get the championship in the first game.

He allowed himself a quick video call to Sal before the pregame warmups. She had wished him luck and blew a kiss to him over the screen. He also took a quick note of who was in the bleachers. The usual relatives of the players were there, along with Maggie, Jo, and Martha. But there were few of the casual fans, the ones who weren't related or close friends to the players.

It was a shame the championship game was on a Wednesday afternoon. The other games were either on weekends or evenings, which allowed more fans to arrive. But they played this game in the afternoon in case Ammonville won to force a deciding game that night. The tournament officials could not wait, Pete had heard. They needed to notify the state tournament committee of a champion by daybreak the next day. So, Central's biggest game would be in front of many fans, but not as many as Pete might have hoped.

But he noticed there were more reporters than usual under the media tent. Pete spotted writers from Lebanon County, Harrisburg, Ammonville, and other towns. Also, there were a pair of local news cameramen setting up their gear.

Maybe there were not as many people were in the stands, but more people would hear about this game.

Pete impatiently stood through the national anthem, then finally took the mound. He reminded himself to not let his vigor overtake him and overthrow on the warmup pitches for the top of the first inning.

But when the first Ammonville hitter got into the batters' box, Pete let loose. Fastballs were at top acceleration. Curveballs dropped with a perfect twelve to six break. Sliders dove at the last millisecond. Changeups looked like fastballs to the naked eye until the batter swung an eyelash too soon. Pete made every pitch fly through the air between the mound and the plate with perfect precision.

With ten pitches, Pete struck out the side. And he was sure that extra throw had caught the corner of the plate and the umpire missed it.

As Pete found out in the bottom half of the first inning, Ammonville also had its top pitcher on the mound as well in this game. Central already knew Ammonville was starting the same pitcher who had started the first game of the tournament. When Pete took a lousy swing at a curveball that was almost as good as his own, he realized it was the best pitcher Ammonville could put on the mound.

Pete was not disheartened. Why shouldn't a championship game be a pitchers' duel? And besides, Pete had room for error. As much as he did not want to lose, a loss would only force one more game. A win would claim the championship.

Taking that confidence into the next few innings, Pete kept Ammonville from ever coming close to scoring. The strikeouts occurred at a slower rate, but the outs were dependable.

It took until the bottom of the fourth inning for Central to get its first baserunner. Phil singled up the middle with one out. Pete stepped to the plate, thinking of hitting a single into right field to move Phil up to third base. But then he saw the signal from Coach Arim at third base.

Sacrifice bunt.

Pete's first reaction was to ignore the signal, as he had done so many times in the past. This Ammonville pitcher got too many outs on his own, so Pete did not want to give him more. But then he remembered Jonas's words about sacrifices. Something about perfect sacrifices, about how they would be needed to reach the team's ultimate goal.

He glanced to Coach Deem at first base, but merely saw him in the coach's box behind Phil with his arms crossed. Pete hoped that his head coach would confirm the signal. But having too many signs go back and forth on the field would tip off Ammonville that something unexpected was happening.

So Pete readied himself in the batter's box, holding his bat as if he was ready to take a full swing. The first pitch was low, and Pete let it fly past him. No one on the Ammonville defense moved as if they were preparing for a bunt. Due to Pete's reputation as an athlete, they probably did not expect him to give himself up.

Pete looked to Coach Arim. Same signal.

The second pitch came towards the plate. It was low again, but this time in the strike zone and one that Pete could put down on the ground. He already had his hands squared around the bat, one near the top and one near the bottom, and nudged the ball back out onto the field.

Pete ran hard to first base and only saw where the ball landed for a moment. Still, that glance told him he had put the bunt too close to the pitcher to hope to make it to first base himself. Phil should make it to second base, he thought. The sacrifice bunt should succeed.

Despite being sure he would be out, Pete hustled down the baseline, because that always was what a ballplayer should do. He did not realize that the Ammonville pitcher had thrown the ball away until it flew well over the first baseman's glove and into right field. Pete was so surprised by the error he took a half-second to make his turn to second. Then, he realized that Coach Arim was waving him to third base. Ammonville must not have backed up the errant throw. Pete slid into third, then looked towards home plate, where Phil scored the game's first run.

Pete stood up, received a high-five from his coach, and instinctively dusted himself. He looked ridiculous, since there was no dirt on the artificial turf. His mind was elsewhere. First, he realized that Central had the lead in this game, and was just a few innings from winning the Region D title. Then, it occurred to him that what he had done was what Jonas had called a perfect sacrifice in one of his talks with the team. He had intended on giving himself up but reached base, anyway.

John stood in the batter's box now. It would only take a single to score Pete and make it a two-run lead. With John batting and James up next, Pete was sure he would make it the next ninety feet to home plate.

Then he noticed the signal Coach Arim made to John. Another bunt. Suicide squeeze. No, wait, that was not the sign. Safety squeeze. Sacrifice bunts with fancier names.

On suicide squeezes, the runner from third charges toward home on the pitch. It meant if the batter missed his bunt attempt, the runner was running straight into the catcher with the ball for an almost certain out. On safety squeezes, the runner must wait until he sees the bunt put down, and then break for home.

Pete was uncertain if any of this was wise. But he could not afford to question the decision now. He slightly increased his lead as the pitcher threw towards home. Pete made a note of the fielders' positions again. They were standing too far back to field a good bunt if John could place it right.

John put another bunt down, and unlike Pete's attempt, this one fell too far away from the mound for the pitcher to field it. He ran from third towards home, and from the catcher's resigned stance he knew there would be no throw to the plate. Pete crossed home standing and turned to look at first base.

The third baseman fielded the bunt and tried to get John out at first. But John beat the throw. Central was winning 2-0 on two perfect sacrifices.

Pete ran into the dugout, where his teammates were hooting and hollering, giving him high-fives and slapping his helmet. Pete wanted to celebrate, but knew he had to keep his concentration for when he got back on the mound. But in the middle of the cheers, he realized that Jonas understood this sport more than anyone he had ever met.

* * *

James almost expected to see a bunt sign from his coach as he approached the plate. But there were no special instructions. He was free to swing away at his own leisure. Maybe three bunts in a row were too much to expect.

A look at the infield showed why. Ammonville had both the first and third basemen playing a step closer to home plate than earlier. Now that the opponent was looking for the bunt, there was no reason to try one.

James took the first pitch for a strike, then swung and hit the pitcher's second offering. At once, he knew he would have been wiser to let it go by him. It would have been a called strike, but he could feel he had hit a ground ball right at the second baseman. James ran to first, but knew the effort to be in vain as Ammonville's middle infielders turned a double play.

That took some joy out of the two-run rally his teammates had put together. But James looked back to his dugout as he and his brother got their gloves. There was no disappointment there. His teammates knew they already had all the runs they would need to win the game.

To win the region.

The remaining innings passed quickly. James had heard professional players say that, in big games, the final outs seemed to be harder and take more time. But it did not feel that way in this game, because Ammonville's batters could do so little against Pete.

Central did little against Ammonville the rest of the game. James struck out in his last at-bat. But with a 2-0 lead and Pete pitching his best, it did not matter.

In the field, James found himself rooting for the ball to come to him, but it only did once. There was one easy ground ball that came right to him, and he made a perfect throw to John at first for the last out of the sixth inning.

In the seventh, as the fielders threw the ball around before Ammonville's batters came up, James's mind did not wander to the prestige of victory. He did not think about the number of newspapers and television stations there at the game. He thought of how long it had taken for Central to do this, and how that length of time made the triumph all the sweeter.

Oh, the game itself was quick. But the years that James had been a teammate to these other boys had filled almost half his lifetime. And from the time they were eight years old to this summer, all their baseball accomplishments added up to mediocrity. Now, they would be champions, not only of Lebanon County but of a region that contained six counties.

It was about time.

James hoped for one more ball to bounce his way, but his brother would steal the moment. After Pete struck out the first two batters, the final hitter hit a grounder to first. John scooped it up and stepped on the bag in plenty of time.

There was no time to resent John for taking the last moment of glory here. James sprinted to the mound with his teammates on the field while the three remaining players rushed there from the bench. The team dog-piled on top of Pete, knocking him to the ground. Their shouts mixed in with the cheers of their fans in the background. James could scarcely imagine a happier or more fulfilling moment.

The players separated so the guys on the bottom could get up and breathe. James looked around him for a moment, and everything seemed different. His teammates looked stronger than they ever had. His coaches looked wiser. In the stands, his mother looked more loving. Martha, Jo, and Maggie looked more beautiful.

John looked tolerable.

It was almost a blur again, receiving medals and the team trophy. One moment, James lined up with his teammates awaiting a medal, and then he had one around his neck. He knew Coach Deem must have put it there, with the announcer speaking his name, but everything was happening so fast. The team trophy was presented to Coach Deem, who handed it to Pete and Andy, and then the whole team circled around them.

The announcer was continuing to speak, saying something about the upcoming state tournament at Salem in Berks County. And then it all hit James again, all the attention he and the team were both going to get. Not just for this win, but for any games it played at states and even into the national regionals. Local baseball fans were learning about Central, and soon baseball fans around the country would too.

Family, friends, and fans were being allowed onto the field. Coach Deem was trying to get the players together for a team picture with the trophy. James tried to spy his mother, but did not find her until he was posing for the photo. She was front and center among the fans with their cameras and phones. James's mother was even in a better spot than the news photographers for taking the championship picture.

After everyone took pictures, two things happened. First, Mr. Antes announced that he had made reservations and would pay for a celebration meal back at a restaurant back in Central. Second, the players sought their parents and family. Some players were stopped by the sportswriters. Most of the rest, like James and John, received the embrace of their mothers.

For a moment, James thought he saw, away from the crowd, Nate and Maggie sharing a kiss. He glanced that way again and only saw Nate. James turned his attention back to his own family and forgot about his teammate's romance on this grand day.

Chapter 30

"Did any of you see Matt jump in left field?" Jo asked. "I didn't know if he'd ever come back to the ground."

"I didn't know I had legs," Matt answered. "I couldn't feel my feet running into the mob either."

"I felt your cleats in my shin when you jumped in," James said. "I'm glad you didn't draw blood."

All twelve players sat around a couple of tables in the center of the front dining room at Emperor's, a bar and restaurant in the town of Central. Maggie, Martha, and Jo had joined them though, on this rare occasion, they were not sitting all in a row. Now they mixed into the group with a baseball player on each side. The players' parents, along with a few other adults like Nate's cousin Lydia and Jonas, were in the back dining room. It looked like Mr. Antes had invited about a dozen other adults to go into the back room. Pete did not recognize the other people and figured that Mr. Antes just had them here to enjoy a party.

The difference between the front room where the players were and the back room where the adults ate was alcohol could be served in the back. But no drinks were needed for Central's players to feel happy now. Pete had not yet come down from the high he experienced from the last out of the Region D championship game. His parents had driven him and Andy home from the game, and during that ride, Pete called Sal and told her about the game for thirty minutes. Then they all drove back to Emperor's to rejoin their teammates, or were driven there by their parents. The teammates almost dog-piled each other again when they got to the restaurant.

And while Pete still disliked Mr. Antes, who himself was in the back room, he would not object to eating on his tab. Burgers, wings, cheese sticks, breadsticks, loaded cheese fries and more were in baskets all over the table. Sodas and juices were everywhere. They had earned it.

"Anyone find any stories on the internet?" Pete asked, hoping Central's rivals knew this celebration was happening.

"I found a video of the last out and celebration," Nate said. He played it on his phone and showed it to his teammates around him. He also showed it to Maggie, who Pete noticed was sitting next to Nate.

"Here's one of the first inning," Sam added. "Though not much happened then."

"Hey, a lot happened that inning," Pete said, stretching over to see the playback. "I got into my groove early. Can't shut the opponent out for a game if you don't shut them out in the first inning."

That led to high-fives between Pete and Sam, and hoots from the other boys. Martha was laughing out loud. Other groups were eating in the restaurant, and Pete glanced around to see if anyone would try to calm them. But those few who looked over were smiling, one older man even giving him a quick nod. It seemed everyone understood that the baseball team had done something worth celebrating, and no one would interfere.

"Oh, here's a video of my bunt," John said. He turned his phone around to show everyone. Pete could barely make it out from the opposite side of the table, but he looked as closely as he could. Though Pete had scored a run on that play, he never had a chance to see John run down to first.

"Look at you go," Pete said. "I don't ever remember seeing you run that fast. Even back when James would beat you up."

"That was ten years ago," James said, pausing between chicken wings. "But I still put fear in him to make him run that fast."

"I was only afraid you'd do something to kill the rally," John said. "And you did, double-play machine."

James waved a dismissive hand at his brother but was working too hard on the next wing to say anything more.

"Anyone find a video of my bunt?" Pete asked. "I'd search myself, but I left my phone at home on my charger." It was true. He had sapped the battery while talking to Sal.

"I didn't find anything," Andy said. "But that play was more about luck than anything. You would have been out on a good throw."

Pete almost protested, but stopped. He didn't want to bicker with his brother today even if John and James still seemed willing to argue. Besides, Andy was right. A good throw and he would have been out by at least a step. Maybe Central never would have scored that inning, and the Region D title would have been in doubt.

While Pete kept silent for a minute, Jules spoke in his defense. "It wasn't luck. Pete put down a good bunt. He ran hard to first. He forced Ammonville to make a play, and they didn't. That's just sports."

Pete turned and gave a quick eyebrow raise to Jules, a silent thank you.

"But I thought," Maggie started, then looked around the room. "Your coaches aren't here, right?"

"No," Nate answered. "Coach Deem and Coach Arim aren't big for these larger celebrations. They'd rather appreciate the wins on their own."

And the last time we had a celebration Coach Baptiste got fired, Pete thought to himself. But he didn't want to mar the moment, so he kept that observation to himself.

"Well then, I'll drink to them," Ted said.

"You drink to Deem, I'll drink to Arim," Phil said.

They each grabbed full glasses of soda and started to chug them down, without stopping. Tom told them that was for adult beverages. Jo told them it was disgusting to take that much sugar in a few seconds. None of their words stopped them.

When they finished at about the same time, the other boys cheered. Well, Pete just laughed. Pete also noticed that Jo, despite trying to act above it all, gave Phil a smile and a hug afterward.

Nate and Maggie. Phil and Jo. Rumors were even starting about Nate's cousin and the one newspaper reporter. Success on the diamond had its benefits. If only Sal were here, Pete thought. That was the one thing that kept this day from being perfect. But even that one shortcoming, though important, also made it all the more clear how wonderful everything else was.

"Were you going ask something, before the carbonation contest?" Martha asked.

Maggie cleared her throat. "Oh, yeah. I thought you guys didn't bunt. Like, not sacrifice bunts. You always pretended not to see the signal or tried to bunt for a hit instead."

"That's right," Jo said, and Pete was sure she and Phil were holding hands under the table. Jo spoke loudly, so she was clearly talking to everyone, but she was still turned to her new beau. "Those bunts were obviously meant as sacrifices. What changed?"

"You weren't there," Phil answered. "Jonas gave us another pep talk yesterday, before the game against Borderville. It was all about bunting."

"Actually, it was about sacrifices," Pete said.

"Whatever," Jules said. "He said sacrifices would be important to beat Ammonville. That and something about perfect sacrifices. Trying to sacrifice but being safe, anyway. I might put down a few perfect sacrifices at the state tournament next week."

"Your opportunity will come," Jonas said, walking in from the back room.

Pete stood. He did not know why at first. Out of respect, perhaps? He put out his hand to Jonas, but Jonas ignored that and gave him a hug.

"I wanted to congratulate all of you one more time," Jonas said, shaking Pete by the shoulders before letting him go. He turned to face everyone at the table. "And to let you know I will be there at the state tourney, to support you."

"Will you have anything more to say to us?" John asked. "Any more lessons or inspiring speeches?"

"Eventually," Jonas said. "But no big team meetings with me on the first day of states. Sometime during the week, we will have a significant talk."

"I look forward to it," Pete said. "Are you going home now?"

"Of course not," Jonas said with a laugh. "The celebration in the back is far from over. And I'll have more people to talk to in a little while."

"Who?"

"Let's say you and your teammates are not the only ones who need instruction, and leave it at that," Jonas said. He gave

Pete a wink, and headed back to the other dining room, out of Pete's view.

"I can't picture him as a heavy drinker," John said. "I wonder how he celebrates."

"Ahem," Martha said. "Am I the only one who noticed what happened while Jonas was talking?"

Pete sat again and looked around, not sure what Martha was talking about. Then he realized it.

"Nate and Maggie," he said.

Martha nodded. "Maggie snuck off first. Nate a moment later."

The table erupted into a long "Woo!"

* * *

The conversation, or random shouting, continued around the table after Nate and Maggie had departed. Everyone else seemed to have moved on from a few jokes behind the couple's back. Some of the barbs were good-natured, while others were best out of the earshot of the parents in the other room. But after the talk had moved on, James was still wondering about them.

Well, not true, James thought. He was more wondering if there would be any pretty girls left for him. Nate had taken Maggie, which everyone saw coming. Phil and Jo were beginning to pair together. That was not a surprise either.

There was still Martha, though. She was seated between Andy and Matt, but she showed no closeness to either of them. It happened to be where she sat down over an hour ago. James did not know Martha that well, but she liked baseball, and she was a red-head.

James tried to push the thought out of his mind. There would be plenty of girls in college. Not that he was looking for lots of women. He wanted to find one who matched well with him the way Sal matched with Pete. Still, the thought of dating the one unattached girl who kept coming to the all the games was tempting.

He was staring. Don't do that, James berated himself. Girls like glances, not stares. Was it John that told him that? Maybe his brother lied.

Martha spoke. James had utterly lost track of what everyone was talking about and remained silent to listen to her.

"But that still doesn't explain anything," Martha said.

That did not help James figure out what was going on, but Ted's response did.

"There's nothing else to it, though. I was in the ambulance. Jonas got in the ambulance, touched me, and my foot was back to normal."

Between Ted's inexplicable recovery and winning the Region D title, Ted's broken ankle itself was almost forgotten. The whole story, from how Ted recovered to any role Jonas may have played in that recovery, was still unclear to James.

"He was wise to do whatever he did in the ambulance," James said, suddenly nervous to speak in front of Martha but forcing himself, anyway.

"In case he hurt me more?" Ted asked.

"No. In case healing you caused a scene. What if Jonas had healed you on the field? Yes, you would have been better even more quickly. You might have even been able to stay in the game. But everyone would have gone insane if they saw Jonas heal you with just a touch. Remember how we all crowded around you when you came back after the game? Every fan, reporter and anyone else there would have been poking around you and chasing Jonas down with questions."

Ted leaned back in his chair, munching a breadstick and apparently thinking about James's explanation. But it was John who spoke next.

"Jonas let the spotlight stay on us. However he does what he does, he's not using it to put the focus on himself. He did not take the spotlight when he healed Ted. He doesn't show off to large crowds when he makes his predictions."

"I think that's the reason we all like him so much," Martha said.

"No, we like him because what he's told us has helped us win games, like with the bunts today," Andy said.

Martha shook her head. "No, there's more to it than that. Your coaches help you win games, and while they may not take all the credit, they'll let the reporters interview them after every game. Jonas is helping you without any acknowledgment at all."

"If I could do what he does, I'd make sure everyone knew it," Jules said.

Martha shrugged her shoulders. "I don't know. A man who can stay humble is, how should I say it? Appealing."

"Wait, are you saying you're into Jonas?" Jo almost shouted.

"No, no, no," Martha said before anyone else joined in the joke. "You're all creepy. He's too old. I'm only saying that's a quality I'd like in a man."

Then she glanced over at James and held her gaze for a second. There was a hint of a smile at the corners of her mouth. Then the glance and smile were gone. James hoped he had not imagined either.

"Well, I can tell you one man who hasn't done a thing to help us but does a great job of drawing attention to himself," Pete said. He was glancing toward the back room doorway.

James did not take his gaze off of Martha. Partially because he liked looking at her and partly because he did not want to see the man who came over to the table now. But Mr. Antes' voice boomed louder than any shout that the teenagers had voiced that evening.

"I wanted to congratulate you boys one more time," said the man, who looked like he had gained five pounds since James had last seen him. "I think all your parents are coming over now to take you home. The party will continue in the back, but it's best if you all go home before it gets too late. I don't want any incidents."

Only then did it occur to James that Mr. Antes' "wife and daughter" were not there. That was fine by James. It was less likely that something regrettable or uncomfortable would happen.

Mr. Antes walked around the table and patted Pete on the shoulder. "You're making my investment in the team look good," he said to the pitcher, then announced to the entire restaurant. "And I'll make sure you're all well-rewarded again after you win the state title!"

The pompous man walked to the exit while many of the adults in the back room started to come over to the team's tables.

"Of course they want us to go now," Matt said. "This is when the adults who stay get too drunk for us to see."

"All the more reason for me to go," Pete said. "Don't want to..."

"...lose your scholarship, we know." John finished for him.

Before everyone finished laughing at their star player's temperance, Pete's parents came in. The other players' parents followed. Martha told Nate's parents he had already left, but left out the detail that he must have gone with Maggie. Apparently, Mr. Antes was right. None of the parents were staying any longer.

James walked out, flanking his mother with John. She had her arms around both of her sons. "I'm so proud of you," she said, kissing them on their foreheads despite how embarrassed they were in front of their teammates.

"Are you sure we have to go now?" John asked his mother. "I'd like to keep on celebrating."

"Of course you want to. And of course, you can't," Mrs. Thun said. "It's already getting way too late, even for you two. Besides, I don't want to stay in that back room any longer."

"Is it getting rowdy back there?" James asked.

"It could. No one I know well is back there anymore. It's only a bunch of Mr. Antes' old friends from around town. That's not my kind of crowd." James's mother turned her head for a moment as if she remembered something. "Oh, I guess Jonas is still back there, and Nate's cousin."

Chapter 31

It was not even close to Christmastime, but Lydia felt a warmth like that season as the celebration carried on into the night. None of the players were there, nor their parents, but several other adults from the town of Central were still drinking and laughing. Though there was no one left whom she was familiar with, she stayed even after Nate's parents had gone just to be in a positive atmosphere.

Some of the happiness of the strangers around her may have even been connected to the Region D championship. But Lydia doubted it. Except for her and Jonas, who was on the other side of the back dining room, she was sure everyone still here was drunk.

Lydia took the last sip of her beer, the only one she had all night. Her days of getting drunk were finished. Once drinking parties at college turned into Saturday nights she could not remember, she made a deal with herself: One drink a day, every day.

There was a time she thought those wild college parties were the high point of her life. By the time she was a senior, Lydia knew that was a mistake. A day like this, though, might be one of the best. She watched the championship game with her family. Nate's team won the title. They got to celebrate at the field, not only with the family but with old friends and other people she had just met in the last week. And now, she was back in her hometown and continuing the revelry close to midnight.

And she had fallen in love.

Lydia felt it for three days now. She wanted to be with Lucas, and she desired to make Lucas happy. For a while now, she had put aside the romantic part of her life. It took too much time from running a business. She also remembered too many mistakes in her past. After the last of those misfires, late in her junior year of college, she decided that she would not pursue a man until she could not resist him.

When she first saw Lucas, during the county tournament, he seemed to be a nice guy. He was handsome too. It was enough to catch her interest. But once they started talking together, she could not stop thinking about him. She knew Lucas would not commit too deeply right now since it would be a conflict of interest for him to date someone who was related to a player. But once the season was over, that might change.

But how would it change, she wondered to herself. Something long-term? Or something that would fizzle? How would Lucas react to a long-distance relationship once she had to go back to Virginia for her business? She always handled each of her past relationships with poor judgement. Lydia was a little too clingy to men who needed a little space. She acted wild around the men who were looking for someone stable. She did not want to make any of those mistakes with Lucas.

A couple came over to her table, interrupting Lydia's thoughts. She tried to remember who they were and failed.

"Tell me again, you're a cousin to which player?" the man slurred.

"Nate is my cousin," Lydia said, trying not to laugh at the gentleman who appeared to be a half-drink away from being completely incoherent.

"He can't remember anything even when he's sober," said the woman, who was under the influence but in much better shape than her husband. "Hey, we were talking over there, do you remember if we ever had a parade through town for a team that wasn't part of the high school?"

"What do you mean?" Lydia asked.

"I can remember having a parade in town when the high school field hockey team won the state title," the woman belched. Maybe she was not in as good a shape as Lydia thought. "Then they did the same thing when the high school soccer team won the state. Did we ever have a parade for a team from in town that wasn't a part of the school?"

Why are they asking someone twenty years younger than them that question? Lydia wondered. Alcohol, she answered to herself.

Out loud, she said, "No, I don't remember them ever having..."

The man did not let her finish. "Well, we're going to change that. I'm going to call the fire chief first thing tomorrow morning and see what we can arrange!" He slammed his fist on the table, gave out a hearty laugh, and stumbled over to the where most of the other diehard drinkers were. Lydia was confident that the man would not be capable of calling anyone before noon.

"They haven't won a state title," Lydia said to the woman. "They're going to states."

"Oh dear, that will be simple."

The woman wandered away. Lydia hoped that when everyone woke up tomorrow, they would realize that states would be a more significant challenge than Region D was. Lydia did not doubt that Central could win. But if they lost two games, she did not want people disappointed in her cousin's team after all they had already accomplished.

She leaned back in her chair, sighing. Little Nate's team is the first team from Central to even make it to the state tournament. That alone should keep everyone satisfied with this season.

Lydia tilted back her bottle again, only to remember that she had already finished the beer within it. That was a good sign it was time to go home. There would be another celebration a week from now, anyway.

But before Lydia stood, she saw that Harry Antes had come back into the room, and he was not alone. There was a girl with him. She looked distraught. Her blonde hair was unkempt, her face was red, her clothes were rumpled. She wore only a short-sleeve shirt and shorts. There wasn't even anything on her feet.

Oh no, Lydia thought. In her frumpy outfit, she had not recognized the girl at first. But now she realized it was Maggie. What had happened?

Harry pulled Maggie by the arm over to Jonas's table. Jonas set down his glass of wine and glared at Harry. It was the first time Lydia saw an angry grimace from the odd but intriguing man.

"What do you think you're doing to Maggie?" Jonas asked, not quite in a nasty way but with an edge to the words. The deep, calming voice held a bit of a threat to it.

Lydia double-checked who was left in the back room of the restaurant. Eight other people were still celebrating, or rather, drinking, and Nate's parents were not among them. She assumed that Maggie's family was not here either, since no one had called her by name. This would be a good time for Lydia to get out. She could not think of anything good that would come out of this.

Then she realized that the other revelers were gathering around Jonas's table, around Harry and Maggie. Lydia changed her mind. This looked dangerous for Maggie and Jonas.

"You've been telling our players how they should behave," Harry said pointedly. "Maybe they've become better on the field because of it. But maybe they are also disrespectful because of it."

"You're the one dragging an eighteen year-old girl into a restaurant against her will," Jonas said, his calmness restored. "Care to explain that?"

"I was driving home and drove by the baseball field. I saw someone on it. This late at night it might be a prank of some kind. Some jealous fan from Hemtown might have been vandalizing the dugouts or something. When I pulled over and got out of my car, I realized there were two people on the field. I caught *her*," Maggie winced as Harry snarled the word, "and one of our players, in the act, let's say, out in right field."

What does he think he's doing? Lydia thought to herself. Maggie is just a girl. Now she gets caught and called out in front of a bunch of adults she does not know. Why would Harry be this cruel to her?

"Coach Deem keeps telling me it's fine that you keep having meetings with the players. He says you're teaching them more than baseball," Harry continued. "Is this one of the things you've been teaching them?"

Now it clicked in Lydia's mind. Harry did not care about Maggie one way or the other, and he was no prude. This incident on the baseball field was a chance for him to push Jonas away from the team. Mr. Antes had fired Jonas's cousin last week, and now he intended to push Jonas himself farther from the team.

Lydia's mind raced to think of a way to help the girl, but she did not want to call the police if it could be avoided. It was most likely Maggie would be fined for trespassing, and her embarrassment would only get worse.

There were a couple of bawdy jokes from the drunks at Maggie's expense. Lydia wanted to slap anyone who said those things, but when she looked up to see who spoke, she noticed even some women were laughing along to the rude quips. Lydia was mad with almost everyone in the room: Harry and his friends. She was also upset that Jonas did not stand up and punch Harry in the nose. She was angry with everyone except Maggie, the target of their ridicule.

"The team had its own rules and own ways of discipline before you came along," Harry continued. "It's no coincidence that this happened shortly after you started influencing the players."

"Speaking of discipline and players, shouldn't the boy involved be here too?" Jonas answered.

"He got away," Harry said.

"Look, I did it," Maggie said, speaking for the first time. "I told him, when they won Region D," Her voice trailed off before she found it again. "Look, I'm sorry. It was a stupid thing to do. Let me go. Please don't tell anyone else. I'll never, never." Any more words were lost in her sobs.

Lydia stood and walked over to the crowd. With a clearer view of everyone gathered around, she realized how bad the situation was. Maggie appeared ready to pass out from exhaustion and fear. The adults around her stopped joking and started to look furious, but not at Harry for dragging Maggie in to the restaurant. They were angry with Maggie herself. Goodness, what she did was foolish, but anyone should be able to understand that treating her this way was abusive.

Then she remembered how the people who had stayed late at the celebration, except for Jonas and herself, were drunk. They would not handle this rationally. Harry, who seemed sober enough, spoke with a softer voice. "Don't worry, Maggie. This is almost done. We only need to hear what Jonas says."

The other adults turned their dagger-like stares to Jonas. Lydia fumbled around in her purse for her phone. Maybe she should call the police, regardless of who would be embarrassed by what had happened. Harry was harassing Maggie, and with the inebriated crowd turning irate, the situation could get out of hand. But she noticed that Jonas remained silent. Would he do something?

"What do you think we should do with her?" Harry continued. "She is guilty. She admitted it. And not guilty only of not being able to control herself. This all happened on grounds that belong to the school district. In case you forgot, I pay the fees to let Central rent that field. I don't appreciate it being treated like this."

Jonas looked at him for a few seconds, then grabbed his napkin and unfolded it. "I admit, there's something to what you say." Jonas tore the paper into several pieces.

Uh, oh, he's getting nervous, Lydia thought. Maggie was in no better position than when she was forced here. Lydia finally found her phone but wondered if she should take matters into her own hands and try to pull Lydia out of Harry's grip.

Then she noticed that Jonas was measuring the pieces he was tearing. He was not panicking. He had a plan.

"Well?" Harry asked, sounding impatient. "I'll allow what you say to go this one time. We can leave her go if you approve of this sort of behavior. Or we can report her and ban her from any of our events."

Lydia suspected the real reason the boy was not here was that Harry did not want to suspend one of the players before the state tournament. She had no way to prove it now. Lydia hoped it wasn't Nate. At the same time, she knew it must have been. But her anger at her cousin for bailing out on Maggie could wait.

Jonas now was writing with a pen on the pieces of the torn napkin. "Here is what I say. Whichever one of you is without fault may report her to the police."

That's it? Lydia thought. She again considered trying to pull Maggie out of there on her own. But if she encountered any drunken rage from the people surrounding her, it could be dangerous for everyone.

Before anyone said or did anything, though, Jonas finished writing on the papers and pushed them over his table. To Lydia's eyes, they seemed to fall about randomly, and she could not read what was on them. But Harry's eyes opened wide. He was furious, that was obvious. He glared at Jonas, who smiled back. For the first time since he came into the restaurant, Harry let go of Maggie's arm and ran out.

The others were slower to react, but they appeared to be looking at the papers Jonas wrote. Slowly, looking more embarrassed than enraged, they started to disperse.

"Call for a ride," Lydia shouted out to them as they walked out.

As the last of the revelers left Emperor's, Jonas stood and turned to Maggie. He placed his hands gently on her shoulders.

"Who is left to report you?" Jonas asked.

Maggie looked around as if she was afraid that some of her accusers were hiding behind a table. The girl locked eyes with Lydia for a moment, but then Maggie smiled. She must have realized Lydia had not been among those who had crowded around her in anger.

"No one is still here," Maggie said. "No one who wanted to humiliate me."

"I will not say anything against you either," Jonas said. "Go, but from now on, wait to give yourself to your husband."

Maggie stepped back, smiling. Lydia could almost feel the relief radiating off the child. The girl turned to leave, but then turned back and hugged Jonas. "Thank you," she said. Tears rolled down her red cheeks.

As Jonas returned the hug, and then let Maggie go to leave, Lydia could not resist glancing at the napkin shreds scattered on the table by Jonas. Now she understood what pushed all the accusers away. Each paper had a word on it. "Glutton," "adulterer," "drunkard," and other accusing words.

"'Drunkard' could have described all of them," Lydia said out loud, then realized she had made a mistake. She looked up and saw Jonas looking at her with a smirk.

"But you don't remember who was shown which paper, do you?"

Lydia had not been watching closely enough to place who saw what. She shook her head.

"That is just as well," Jonas said. "You know all people do some wrong things. Seeing those words should not change your opinion of anyone here tonight. And don't think I did this tonight out of anything other than compassion for Maggie. I don't hate Harry or any of the people who were yelling at Maggie. I have compassion for them too."

Lydia mulled that over for a second and sat down at what had been Jonas's table. "I guess I can see that. What I don't understand is how you know what each of those people was guilty of. But since you helped Maggie out of what was a horrible situation, I won't grill you about that. Can Maggie get home? Mr. Antes probably drove her here."

Jonas started to make his way out of the restaurant. "You needn't worry. She lives one block from here. For now, it would be best for you to go home and rest. I will see you again at the state tournament." Jonas stopped before he left the room. "Oh, and Lucas will see you too."

Lydia smiled. It sounded as if this mysterious man was encouraging her romantic thoughts. "It's not so surprising you know about that. I think everyone at the game knows we're hot for each other."

"You were made to be attracted. Just pay attention to what's in front of you."

Jonas walked out after that odd statement. He puzzled Lydia, though she could not see any of the negatives that Harry and a few of the players' parents did. He seemed to be teaching Nate and the other players good things, almost like baseball advice and fatherly wisdom all wrapped into one. He may or may not have done something to fix Ted's leg, and now he pulled a vulnerable girl out of a dangerous situation without raising a fist.

But then he said odd things like, "Pay attention to what's in front of you." Jonas was standing in front of her when he said that. Was he flirting? He didn't say it in a flirty way. It sounded more like a warning.

She glanced down at the table. There was one paper in front of her seat. She idly picked it up but did not look at it yet. Her mind was now returning to her cousin.

It must have been him. Nate and Maggie had been getting close, even in public. Mr. Antes also said the incident happened in right field, where Nate always plays. He may or may not have talked her into getting together, but Nate must have come up with the foolish idea to be out there on the field. But for him to abandon the girl when they were caught? That was unforgivable.

She balled her hand into a fist, crushing the unread paper. All the joy she had felt after watching Nate and Central win Region D and all the comfort she experienced in celebration had dissolved. All that was left was a fury that someone in her own family could act that way.

Lydia stomped out the door and got to her car. She sat in the drivers' seat, but took a moment before starting the ignition. After catching her breath, her anger changed to disappointment. Nate had to know better. Maggie too, but Lydia was confident she was following along to Nate.

Thank goodness, she thought, that I've handled my life in the right way, and not the way Nate did.

She was about to drive away. Where to, she did not know. She was too upset to go back to her parents' house and go to sleep. She considered riding around town or past the farmland near Central. She needed to calm herself. But as she reached down to the transmission, she saw a little paper. It was the one that Jonas had written on when he said to pay attention to what was in front of her. She realized that it was the paper that Jonas was referring too. Lydia must have picked it up and dropped it back in the car.

She unfolded the paper. Her heart stopped. She told herself that it was a coincidence. No matter what Jonas knew about the baseball team or about people who lived here, he could not know what she had done.

But Lydia was lying to herself. Jonas knew her past, and he was calling her out with a word so familiar, yet one she never applied to herself.

"Thief."

Chapter 32

Pete parked next to the gas pump, half-paying attention to what he was doing. People looking at him only saw a young man filling his tank. Inside he was furious, fighting with his teammates in his mind.

He silently repeated everything he knew, thinking he must be missing something. That was the only way to explain why no one else was taking the situation seriously. He squeezed the pump handle more to vent his frustration than to refuel his car. Pete kept thinking to himself, "They were on our field. And then Nate ran away."

After the tank was filled, Pete almost slammed the nozzle back in place. Maggie was not a member of the team, and either had not run away or had been caught. Pete could not know if she had been coerced into doing something that foolish or if she had been willing from the start.

But Nate, he should know better. He should have a little respect for the field he's been playing on for years. More than that, he should stand up for his girl instead of running away. But even that was not what filled Pete with hot anger. Two days had passed, and his ire had not cooled.

No one wanted to do anything about it.

At least not to Nate. Maggie had already been publicly embarrassed. At least that was what Pete had heard second-hand. Neither his teammates nor his own parents had still been at the party when Mr. Antes dragged Maggie there to humiliate her. The story was that only a calm reaction from Jonas Davis kept the situation from escalating.

But as for Nate, Pete was angry and didn't want to get into the car right away. He'd probably take his ire out on the gas pedal and get pulled over for speeding. Pete hadn't paid for his gas yet, anyway. He stomped into the gas station, then walked down an aisle or two. Pete was not hungry or thirsty. He needed to move.

"You look like a man who needs someone to talk to," a voice said from behind him.

Pete turned. He did not see him come in, but Jonas was right behind him. "Oh, yeah. Hi. It wasn't the best practice today."

"It's not how well you or your team practiced that was the problem, was it?"

Pete looked up and down the aisle. No one was close enough to listen to them. "I've heard you were there when Mr. Antes forced Maggie into Emperor's. Is that true?"

"Yes, I was there."

"Well, it was Nate that was with her on the field. No one wants to do anything to him. Coach Deem said he can't do anything because it wasn't during a team event. Most of my teammates think Nate's only crime is that he got caught. They're almost happy for him that he got the girl and got away from Mr. Antes. Nate said even his parents aren't going to punish him. Some sort of 'boys will be boys' attitude."

"And what would you do?"

"The first thing I did, when I saw him today and we were getting ready for practice, was ask him if all this was true. He said it was, and seemed rather smug about it too. I told him he owed the team and Maggie an apology. He said he didn't owe anyone anything."

Pete reached to the shelf for a bottle of water and squeezed on the plastic hard enough he thought he would make it burst. Jonas must have noticed the rage.

"You are justified in your anger," Jonas said, "both for what Nate did to Maggie and to the team. Even if the other boys don't recognize it yet, you understand the situation better than any of your teammates. But if Nate were to apologize, and turn away from the wrongs he has done, you would have to forgive him."

"Nate hasn't done that," Pete said. "Not yet."

"He will. Nate needs correction. Not to give out punishment, but to let him dwell on his missteps. If Nate is going to become a new man, he needs to understand that there is something wrong with the old man. At the same time, he needs some grace so he will want to become that new man."

Pete thought about it. "I know how I would handle this if I were the coach."

Before Pete could tell Jonas what he was thinking, Jonas spoke again. "Then do it. Whatever you have in mind."

"But I can't. I'm not a coach. We don't even have official team captains. I have some influence on the other guys, but I can't give out corrections and punishments. I don't have that much power on the team."

"You do now," Jonas said. He grabbed Pete by the shoulders. "I give you the authority to decide what will be permitted for the team, and what will not be permitted for the team. If you say someone needs discipline, your coaches will carry out the discipline. If you say someone needs forgiveness, he will be forgiven."

For a moment, Pete felt an energy surge in him. His fingers and toes tingled, but then the sensation passed. Maybe it was an adrenaline rush.

Jonas took his hands off of Pete. "Speak to Coach Deem before the state tournament starts. He will do what you ask."

Pete decided. He would talk to Coach Deem privately before tomorrow's practice, the last workout before states. Nate would not be happy, but he would at least get a second chance.

Probably.

Pete wanted to ask Jonas how he was sure that Coach Deem would listen to him, but he had already disappeared.

Part IV

A Perfect Sacrifice

Chapter 33

The Meadville water tower slowly rose on the horizon, and Lucas knew his trip to Salem was about half-finished.

Once he had made his way through the city of Lavernon and its endless traffic lights, Lucas felt the rest of the trip was a pleasant drive. It was long, especially if he had to repeat the hour's jaunt back and forth five days in a row.

That was all up to the Central baseball team. The state tournament would be another double-elimination tourney, like the Region D tourney that Central just won. But the competition, presumably, would be tougher. Lucas did not know for sure as he had never seen any of the other teams in the tournament. He barely knew where half of them were located. He had found the records of the other seven teams, but without knowing the quality of baseball from the other regions, that did not tell him much.

But the focus of his writing would be what Central did, win or lose. If Central made it to the fifth and final day, at least it would make for a more exciting story. If Central added a state championship to its already impressive collection of trophies, it would be a story in itself. But, unlike Region D, here there was a special reward for being the runner-up. Both the first- and second-place teams would qualify for the Mid-Atlantic Regional in Lincoln, Virginia.

Anyway, he could not complain too much about the time it took to get to these events. The extra travel time that trips to Salem and then Lincoln would take would be a mere annoyance that would be relieved with his expense vouchers.

Lucas realized he was getting ahead of himself again. He needed to focus on today's opening round of the tournament, in which Central would play Great Lakes, a team close to Lake Erie itself. But there were other things to consider today, other than what happened on the field. He wondered if anything else would happen involving Jonas Davis. Lucas assumed the man would at least be at the state tournament, so he would keep an eye open. So far, all Lucas had pieced together was Jonas acted as a mentor or

counselor to the players. He happened to be present when Ted
made an impossibly fast recovery from a broken ankle.

If nothing else happened that Lucas could track down, he
would pass it off as an odd set of circumstances and nothing more.
He must have missed something when Ted was hurt that would
have explained the event more rationally. But if anything unusual
happened again around Jonas during this week in Salem, then he
would have to probe into what this man was all about.

That was not what he wanted to spend his time doing. He
wanted to observe how the pitchers approached each batter and
other subtleties of the game. He wanted to hear the crowd's
reaction when each run was scored. Summers were for baseball,
after all. But Lucas could not shake the feeling that something
important was going on with Jonas.

Lucas decided he was lying to himself. Not about the
potential importance of Jonas, but about what he wanted to be
doing. Lucas wanted to be watching the game, but with Lydia and
not sitting at the media table. Hopefully, he would sit with her
again for a game or two.

He was now driving through Womelsdorf, about to enter
Robesonia, on the western side of Berks County. That meant he
must have spent ten minutes without thinking of Lydia. He knew
she would be at this week's games because she had sent an e-mail
to him asking if he would be working at this tournament. After he
replied that he would, her last, one-word response was exactly
what he wanted to see.

"Perfect."

That one word told Lucas all he needed to see. Lydia was
not tolerating or mildly enjoying their conversations back at
Ammonville. She wanted more time with him. But Lydia also
seemed to understand that these meetings at ballgames was all he
could offer right now. When the season was over, he would ask her
out on a real date before she travelled back to Virginia. Now Lucas
was almost sure she would say yes. But that could not happen
while he covered her cousin's baseball team.

It was fantastic to fall for a woman who understood the
game and the limitations that his job gave him. Once this baseball

season was over and those limitations disappeared, they would discover if there were more ways in which they connected.

All that presumed that she was still nearby and not back at her home by the time this season ended. He did not want to rush into anything, nor pressure Lydia to rush into an intense relationship. But they might only have a limited time.

Lucas was finally at Salem, which was west of the city of Reading. He passed by the infamous Road to Nowhere and turned right off of the main road several blocks later. Two more turns through a development, and he was at Falcon Field.

For the next five days, this would be Lucas' second home. This would be the place where Central would prove whether it deserved a state championship or a trip to the Mid-Atlantic Regionals. He parked in the main lot, across the street from the field, stepped out of his car and looked over the outfield fence to the field itself. The Central team was in the middle of its pregame warmups for its tournament opener.

Yes, he thought, a good story will be told from here.

* * *

"Guys, head in, except for Pete and Nate. I need to talk to you."

While the other players came in from the pregame warmups and jogged to the dugout, Coach Deem pulled Pete and Nate in close. The coach spoke in a hushed but still commanding voice. "Nate, you heard me give the boys today's starting lineup. You're not out there today."

"I know, Coach," Nate said. "Why?"

"Pete made that decision. We talked about it yesterday. But Pete, if you're going to make these calls, you've got to look your teammate in the eye when you do it."

Nate turned to Pete, who looked uncomfortable but spoke, anyway. "Our team doesn't treat our own field with disrespect. We don't disrespect women. Today and tomorrow, you don't get on the field. Not as a starter or a pinch hitter. Not at all."

"What?" Nate shouted, and Coach Deem was worried that he would make a scene. But Pete continued.

"That means we have to win at least one game for you to ever get back on the field. We should win. But even then, you must apologize to the team for what you did. If you do, you're back in the starting lineup for the third day of this tournament."

Nate was staring at Pete. Coach Deem kept looking back and forth between the two. He was impressed with Pete's words. They carried more authority than he had expected, considering how nervous Pete appeared to be.

Almost like he was a new man, maybe. Wasn't that what Jonas had said?

Coach Deem was expecting more of a protest from Nate, but perhaps he felt that same authority from Pete. Nate only asked, "What about Maggie?"

"You should apologize to her too," Pete said. "But that's a private matter between you and her. If you apologize to us, I will take you at your word you also apologized to her. Now go into the dugout and take care of the scorebook. Give Coach Arim a break."

Shoulders slouched, Nate walked back to the dugout. Nick slapped Pete on the back. "Nice work. You did what I probably should've done. After that, pitching will be easy."

"For a moment, I thought about being harsher with him," Pete said. "I considered just throwing him off the team and being done with it."

"That might have been too much," Coach Deem said. "What made you change your mind?"

"No matter what mistakes he's made, Nate still needs to have hope."

* * *

As the game started, Lydia could not decide if it was a coincidence that Nate was not starting, or if someone realized he needed correction.

For a time, she had considered not even coming to the state tournament or at least skipping the first day or two. She wanted her anger at her cousin to cool before watching him again. But that would mean fewer chances to talk to Lucas, who was now in the press box. It was worth the drive to Salem even if there was no game to watch.

Besides, she still enjoyed the sport and wanted Central to win. But if Nate were playing, it might have spoiled the experience for her. As it was, Lydia was sitting on a lawn chair well down the left-field line, away from most of the fans of either Central or Great Lakes. It was not the best view of the game, but she did not want to be near Nate's parents. She had lost a great deal of respect for them when they gave out no discipline.

But from any seat, Lydia could tell that the game was going well for Central. James and John had run-scoring hits in the first inning. After that, it seemed that the Great Lakes batters were having a hard time getting good swings against Pete's pitches.

The score was already 2-0 in the second inning, and Central had two runners on base when Lydia heard the voice behind her. "Hello again."

She turned, already knowing it would be Jonas. "Hello," she answered. "Did you give the boys a pep talk before the game?"

Jonas shook his head. "I will talk with a few of them after the game, but I didn't have any words for them before they started." He gestured to the scoreboard. "That two-run difference is as close as this game will ever be, anyway."

As he uttered the words, Matt hit a ball down the right-field line, scoring two more runs. "I wasn't sure if Central had it in them to do well here," Lydia admitted after the cheering stopped. "But maybe I had too little faith after Nate's stupidity. Wait, did you know it was Nate with Maggie?"

Jonas nodded and sat on the grass next to her. "Maggie and her friends, Jo and Martha, joined us for some of my talks, just like you did once. Nate and Maggie were getting a little touchier with each other. I wouldn't have to see into their hearts to know Nate was with her."

"Can you actually see into people's hearts? Into theirs? Into mine?" Lydia asked. She almost could not believe that she even asked those questions, but it somehow seemed possible.

Jonas smiled. "Do you believe I can?"

Lydia hesitated. Jonas was a strange man, but a good man as far she could tell. "It would explain a lot, even if it doesn't make any sense. But no one can know what someone else's deepest secrets are. Some of us are just better at guessing."

There was the slightest shift in Jonas's eyes. His stare penetrated her, not the way a boyfriend's gaze would, nor the way an accusing authority figure's glare would. Instead, she almost felt his presence within her. "Within your heart is judgment. You are becoming consumed with a need to see Nate punished."

Lydia's heart started racing. She had argued with Nate two days ago, but she had not expressed her feelings about the matter to anyone else. She did not even discuss the issue with her own parents, whom she was staying with during her time off. "That's not the only thing in my heart."

"No, you have other desires there. Some good, but others that will cause you harm."

Jonas was treading close to inappropriate territory, but Lydia did not back away yet. "What in my own heart could hurt me?"

"It is inside the heart we decide to do the wrong thing, often the thing we have told ourselves over and over is fine."

"Look, I came here for only two reasons, to watch this game, and to give Maggie words of encouragement if she were here."

"Oh, she's here," Jonas said. "Look down past right field. See the last three people, sitting on their own on the opposite hill?"

Lydia glanced at the scoreboard first and saw the score was 5-0. Then she looked to the other side of the field. There were three girls out there. It was hard to tell at first since they were in the shade, but after a moment she could see it was Maggie with her two friends.

"Maggie is getting the support she needs from other people," Jonas said. "It is not your words she needs to hear. And, as far as Nate's correction, Pete has taken care of that."

Lydia looked at the field again, where Pete was coming back onto the mound to pitch in the third inning. "So he's the one who came to his senses."

"Yes, Pete decided to keep Nate from playing two games. But your cousin will get several more chances to play. Central's season is far from done."

Lydia mulled it over. A two-game suspension. It was not just any two games, but two games in Central's first-ever state tournament. That was probably about right as far as the team was concerned. She still thought the family should have done something too, though. This next generation growing up was getting reckless. Mature people like herself would soon become a rarity.

"Why do you belittle your cousin for putting a splinter in his hand, when you have placed an entire bat through your own?"

Lydia was getting nervous now. She was not sure what that meant, but it was not a compliment. "What are you saying about me?" she asked, putting an edge in her voice she had held back until then.

Jonas stood. "Nate needed correcting, and discipline would serve him well. But you only wanted for him to be punished. Pete suspended him to give him a chance to make amends, not to punish. You, however, wanted to punish Nate for his wrongdoing, while trying to forget about your own."

Jonas had somehow seen inside her heart. He found out what had happened back in Virginia. "You know."

"Everyone seems so surprised by that," Jonas said with a smile. "It's not just about the money you took, though you need to correct that. You need to understand why you have done what you've done."

"Wouldn't it be enough to give the money back and say I'm sorry?"

"Are you sorry?"

Lydia hesitated. She had been feeling conflicting emotions ever since Jonas's note brought back memories of her past. But, it was at least a little true that she regretted her mistakes.

"Yes, I am," Lydia said. "Though, to be honest, I'm not sorry enough."

"That is part of the reason you must understand why you took the money. Some people steal out of greed, but not you. The same mistake you made then can happen again and ruin what you are building with Lucas."

"You going to preach at me that dating him would be wrong?"

"Not at all. Romantic love is one of the things that most people were made for. But think about what I've told you, or else you will lose him."

Jonas gave the quickest smile and walked away. On the field, Pete struck out another batter to end the inning, but Lydia barely noticed. Jonas had been right about everything. It was as if he had seen more deeply into her heart than she did.

What was the connection between money she had taken years ago and her relationship with Lucas now? Was she supposed to feel worse about what she had done? Should she keep her silence from now on about what Nate and Maggie had done?

For several minutes that seemed to be several hours, all these questions and more echoed in Lydia's mind. But for now, she could not find the right answers. Or, at least, not answers she wanted to accept.

After a time, she stopped dwelling on those issues. She tried to refocus on the game and enjoy what appeared to be another Central victory. But then she realized that she also had no answers for the most puzzling question of all.

How did Jonas know the truth about everyone?

Chapter 34

After Coach Deem finished his post-victory speech, the players started to leave Falcon Field. But Pete decided to stay behind. He wanted to watch the next game between Puraton and Royersville. He had never seen Puraton in person, but knew their reputation as a consistent winner at the state level. Pete was curious to find out what Central might be up against later in the tournament. He recalled talking with Andy, James, and John when the season had just started, and mentioning Puraton as the team they should imitate. Or at least, they wanted to imitate their success.

But for now, Puraton was only worth some interest, not his undivided attention. The next day, Central would not be playing either of these teams, but instead the winner of Uptown and Beach Side. That game would not take place until late in the afternoon. And while Nate took being benched a little better than Pete had expected, it still bothered Pete it had to happen at all. Staying at the park for a while might help him process the next step they would have to take: transitioning to having Nate playing again. There would have to be a distinct apology, but once that was done, no one should speak of the incident again.

John and James stayed behind to watch the next baseball game too. Pete's parents drove home with Andrew and said Pete could come back with the brothers as long as he was back by dinner time.

Maybe they would watch more baseball, or perhaps they would go a little farther east to see if there was anything fun to do in Reading.

They had not made up their minds about any of this. But all three boys decided it was getting hot in the third-base bleachers, especially since they were still in their full uniforms. They either had to go to the air-conditioned relief of a shopping mall or up the hill behind them where the trees would give them shade.

"Glad it didn't get this hot until I was finished pitching," Pete said. "Want to leave now or move seats?"

"I'd rather stay a little," John answered. "We might run into one of these pitchers in the next few days. I'd like to see what they throw for a few innings."

"Me, too," James said. "But not for too long. There's no reason to get tired in the sun when we will play again tomorrow."

All of them grabbed their equipment bags and walked up the hill. The game between Puraton and Royersville was about to start, so they all hesitated for the National Anthem.

"I'm surprised neither of our coaches stayed," Pete said to the others. "You'd think they'd do a little scouting of the other teams here."

"They only did a little scouting during Region D also, and that went well," James said.

Pete decided that was true enough and turned to go up the hill. While looking for an empty spot, he noticed there were two men also in baseball uniforms up near the top. But they were not in Armed Services baseball uniforms. One was wearing the jersey of the Philadelphia professional team, and the other was wearing a Pittsburgh jersey.

They had their backs to him and seemed to be in a conversation. They were probably fans of those teams, but they each had the build of a professional athlete.

John walked by Pete, but must have noticed the same thing. He strode closer to the two men and then waved Pete and James over to the gathering. With a closer look, Pete realized these were indeed two professional players. Their names escaped him for the moment. He should have noted the back of the jerseys. But it was the Philadelphia third baseman and Pittsburgh right fielder.

And they were not alone. Jonas was there, dressed for the midday heat. His shirt was white as usual, but his shorts and sandals were white as well. The three men were having an intense, though pleasant, conversation.

"I am so happy to see you doing this here, at last," the Philadelphia player said. "These young men need instruction, in so many ways. So few know how to slide into a base right, nor how to treat a woman right. No one can guide them on the field or off of it better than you."

It took Pete a moment to realize it was Jonas who was being addressed. He knew these professionals? And they respected him?

The next words, spoken by the Pittsburgh player, confirmed those thoughts. "And when they learn from you, they also learn from your father. Am I happy to know you both now, but how I wish you could have done this for me when I was younger."

Jonas clasped a hand on each man's shoulder. "We will all share this joy, at many other baseball fields than this one, and many other places than Berks County. I promise you. But what has happened so far is exactly what should be happening. You have done your parts well and are continuing to do your parts well now." Both professionals were beaming. They did not look like they were talking to a random fan or even a respected baseball figure. They were smiling like they were had been complemented by a legendary Hall of Famer of days long gone.

Jonas spoke once more. "In due time, all but one player on this Central team will join you."

Pete was amazed. Did Jonas just say nearly all the players would become professionals? That was high praise. Even as part of Pete's mind told him this was unrealistic, he found himself getting caught up in the moment. Thoughts were racing through his brain, but Pete had to say something to these esteemed players.

"Could we talk with all of you?" Pete said. "If you are staying for all today's games, we could stay up here with you. Teach us what you know, anything that might help us in the state tournament, or when I go back to college, or anything to help us in our careers." His words trailed into silence. He knew he was rambling and even being rude by butting into the conversation, but he had no idea what to say. However, he could see both John and James, as awed as he was, nodding to his suggestion.

The two professionals turned to Pete, both still smiling, but saying nothing. But then Pete heard a voice, one he had only heard once before today. It was the voice of the old man, the man Jonas said was his father. "Listen to my son."

Pete thought the voice had come from right behind him as it was so intense. He spun around, expecting the old man to be face-to-face to him for the first time. But no one was there. Confused, he turned back around to Jonas, but now the Philadelphia and Pittsburgh players were both gone.

He looked back down the hillside. There was no sign of the professional players. "What? What just happened?"

"Oh, they have a game against each other tonight in Philadelphia," Jonas said. He was so casual it seemed he was used to public figures appearing and disappearing.

"But, why were they here with you in the first place?" James asked. "Do you know them?"

"Yes, I know those players. I gave them what they needed to do their work though I did it differently than I have for you."

"Did you mean what you said to them?" John asked. "That all of us will play professional baseball?"

"I thought you said all but one," Pete said.

"Don't tell your teammates about that yet," Jonas said. "And do not misunderstand it. I did not say you will be in Philadelphia or Pittsburgh or any city that has a professional baseball team. I'm not even promising you'll play for a minor-league team. But yes, eleven of the twelve of you will be with them, my father, and me in due time."

It sounded like Jonas was going back on his word a bit, but Pete could not be sure. The man had a knack for being inspirational and confusing all at once.

"Now," Jonas continued. "Let's go back down there to the front row. Let's watch a few innings of this game together. You might learn some things about a future opponent. Royersville's side of the field is emptier."

"Mr. Davis, we came up here to get in the shade," James said. "It's too hot."

"Yes, it's good to be up on the hill where it's cool and comfortable for now," Jonas said. "But you have work to do, don't you? You stayed to scout these teams, so now we have to go down the hill where we can see clearly what pitches are being thrown."

Jonas walked down the hill. Pete, John, and James all looked at each other for a moment, trying to process the last five minutes. Pete filed it in his mind along with all the other odd things that had been happening and followed. He heard the footsteps of the other two players behind him.

Jonas sat in the front row on the third-base side, and Pete sat next to him. The game was already in the second inning, and Puraton was winning 1-0. There looked to be about two hundred Puraton fans on this side of the field while there were only twenty-five Royersville fans on the first-base side. Since Puraton was only about twenty minutes away from Falcon Field, Pete was not surprised.

But Jonas was right. Of course, he was right. From here, they could see if a pitcher was throwing fastballs, curveballs or sliders. If they had stayed on the hill, they might have been in the shade, but they would not have learned nearly as much.

There was one detail about the encounter on the hill Pete realized no one had addressed. "Jonas, is your father here?"

"Yes. My father is up in the press box now."

"But, I thought you told us we would not see him again this season. You said that when we first met you, with Coach Baptiste."

"And have you seen him?"

"Well, no," Pete looked up at the press box, two stories above the field and behind home plate. He could not make out any images behind the window. "But I heard him. I heard him say the same thing he said last time, to listen to you."

"I'm going to let you in on something," Jonas said. Leaning in towards Pete, he whispered, "That's good advice."

Pete chuckled. "I've figured out that much, even if I don't understand everything you've taught. I just wondered why your father is here if he isn't following Central anymore."

"Well, it's not Central playing right now, is it?" Jonas pointed out. "My father has other teams and other players with whom he is concerned."

Jonas said no more and seemed to watch the game now. Pete wondered to himself what Jonas's father was doing with the other teams. Then he cast the thought aside and decided to enjoy another inning or two before driving back home.

Chapter 35

James took his lead off second base. It felt like he had been standing out in the field for thirty minutes. He led off the second inning with a double, then remained at second base while one teammate walked and another struck out. Now, Ted was batting and had worked a full count against the Uptown pitcher.

The late-afternoon sun was still warm and making James's eye black smear. He wiped his brow and took a glance back at the outfielders. He could tell where a potential hit would allow him to score, and where a hit might force him to hold up at third.

But he was not going anywhere on the next pitch. Ted fouled it straight back.

This is one of those innings people who don't like baseball always complain about, James thought to himself. We need something to happen here.

James again took his lead off second base, and this time had somewhere to go. Ted hit a hard grounder out of the second baseman's reach. James did not watch the ball any farther than that as he ran toward third base and looked up at Coach Arim. As James had guessed from when he checked the outfielders' positions, the coach was waving him home. James made his turn around the bag and headed toward the plate. Jules, the on-deck batter, was there to signal him that he could score standing.

There was no throw to the plate, which James stepped on at a full run anyway just to be sure. He turned and checked what else had happened on the field. The Uptown outfielder threw the ball into third base, keeping the other runners from advancing any extra bases.

James gave a high-five to Jules. "Bring in another," he said, then walked over to the dugout to receive more high-fives from his teammates.

That run made the score 1-0, and the game was only in the second inning. To James, it felt like Central was winning by a dozen runs. The whole team had been playing so well for so long it was hard to believe anyone could beat them, especially once they already had a lead. James was convinced Central was well on its way to its second win at the state tournament.

James sat down on the bench and watched the action on the baseball diamond. The count was one ball and one strike on Jules, with the runners still at first and second with one out. Then he saw Coach Arim make the signal for a sacrifice bunt.

Odd, James thought. If Jules sacrificed here, the runners would move up, but there would be two outs. However, James noted the Uptown infield did not look ready to field a bunt, and the same strategy had worked in the Region D final.

He wondered if Jules would actually try the bunt. But as the pitcher started his delivery, Jules squared up a bunt and pushed the ball towards third base.

That usually would be the smart thing to do on a bunt with a runner on second base. That made it difficult for the defense to throw a runner out at third, because no fielder was left to cover the base. But Uptown's third baseman was surprisingly quick and fielded the ball with his bare hand. Instead of throwing to first, he whipped a throw to second. The play surprised everyone, but the Uptown second baseman was covering the bag. He caught the ball for the force-out on Ted on his slide. The second baseman then threw to first base, and the umpire called Jules out on a close play.

Some Central fans jeered the umpire, yelling that Jules was safe. James could not tell for sure, but he knew it did not matter.

There was no way Central would lose. Not today, and probably not in this tournament at all.

* * *

"The game is still played well, but it was better about thirty years ago," Lucas said as he marked the last out of the sixth inning in his scorebook. It was a comment he had made several times before, but this time it was not to another sportswriter. It was to Lydia.

"Why's that?" Lydia asked, and her eyes made her seem to be genuinely interested in Lucas' opinion.

"I think each generation gets more interested in the big, showy play. Basics and fundamentals are set aside."

Lydia nodded. "Kind of sounds like society as a whole."

"In a way," Lucas answered, but as he spoke his left hand accidentally rubbed against her right arm. No, he corrected himself. He may have done it unconsciously, but not by accident.

It was getting difficult for Lucas to stay away from Lydia. He opted not to sit in the press box after the second inning of Central's game against Uptown. He left Marcus and a few other writers up there so he could look for Lydia.

Lucas knew he should wait until after the game to talk, at least for this long. He understood he should not be sitting on the grass on the hillside with Lydia. He knew he should not be with a woman who was related to an athlete he was covering.

Lucas could not stop himself. The pull towards her was about more than Lydia's beauty or Lucas' loneliness. He enjoyed talking with her. They had already been talking about concerts, summer memories, and trips they had taken to nearby Reading when they were children. That she also liked to talk about baseball only made her more irresistible, though mentioning other sports bored her.

He touched Lydia's arm again, ever so gently as a caress. Not inappropriately, not considering the tension he was sure they were both feeling. It was a conscious decision this time, though.

Lydia smiled. She leaned into him, her hair falling onto his shoulder.

Lucas did not care anymore if this got him in trouble with his employer. At least, he was not as worried about that as he had been a week ago. Being with Lydia felt too good. Better yet, it seemed that it felt good to her. This was beyond making him happy. He wanted Lydia to be happy too, and he was sure that was exactly what he was doing.

Until, as she was leaning back, Lydia's purple purse tipped over and spilled its contents onto Lucas' legs.

Lydia brought her hands to her mouth, half-embarrassed and half-laughing. "I'm so sorry, I'll get it."

Lucas helped her collect the items that had fallen, but kept an eye on the field too. Central was three outs away from a second win in the state tournament.

Lydia apologized again, quietly. "Sorry. We had a nice unspoken moment there."

"I think there will be more," Lucas said.

Lydia's eyes narrowed in on him. Her smile this time was more than happy. It was mischievous. She mouthed the words, "Many more." Then, she looked down, and Lucas thought he heard, "maybe."

Lucas was having trouble returning his eyes to the game, but for a moment the writer in him won, and he noted a groundout.

Then he noticed Lydia had turned away and had changed to a pensive look. Afraid he had offended her by looking back to the game, he explained, "I just had to write that last play."

"No, it's not that," Lydia said. "It was something he said to me. Something that's been in the back of my mind since yesterday."

"Who?"

"Jonas," Lydia answered. "I'll tell you about it sometime. But I need to process it myself first."

Lucas nodded. If he wanted Lydia to trust him in a long-term relationship, he needed to show her he knew when not to press.

"Oh, I didn't even realize he was over there," Lydia said. Lucas followed her gaze further up the hill. Jonas was there with one of the teen-age girls who always watched the Central games.

"That's her," Lydia continued. "That's the girl who was with Nate. Maggie."

"The same girl you told me about, being harassed at the party?"

Lydia nodded. "Same girl. I wonder what they're talking about. It looks like she's upset."

The home-plate umpire called a third strike. Lucas wrote a backward "K" in his scorebook and looked back to Jonas and Maggie. Maggie was crying and hugging Jonas.

"I don't think she's upset," Lucas said. "She's showing gratitude."

Lucas remembered the notes he had taken about Jonas Davis. It was still a smattering of almost random facts and guesses, more of the latter. It was time to find out more about this man.

"I've put it off," he said. "I need to speak to him in person. That's if he'll talk. I still don't understand what happened with the injured player at the Region D tournament. For that alone, I want to speak to Jonas. But that he has such an influence over people, or at least seems to."

"He does," Lydia interrupted. "I see it in Nate, and in the other players. They seem to revere the man. I'm not sure they know much about him, though. They only say his teaching is reaching them in ways others can't."

"But is he teaching them about baseball, or teaching them about life? Or is he someone who shouldn't be trusted? All these things are being whispered by fans when I'm walking around the park before and after games."

There was the crack of the bat from the field. The Uptown batter hit a high fly ball to left field, where Sam needed only to take two steps and make the catch for the final out. Lydia stood up to applaud the 9-3 victory for Central. After a moment, she turned back to Lucas. "Now Nate's two-game suspension is done. If Pete and Coach Deem let him, he will play again tomorrow."

"I'm glad everything worked out that way for him," Lucas said, getting up himself now. "He did something stupid and needed correction. But I'd hate to see any kid's season end that way."

Lucas looked back toward the hill. Jonas was walking down, Maggie no longer with him. "Lydia, I have to speak with Jonas for a moment, to see if I can set up another time to interview him. Then I have to talk to Coach Deem. So, may I watch with you again tomorrow?"

Lydia grabbed his hand, and it felt to Lucas as if hers melted into his own. "We are beyond having to ask. Good night." She held her gaze on him for one second that said everything and nothing all at once. Then she let go of his hand and walked away towards a group of Central fans farther up the left-field line.

Lucas forced himself to focus on the task at hand. Coach Deem would talk to the team for a few minutes after the game, so now was a chance to grab Jonas. He could start putting the puzzle pieces together about what was going on with this stranger.

But Jonas was already walking towards him. Not taking the chance, though, Lucas headed in his direction. "Mr. Davis, may I have a word with you?"

"Of course. And, Lucas, please call me Jonas."

"Jonas, then. Um, I'm sure you're aware of how your close relationship with the players on the team has been controversial."

"Yes. All people who try to do something good will have someone speak poorly of them."

"Well, would you be able to sit down with me for an interview? I can't promise there will be a story in print about this, but if there is, I need to have your point of view."

"Actually, I need to talk with you. What you write will be read by many. There are many ways my teaching will be spread, and many through whom it will be spread. You are one of them."

That was a little too enthusiastic for Lucas, but he had asked for it. "I will write my story on Central's game up in the press box, during the night game. Will you still be here?"

"I will wait for you." Jonas smiled. "You know, I will even have words of wisdom for you."

For a moment, Lucas hoped it would involve turning journalism into a millionaire's profession. He pushed the crazy thought out of his mind. "I will see you then."

Lucas was about to go down to the field and get to the Central huddle to make his interviews. But Jonas stopped him.

"I should tell you one thing first. The name of my father."

Jonas spoke the name. Lucas' ears heard, but it took a few seconds for his mind to process it. "He has a son as young as you?"

"Everybody asks me that. Yes. I am his one and only son."

Jonas nodded, then walked to the field. If Jonas was telling the truth about his father, it might not explain everything, but some recent events might make sense.

Chapter 36

After years of hearing warnings from adults about how he was not invincible, James almost felt like he now had evidence he was unstoppable.

Well, not James alone, but he was part of an invincible baseball team. Gathering his equipment together and walking out of the dugout, he tried to process what the team had done already. Not only was Central the Region D champion, but now they had beaten two other regional winners.

Coach Deem was calling the team together for a meeting on the hillside on the third-base side. It was close to, but not quite as high, as the odd appearance of the professional players from yesterday. James sat down with his brother John on one side and Jules on the other.

"Boys, you're making an old man proud," Coach Deem said. "When this year started, I believed we should win the county and had a realistic chance of winning the region. But I never gave much thought about winning here. You've surpassed everyone's expectations, except, perhaps, your own."

"I hear the national tournament is a fun time, coach," Tom said. "Why don't we all put that on our calendars now?"

"Don't get ahead of yourselves now," Coach Deem said over a few players' chuckles. "But now we can start looking at the national regionals. If we win tomorrow, we will clinch a spot in the Mid-Atlantic Regional. We could make it even if we lose tomorrow, but let's make it easy on ourselves. John, you'll be pitching tomorrow. Stick around for a few innings of this game and get a look at the hitters on both sides."

"Will do, coach," John said.

James looked back to the field. Red Eagle and Puraton were warming up for the other winners'-bracket game. His brother would pitch against one of them. A week ago, James would not have given John much of a chance against teams with such historic success. Maybe Pete could handle them, but he was still resting from pitching the opener. Pete would not throw again until the last day of the tourney.

But with the way the team was playing right now, Central had a chance against anyone. Central might even be the favorite against anyone.

"Not much more to tell you guys," Coach Deem said. "Get here two hours before tomorrow's start time. We will be the last game of the day." The coach looked over the heads of his players, "is it ready?"

"We have a problem, coach," an adult called back.

James looked around the hill. All the players' parents and many of their friends had stuck around and were gathered outside the team's meeting.

"I think we all got so excited about the game, we forgot to bring the food along," Tom's mother said.

"Are you serious?" Coach Deem asked. "Well, hopefully, we'll be here a few more days. We can do it after a different game."

"Do what?" James asked.

"Guys, we were planning to have a surprise picnic here after today's game. But it looks like the food is all back home."

"Wait a minute," a voice called out. A familiar voice. "I might be able to scrounge up something." James and others turned to Jonas. "Give me a moment and a little help, then we can eat."

"It's all right," James said. "We can just grab something on the way home."

"No, no, we will feed everyone here," Jonas said. He looked at each of the players. "Andy, would you help me?"

Andy shrugged his shoulders and got up, then walked away with Jonas towards one family that had come to the game. James thought he recognized them, but he was not sure. They weren't relatives of any player, but they might be fans from Central.

James turned away, unsure what Jonas was doing this time. The other players walked back to families, buddies, and girlfriends. Except for Jules, who was steaming right next to James.

"What's the matter?" James asked, hoping the flaring red on Jules' face was from the summer warmth.

"Perfect sacrifices," Jules snarled. "I couldn't have put that ball down any better."

It took James a moment to remember, but then he recalled the play. It was the second inning, with runners on first and second, one out. Jules put a bunt down to move the runners up, but Uptown's third baseman fielded it to get both a runner and Jules out for a double play.

"Oh, don't worry about that," James said, patting Jules on the back. "You did exactly what you were supposed to do. Sometimes the other team makes a great play, too."

"But if that's what's going to happen, I should swing away whenever I bat, no matter who's on base."

"Calm down," James said. "We won. That bunt set up other guys getting key hits. Did you see the third baseman was playing in when we hit two RBI singles by him later in the game? If you hadn't bunted early, he would have been playing farther back."

"What good did that do for me?" Jules interrupted and stomped away.

James stared for a moment, then tried to forget the argument. But Jules' attitude was disturbing. It might be a cliché, but if Central was going to continue this run through the playoffs, everyone would have to put the team first. The frustration might have been understandable if the failed bunt had cost Central the game, but they had won. What difference did it make?

Now James noticed Martha was walking back in his direction. Jules was forgotten. There were people around, but no one was close enough to eavesdrop. It was time to ask her out.

"Hey, Martha," he started. She turned to him and smiled. "When the baseball season is over, I was wondering if you would like to go out for dinner sometime? Just the two of us?"

James impressed himself. He had been afraid he would stumble over the words. But then he saw Martha's smile fade.

"Or just out for a cup of coffee?" James added.

Martha shook her head. "I knew this was coming," she said. She came up close to James, but only to whisper to him. "I knew you were looking at me back at Emperor's. Look, I like you.

I like all the guys on our team. But there's a reason I haven't been dating any of you."

"Why?" James whispered back.

"You're all too vain. You're great at playing baseball, but you think you're better than what you are. I know girls who like the guys who always talk themselves up. But it turns me off."

James did not know what to say. He took a two steps back.

"I meant it when I said I like you. There are many good things about you. If my friend is puffed up with pride, I can deal with that. I will still see all the positives in you. But I'm not going to start a relationship with someone that vain."

James was flustered. They stared at each other for a moment in the most awkward silence James could remember. He knew there was a chance Martha would turn him down. But calling him vain and saying he was too proud? He was a great baseball player, and he was playing on the best baseball team. Why shouldn't he be proud? And he could have been a great boyfriend to her.

"Try this," John said slapping a sandwich in James's hand. He had become so worked up, he did not see his brother walking toward him. James hoped John had not heard anything he and Martha had said.

"What is it?" James asked, not even looking at what John had given him.

"What do mean, 'what is it'? It's a sandwich, you goof," John said.

James took a bite of it. The fish was fried and spicy. The bread tasted like it came fresh out of a bakery.

"That is good," James said. "But I don't remember the concession stand having these."

"They don't," Martha said.

"Did Mom bring them?"

"No," John answered. "She hasn't brought any food since we embarrassed her at the Lavernon doubleheader. But now everyone around here has them. I'm not sure where all this food came from. This is my second," John took another bite and continued. "I wonder who brought them."

"What do you mean, 'I wonder who brought them'?" James chewed and walked up and down the third-base line, looking for Jonas. At first, he did not find Jonas but saw all his teammates, their families, and fans eating the same kind of fish sandwich John had given to him. Then he noticed they were even being given to the Red Eagle fans, who were on the third-base side for the upcoming game.

Finally, James spotted Jonas, who was sitting almost all the way down the left-field line with Andy and the family James noticed earlier. He ran over to them.

"No one has said anything yet," James said. "But I'm guessing we have you to thank for all this."

"You should thank this boy," Jonas said, gesturing to a child who looked to be about eight years old. Only then did James notice the family, including the boy, seemed to be pale with shock. "He offered to share his sandwich with someone who didn't have any food. You could say that's what he's doing right now."

"Jonas is skipping part of the story," Andy said. "He took the sandwich, then put it back in their cold case here."

"After that, he kept pulling out sandwich after sandwich," said a man, who James assumed was the father of the family. "Over and over and over."

James looked back around over all the people eating on this side of the field. There were hundreds, and all of them seemed to have a sandwich if they didn't have two.

"There is no way there were that many sandwiches in there," James said.

"And there's no way Ted is walking after his injury in Ammonville," Andy answered.

They turned to Jonas, only to discover he had walked away.

"We packed four sandwiches," the mother of the family said. "Just four. We had eaten three. There was only one left. I don't understand what just happened."

"I think we're getting used to not understanding what's happening," Andy said.

James felt somewhere between amazed and frightened. What sort of person was Jonas Davis? So much of what he did, or seemed to do, made no sense. But he was doing no harm, so was there anything to be afraid of?

Pete came over, trying to hold several fish sandwiches at once. "We seem to have leftovers," he said, putting the sandwiches in the cold case. "I thought we should give them back to you."

The family looked at James, Andy and Pete, still taking in the scene.

"I'm not sure I'll be bringing my kid back for tomorrow's game if this odd man is going to be here again," the father said.

"But why?" the boy answered. "He fed everyone and didn't ask for anything in return. And we even go home with more sandwiches than what we brought."

James smiled. The young child was right. What caused people to fear Jonas was not that he was dangerous. If anything, he seemed to be the opposite. But it was difficult to understand what he did, and that was enough to be scary.

"Well, we thank you for the food," James said. "And hope you come back tomorrow. I promise it will be a memorable game."

* * *

From the field, after he had interviewed Coach Deem, Lucas observed what Jonas was doing. He saw the people crowding around him as he pulled item after item out of a cooler. At first, it seemed like a magic trick, but soon it appeared to be utterly impossible. The cooler could not have contained the amount of food Jonas provided.

Next to him, Marcus watched the whole event unfold. "Is this the person we've heard whispers about?"

Lucas remembered the words Jonas spoke to him only minutes ago. Something about there being many through whom his teachings would be spread.

"Marcus," Lucas said. "If you can, you may want to write your story from here at the field and wait afterward. We should both be able to talk to him.

Chapter 37

Jo and Martha had wandered off after they had realized Jonas was somehow providing food for everyone at Falcon Field. For all Maggie knew, he was making food for everyone in Berks County. But she walked to the parking lot. She did not need to see this new surprise to understand Jonas was a wonder-worker. A wonder had already been worked in her.

The words Jonas had spoken to her at the end of the game put Maggie at such ease. They meant even more than when he had put an end to her embarrassment at the restaurant celebration. Then, she was still angry at herself, a wave of anger that continued until today.

She had driven to yesterday's state tournament opener on her own, processing mixed emotions about going at all. She hoped there was a place where she could watch the game alone and still feel like a part of the team's success, even as a fan. But it was impossible to stay on her own. It was possible to sit away from the other fans since there was enough space around a baseball field to get away. But her friends would not let her sulk alone.

Martha and Jo had found her and gave her words of encouragement throughout yesterday's game. What they said was like what her mother had told her when she found out about Maggie's recklessness. There are a lot of men out there who don't understand how to treat a woman. Don't let them take advantage of you, but when it happens, you can't blame yourself.

Maggie saw the truth in that. But what neither her mother nor her friends understood was she was equally guilty about everything. Nate may have chosen a foolish place, but they did everything by mutual consent. She had intended for it to happen.

She had come to the game with Martha and Jo today, but sought Jonas in the later innings. There was a lot she needed to work through. Even though it meant opening herself to a man instead of a woman, Maggie could not imagine a better person to turn to than Jonas. It was the right decision.

Wait. Maggie had come with her friends, in Martha's car.
Maggie looked around the parking lot and found it unattended. She
could not leave until they came back from Jonas's impromptu fish
fry going on back at the field. Maggie considered going back when
she heard a voice.

"Maggie, you know we need to talk."

She turned and saw Nate, shoulders slumped. Maggie saw
no one else she knew, just a handful of fans making their way to or
away from the field. Maggie took a step up to Nate and whispered.
"I know you were suspended, but you should be happy that you
won."

"I am," Nate said. "And I'll be playing again tomorrow. I
apologized to the team before today's game, and Pete said after
sitting out two games, that was enough to let me back in the
starting lineup. Coach Deem agreed."

"I'm glad. I had a lot of anger towards you at first. But I'm
past that now. I didn't want you suspended at all."

"But I deserved it. My parents thought I shouldn't have
been suspended, but I deserved more than what I got. It isn't the
team that needs my apology the most. It's you. I'm sorry I did this
to you."

"You didn't do it to me. We did this together. It was a
mistake. Not just being where we could be caught, but doing it at
all. I never should have even mentioned it to you. But it was our
mistake. We both chose it. I chose the time, and you agreed. You
chose the place, and I agreed. But we didn't coerce each other.
Maybe you need to apologize, but only for the same things I have
to apologize for."

"But I ran away. I never should have run."

Maggie shook her head and looked down at the pavement.
"No, you shouldn't have. But I'm not innocent there either. I was
starting to run too. You were just faster, so Mr. Antes caught me
instead."

There was silence for a moment. Maggie was unsure how
Nate would react to that admission.

"I couldn't see that in the dark," he started. "But looking
back now, I doubt Mr. Antes wanted to catch me, anyway. He

didn't want me in trouble. He wanted to embarrass Jonas through you."

"Jonas's words rescued me."

"I heard. Jonas called Mr. Antes and everyone else out as hypocrites."

"He did that, but that's not what I mean." Maggie lifted her face and looked Nate straight in the eyes, the first time she had done so since their night together. "I have still been working through my guilt and anger. At the restaurant, Jonas protected me from the judgment of others, but not my own. I was with you knowing full well you were only a friend. We will never be a couple. And even though I didn't get away, I would have left you behind if I had been a little faster."

"And you told this to Jonas?"

Maggie nodded. "He told me there was nothing I could do that couldn't be forgiven. Well, he said I had to allow myself to be forgiven. I said this was so over the line for me. A year ago, I might have believed I might make one of these mistakes, but I could not accept I had made so many together. He said it wasn't my standards that mattered. There was one true standard, and we all fall short of it, but we can be forgiven for all the shortcomings we have."

"Do you think he's right?"

"I felt the weight of my guilt being lifted as he spoke. I asked about each thing I did wrong, from the actual actions I took to the thoughts I had. He said all I needed to do was to choose to be forgiven. Then he said, 'I forgive you.'"

Nate raised an eyebrow at that. "He forgave you? But you, I mean, we didn't do anything to him."

"I know that, but when he said it, the entire weight was gone. I still remember all of my mistakes, but the guilt, the shame, the anger, it all disappeared. And I understand other things more clearly now."

"Like what kind of man you should be looking for? Because we can be sure he shouldn't be like me."

Maggie smirked in spite of herself. "You still have plenty of good things to you. I don't want the anti-Nate either." She paused as Nate chuckled. "But I figured out something he told us a while back, the first time he spoke to me. Jo and Martha were there too. He was telling us about our worth, how it wasn't found in clothing or style or popularity. Our worth was in us from the beginning of our lives."

"He's said similar things to the team."

"Yes, and I thought I understood it, but now I realize I only got it on a surface level. Now I understand it more deeply. Even after I first listened to Jonas talk about my value, I still was measuring my worth by whether I had been with a boy or not. After we were caught, I was convinced I had no value because of all the people who looked down on me for what happened. But even those things don't change our value."

Maggie stopped. She felt like she was rambling on too long. Now Nate was looking down, avoiding her stare.

No, Maggie decided. She had to keep going.

"I also understand why he told me about the coach who left ninety-nine players behind to find the one player who was lost. He told me that before you and I were caught, but he knew I would be lost. Even with all I've done wrong, it was important to Jonas that he would be there to help me when Mr. Antes tried to hurt me. That was more important to him than it was to celebrate with the players and parents who weren't in any trouble. My value, our value, to him does not depend on how much good or evil we do."

Now she was rambling, but she needed to ask one question.

"Nate, do you believe that?" she asked.

"Not sure," Nate mumbled.

Before Maggie said anything else, they both realized that Martha and Jo were coming back to the parking lot. "I guess I should go before we start any more rumors," Nate said as he walked away, with Maggie's friends staring at him, agape. "Wait," Maggie said. Nate turned to her. "We did the wrong thing together once. Let's do the right thing now."

"And what would that be?"

Maggie took Nate's hand. She didn't care who saw them or what anyone would infer from them being together. Pulling him along behind her, Maggie led Nate back to the field, to where

Jonas was standing on the hill. There were still other people milling about around him, in awe of the food that had appeared. But Maggie was able to get next to Jonas, and Nate came up face-to-face with him.

"For anything he's done wrong to me, Jonas, I have forgiven him," Maggie said. "But he still needs to hear it from you."

Maggie turned to look at Nate, who was crying. He seems so broken now, she thought. She hoped she had not made things worse.

"I'm not worthy to be part of the team anymore," Nate said to Jonas through his sobs. "What Pete told me, and all that time on the bench, it made me understand. It was so much worse than being caught. No one on the team is perfect, but no one else has done something like this. If you tell me I should quit the team, or I should never be here to listen to your teaching again, I will go away. It's what I deserve."

He is in worse shape than I realized, Maggie thought. But Jonas brought comfort again.

"Nate, you have told me what you deserve. But what do you want?"

"Forgiveness."

"You already know what you've done wrong, Nate. Turn away from those decisions. Wait for your wife and follow me. I forgive you."

Nate's arms flew around Jonas in an embrace so quickly, Maggie thought for a moment that she imagined it. But she saw the relief Nate was feeling, just like the relief she experienced when Jonas had forgiven her.

Chapter 38

The ball sailed over Pete's head, and he sprinted back to the center-field fence, hoping that the ball would hit the wall instead of flying over it. He was quick enough to get to the ball as it rebounded off the wall before it hit the ground. But as he turned to make a throw back into the infield, Pete knew he was not quick enough to stop Puraton from scoring its third run of the game. John had struggled all game. From his center-field position, Pete had a good view of John's pitches as they passed over the plate. The fastballs were fast, and the breaking balls were breaking, but neither did much to fool Puraton's batters. They had scored two runs in the first inning. Now in the third, they led Central 3-0 and even had another runner on second base.

Pete felt almost powerless out in the field. Maybe, if he were pitching, Puraton would not be so successful. Pete doubted he would throw a shutout as he had against some other teams, since it seemed like all nine batters in the lineup were threats to get on base. But he knew he could pitch better than what John had so far.

It did not matter, at least not today. Pete was still ineligible to pitch until the fifth day of the tournament after throwing a complete game in Central's opener. This was only the third day. If Pete was going to help turn this game around, it would be with his glove and his bat.

The moment that thought crossed Pete's mind, he had an opportunity to impact the game with his glove. Another fly ball was hit, this one to Pete's left. As he chased it, he realized this one was not hit as hard as the last one, but it tailed away from him. Pete looked over to Nate, back on the field for the first time since his suspension, but the ball was not tailing enough for him to make the play either. The ball landed between them.

Pete fielded the ball on one hop, but before he threw the ball back to the infield, he knew Puraton had already scored again.

Two groundouts mercifully ended the inning, and Pete jogged back to the dugout. His teammates looked dejected, which he was not used to at all. But, they had the top of the order coming up to bat. A little spark here could turn the whole game back to Central's favor.

"Look alive, guys," Pete said, grabbing a bat and getting to the on-deck circle. "Let's get a couple of guys on base and make this pitcher work. Find a way to first, Phil."

Phil was the first batter up in the bottom of the fourth. It was the second time he and the Central players would get to face the pitcher, but the experience seemed to do no good. The first two pitches barely caught the corner of the plate for two strikes. Then Phil swung a borderline-high pitch that turned into a weak ground ball to second for the first out.

That was how this pitcher recorded most of his outs. He had pinpoint control that led to difficult counts out of which to hit. It did not always result in strikeouts, but it led to poorly hit grounders and pop-ups.

Pete dug into the batter's box. He knew the first pitch would be on a corner, but whether it would be inside or outside, high or low, was a guess. He expected the ball to be high and outside, but when he realized it would be lower than that, he checked his swing. The umpire called it a strike, and Pete agreed, but taking a strike was better than hitting the ball weakly again.

Pete leaned in over the plate a little more, guessing again on an outside pitch. By the time he realized that this pitch would be far inside, it was too late. The fastball hit him in the head. He did not feel it at first. There was a moment's shock before he physically felt the blow. His batting helmet stayed on, and the ball deflected away. Coach Deem hurried there in a moment.

"Pete, where are you?"

He is worried I have a concussion, Pete thought. "Salem, in Berks County, Pennsylvania. At home plate, about to go to first base."

"When's your birthday?"

"June twenty-ninth."

"Girlfriend's name?"

"Sal."

"You're fine," Coach Deem said, and they walked to first base.

The pain had not been intense and had already disappeared. Pete wondered if the pitch was not as fast as he first thought. It was not a fastball, but a slider he never identified.

John batted next. Pete got no signal to do anything but wait to see if John would put the ball in play. The outfielders were playing shallow. On a ground ball through the infield, Pete would be able to go no farther than second base, but if John could get the ball over the outfielders, he had a chance to score.

It did not matter. On the first pitch, John was plunked on the head. This one was definitely a fastball.

Pete was free to walk to second base, but did not move at once. He wanted to know if John was all right but stayed at first base for a moment to give the coaches room to check John out. Coach Arim got there first. When he did, John was already trying to wave him away. Pete thought he heard John say he was not hurt and also thought he heard Coach Deem tell the umpire that the Puraton pitcher should get at least a warning.

It was not completely clear to Pete what anyone said, because there were dozens of voices yelling from the stands. It was louder than the cheering for a great play. Mothers were screaming for the pitcher to be ejected. Fathers were questioning the toughness of the pitcher. From the opposite side of the field, Puraton parents shouted that Central's fans were being too sensitive.

Pete glanced over to the Central dugout. His teammates were angry, but still silent. Good. They ought to be mad over this, but shouting would not help. Their focus had to remain on the game, not the antics.

After John talked with the coaches for a minute, he walked to first. Only then did Pete make his way to second. If nothing else, a scoring chance for Central had developed. There were two runners on with only one out, and the clean-up hitter was batting.

James was hit on the shoulder by the next pitch.

Fans on the Central side of the field were jumping out of their lawn chairs now. Pete could see Mrs. Thun run down to the chain-link backstop behind the plate. James was not hurt and was probably the most fortunate of the three hit batters. The muscles around the shoulder gave padding against a baseball, and no one would worry about a concussion from a play like this. But that appeared to take away none of his mother's ire as she shouted at the pitcher, catcher, home-plate umpire and anyone else who would listen.

James gave his bat a toss toward the dugout and glared at the pitcher as he ran to first. Not walked or trotted, ran. He's angry. We should be angry, Pete fumed, and that pitcher should be ejected.

The home-plate umpire grabbed a new ball and walked halfway between home and the mound. He pointed at the pitcher, then at the Puraton bench, then at the Central bench. Pete could not discern the words over the din of over two-hundred angry voices in the crowd, but he understood from the gestures. Warnings had been issued. The next time the umpire decided that a pitcher was aiming at a batter, that team's pitcher and head coach would be tossed out of the game.

Pete tried to ignore the injustice of it. Three of Central's batters had been hit with three straight pitches. Not only was the Puraton pitcher staying in the game, but Central could not hit even one of Puraton's batters without being tossed.

Worry about that later, Pete told himself. We have the bases loaded with just one out now. The pitcher has to be worried about throwing pitches inside that the umpire might think of as another beanball.

But the new situation did not seem to affect the opposing hurler. Six strikes later, the inning ended.

* * *

Jules slammed his glove into his bag. The frustration from the last two games, ever since his failed sacrifice bunt yesterday, was boiling over into a rage. He had been on the field for only half the game, and this time, it was a shocking defeat. Jules didn't care how good Puraton was, or what their reputation was. No one should be able to beat Central by seven runs.

The last pitch he saw before being removed from the game was high and inside. Unlike a few of his teammates, he had dodged it for ball four, but it was like the proverbial salt in the wound. Especially since he was taken out of the game for a pinch runner a moment later, so he never had an opportunity to get even with the pitcher. Not that he ever made up his mind how he would do that, but he would have found a way.

Everything started going downhill ever since Jules tried to put down a "perfect sacrifice," as Jonas had called it. For a time, he thought Jonas had a secret approach that made the team invincible. Now, he suspected that it was a coincidence. This stranger appeared when Central was hitting its stride. Jonas had nothing to do with their wins, nor their losses.

No, Jules amended in his mind, as he zipped up his bag and walked out of the dugout. He does have something to do with the losses. He put it in our mind to look for those sacrifice bunts. We have not been working our way around it when the coaches signal us to bunt. Less swinging away, less big hits. Talent still carried Central past most opponents, but a better team like Puraton took advantage.

Central was losing its aggressive streak, and that had started with Jonas's meddling.

Jules wanted to get to his car and drive home. It was late, the sky long since dark. He and everyone else would need to refocus to keep the season going with a win tomorrow. No one wanted the season to end, but they especially did not want to finish with two straight losses in a double-elimination tournament.

"Deep thoughts?" someone said to Jules. Where he had parked, there was little light so he could not see who had addressed him. "Amazing how quiet you are after a loss, considering how loud you can be after a win," the voice continued.

Jules recognized the voice now, though Devon Hellickson still hid in the dark. Come to think of it, he had not seen Devon ever since the first time he had met Jonas. It would have been nice if he had been around for this playoff run. He could have sneaked more beer to the team for even more fun at their celebrations. But Jules was not having any fun today.

"I take the game seriously, Mr. Hellickson" Jules said. "I should be upset when we lose. And happy when we win."

"Puraton really is some team, isn't it?" Devon replied from the darkness.

Jules opened the back of his car to throw in his equipment bag. The light from within finally revealed Devon, standing a little too close to Jules for him to be comfortable.

"They're good enough that I can't say we should beat them," Jules said, instinctively taking a step back. "But I can say we should be closer to them than what we were today."

"And why didn't you play better today? Who has caused you to lose your edge?"

Jules said nothing, but looked at Devon suspiciously. He was dressed in trendy clothes like he always was, but Jules saw nothing out of the ordinary with him.

"You know what's happened," Devon continued. "Jonas is not teaching you anything but how to make yourself weaker. But it's worse than that. He is a violent man."

"Violent?" Jules answered. He had seen nothing violent from him.

"Why do you think I've been away these last few weeks? I meant to be there for all your playoff games. He confronted me, threatened me, told me to stay away from you, every one of you. That's why I haven't been able to bring you your gifts."

"A beer or two would have been good after winning regionals," Jules said, looking around and hoping no one heard that.

"But I wasn't going to stop there," Devon said. "I'm your friend. I know what this team has been craving. Attention. Prestige. Fame. You want your names to put on billboards across the country. You want baseball fans everywhere to read about Central. I have ways to getting that done."

Jules was intrigued, even tempted. It seemed like Devon had enough money he could make a publicity campaign if he wanted. Another thought struck him. There was something he found even more tempting than fame.

"Based on the way you dress, I've always assumed that you must keep money stashed aside," Jules said.

"Of course I do, even more than Harry Antes has," Devon answered, grinning. "Anything in this world, I know how to get. I could make you famous in a few days even if you had no exceptional talents."

"We're talking about money," Jules insisted. "I'll be going to college soon, but my parents have only been able to save up so much. And committing to the team has kept me from working a regular job."

"So it's cash you want," Devon said. He pulled a wallet out of his back pocket. Leafing through it, he continued, "Money is the best of my tools. So many people want it." Then he lowered his voice. "So few know how to use it."

He pulled out a wad of paper bills, showing them to Jules in the light from the car. Devon counted them, and Jules could see they were hundred-dollar bills.

"Thirty," Devon finished. "Three thousand dollars, for you."

"You carry that kind of money to a baseball game?"

"I wasn't at the game! Weren't you listening?" Devon almost screamed. Then he recomposed himself. "That's the whole point. I can't risk an encounter with Jonas. I waited out here for you. I wanted to speak with your whole team. Especially Pete. But for now, I can only risk this one meeting with you. And, to answer your question, I make it a point to always have what people will want."

"Well, thank you," Jules said, stepping forward to take the money.

Devon crumpled the money in his fist. "Oh, this time it's not a gift. It's a payment. You need to understand that before you take it."

"Payment? What do you want me to do?"

"What you already want to do. Find a way to remove Jonas from the team permanently. Then I will be able to interact with everyone again. I can help your teammates regain their focus and their aggression. Get rid of Jonas, then I can get this team to the national tournament, even to win the national tournament. Baseball fans will know your name from coast to coast. I can get more money to you then as well. Anything you want, I can give it to you. But not with Jonas still in the way."

Jules considered everything Devon said. "I'm not sure how I can keep someone from being at the games. And we play again tomorrow afternoon. That's not much time."

"Then you better win tomorrow, and figure out something for tomorrow night," Devon said. His tone was a little threatening, leaving Jules unnerved. But he felt better when Devon put the money into his hands. "But if you can get him out of the way before the final day of states, the championship round, then you will get everything you truly deserve."

Jules counted the money to be sure Devon had given the full amount. There were, in fact, thirty one-hundred-dollar bills. Tonight was not so bad after all.

He looked up and was about to speak, but Devon had disappeared again into the darkness.

Chapter 39

Would Jonas bail on us after a loss? James wondered to himself. It did not seem like him. But Central had not lost a game since Jonas first showed up before the county playoffs, so there was no way of knowing what he would do right now. Even after dozens of conversations with him, there was still a great deal of mystery around Jonas. Any new situation could bring unexpected results. But the game against Puraton had ended almost thirty minutes ago, and there was no sign of Central's unofficial mentor.

James rolled his left shoulder around twice. The sting from the pitch that hit him was gone, though a prominent bruise was still there. James was not as confident as his teammates that the Puraton pitcher was aiming for their heads, but he was convinced that he was trying to hit them.

He wondered for a moment if the newspaper writers who were there would mention all the hit batters. Guess it depends on how much they like to write about controversies, James thought. Then he reflected on how this score would appear across the state. Big stories would be published back home in Lebanon County and here in Berks County. Then he realized that there would be stories in Dauphin County too, since that Harrisburg reporter was also here. Maybe other newspapers and websites would have stories about Puraton beating Central.

Shameful, James thought. We can't have people out there seeing Central on the losing side. But it was still possible to win the state tournament out of the losers' bracket. A state title would redeem the team's reputation in the next couple of days. Then they all would be known as winners.

Most of his teammates had left, and since their game was the last contest of the day, there was little reason to hang around the field tonight. A few of the lights were still on, but it was past eleven and Central would play again tomorrow afternoon to try to avoid elimination. It was not an early game, but there was an hour drive home tonight and an hour drive back the next day. James did not want to waste minutes he could spend recuperating for such a big game.

Depending on how one looked at it, tomorrow's game was the most crucial game of the year. Even when Central won the Lebanon County and Region D titles, Central could have lost those games and had another chance. Not so in this upcoming game.

Yes, James decided, tomorrow was the most important day so far.

"Hey," John called from near the left-field gate. "You ready?"

"Yeah," James yelled back. He started walking the path when he saw Peter and Andrew running the opposite way.

James turned to see where they were going and then saw Jonas. He was walking back from the first-base side of the field where the Puraton fans had been sitting and where a handful of their players were still packing equipment.

James decided to follow his teammates. Jonas's wisdom after a loss could be more valuable than what he taught while they were winning. His brother could wait in the car.

"We were looking for you," Pete was saying when James caught up to them. "You saw everything, right? All three players who were beaned?"

James pulled up his left sleeve to show his bruise, in case Jonas needed proof. "It doesn't hurt anymore, but it might be sore tomorrow."

"When you decided to play a sport, you knew there would be a cost," Jonas said. "Pitches sometimes hit batters, even in the head. It is part of the game. Not all injuries will disappear like Ted's did."

"Well, yeah," Andrew answered. "But, it's not that we got hurt. We have another problem."

"It's that pitcher for Puraton. He was aiming for us," Pete said. "He had great control all game, then suddenly we were getting pitches that were way too high and inside."

"Suppose he did try to hit you," Jonas said. "What do you want me to do about him?"

"You've given us guidance on so much," Pete said. "What should we do when we face them again? How can we get back at him?"

"Hang on, Pete," John said, having come over earlier in the conversation. James had not noticed. "We don't know if we will play them at all. We have to beat Red Eagle tomorrow or our season is done."

"I'm certain we will beat them," Pete said to John. Then he turned back to Jonas. "We could still play Puraton in the state finals on Saturday. Or even in Mid-Atlantics next week. How can we best handle him?"

Jonas sighed and looked down for a moment. "The best way to treat him would be to treat him how you treated the pitchers from Vigortown."

James's mind raced. The games from the regular season and county playoffs seemed like a lifetime ago, and Central had not played Vigortown since then. But he couldn't remember any incidents with those pitchers.

"Jonas, I don't think there were any hard feelings between Vigortown and us," James said. "They might have been the second-best team in the county, but I don't remember them aiming for our heads."

"That is correct," Jonas said. "You should play against Puraton, or any other team, the way you want them to play against you. Of course, both teams will try to win. But you should not try to hurt any of your opponents."

"What about spiking him when he slides into a base?" Andrew asked.

"No!" Jonas said, as harshly as James had ever heard him speak. "Leave him go. If you feel he has wronged you, forgive him. Only then can you expect to be forgiven if, in the heat of a game, you do something that hurts another player."

"Forgive?" John asked. "This is baseball, not dinner at the guidance counselor's house."

"I think I understand what you're saying," Pete said. "But he started this. We didn't do anything to him all game. We need to balance out what he did."

Jonas shook his head. "You will never reach your ultimate goal with those thoughts. If a pitcher hits you, tip your cap to him and go to first. Stand in the batter's box during your next at-bat the same way and give him the chance to hit you again."

This was getting beyond James's ability to grasp. Was Jonas telling them that if they kept getting hit by pitches, they were proving their toughness to the other team? Were they intimidating the opponent by taking it over and over without response?

"What's that pitcher's name?" John asked.

"Corey Newcomer," Jonas said.

"We could ask him," John said, gesturing to where a few of the remaining Puraton players were walking up the path. The pitcher, Corey, was among them.

James looked at Corey and felt himself steaming in his heart. He did not want to start a fight, but he wanted to go over and share a few words with him. Jonas turned to James and stared at him so intently James felt a tremor. There was still a fire inside James, but he remained still and silent.

Corey did not. He parted from his teammates and walked over, grinning. Smug jerk, James thought. If he comes over here and taunts us, I'll put a bruise in his forehead.

But Corey spoke only to Jonas. "Sir," he said, "I don't understand how you knew it, but, my brother is fine now. My mother called me just after you walked away. He woke up, and the fever was gone. He will probably be here tomorrow for the game."

"That is good," Jonas said, hugging the Puraton pitcher. "Few have trusted me so quickly. I am happy for you."

"Thank you again," Corey said. "Whether you did it yourself or somehow just knew, thank you."

Corey ran off to catch up to the other Puraton players. The only people left at the field were Jonas, James, John, Pete, Andrew, and a few maintenance workers tidying up the grounds. James knew they would have to leave soon before the workers turned off the lights, but he had to know what Corey meant.

Pete asked before James did. "Does he know you? Is that why you don't want us to throw at him?"

"No, tonight is the first time he's ever seen me," Jonas said. "But he has a brother who's six years old. The young boy has had a bad fever for several days, and their doctors weren't able to make it go away. Corey did not see the professional players here with us two days ago, and he was busy warming up when we were giving the food to everyone yesterday. But he heard about these things and believed from what he had heard I could help, so I did."

"You took away the fever of a child you never met?" James asked incredulously. This was getting out of hand. Unlike Nate's healing or the mysterious production of food, there was no evidence of this curing in front of him.

But James's question was drowned out by his three teammates, all of whom were talking over each other. They were complaining about Jonas helping someone on the other team.

"Are you so worried about the baseball game you would let the boy suffer?" Jonas asked.

That silenced the other three boys. Then Jonas turned back to James. "And as for your question, how many people will believe you when you tell them about how all those people were fed yesterday?"

"Not many," James squeaked out.

"Then trust Corey's words about me," Jonas said. "You are all my friends, and I will do much for you. But there will be things I do for others who do not come from the same town or play on the same team you do."

There was an awkward silence, the five of them looking at each other, though only Jonas's gaze had any authority behind it.

"Hey, guys," one worker called from the field. "We're going to be turning off the lights in five minutes. You better go."

All of them walked up the path to the left-field gate and the parking lot. Before they got to the cars, Jonas spoke to them again, but now in the powerful, yet compassionate, voice they were used to hearing. "You and your teammates have learned much and have done much. But there's more to learn and more to do, and time is getting short." He paused. "Get here earlier than your coaches say to tomorrow. I must speak to the whole team before you play Red Eagle."

The reassuring tone gave James confidence they had not disappointed Jonas, or at least if they had, Jonas was now past that. But Jonas's sudden determination to speak to all the players before tomorrow's game made him wonder. Did Jonas think they were in danger of losing again and ending their season?

Chapter 40

Pete, along with Andrew, James, and John, had sent messages to their teammates the night before about how Jonas wanted to speak with them. Pete was pleased to see all his teammates were at Falcon Field an hour before their coaches had told them to arrive this afternoon. He was looking forward to hearing what Jonas had to say. Though Jonas seemed to be too forgiving towards the Puraton pitcher, otherwise his words had always been enlightening.

Today would be the first time all year that Central had to win to keep its season going. "Win or go home," as broadcasters liked to say. Perhaps Jonas was saving his most important lesson for a game with these kinds of high stakes.

Walking through the entrance, already in uniform and with their equipment, Pete and the rest of the team were greeted by Jonas. He led them over to the hill on the third-base side. He embraced each one as they came over, put down their equipment bags and sat. Jonas sat in the center of them, next to a cooler.

There was a moment of silence, almost of anticipation. Pete wondered what Jonas would say. Maybe he would give a new strategy on the field. Perhaps he would tell something he had been discussing when the players from Philadelphia and Pittsburgh had been here a few days ago.

In that brief, soundless time, Pete noticed that Jonas was wearing a shirt with a couple words on it. It seemed out of the ordinary for him. Jonas had always worn plain white shirts with nothing that would draw even a little attention. But today, his white shirt had a message in black script, *"Everybody dies..."*

Despite the dots at the end, there was nothing on the back to finish the phrase. Before Pete could wonder if there was a hidden message in those words, Jonas broke the brief silence. "I have looked forward to telling you this lesson, but it also grieves me. I will be with you today, for this game. But after midnight tonight, I will have to leave you for a time."

"Leave?" Pete asked. "You hadn't mentioned any plans about leaving."

"We thought you were going to help guide us through the whole season," Andrew said.

"You've always said about getting us to our ultimate goal," Matt added, notebook in hand as usual during Jonas's talks. "I always thought you meant the national tournament."

"I must go," Jonas said, waving his hands down to stop further questions. "I will miss you, but this will only be for a short time. And it is for your benefit I leave. You will be sad while I am gone, but that sadness will turn to joy when I return. Then I will be with you for a while before leaving again."

"Where are you going?" Tom asked. "May we go too, when our season is finished?"

"Except for one of you, you will all go with me," Jonas said. "And you know the place where I am going. Your understanding of it is not complete yet, but in time it will be."

Pete was growing concerned. Was Jonas beginning to lose his mind? Or was he speaking a little more vaguely than Pete could follow? Perhaps he was saying he would help them get to the national tournament, but at the moment, the team could not appreciate it. Maybe Jonas meant they could only enjoy it once they had earned it through the state and Mid-Atlantic tournaments.

But he also said one of them would not be going.

"Jonas," Pete interrupted. "Why wouldn't we all be going with you? Why did you say, 'except for one'?"

Jonas hesitated. To Pete, he looked upset. Jonas took a deep breath before answering the question.

"Before I leave you, all of you will leave me," Jonas said.

This time, all twelve players spoke. Pete and all the others said they would not leave him.

"We've stuck with you, even when our parents have questioned you," Tom said.

"We don't care what Mr. Antes thinks," Andy added.

"You saved Maggie and me from being reported to the police," Nate said. "I owe you too much to walk away."

Pete stood. "Jonas," he said after the others had finished. "I will not leave you. I don't understand everything you've taught us, but I will stand with you in anything you want me to do. I'd even take a bullet for you."

Jonas stood next to Pete. He grinned for a moment, but then frowned again. "Pete, in time, yes, you will work alongside me. You will also do work I give you when I am not nearby. But tonight, before tomorrow's dawn, you will say you don't know me. You will tell other people you don't know who I am, and you will say it three times."

The statement shook Pete. Why was Jonas questioning his character or his loyalty? If he did not believe Jonas was a great teacher, he never would have made sure the whole team was here for this meeting. But Pete felt he was holding up other things that Jonas wanted to say, so he sat back down mumbling to himself, "No, never."

Jonas did not sit down, but knelt over to reach into the cooler. He pulled out a large roll of pita bread and tore it into smaller pieces. "You have a difficult day ahead of you. Eat this and remember both my father and me when you eat bread in the future."

Pete saw Jonas hand the bread to each of his teammates, then lastly, to him. Jonas was no longer frowning, but rather, smiling compassionately. It reminded Pete of his own mother's face whenever he had been hurt, and she tended to his care.

They all ate the bread, and Jonas ate a piece as well. Then he pulled several empty plastic cups from the cooler, followed by a large bunch of grapes. Jonas squeezed the grapes into the cups, producing a several drops of juice into each one. Pete thought the grape juice looked like blood on Jonas's hands.

"Drink this. When you drink in the future, remember me, and my father, and what has been done for you."

Jonas handed the cups to each team member. Pete looked at the small amount of juice he had been given. Then he drank it, and he considered the things Jonas had mentioned. Though he still knew only a little about Jonas's father, what Jonas had told them made Pete believe he was a good man. Jonas himself was selfless.

Some of his messages, like today's, were confusing. But he had been helping them win games and straighten out their behaviors and attitudes with no reward for his guidance.

After finishing the drink, Pete turned to his right shoulder, where John was. One thing was still bothering him, but he had already made too much of a show of himself. He whispered to John, "Could you ask him about the one he thinks won't be going with us?"

John nodded and moved over to Jonas to sit down next to him. John whispered to Jonas, and the response was whispered back, but Pete could still hear it.

"There is one among you who will try to get rid of me," Jonas said. "While all of you will run, only one will deliberately act against me. He will never go where you all wish to go. It would be better for him if he had never joined this team."

That did not answer the question, but Jonas stood up and spoke aloud again to the whole team. Pete guessed that no more clues were forthcoming.

"From now on, whenever I see my father, I will speak to him on your behalf. I will also speak to him on behalf of those who hear of me because of you. But for now, there is one more thing I must do," Jonas said. Then he reached over and took the equipment bag of Jules, then of Ted, then Phil and Sam. With two slung over each shoulder, he carried them down to the field.

"We can do that," Little Jimmy called out to him.

"But you must let me do it today," Jonas said.

Jonas put the bags in the third-base dugout, then walked back up the hill to take the bags of Tom, Nate, Matt, and Jimmy. Jonas had some muscle to him, and the weight of the bags was not outrageous. Still, it was difficult to carry four at one time, if not only for the weight but for the space the bags took on his back.

After that trip, with the team watching confusedly, Jonas took the bags of John and James. Then he took Andrew's, the largest of them all due to the catcher's protective equipment. He reached for Pete's bag, but Pete stepped in front of it.

"No," Pete said. "You don't need to do this. Whatever lesson you are teaching us, I'm not going to make you carry my things. It's my responsibility to carry them. If we had a junior varsity team or an equipment manager like we did in high school, they could do it. But I can't ask you to do such a menial task."

"If you do not let me carry them this time, can you say we are friends?"

Pete pondered the words for a moment. Maybe he had a point. Well, Jonas always had a point, but Pete could not always see it. But friends shared burdens, physical and otherwise. He picked up the bag and put it on Jonas's back. Then he took off his cap and placed it on Jonas's head. "If my friendship with you will be measured this way, then also take my hat."

Jonas smiled and carried the equipment back down to the dugout. This time, the team followed. "You'll eventually understand what I'm doing here and do it yourself. Though you will not be carrying bags of sports equipment. When the time comes, you will help to reduce the burdens of others."

"Whose burdens?" Andy asked.

"Many people's. But the first ones you will help are people who you have met before," Jonas and the team made it to the dugout. He dropped the bags on the ground. "Now concentrate on this game. Get ready for batting practice and your infield-outfield warmups. You don't need any more lessons today."

Jonas was about to leave the field when Jules called out. "Do you think we will win?"

At first, Jonas seemed to miss the question. But as he was walking by Pete on his way to the gate up to the bleachers, he whispered, "Do you think he should not have ever joined this team?" Then he walked away.

Pete looked back over to Jules, who apparently had not heard and was getting his glove. Did Jonas mean he was the traitor?

* * *

More so than usual, Jonas's words seemed mysterious to James. But today was not the time for him to figure out how they applied to his life, if indeed they did.

For the first time all summer, Central had a must-win game to play. And, for the first time this season, Central was angry. Sure, a couple of times before there were individuals who were upset, but this was the first time that every single person on the team was furious.

Red Eagle was not the team who had earned their ire, but they were the team in the other dugout. James intended to make them pay for what Puraton had done to them yesterday.

Puraton could pay its share tomorrow.

Jonas's words and his unexpected help in carrying the bags and equipment to the dugout were already forgotten. James and his teammates developed a laser-like focus on beating Red Eagle.

When he was on the field, James wasted no time sending any ground balls hit near third base over to first base for an out. He threw more quickly than necessary for most of the plays, and he could hear Coach Deem call out to take his time. But there were no errors on his throws. They were precise, with a velocity that reflected the anger he felt at the lopsided loss from yesterday. It was similar when he came up to bat. Frustration made him focused, not wild. Each plate appearance, he waited for the perfect pitch in the perfect spot. Then, he punished the ball.

That did not always work out. One time, James's line drive was caught by the second baseman. Another time, he hit a deep fly ball to left field that hooked foul and out of play. But once, he put a line drive back up the middle, just over the pitcher's glove and between the middle infielders for a two-run single.

It was James's last at-bat that finally allowed him to let go of some of his anger.

The count was two balls and no strikes. James expected a fastball, about stomach high and on the inside half of the plate. The pitcher, as if he were on the same team instead of the opposition, gave him that pitch.

James took a swing that a professional hitting coach would have been proud of, level but quick and powerful. Again, the ball flew out to left field, but this time it stayed straight and sailed over the fence for a solo home run.

For the first time all day, James listened to the crowd and the cheers of family, friends, and strangers for his first home run of the postseason. As he rounded the bases, his passion cooled, and he reminded himself to enjoy the moment.

He enjoyed another moment a few minutes later when a pop-up came over to him, and he squeezed it to complete a 9-1 victory.

Central had survived. A part of James's anger disappeared. The embarrassment of the lopsided score yesterday against Puraton vanished.

But the rest of his anger, the anger over being target practice for the Puraton pitcher, remained. Something would have to be done about that.

* * *

This was rare, Pete thought to himself.

He was not contemplating how few teams would be still be playing on the last day of states, or how fortunate Central was to finish no worse than third here.

It occurred to him how rarely he played in a game, on the winning side, and felt no high from it afterward. Maybe when he was still a child and could easily be distracted by the next thing his family did, but not since then. High school, college or Armed Services, a win at any level colored the rest of the day in brighter tones.

Everything remained monotone this time. The victory over Red Eagle, though decisive, brought little joy. It could be because they were still in the losers' bracket, where there would always be more pressure. Perhaps it was because clinching a finish in the top three meant only a little when it would be the top two that would advance to Mid-Atlantics.

More likely, though, it was that Pete and all his teammates were sitting on the hill on the third-base side of the field watching Puraton. That was the team that had embarrassed them. Puraton had taken cheap shots at them.

And worse, Central was in a position to root for Puraton. Not out loud, but each player knew they were better off if Puraton beat Salem. If Puraton won, Salem would have two losses and be out of the tournament. That would put Central no worse than second place and assure a trip to the national regionals.

It would also mean that Central would need to beat Puraton in back-to-back games tomorrow to win the state title. A chance to beat them twice would make Pete feel better.

The sun was getting low in the sky, and Puraton was already winning its game against Salem in the third inning. When the coaches left, Pete told them that all the players would stay to watch the whole game, to get any advantage they could over their opponent.

It was not a lie.

Coach Deem and Coach Arim agreed that was fine as long as everyone got back home in time to get enough rest for tomorrow's action. Each player checked with his parents, and now, ten of the twelve players were watching the game from the hillside.

James was up in the press box, being interviewed by the two sportswriters that had been following the team during the playoffs. It was one of the perks of hitting a home run, even if the result had been decided by then. Pete was not sure where Jules was, which made him a little nervous. Jonas had hinted that something was not right with Jules.

"That was fun," James said, pulling Pete out of his thoughts as he walked up the hill.

"Are you a celebrity now?" asked Andy, sitting next Pete.

"For a day, anyway," James said, sitting and smiling. "Talking with the sportswriters actually helped me appreciate the home run more. I was so angry today I didn't realize what I had done until I was trotting around second base."

"I hope you have one more of those in your bat for tomorrow," John said.

Pete looked at the other Thun brother. "I'm hoping we can be as laser-focused as we were today. If we have to beat Puraton twice, and it looks like we will," Pete gestured to the scoreboard, "we will need to do everything right. There can be no errors in the field and no mental mistakes."

"You're pitching tomorrow," Tom reminded him. "We should kill them."

"Don't take anything for granted," Pete warned. "And besides, even if I pitched a perfect game, we would still have to win the second game. Everyone needs to be ready, even guys who aren't usually pitchers."

"It's a shame that that Newcomer guy isn't eligible to pitch tomorrow," Andy said. "We could throw a couple of pitches high and inside on him."

"Clip him, just a bit," John said. "I wish I would have done that yesterday. Stupid umpire's warning scared me out of it."

"We're not going to throw at them," Pete said. The other players stared at him, surprised. "I want to get back at them too, Newcomer especially. But I have to assume the tournament officers will tell tomorrow's umpires about what happened yesterday. They will be looking for us to deliver payback. We would be risking early ejections."

"What are we going to do then?" Nate asked. "I mean, winning the games goes a long way, but that still doesn't make us even."

"I agree," Pete said. He hesitated. "Is Jonas still here?"

"He told us what he thought yesterday..." Andy answered.

"I know what he said, but I'd still like to hear from him one more time. There may be a more subtle way to get revenge."

"The reporters mentioned Jonas," James said. "Just now, when I was being interviewed. They said they were a little late finding me for an interview because they were talking to him after our game ended. I think they like him. They may be writing a story on him or something."

"But did they say where he is?" John asked.

"I think they said they saw him wander off away from the field. Not to the parking lot. Both writers asked me if he lived around here, but I told them we never found out where he lives now. I don't even remember seeing him drive a car. Coach Baptiste was the only one of us who knew him before last month." James turned to his other teammates. "Nate, your cousin was there too while they were interviewing me. I think Lucas bought Lydia flowers."

Nate put his hands up in front of him. "Look, I've got too much going on with the baseball and the other thing that happened to worry about who's flirting with Lydia. She'll take care of herself."

"Nate is right," said a voice behind the players, and Pete jumped from shock. He stood and turned around to see Jules, no longer in any of his Central uniform but rather a nondescript shirt and shorts.

"Where have you been?" Pete asked.

"Eavesdropping," Jules said. "I was sitting behind the Puraton players' families. They didn't recognize me without the uniform. While I there, I figured out a way we can get even with them."

Pete sat again. "What did you hear?"

"It turns out that the mother of that pitcher, Newcomer, drives several of the players back and forth to their games," Jules explained. "They have a van, not his family's but the team's van. For some boring reason I didn't quite follow, they are leaving it here tonight, and not using it to drive anyone back home until after tomorrow's games."

"So what?" John asked. "What do we care about their van?"

But Pete understood. "We could hit back without hitting any person. Guys, I see where Jules is going with this. But we have to make sure we're all together."

Chapter 41

Pete drove back around to the parking lot behind Falcon Field's left-field fence. He remembered how long it had been between the end of last night's game and when the field workers said they were shutting down the lights. Pete had a rough idea for how long he had to drive around Salem to make sure the field would be dark and deserted when he returned.

Pete's headlights showed that a single van was still in the lot. He parked a distance away and turned off the headlights. They were still in a residential area, and it might get noisy in a moment, so it was best to not do anything else to draw attention. He and Andy got out of the car.

Soon, four more cars parked near Pete's car, not in the parking lot but along the street next to it. That was the best place, Pete decided. No one wanted to accidentally damage their own cars.

His teammates stepped out of their vehicles, and everyone grabbed their bats. There were two or three players in each of the other cars, except for Jules. He had been riding alone.

They all walked to the van and circled around it, but no one made the first move. Most were holding their bats by their side, a couple over their shoulders. Jules was patting his bat into his hand.

"Well, are we going to do this or not?" Phil asked.

"Wait," John said. "Are we sure this is the van that belongs to Puraton?"

"Newcomer's mother said they were leaving the team van here tonight," Pete said. "There aren't any other vans around here. But let's see if we can tell."

The night was not pitch-black, but even with a new moon in the sky, they needed just a little extra light to investigate. Matt pulled out his phone and turned on the flashlight in it. He shined it on the back, and among a half-dozen stickers there was one that said "Puraton baseball" and another that said "Armed Services baseball." The others stickers were in the shapes of baseball batters and pitchers.

"Puraton is not that far away," Sam said. "But we are in Salem. How many vans can there be here with those stickers?"

Jules was hopping on his tiptoes. Pete noticed that Jules was wearing his batting gloves. Apparently, he wanted to be thoroughly prepared.

"We better get started, and do it quickly," Jules hissed.

For a second, no one did anything.

Then Jules stepped forward and slammed his bat into the rear windshield, shattering it. The sound echoed.

"Quick!" Pete hissed, and everyone took a couple of swings at the van.

Pete slammed in the front windshield. Andrew shattered one headlight while Tom hit the other. James and John smashed the two front windows while Matt and Nate took out the rear windows. Little Jimmy took swings into the backup lights. With the easier glass targets gone, Sam, Phil, and Ted hit the doors, denting them.

Taking a step back, Pete looked at the damage they had done. Newcomer probably deserved it, and by extension the rest of the Puraton team did. Still, he hoped his parents or Sal never found out about this. He especially hoped his college's administration never did either. That would be the end of his scholarship. But something had to be done, and now it was.

"All right, that's enough," Pete hissed, and his teammates stopped hitting the van.

"Come on, we want to get out of here now," Jules said. The voice came from behind Pete. Jules was already back at his own car. Pete saw Jules had left his bat by the smashed van. He was about to call for Jules to grab it, but then something distracted him.

Though there were no lights on at the parking lot or the baseball field, the light from inside Jules' car had turned on when he opened the door. Towards the edge of that light, Pete saw a figure running towards them. At first, he could not see the man's face, but he saw the words on his shirt.

"Everybody dies..."

Oh, no, Pete realized, it's Jonas.

Jonas ran by Jules, not looking at him, and did not stop until he got to Pete. Several of his teammates had run back to their cars as Jules had said. Pete could not follow them, feeling glued to one spot.

"You've made a great mistake," Jonas said, looking at the damage on the van. A couple of the players had started their cars and turned on their headlights while trying to get away. The new light showed the results of their actions: The van may have been totaled. Everywhere there should have been glass there were holes, and on the ground, there were glass shards for several feet circling the van.

"How did you know?" Pete asked.

"I was not far from here," Jonas said. "I was speaking with my father on the phone. Then I got a phone call from Jules to tell me to come here. But I did not need it. You still held anger in your heart towards Corey. I knew this would happen."

Jonas turned to where the players' cars had been parked. Now there were only two left. Pete's car was still there, where Andy was already hiding. Jules was still there as well, still standing with one foot in the car and the other out. His engine was running.

"You made one other call, didn't you?" Jonas called out.

At that moment, a siren sounded, and a few seconds later, red and blue flashing lights filled the darkness. A police car turned into the lot. Pete ran, leaving the damaged van and Jonas behind him.

Before he heard any orders from the officers, Jules shouted, "It was him! I saw him!" Then Jules got in his car and pulled away.

Pete stopped and turned back to the scene. The two officers both had guns drawn, but neither of them was pointed at him. Nor were they aimed at Andy, or at Jules' escaping car. They were all trained on Jonas, who had his hands raised.

"I am the one you want," Jonas said. "You can take me. I will not resist arrest."

"Cuff him and read him his rights," one officer said. The other policeman lowered his gun and arrested Jonas.

What have I done? What have we all done? Pete thought, his mind racing while his body was paralyzed.

294

"Pete," Andy hissed from the car. "Don't stare. Let's go now."

Pete glanced back towards Andy, then at the image of Jonas in the flashing red and blue lights having handcuffs put on him. One officer was reciting the Miranda rights loudly enough that Pete could hear him.

After a moment, Pete looked down at the ground, unsure of what to do. Then, Jonas shrieked in pain. Pete looked toward him again.

"Give me your cuffs," one officer said to the other. "Something's wrong with mine. I think they cut him."

"Be more careful," the second officer said, handing another set of handcuffs to his partner.

Jonas might wind up in jail for what everyone else had done, Pete realized. It would cost Pete everything, his baseball career, girlfriend, family. But he knew he should tell the officers what had happened.

Then the officer who had spoken earlier noticed him near the road. The other teammates, save for Andy, were long gone. Apparently, the policemen decided it was more worthwhile to grab the people were still here than to chase down anyone who was getting away. Pete, however, had not gotten away.

"Hey, kid," the officer called out. His gun was holstered again, but its presence had Pete a little unnerved. "Are you the one who called in the tip?"

For a fraction of a second, Pete imagined slamming a bat into Jules' kneecaps for getting all this started. But then his brain started working on his current situation. There was only one right thing to do.

It was the one thing he could not bring himself to do.

"Oh, officer, I don't know about anything happening on here."

The words tasted vile coming out of his mouth. But what choice did he have? If he told the truth, not only he might lose everything he was working for, but his teammates might too. His brother, waiting in the car, might lose everything, and he had not finished high school yet. And his poor parents, how would they take this?

"But do you recognize this man?" the officer asked. "Do you know who he is?"

I've got to leave, Pete thought. But he could not as long as the police were asking questions.

"I don't know him," he responded.

"Wait right here," the officer said. He did not walk away, but turned away away from Pete. Pete did not risk moving or even turning. He was sure that Andy was nearly sick in the car.

"Is the suspect dangerous?" the officer called back to his partner.

Pete looked back towards the scene of the crime. The other officer was leading Jonas to the back of the police car. He answered, "Nah, he took the arrest in stride. Nice change of pace, actually. He had no weapons either. He doesn't seem to be carrying anything at all."

"Put him in the back. You, come with me," the officer said to Pete, and they walked over to the police car in which Jonas was now seated. Pete thought the officer had missed that Andy was still his the car. He risked a glance back and saw his car was dark. Andy must have closed the doors and kept his head down before the police noticed that the car was occupied.

Once they reached the police car, the officer shined his flashlight through the window at Jonas. Pete's mentor squinted but looked back at him.

"We got a call from an anonymous tipster that one man was planning on vandalizing an automobile here," the officer explained. "We should be able to ID him one way or another at the station, but if you know anything, it could help us."

Pete looked at Jonas, knowing all the truth, but still only saying, "I don't know this man. I have no idea who he is."

Pete expected to find anger in Jonas's face. His gaze instead took the same look it had during their pregame meal from hours ago though it now seemed like years ago. Jonas was looking at Pete with sad, yet compassionate, eyes.

296

"But have you seen him around here?" the officer asked.
"Does he seem a bit familiar?"

"What kind of person would I be if I hung around with
criminals like him?" Pete said harshly, not realizing until after the
fact how nasty his tone was. It was not the best way to address a
police officer.

But the officer did not seem to mind. He asked Pete
questions that were not directly about Jonas. Where had Pete been
all day, when did he come over to the parking lot, and on and on.
Pete barely heard the questions. His answers, both the true ones
and the lies, were hardly loud enough to understand.

The policeman continued to write what Pete told him. It
seemed to go on for hours. "I'm going to need to see your ID, in
case we, or a lawyer, need to call you as a witness. Even if you
don't recognize him, you were still nearby when the crime was
committed. Your name won't be in the news, this is just for our
files."

Pete handed over his driver's license, and the officer copied
down all the information. He panicked when he realized that it
gave away that he lived about an hour away, which might make his
presence there at all suspicious. But then he remembered that he
had already told the officer he was part of the state baseball
tournament. That might be enough of an excuse.

"Are we taking him, too?" the officer's partner asked.

Pete could not breathe.

"No," the officer said, handing the driver's license back to
Pete. "The tip said one person, and we have one person not
resisting arrest. There's also only one bat on the ground here, so it
doesn't look like a group effort."

Pete remembered Jules' batting gloves, and how Jules had
dropped his bat next to the van. He had thought of everything, and
Pete fell for his trap. Pete could not think of any way to get the
police to go after Jules without having punishment fall back on
himself. He remained silent, despite his inner fear and rage.

"I think this kid just stayed out too long after today's
games," the officer continued. He refocused on Pete. "You did the

right thing by staying to give me a statement, though. You seem like a real stand-up guy. Good night and drive home safely."

Pete turned away. He could not force himself to look at Jonas or even the police car again. The officer's words burned inside him, only making the guilt all the more crushing. He walked across the parking lot to his car. Getting in, the indoor light brightened. Sure enough, there was Andy, huddled down in the passenger's seat.

"What?" Andy said. "No more cowardly than the guys who drove home."

Pete got in his car and then saw that the police car had pulled away.

"Andy," Pete said. "Take the wheel. Drive us home. I don't think I can."

That was the one right decision Pete made that night. On the drive home, he could not see through all his tears.

Chapter 42

There was still a game to play.

James tried to focus on that during the drive to the field and during the warmups. But no matter how many times he thought it, no matter how many times he reminded himself that it was the state championship, he never believed it. At least, he never thought the game mattered.

When the time came for Central to take its infield-outfield pregame warmups, James noticed that one of his teammates was not present. Jules was not there. He was probably hiding from the rest of them. In retrospect, it seemed like he had set up the whole thing. Jules had agitated everyone when they were already angry, told them about the van being left in the parking lot, and then pointed out Jonas to the police. At least, that was how Pete had described it to James.

But James did not feel too self-righteous at the moment and could not dwell on what Jules did wrong. James had done enough wrong on his own.

There was still a game to play.

James assumed there would be only a single game. If Central was going to win the state title, they would have to beat Puraton twice today. But that seemed almost silly. Puraton was the best team they played all year, and James knew neither he nor his teammates were in the psychological condition to win against them.

It was the only time James remembered starting a game convinced his team could not win.

But the game still had to be played.

* * *

The infield and outfield practice was almost done and already Coach Deem could tell that something was wrong with his team.

One part of that was obvious to anyone paying attention. Central was missing a player. Jules was nowhere to be seen, and so far had not left any message about why he was late or when he would arrive. His family was not here yet either, but his parents may have intended on coming right before the first pitch. Players did not have that luxury.

But even more upsetting than Jules' absence was that the other eleven players were distracted. There was no spunk as the players fielded the practice grounders and pop-ups. Their throws around the field were weak and not as precise as usual. Perhaps they stayed out too late last night, he considered, but there seemed to be more behind this than lethargy. The players' bodies were not the only thing tired. It seemed that their spirits were exhausted.

"Two minutes!" called out one of the tournament officials, signaling that Central's warmup time was almost over and Puraton's about to begin.

Coach Deem took a glance back to the dugout, and then to the fans on the hill behind it. He guessed there were well over two-hundred fans from Central here for a Saturday afternoon game, to say nothing of a greater number of Puraton fans. But Coach Deem would trade in all the fans in attendance to find Jules somewhere. Central faced long odds today, since they needed two wins to take the state title. Being down one more player might not be the deciding factor, but it would do Central no favors either.

Coach Deem hit the last practice fly ball to Nate, who then ran in as the last player to return to the dugout. The coach ambled behind him. If there was going to be a problem with a player, Coach Deem would have guessed Nate. But everything seemed to be resolved over the controversy with him and Maggie.

Assuming Maggie was not pregnant. Not that that would be any concern of his as a coach.

As far as the team was concerned, though, Nate had returned to the fold. The players felt the two games he sat out was enough to earn his starting spot in the outfield. But now Jules had disappeared. Had there been an accident on the way to the game?

Not likely, he figured. With all these fans that drove east after the players, someone would have mentioned about an accident on the road by now.

I can only manage the players who are here, Coach Deem reminded himself. He called them into a huddle around him.

"Anyone hear anything from Jules? Any texts or phone calls?" he asked.

A few players shook their heads.

"We can't worry about him now," the coach continued. "It looks like you're not quite game-ready, boys. Maybe it's Jules not being here, or that we already know we're moving into the Mid-Atlantics. We haven't played too many morning games before, so maybe your alarms woke you up too early. But whatever it is, remind yourselves of this: most players in our league never even get to be in the championship round of the state tournament. Take a deep breath. Sit in silence. Or pump each other up. Whatever you need to do, do it. Get focused. This is our chance to do something no Central team has ever done before, and it looks like half the town is here for it. Give it your best."

The boys listened. Coach Deem could see that. But the words did not get through to them. Pete looked like he was ready to cry. Not the mood he would have chosen for his starting pitcher. All the players walked into the dugout. Most sat while others stood, but all were silent.

Coach Arim came up next to Coach Deem. "What is going on?"

"No idea," Coach Deem kept his expression neutral. He did not want the players to see him get down, too. But he whispered. "But between you and me, I'm glad we've already got our trip to Virginia booked."

* * *

"So, do you have your trip to Virginia booked?" Marcus asked as he scribbled the lineups for the game into his scorebook.

And it really was scribbling. Lucas would not have been able to read the other journalist's notes if there had been a million dollar reward for it. Fortunately, there was a computer printout of the lineups in the press box he could use for his own scorebook.

"I had to set it up last night, and I reserved a room at a motel near the field," Lucas answered. "I called my editor before I drove here this morning. He said the company would reimburse me."

"I'm waiting until I hear from my boss before I set up anything," Marcus said. "I'm not thrilled about it. It will be a lot of time away from my family. Central better show me some good baseball next week, regardless of what happens today."

"It would make the drive a little more worthwhile," Lucas answered, finishing the lineup. He turned to his computer, getting ready to send out live updates over social media. But the first item on his screen was something different. He cleared the screen before Marcus, or anyone else, would see it.

It was Lydia's address. She lived a few minutes from the field in Lincoln, Virginia. It was true that Lucas had booked a room at a motel, but he might not be spending all his time there.

He looked back to the crowd, where he saw Lydia sitting with her family, the family of Central's right fielder. She told him after Central's win the night before that they should not sit together for the state final. He was too distracted to do his job correctly when he was beside her, and this was too big of a game to not have his focus on the field.

Lucas agreed, knowing full well that Lydia was on his mind too much already for him to not be distracted.

Lydia gave him a smile and a wave, then she made a typing motion to tell Lucas to get to work. He smiled back, then sent out updates to his social-media followers about the team's records, the pitchers and the starting lineups.

As he was typing up one of those notes, the thick scent of a cigar drifted straight into his nose and seemed to go right into his brain. Lucas hacked harshly, but could hear Marcus say, "I don't think those are allowed in the park."

"I enjoy it," said a voice that Lucas dimly recognized. He turned and saw Mr. Antes, the sponsor of the Central team. Who invited him up here? "I need you guys to write something for me."

"We don't..." Lucas started, then he coughed again. He composed himself. "We don't write for you. But if you have a story tip, feel free to share."

"Well, I expect to see this in the paper and online and everywhere soon," Mr. Antes said, dropping the ashes from his cigar next to Lucas' foot. "That Jonas Davis guy was arrested last night. The faker was caught beating up a van that belonged to Puraton's team. The man finally got what was coming to him."

"What?" Lucas asked. "That sounds out of character for him. And I have spoken with Mr. Davis a few times."

"Sounds like you were taken in by a charlatan," Mr. Antes answered, smoke blowing out of his mouth with each syllable. "Anyway, the word's going around town, and around the crowd here. Our people know about it, and the Puraton people know too. I'd like to be there when he's sentenced. Hope they keep him locked up for what he's done to us."

"And what did he do to you?" Lucas asked, watching to make sure the ashes from Mr. Antes' cigar did not become a fire hazard.

"Well, you have to assume those meetings with the players were all about breaking the law now. And he sure wasn't doing anything to make them a better baseball team."

"I didn't realize that not making baseball players better was a crime."

Mr. Antes was about to snap back at Lucas, but Marcus interrupted them. "Sir, while you've been talking, I've searched the Berks County and Lebanon County news websites. There is no report of an arrest for damaging a vehicle anywhere."

"Well, it happened, trust me," Mr. Antes said. "A man named Devon Hellickson told me face-to-face this morning before I got to my car."

"And is that man, this Devon Hellickson, here?" Lucas asked.

"No, he said he had business today. Something about Mr. Davis's father meeting with him and he could not get away. That old, senile man is probably angry that his son got caught. Anyway, the game's going to start soon. I'll be looking forward to your stories. All of them."

The man walked away, going down the steps to the crowd. Lucas was glad he left. "What an arrogant pig," he said to Marcus. "There's no way I'm writing a story on second-hand hearsay. I'm not even going to bring it up to my editor."

Marcus nodded. "It still could be true. But experience tells me that there is only a little truth behind this, and a lot of unknowns."

Lucas turned to the game. He hoped that the rumor, and so far that's all he could call it, was false. Lucas liked Jonas. If he had a chance to write about him, he hoped it would be something to praise him, not condemn him.

* * *

All the sounds from the stands failed to reach Pete's ears, or at least they did not enter his mind. The opening lineups and the national anthem both started and ended without ever sinking into his consciousness. But in this game, it was for all the wrong reasons.

Usually, his focus on the game was so sharp, any yelling from the crowd or any unwanted chatter from the other team's dugout was filtered out.

Today might be the day of the state championship, but Pete's mind was still in last night. He was not remembering the blows he and his teammates delivered to the Puraton van. That may have started the problems, but the vehicle was almost incidental.

It was the image of Jonas, being handcuffed and being put in the police car, that shaded everything he saw. It was the sound of his own voice, claiming to know nothing about Jonas, that drowned out all other noises.

Natural ability allowed Pete to throw some pitches over the plate, even under duress. But in the first inning, even the strikes did not wind up where they were supposed to be. A fastball meant to be at the knees floated stomach high for an easy hit. A slider on the inside corner was out over the plate and slapped for a double.

Pete was not sure if anyone other than Andy noticed the difference, and he did not care. Even a state title game seemed hollow after watching his mentor being arrested for a crime he did not commit. Jonas was probably sitting in a jail cell right now because Pete had run away from his responsibility.

He knew his teammates felt the same way. Mostly, anyway. A few teammates were more afraid of being caught, but that did not occur to Pete. Whether he got away with it or not, he had still betrayed Jonas.

On a pitch that sailed high and wide, allowing a baserunner to move up to third base, Pete had the distracting thought: Why not turn myself in to the police? Maybe he should wait until after the game, but he should do it. Own up to what he did and end the charade.

But by the time the ball was thrown back to him, Pete already had two answers for that, one more legitimate than the other. The first, the one that would have been harder to justify, was he did not want to take down the rest of his teammates with him. If he confessed, it would lead to everyone being caught.

But the second reason, the reason that kept Pete moving at all, was Jonas chose not to report him. He had the chance last night to tell the police who had really damaged the van. Presumably, he had the opportunity ever since then. Jonas, apparently, felt it was not worth it to turn in Pete or anyone else.

That did not make sense to Pete, and he was too upset and distracted to think through any of it.

Andy gave Pete the signal for a pitch, but he could not recognize it. He waved Andy out to the mound for a quick conference. Pete stayed on top of the pitching rubber, and Andy stopped at the base of the mound. With their difference in heights, it would have looked comical if not for all the stress they faced.

"What's that signal?" Pete asked through his glove.

"Slider," Andy answered through his catcher's mitt.

"Slider is three fingers. You gave me all five. That's nothing."

Andy shook his head. "Sorry. My mind's all out of blown up."

Pete nodded, ignoring the mashed-up cliches. Andy's distraction was much like his own.

"Let's just get through this," Andy said. "I hate it as much as you do, but there will be more games after this one."

As Andy walked back to the plate, Pete considered those words. He could hardly imagine his brother talking about the state championship game like that.

He also believed Andy was wrong. There was no way he hated this as much as Pete did.

* * *

Puraton was already winning the game 5-0. Ted was warming up in the bullpen to replace an ineffective Pete.

It was now the bottom of the second inning, and James was leading off for Central. But all the game strategy, if there was any strategy left that could help his team recover, was distant from James's distracted mind.

James usually wanted to keep the crowd out of his mind during the game. Now he was looking all around the field as he stood in the on-deck circle. James knew he should focus on the pitcher's warmup throws and try to get his timing for his swings. But he could not pull his eyes away from the people sitting on the hill and in the bleachers.

Were there any policemen here? Would they come onto the field during the game and arrest him? Would they arrest his brother and all his teammates?

He had not spotted anyone, and he did not recall any police or security during the previous days of the tournament. But James could not be sure that, before the day was over, he would not be escorted to jail in front of everybody.

When he was fielding at third base, James even tried to listen for any comments in the crowd about the van. He thought a few Puraton fans were talking about the damage he and his teammates had caused. But it did not sound like anyone was connecting Central to the crime. He also did not hear Jonas's name mentioned, for whatever that was worth.

The pitcher finished his warmups and James snapped out of his thoughts. He walked to the plate, but more out of muscle memory than having any interest in trying to hit off of Puraton's top pitcher.

No one had talked to anyone in authority, James thought to himself. That was obvious. Neither he nor John ever said a word to their mother, who only observed that they came home late last night. She seemed to think the team had celebrated clinching a spot in the Mid-Atlantics at a fast-food restaurant. She did not even give them a hard time about missing curfew.

James never saw the first pitch. "Strike one," the umpire said.

He again resettled himself in the batter's box. His teammates would not have told anyone either, not their parents, the coaches or the police. What happened with Nate and Maggie spread through the town like wildfire, and that involved only one player, not the whole team. If anyone had whispered a word, something would have come of it by now.

"Strike two," the umpire called after another pitch that escaped James's notice.

What about Jules? Had he been arrested? If so, he had not said anything to the police about the rest of the team, apparently. But what if he was in custody and decided to tell everything later? What if there had been a Puraton fan there late last night who no one saw, and would report all the Central players after the game?

"Strike three, the batter's out," the umpire called, making the motion for a strikeout looking.

James turned back to the dugout, glad to be out of the view of the crowd again.

* * *

Everything after the game was a blur to Coach Deem. Not in the sense that everything happened too fast, but because everything seemed so unclear.

How could Central play like this in a game this important? The question kept going back and forth through his mind during the postgame ceremonies. Puraton received their gold medals and trophy after Central received its silver medals and smaller trophy. One of the Armed Services officials announced the dates for the Mid-Atlantic Regional coming up in Lincoln. But Coach Deem was only half paying attention. The status of his team fell from inspiring to disturbing in one day.

First, he still did not understand what was going on with Jules. He pushed that out of his thoughts during the game, but when there was still no sign of him or his parents after the contest, he became concerned. Coach Deem decided to make some phone calls the next morning.

But even apart from Jules' vanishing act, the performance of his team had been poor. It was true Puraton was good enough to make other solid teams look bad, but Central had looked uninterested several times. There had been too many errors and too many late swings on pitches that were not that fast. That's how a team can lose 9-0. Coach Deem had seen players go through funks like that before, but never the whole team at once. It could not have happened at a worse time, the state championship. That opportunity was something even the youngest players may never get again.

Maybe the team was burned out. Most Armed Services baseball seasons don't last this long. Burn out could happen to a pitching staff used to three or four games a week when faced with five games in five days. Or the boys had decided to celebrate a night early. Once they found out they had clinched one of the two spots in Mid-Atlantics, the players may have stayed out late to party. That would at least explained all the bleary eyes during this morning game.

When Lucas and Marcus interviewed him after the ceremonies, Coach Deem shared that last reason to explain why Central played far below its skill level. He did not say anything about a party, but that knowing they were going to Mid-Atlantics may have affected their concentration. Coach Deem was not lying, just giving the best explanation he knew. He spoke well of Puraton also, not wanting to sound like his team's poor play alone gave away the state title. Puraton had earned it. There was no reason to give them any bulletin-board material, if anyone still used bulletin boards, in case they played each other again in Lincoln.

It was after those interviews were over that Coach Deem finally talked to his team. He chose not to dress them down for their poor play. Something sapped them of their energy, and he would rather speak to them about regaining their focus after they got away from the field for a day or two. There was time before they travelled to Virginia.

Besides, two months ago he had not even considered making it this far. Coach Deem could not be too angry. It was also possible, though he hated to admit it, Central was now reaching a point where the talent level of the opposition was too good for them. He guessed they would find out for sure once they took the field at Mid-Atlantics.

As Coach Deem gathered the team around him, he took one more quick glance at the fans who had stayed after the game. Among the parents, girlfriends and other spectators, he never spotted Jules or his family. He spoke to the team, reminding them more significant opportunities were ahead.

* * *

Andy pulled the car over into a restaurant parking lot in Womelsdorf. They weren't even back in Lebanon County yet. Pete would have preferred if his brother had driven them straight home. Andy must have something to say, something he did not want anyone else to hear and might distract him from the road.

"Man, you're not stewing over the game," Andy said after putting the car in park, leaving the engine and air conditioning running. "What else would you have done last night? What else should any of us have done?"

For the first time since they pulled away from Falcon Field, Pete turned away from the window and to his brother. "Not damage the van?"

Andy tilted his head as if this was the first time that occurred to him. Pete almost asked if it was, but let it go.

"All right," his brother answered. "But once that happened, what else were we supposed to do? The police let us go. They didn't come back to today's game, so I think we're safe."

"But for all the wrong reasons," Pete said. "Jonas had nothing to do with it, and he was the only person who was arrested." He paused, looked away again, not wanting Andy to see his tears two days in a row. "Did you find anything about him in the news?"

"I checked on my phone before we left the field. I found nothing, though somehow word got out because people were talking about it after the game. They were saying all sorts of lies about Jonas. And Mr. Antes was smiling while smoking his cigar listening to them. Look, I'm not saying we did the right thing. What I am saying is that we still have a chance to make something of ourselves, and of this season. And you still have your scholarship."

Pete shook his head. "The games, the season, the scholarship, none of it seems very important right now."

"It was a tough night to recover from," Andy said. "We all played like it. And, whether we like it or not, Puraton is a good team that could have beaten us even if we're playing our best. But we still could get our heads back on straight and play well at Mid-Atlantics."

"Virginia is the last place I feel like going now," Pete said. "We should have stayed. We should have admitted what we did."

"Jonas told the police he did it," Andy argued. "They probably won't even call us in as witnesses."

"And you think there is no problem with that?"

"Of course not! But it's the best we can do with what we've got now. We were given a second chance, so we may as well take advantage of it."

"But it's not about us," Pete said. "It's about Jonas. We knew him. He was teaching us good things. He was helping us to achieve more. We knew he was making us think about things differently. But the police only saw a stranger next to a bashed-in van. Mr. Antes only sees someone he resents. We should have stood up for him."

"You need more rest," Andy said. He put the car back in drive. "Relax until Mid-Atlantics. No late-night calls to your girlfriend, no agonizing over what's already happened. We get a win or two next week, and we will all feel better."

Andy drove them the rest of the way home, but Pete knew he would not find any rest for a long time. A man who was his friend, but for whom he had never done anything, would probably wind up in jail in Pete's place. And Jonas had allowed it happen. Why would he do that?

Part V

The Ultimate Goal

Chapter 43

"I hate traffic circles," Lucas said to no one. Again, he was alone in his car. He was driving to another Armed Services baseball tournament. But this drive took him through two traffic circles in Virginia, and both times, Lucas missed his exit the first time around the spiral.

There were traffic circles in Pennsylvania, too, but Lucas knew how to avoid them. This trip to Lincoln for the Mid-Atlantic Regional was new territory for him. He spun three-hundred sixty degrees and still was not sure which road to take until his third time through.

The drive itself was not that long, clocking in a little under two hours. This time, Lucas would be staying at a motel a few minutes from Firefighter's Park. For that, he was grateful. But making this drive down Route 15 was taking on an otherworldly effect.

Maybe that had more to do with the Central team he would be covering for at least a few more days. When the Armed Services baseball season started, Lucas did not expect to still have a team playing this deep into the season. He also did not expect that his bosses would approve of a trip to another state if a team lasted this long. But subscribers emailed and commented with good feedback on his game stories and features about Central's run through the postseason. Considering that, both the editors and the accountants agreed it was worth the mileage and the hotel stay.

Lucas found he had no way to guess how long Central would last at the Mid-Atlantic Regional. He knew the records of the other seven teams, but no more than that. There was no way of knowing how good the competition would be until Central took the field against East Hudson, a New York team, later this afternoon.

Except for Puraton. They would be at the Mid-Atlantic Regional as well, and Lucas had already seen that they were every bit as good as their reputation implied. But the way the bracket was organized, Central could not play Puraton any earlier than the third day of the event. That would only happen if Central lasted that long.

And who could tell if the state champions from Delaware, New Jersey, Maryland or Virginia weren't even greater threats than Puraton?

But no matter who Central played, Lucas knew they would be short-handed. When he called Coach Deem for his preview a couple days ago, the coach confirmed that Jules Iscar was no longer associated with the team. The coach did not explain why, even when Lucas gave him the chance to talk off the record. Since Coach Deem was under no legal or moral obligation to do so, Lucas did not press the matter.

Lucas also did not press when Coach Deem declined to comment on Jonas Davis, who had been absent from the state title game. He remembered what Mr. Antes had said on the last day of states, and had heard other rumors about an arrest, but any details around it were vague. Some of what had been whispered at the field and some emails he had received from readers were contradictory. Lucas had asked a couple of questions and tried to find something in a police blotter about an incident, but nothing ever turned up.

He also asked the top crime reporter in his office to keep an eye out for any information, but she never found anything. Jonas thought she never looked that hard. The crime itself happened in Berks County, well outside the newspaper's coverage area, to a van that belonged to a team from far away. Since no one knew where Jonas currently lived, it was possible the accused criminal was not from the coverage area either. The crime writer seemed more concerned with an investigation into the Lavernon fire from a month ago, meant to find out if that blaze had been arson or not.

Even so, when he told the crime reporter the details about Jonas, she said he sounded like a man who could be arrested for fraud. Lucas did not mention food appearing out of nowhere or a severely injured athlete's impossible recovery. In fact, he had made no other comments about Jonas to anyone else who did not attend at the games. In truth, Lucas still was not certain what to make of the man.

But, he had to be a good man, Lucas knew, from the words from Jonas's own mouth the one time he interviewed him. If Jonas told the truth, and there was still no evidence he was lying, the messages he had been giving to the team were positive. He pointed the kids in the right direction, not acting like a cult leader. During that interview, Jonas seemed to be just another man who happened to have intangible qualities of influence. Lucas found himself mesmerized by some of Jonas's teachings.

Even then, how did one explain the...Lucas did not even know the word to use. Tricks? That meant deception. But Jonas showed no other signs of trickery, at least not from what Lucas gathered. During the interview, all Jonas said to explain those mysterious events was they were both things he had learned from his father.

In light of who Jonas's father was, or at least who he claimed his father was, it might be true. It was still tough to explain to those who never knew Jonas's father, but at least everything could start to make sense. So far, though, Lucas had told no one about Jonas's father. Not even Lydia.

Lydia seemed to believe in Jonas, having seen him stand up for those who could do nothing for him or the team. Lydia admired the man for defending Maggie in a situation where Jonas might have gone with the majority and let her be humiliated.

Lucas smiled. The road in front of him happened to stretch out in a smooth straight line, but his calmer driving path was not why his mood lightened. It was the fact he and Lydia had already connected over something other than a love of baseball. They both saw what many people failed to see, that Jonas was a good man, not a deceiver. Some parents and Mr. Antes saw a threat of some kind in Jonas. But they were wrong. Lydia and Lucas could not explain everything that happened around him, but they had the insight to understand that Jonas was a good leader. He got caught in a bad situation back in Salem, and all the facts had not come to light yet.

It was amazing that a discerning woman was interested in a local sportswriter, Lucas thought to himself. But she was interested. There was no question about that anymore. It was frustrating he could not so much as hold her hand or hug her without looking over his shoulder at the same time. With every gesture, he needed to make sure he did not cross a line, a line not set there by Lydia but by his work. He had taken a chance during the state tournament sitting so closely with her, but he burned for more than that. He was happy to find out that Lydia would be watching the Mid-Atlantic Regional too, but it was disheartening to think of being separated when they were away from the games.

But Lydia had given him his address, not far from Firefighters' Field. They might get away with it, he realized. Lydia was a cousin to Nate, not an immediate relative. She held no position with the team and even lived in a different state. His bosses might look the other way if they considered those circumstances. The thought of gambling his job scared Lucas, but he might take that risk, anyway. It felt like Lydia was worth it.

And then he remembered the last thing Jonas said to him before they parted from the interview last week. Marcus was no longer there, and only Lucas heard it. After being lifted by Jonas's words, a mix of great justice and even greater forgiveness, Jonas hit Lucas with words that crushed him. Words that, if he followed them, might keep him from the one whom he wanted most.

* * *

The infield-outfield workout looked the same as any other pregame warmup to the fans in the stands. But James sensed the difference in himself, and saw it in each of his ten teammates.

They did not want to be here, not in Virginia and not at Firefighters' Field. None of them wanted to play baseball today.

It was quite a sad realization for him, considering this was the first day of the Mid-Atlantic regional. Between fielding the grounders that Coach Arim hit towards him, James pondered the irony. They were farther along in the Armed Services baseball playoffs than any Central team before them, but now all the enthusiasm had disappeared.

James had hoped that the days off between the horrible ending at states would give everyone time to refocus and get their desire back. But time did not heal these wounds, or not quickly enough to help Central. No one was even talking anymore about Jonas being arrested, or how they did not stand up for what they knew to be true. The feelings of loss, betrayal, and guilt were still there, but now everyone internalized them. James and John had not even spoken to each other, nor their own mother, about what had happened for days.

It would feel good to take our frustrations out on East Hudson, James thought. But he doubted it Central was up to that challenge. Even an excellent team would struggle when distracted.

Coach Arim dismissed the infielders from the field to the dugout. James set his glove down on the bench and turned toward the field. Firefighters' Park was pleasant, even if James was not in the mood to appreciate it. It was a natural grass and dirt field, like their home field and Falcon Field were, though a little smaller than James expected. The fences made for a tempting target. Maybe jacking one over the fence would lighten everyone's mood.

Probably not, he decided. A home run, even a grand slam, even a win would not change the guilt. If they somehow found a way to win this whole tournament, James would still know in his heart they were all guilty of busting up that van. He was still guilty of leaving Jonas behind to take the fall for it.

James could hear some fans above him, his mother's voice among them. Like the team, several of the families were staying in hotels in Virginia. Others were traveling back and forth from Central when they could make it away from work and to the games. James tried to keep that out of his mind. The last thing he needed was to worry about other people's investment of time, travel and vacation hours into the team.

The truth was, James almost felt nothing right now. Loss, betrayal, guilt, all of it was merging into a malaise. Not that James wanted to be so hollow entering the biggest tournament of the year, but he had no inspiration. Based on the lack of dugout chatter, he was sure his teammates felt the same way.

Martha was right, he realized. When she told him he was arrogant, back at the state tournament, every word was true. The whole Central team had become vain. They all believed they were the best team anywhere, but Puraton crushed them twice. James had even started to think he and his teammates were better people than anyone else. Then they all abandoned Jonas.

The pride of Central had blinded them to how things really were. It had caused them to make so many wrong decisions, and those decisions were having their consequences now. James wanted to hit himself over how stupid he had been. He thought about how disappointed his mother would be if she knew what the team had done. He remembered his late father, and how disapproving he would have been if he had lived to see this. After the coaches and umpires met at home plate to exchange lineup cards, each team's lineup was announced over the loudspeaker. When his name was called, James ran out the baseline and turned back towards the dugout. He saw over a hundred Central fans in the bleachers above it. That was not as many as watched the Region D or state tournaments but the long drive had to be considered. From the edge of his vision, he could tell there were a similar number of East Hudson fans.

The sun shone, but the temperature was mild. There was a gentle breeze and the welcoming sound of a local Armed Services officer reading an announcement, welcoming the crowd to the Mid-Atlantic Tournament. A local school student sung the national anthem. A perfect day for a game.

James still wanted nothing to do with it.

* * *

A week earlier, Coach Deem could scarcely believe a team he coached would be in the Mid-Atlantics. Now, he could hardly accept how much the team looked like it did not belong there.

Already, Pete had walked the first two East Hudson batters on only eight pitches. Coach Arim had gone out to talk with Pete on the mound, hoping to calm the star pitcher. Sure enough, the next pitch was a strike, a strike that the batter hit toward third base.

James fielded the ball, but seemed to forget about the runners. He did not run to third for a force-out, nor did he throw to second to start a double play. Instead, he threw the ball to first, and that throw sailed high and pulled John off of the bag.

East Hudson was the New York state champion. Six of the eight teams here were state champions, so Coach Deem knew every game could be a challenge. To lose two straight games here would be understandable. But the sloppy play was not.

Pete's next pitch was in the dirt, and it bounced away from Andy. All the runners moved up one base, and Central already trailed 1-0.

Coach Deem took a step out of the dugout. "Stay calm," he yelled to his fielders. "Just get an out."

The next batter hit another ground ball to third base. James took a quick glance at the runners, who held their ground for the moment. Then he threw towards first base, but this time the ball bounced fifteen feet before reaching John and caromed into foul territory.

"Come on, James, the base ain't moving over there," Coach Deem said as the two runners came around to score and the batter made it to second base.

That new runner scored later, and Central was down 4-0 by the time they batted in the bottom of the first.

Walking out to the first-base coach's box, Coach Deem still felt that Central was in the game. Firefighter's Field had shallow fences compared to the fields in Ammonville and Salem. If somebody got a hold of a good pitch, this became a good game again.

But his optimism faded. Phil struck out on three pitches. Pete did not strike out as quickly, but was rung up looking on a fastball right down the middle of the plate. John followed with a half-hearted swing that made contact, but only deadened the ball right in front of the plate. The East Hudson catcher fielded the ball and threw to first for the final out.

What had happened to this team? This was deeper than Jules going AWOL, which itself was a situation that still had no resolution. The players were uninterested. Or burdened. Maybe distracted. It all seemed more confusing than it had at the state tournament. When Central played poorly in the state final, they were in their fifth game in five days. Today, they were rested.

Maybe Central had the talent but not the grit to keep playing into August when most teams had finished. They may be burned out, as he had feared.

But even if they were, it was embarrassing to see them play like this in their most prominent tournament so far. It was more humiliating since well over one hundred fans had made the trip down to Virginia for the game. Central appeared to have the same number of supporters as East Hudson in the stands, but the degree of cheering was in the New York team's favor.

The first batter of the second inning walked on five pitches by Pete, and the one that was called a strike looked like a questionable call by the umpire. Somehow, as weakly as Pete had pitched in the state final against Puraton, he pitched worse now. The next batter swung at a pitch out of the strike zone and hit it toward Tom at second base. Coach Deem tried to will the ball into being a double play from the dugout, but the ball hopped between Tom's knees into the outfield.

Pete put the next fastball in the center of the strike zone, but not fast enough. The fly ball did not land until it was well past that shallow fence in left field.

As the East Hudson team congratulated the home-run hitter, Coach Deem checked with Coach Arim on how many pitches Pete had thrown. It was not too many. Pete was not going to get back into his regular groove today. But if Coach Deem took him out now, it would open up some new options.

"Time out, ump," he said, and he ran out to the mound, and pointed to Sam in center field.

"Sorry about this, Pete," Coach Deem said.

"I understand, coach. I think I deserve it," Pete answered.

Usually, Coach Deem would not have wanted to hear those words from his starting pitcher in the second inning. But being down 7-0 already, some straight talk was not so bad.

"Take center field," he told Pete. Then he handed the baseball to Sam. "Do your best."

Sam nodded, though his expression was one of surprise. He did not expect to pitch in the opening round of regionals. No one expected Pete to falter.

But Coach Deem felt like he needed to take the long view. This game was lost. He did not want to waste the arm of Pete or any of his other regular pitchers. And if the team could rebound with a win tomorrow, Pete would be eligible to come back the following day.

And Coach Deem could not believe Pete would pitch like this three times in a row.

* * *

Pete knew he should be more disappointed about how he had pitched. He collapsed into his hotel bed and tried to visualize the pitches he had thrown throughout the game, but little would come to mind.

Even without the images in his head, he knew the facts well enough. He had faced ten batters, and seven had scored. His fastballs were not much faster than his changeups, allowing East Hudson batters to time each pitch perfectly. His curveballs and sliders did not change direction much, so he never deceived an opposing hitter.

There were a few errors in the field, too, which did not help any. But Pete was not about to point fingers at anyone. He knew why everyone had played lousy. He could not feel sorry about the game, because he felt so much worse about what they did to Jonas. Any feelings about sports were washed away by his guilt.

Andy sat in another corner of the hotel room, looking at his phone. His brother should try to sleep by now, with a morning game coming up tomorrow. Pete was in no mood for leadership right now and let Andy continue staring at the screen. His brother was trying to take his mind off everything. Pete couldn't blame him for that.

James slept on the other bed, and John laid on the ground, refusing to sleep next to his brother. Neither of them wanted to be at this tournament either. John had even told Coach Deem that he could not pitch tomorrow's game. Matt would take the mound.

Pete thought back to when the four of them talked together, early in the regular season, about how anxious they all were to win a championship. Now they won their county and region championships, and those medals were worthless because they had led them to betray a friend. Even with the chance to pitch in this tournament, John could not bear to take the mound. Pete understood better than anyone else. He had only barely found the emotional strength to pitch today, and it did not end well.

At this point, Pete was sure that the police would not come looking for them for damaging the Puraton van. But there was still a chance he would be called as a witness in a trial. That would put his scholarship in jeopardy if the real facts of the incident came to light.

Not that Pete could argue with anyone who wanted to revoke the scholarship. He had told Coach Deem he deserved to be pulled out of today's game, and in the same way, he deserved to have the scholarship pulled away from him. Relative to what might have happened to him, that would be a small price to pay. Though the crime he was most likely to be punished for was damaging a van, the offense he was most guilty of was lying about not knowing Jonas.

That guilt kept him from having any conversations with his parents, with whom he had said only a few words to after the loss to East Hudson. He had not spoken to Sal since the incident either but sent a few short texts about the 14-0 final score. If it had only been damaging the van, Pete could have looked his family and friends in the eye. It was stupid, but a van was merely a vehicle. He refused to talk about how he had bailed out on a friend.

He glanced over at Andy, who looked up from his phone for a moment and shrugged. There was nothing to say anymore. All the players already had their conversations in the day or two after Jonas's arrest. Now, they were all dealing with this failure and guilt as individuals. Or they were not dealing with it. Whatever.

For a moment, Pete wondered if he had pitched lousy today to punish himself, to punish his teammates for what they did.

Subconsciously, he may have been trying to lose. Central should not be here, and they had no business going to the national tournament in North Carolina.

He put the thought away. It didn't matter anymore. Tomorrow's losers'-bracket game against Lincoln didn't matter either. He closed his eyes and was relieved when sleep overtook him.

Chapter 44

Lucas nervously tapped his pencil at the cafe's high top table. Caitlin's Cafe was cozy, one of the few coffeehouses in the area to be open this late, though there were a ten or twelve other customers at this late hour. They seemed relaxed. Lucas was anxious on more levels than he cared to think admit.

He was putting his job on the line by agreeing to this coffee date. But when he got the email from Lydia after he finished his story on Central's loss, he could not stop himself from going.

He must have arrived too early, as it seemed an eternity he waited for Lydia. Lucas put the pencil in his pocket, not wanting Lydia to see how worked up he was when she entered. Lucas wondered if it would be easier if she did not show. It had been a while since he had been in a close relationship, and they had all ended badly. Being let down with a no-show would be a softer disappointment.

No, that was not true. Losing Lydia would be crushing, no matter how it happened. He loved her. Lucas was sure. He was ready to express that love any way he could. But words from Jonas echoed in his mind.

Lydia came in the door, and she beamed a smile at Lucas. He stood up, and when she approached, he put his arm around her. She nestled into him and continued to smile, then it flickered away for a moment, only to return.

Neither of them said anything as they approached the barista to get their drinks, then they sat back down at the high rise. Lydia set her purple purse on the table next to her cup.

"I know we have things to talk about," she said in a quiet tone. "But I think you'll want to know what I learned from Nate after the game today."

Lucas loved that Lydia shared his passion for baseball, but he did not expect to get a tip on the team now. "Well, if anyone asks why we're here, it gives me a good cover story."

324

Lydia smiled again. "I guess it does, but I mean it. He told me everything about why the team is struggling, and why Jonas Davis is gone."

"Central is playing bad, or at least looks like they're playing bad, because they are now playing state champions," Lucas said. "Puraton was the best team in Pennsylvania. East Hudson was the best team in New York. They would make many good teams look worse than what they really are."

"There's more to it," Lydia said, pulling a paper out of her purse. "I wrote what Nate told me after he left like you would so I wouldn't forget."

"I probably would have started my voice recorder, if Nate gave me permission to do that."

"It was the best I could do. Please don't use Nate's name if you ever need to publish this."

Lucas nodded, then took the paper and glanced through it. Her handwriting was immaculate, but the message did not make sense. "I'm not following this. What does a Puraton minivan have to do with anything?"

"I scribbled it down, but here's what happened. After the first time we played Puraton, the team was angry about the pitcher who threw so many times near their heads. The guys thought it was on purpose. Then the night before the state final, they saw Puraton left a van in the parking lot. The boys, well, they're testosterone-filled teens who can act before thinking."

Lucas looked at the notes some more and then connected the dots. "They busted up a van belonging to the Puraton team. Did Jonas tell them to do that? Is that why he's gone?"

Lydia shook her head. "No, just the opposite. Nate said Jonas was not there until after they did the damage. Then he arrived, and after that, the police were on the scene. When the boys ran away, Jonas stayed there and took all the blame for the crime. He was arrested, and no one has heard what happened to him since then."

Lucas sipped from his coffee. He was trying to look calm and contemplative in front of Lydia, but inside his mind was racing with confusion. "So, the team is playing bad baseball because they think they don't belong here?"

"In part. I think all the players are also afraid the police will come looking for them. Half of the time, they can't concentrate on the game. The other half, they feel they don't deserve to be here."

"And they're right. At the very least, they should be on probation."

Lydia bit her lip. "I told you because I thought it was the honest thing to do. And because I trust you. Are you going to write a story on this?"

Lucas shook his head. "No. Or, not yet. I believe you, but I would need verification on these facts. And seeing as I haven't been able to find anything on a police blotter for the last few days, I doubt I'll get any evidence soon." He looked over the notes again. "I don't understand this from Jonas's perspective. Why would he take the blame? I could understand appearing in court with the boys, or even being a character witness trying to get a lenient sentence. But taking the guilt upon himself?"

"I know. Jonas is a teacher and mentor to the team, but he did not owe them anything," Lydia said. She exhaled. "It didn't change much, but I'm glad I told you. I feel a little better now."

Lucas was still pondering the new information. "Considering who Jonas's father is, I shouldn't be surprised. His father often did inexplicable things as well."

Lydia titled her head. "You knew his father?"

"I've never spoken with him, but I know who he is. People say he seems to be at every game or was until Jonas appeared. The stories I've heard are all second or third-hand. But he was an officer in the Army a long, long time ago. The way his stories are told, during maneuvers his men one time crossed a lake without a ship. Another time, they scared off an enemy camp of over a thousand soldiers with only a regiment. He tells many stories like this, to anyone who will listen."

"'Tells?'" Lydia echoed. "He's still alive then?"

"Yes, though he's very old. Jonas seems too young to be his son, but I have yet to hear anything contradicting that they are family. As a journalist, I'm paid to be a little suspicious of things.

But at the same time, I have to remember something being unexplained does not make it untrue."

They stopped speaking for a moment, drinking from their cups. Then Lydia stared into Lucas' eyes, and half of his mind urged him to make a move now, while the other half told him to take caution.

"Jonas is a good man," Lydia said.

Oops, I misread that, Lucas thought to himself. But was he said was, "I know. I interviewed him. His words and ideas were inspiring, though they were a little idealistic."

Lydia stretched out her back. She seemed uncomfortable. "Maybe you need to aim for the idealistic to get what you want in life."

Lucas was not sure what she meant, and after an awkward silence, Lydia looked around and reached across the table. Lucas took her hand as she spoke.

"You know I want to be with you." She took her hand away and leaned back. "But, Jonas has changed me. He's made me see some things. Things about me, things that need even more change."

Lucas cut her off with a wave of his hand. "No, I know what you mean. He spoke to me too."

Lydia's eyes widened. "He always covers all the bases, doesn't he? What did he tell you?"

"Well, I'm not sure how I was supposed to take it, but he told me about being patient with you. But he didn't tell me exactly in what way. Maybe he thought we were getting too emotionally involved or if we would rush into..." Lucas remembered there were other people in the cafe and lifted his eyebrows to make his point.

Lydia looked toward the floor. "He used that word? 'Patient'?"

Lucas nodded, and following the advice Jonas had given, waited for Lydia to continue.

She sighed twice. There was a tension Lucas could see. Lydia squeezed her mouth into a straight line as if she was unsure if she should speak at all. Lucas wondered if maybe he should encourage her to let out whatever was bothering her. But before he could, her confession came out.

"I've stolen people's money."

Lucas let the words fade off into the air. There was a shock for a moment, but it passed. He did not expect to hear this, but he also did not expect Lydia to have a perfect past, either. And she had not taken his money, so no ire swelled up in him. He was tempted to ask for more detail, but Jonas's voice whispered in his mind again. Patience. So he waited until Lydia composed herself and continued.

"I'm sorry if I made you feel like I'm someone I'm not," she said after a few awkward moments. "But you mean so much to me, I have to tell you the truth. The whole truth. My company started with the investment of some of my own money, but that wasn't enough. So I got investments from friends, people in my hometown and anyone I could reach. It was hard to find people willing to contribute, so I made some promises. I told them I would give back a percentage of the profits when I started coming out ahead."

Lucas nodded, but he remained silent, listening not only to the words but to the disappointment in Lydia's voice. He realized she was not only sorry for making him feel like she was someone she was not. She was sad she was only now figuring out the same thing.

"I meant to keep the promise when I said it. It was not a big scheme on my part. But early on, I was having quick success. I made bigger sales than I expected. More stores were ordering my clothes and accessories than I ever would have guessed. I would make a profit sooner than I had anticipated. But then I realized, if I gave back to the investors, I'd lose most of the new profit I had made. None of them knew I was already in the black. So I kept it."

Lydia lifted her eyes back to Lucas, and he saw a woman who seemed to expect him to walk out. But he stayed and even reached out to grab her hand again. "We all do things we shouldn't have. I haven't had the courage to tell you any of my mistakes yet. This sounds like something you can correct, anyway. And I'm happy you trust me enough to tell me now."

A smile formed on Lydia's mouth before disappearing again, but she gripped onto Lucas' hand. "I love you. But it was Jonas who called me out on what I've done. That man seems to see everything in everyone's soul. He was right. I'm a thief. I said I was sorry to him, and to you, and I will have to say it to all my investors when I pay them back what I owe."

"That's the right thing to do."

"But there's more, and it breaks my heart," Lydia said, a tear coming down her right cheek. "I didn't keep the money out of greed. I was determined I was going to succeed young. I wouldn't be the successful business person who worked in obscurity for forty years and then made it big. I would make a name for myself while I'm still in my twenties. I was impatient. I kept the money because it let me grow my business now. I wasn't willing to take the time to succeed honestly."

Lucas reached across and dried the tear from her face. "You'll give the money back. Sometimes, we all have to learn to be patient. And you'll still be a successful businesswoman."

"I am learning I need to be patient. But it's not just with money. It's with you."

That stopped Lucas' thoughts more than Lydia's confession had. Was she breaking it off with him?

"You said Jonas told you to be patient with me. I don't think he meant listening to me pour my guts out here. I've been impatient in my past relationships. Emotionally, physically, everything. I dove in too strong. And then, they always end."

This time Lucas did not want to speak, but he had to be open with her. He owed it to Lydia. "It's been a while, but, yeah. I was 'impatient' in the past."

"I don't want us to end that way," Lydia said. "So, promise me this: stay away for now. I need to fix the mess I've made with the investors. Not fix it, but make it right. And I have to start now."

Lucas nodded, understanding but not accepting. "But after this tournament, I'll be back in Pennsylvania..."

"I realize that. It's part of the price we will have to pay for being patient. But I have extra work to do here, and I need to do it myself. I've decided giving the money I owe back isn't enough.

That's only fixing a problem. I'll give each investor four times the amount I owe them. That will be as close as I can get to making it right."

Lucas nodded. "I am so proud of you. And I love you."

"And that is why I hate having to ask you to make this promise. Stay away until I'm ready. Keep away until I have paid all my debts. It will take time."

That hurt, but Lucas understood. "I promise, I won't come back until you've made amends with all your investors."

"And also, promise me when we are together again, we will do everything we can to be...patient." She returned the lifting eyebrow gesture Lucas had made earlier.

That one really hurt. But patience with Lydia would be better than impatience with anyone else.

"I promise to be...as patient as I can."

Lydia smiled, then stood. Lucas rose next to her. She put her arms around him, then nestled within his arms. She whispered, "I think one day, we will both be happy over everything we decided tonight. But for now, this is all I can give you." She moved her mouth to his, kissed him, and then returned to whispering, "Farewell."

They let each other go, and Lucas watched her walk away, a mix of disappointment, loneliness, hope, and excitement all fighting within him.

Chapter 45

From the moment Maggie had heard Central lost its opener at the Mid-Atlantic Regionals, she knew she should be there for this game. It might be the last game, and she could not bear the thought of being in another state when it happened. Still, Maggie had put off the decision to make the drive down to Lincoln until that morning. She was able to make it to Fireman's Field well before the game, but only by exceeding the speed limit more than usual.

Maggie made sure parents were fine with her taking the long trip. She was on a short leash with them, but to her surprise, they said she could take the older car down for this game only. Her parents had not been harsh with her after she had been caught with Nate, but there were a few lighter punishments. Not being allowed to drive the new car was one of them. The other was that they only allowed her to drive down to Virginia for this one game. If Central won and continued its season, she was not to return or join Martha and Jo in the hotel room they had reserved.

Even after being forgiven, Maggie learned there were consequences for her actions. But by now she knew she was not pregnant. She was grateful for that.

Based on the score of Central's loss to East Hudson, Maggie doubted that there would be another game, anyway. She was not wasting gas because she thought the team was going to win several losers'-bracket games in a row. She was going because she believed they would lose and that this was the end.

Through all the highs of this season, and through all the mess she and Nate had made of it, Maggie was convinced she should be there for the final chapter.

Nate had, in fact, texted her late that night, while she was asleep. He thanked her for guiding him to Jonas when they still had the chance. Nate said he realized that he really had been forgiven and resolved to pursue any woman he fell for in a more traditional manner.

But there was more to the string of dozens of texts she found in the morning. The rumors were true. Jonas had been arrested. But there were other things Nate was confessing. He had damaged a van with a baseball bat, along with all his teammates. Then they all left Jonas there to take the fall for it.

Apparently, Nate also said these things to his cousin, Lydia, but now felt he needed to tell Maggie. Nate may feel forgiven about their tryst, but he and the Central team were mired in guilt over what had happened to Jonas. Maggie never sent a reply. She did not know what to say. She hoped her presence would be as much of a show of support as any words she could offer.

But she worried about Nate. He was fortunate that he was not in jail. If only he, and she, would have listened. If only everyone would have followed Jonas the first time he spoke, they would all have been in better shape.

Somehow, this baseball season kept coming back to a man who was neither a player nor a coach. Jonas was probably in jail now. If the story of this season had been a movie, Maggie wondered if he was the only person in it who would be a hero.

Finding a spot in the lot outside Firefighter's Park, Maggie took a deep breath as she turned off the engine. It had been a long ride, but it was worth it. She was sure she should be here now.

Maggie got out of her car, bought her ticket at the gate and walked down the third-base side of the stadium, behind the bleachers. Before she even had the chance to look for a seat, Martha and Jo appeared.

"You made it!" Martha exclaimed, running up and hugging her. Maggie returned the affection. Even knowing forgiveness, even with time having passed since her terrible mistake, the embrace of her friend was touching.

"Are you all right?" Jo asked.

"Yes," Maggie answered, letting go of Martha's hug. "My parents said I could come down for one game. And Nate told me a lot of things."

"About what?" Martha asked, then lowered her voice. There were people around, fans of both Central and Lincoln.

Maggie was sure that what followed was something they did not want anyone to know. "About trying to destroy a Puraton van?"

Maggie nodded. "Nate texted me about it last night. And that Jonas was arrested for it even though he wasn't involved."

"Then it is true," Jo said, also quietly. "Phil called me last night. I thought he would finally open up to me, like completely. Which he did, but what he opened up about was what happened at the state tournament."

They spoke longer, sharing details about Jonas's disappearance, Jules' vanishing, and Central's losses.

"But I don't understand why no one ever saw a police report, a court date being set up, sentencing, or anything at all," Martha said.

"Well, it was in the middle of Berks County," Maggie said. "It may not have been in our local news."

Jo pulled out her phone. "I'll do a search. We can find out if there's a trial date." her voice trailed off as she typed on her screen.

Both Jo and Martha put their heads down, looking to see what results would appear. Maggie kept looking around. She still had not seen the field and was trying to get a glimpse through the bleachers, but she was standing at the wrong spot to see. But while looking around, she noticed two men she did not recognize walking toward them. They wore simple white shirts, with no team names or any decoration on them. They also dressed in jean shorts and sandals, like what Jonas had worn every day.

The two men came up to the girls, and one said, "What are you doing?"

Jo and Martha were startled, but before anyone replied, the man continued. "Why do you look for those who are free among those who are imprisoned?"

"He is not there," the second man said, gesturing to Jo's phone. "He is here."

As suddenly as they had approached, the two men walked away, toward the concession stand.

"Do you think they know something about Jonas?" Martha asked.

"I have no idea," Maggie said, her eyes following the strangers. "I've never seen them."

Jo ran over to the concession stand, but the men had turned a corner. Jo followed and moved out of Maggie's view, only to return a few seconds later. "They're gone," she said as she walked back. "And I'm not running around after strange men."

Maggie wondered for a moment. The men never mentioned Jonas by name. There was no way of knowing if they were talking about him or someone else. They may have been messing with the minds of a few teen-agers.

Martha shook her head. "Look, let's try to forget about all this. Whatever happened to Jonas, whatever happens to him, we can't do anything about it. The guys may only have this one game left to the season. Let's enjoy the game and cheer for them as loud as we can."

Maggie was not sure if she could switch gears so fast. She wanted a minute to process the odd encounter with the strangers and get beyond that to thoughts about where Jonas may be now. Meanwhile, Martha pulled out two tubes, one red and one blue.

"We thought, since it's Mid-Atlantics and all, that we should do something special for the boys," Martha said. "So we brought some face paint with us. Want any?"

"Um, not my thing," Maggie said. "I never even liked eye-black when we were playing softball."

"We will only be a minute. Then we will sit in the first row right by third base," Jo said.

Martha and Jo walked to the ladies' restroom, and Maggie slowly walked through the bleachers to find her seat. She looked at the field, which was a beautiful sight, but her mind was elsewhere.

Nate had been telling the truth. Jonas had been arrested for a crime he had not committed. No one was doing anything about it, and she did not know what she could do. In the back of her mind, she noticed that the field was just now being prepared for Central's game and that the team was only milling around their dugout. They were not warming up yet. But Maggie could not think about such things. All this was going on while an innocent man was sitting in jail. She assumed, based on how Jonas dressed so plainly, that he could not make bail. They all knew this, Maggie thought, yet everyone was trying to go on with life as usual.

Her heart was much more broken by this than by anything she had done with Nate.

She took a step back, to be between two sets of large bleachers where she hoped no one else would see her. She let the tears out then, unable to control her misery.

Maggie did not know how long she stood there, crying, and the longer she cried, the less she cared if anyone noticed her or not. Usually, a good cry would help her feel better and get more perspective on a situation. But the longer the tears rolled, the worse she felt.

"Why are you weeping?"

She barely made out the voice over her own sobs. Maggie opened her eyes, but the tears still forced her vision out of focus. She turned and saw the image of a man in the light behind the bleachers. "I'm sorry," she said, recovering her poise. "They've taken away the one person who would have made everything right, and I'll ever see him again."

The man stepped forward and spoke again. "Maggie."

This time she heard clearly. She wiped the last tears from her eyes and saw him. The man walked from the light into the shadows of the bleachers around Maggie, yet it seemed as if the light followed him.

"Jonas!" She embraced him, putting her arms around him and burying her head into his chest. "Are you free? I mean, you're not going to go to jail, you can stay with us, right?"

Jonas eased her away, "Don't cling to me yet. I have a lot of work to do for my father today, and you will help me."

"So, you are free? You don't have to go to prison for what happened with the Puraton van?"

"Of course not. But I will explain why later when I can speak with all the boys and you at the same time."

"Is that really you?" came a voice from behind them. Maggie looked past Jonas, still wanting to hug him but respecting his request not to, and saw Martha and Jo walking towards them. They both had half their faces painted in red and the other half in blue. Under less emotional circumstances, Maggie would have thought they looked ridiculous. Now she barely noticed.

Jonas turned towards the other two girls. "Yes, I am me," he said, smiling. "There is much for all of you to learn. Martha and Jo, I will talk with you now, before this game starts." Then he turned back to Maggie. "But you, Maggie, I need you to go around the field and call out to all of Central's players. Tell them I am here. The time to finish my work is coming."

Jonas's smile was infectious. Suddenly, everything was right again. The innocent man was free. That same honest man could provide everyone with the guidance they needed so they would avoid any more mistakes.

And the baseball team? Well, of course, they were going to win now. Right?

She ran out past the bleachers and into the sunlight. She found the closest spot to the field where she figured most Central players would hear her. But she yelled loudly enough, boldly enough, that many of the fans there heard her as well.

"Jonas is back! He is here! Nate, James, John, anyone! Jonas has been set free!"

* * *

The moment Maggie's words reached Pete, he ran off like a shot. He ran away from his teammates and coaches, over to the gate up the left-field line. He exited the field continued toward the bleachers.

Pete heard his coaches and teammates calling after him. It was not the best behavior for a team leader, suddenly running away before the pregame warmups. Pete didn't care. He reached Maggie and locked eyes with her. "Where is he?"

Maggie pointed to the gap between the bleachers. "I spoke with him there."

From where he was standing, Pete could not see between the bleachers. Before he moved again, though, a teammate ran by him so quickly that he did not immediately know who it was.

Whoever it was rushed by and stopped where Maggie was, looking between the bleachers. Then Pete realized it was John.

Pete glanced back to the field. None of his other teammates were following them, nor was anyone coming to stop him and John. He trotted in front of the first set of bleachers and looked down the space between them and the next group of seats. Not hesitating, he walked into the shaded area. No one was there.

"Are you sure about this?" he asked.

Maggie and John walked to Pete. "Jonas found me," Maggie said. "I hugged him. He told me to tell you that he's back."

"Why wouldn't he have told us himself?" John asked.

"He was talking to Jo and Martha," Maggie answered. "I think Jonas came here because he has things to tell us."

Pete kept looking back and forth, glanced out the other end of the walkway between the bleachers, back to the concession stand and ticket booth. He could not find Jonas, nor Jo or Martha.

"Maybe you're just seeing what you want to see." The last word stretched out, as Pete became distracted by something on the ground, behind the bleachers. At first, it looked like a rag, but he realized there were words on it. The folded cloth was a shirt. He picked it up and straightened it to read the print.

"Everybody dies..."

He carried it back over to John and Maggie. Maggie looked confused as did John at first. Then John's eyes widened. "That's the shirt he wore when he was arrested," he said.

John turned and rushed in front of the bleachers, looking through the crowd. "He said this would happen. When we ate with him before the Red Eagle game, he said he would leave, but he also said we would work with him again." John waved Pete and Maggie to him. "I can't find him now, can you?"

Pete looked around Firefighter's Park. There were about one hundred Central fans there, and perhaps twice that number for the host Lincoln team. But among them, he could not spot Jonas.

"I don't see him," Pete said, gripping the shirt. "Not yet. But I know he's here. He is free."

Chapter 46

One of the most exciting times for a baseball team was when a big play led to more big plays. James had seen it and had been a part of it several times. A sliding catch to end one inning led to a double to start the next inning which led to a stolen base, and it was capped with a home run.

That was not exactly what was happening in Central's game against Lincoln, but it felt similar to James. Intangible but real momentum was on his team's side. It did not start with a big play, or a pregame speech, or any of the usual sources.

It started with Maggie's call out to the field, her proclamation that Jonas had returned.

Only Pete and John had dared run away from the pregame warmups to try to find him, and at that time had not seen Jonas. But finding one of Jonas's shirts, along with Maggie's certainty she had seen him, lifted James and most of his teammates.

The most important news was Jonas was now all right. But in learning that, James was also convinced that Central's fortune would change. They were going to win.

Though they did not score in the top of the first, Central did precisely what it needed to do in the bottom of the inning. Sam retired Lincoln's batters in order, but it was his news in the dugout afterward that confirmed everything James believed. After the third batter of the inning struck out, Sam spotted Jonas, in a seat behind home plate.

From the dugout, James could not see that part of the crowd. But after Nate singled and then scored on a hit by Phil, Nate confirmed that Jonas was there.

In the bottom of the second, James ran out to third base and looked at the seats behind home plate. He did not spot Jonas right away, and since he could not allow distractions during game action, he put it out of his mind.

After another one-two-three inning by Sam, James ran into the dugout and grabbed his bat, knowing he would come to the plate in the top of the third. But as he did, he heard Pete say he had seen Jonas. Now he was over their third-base dugout.

James took his place in the on-deck circle. He paused for a moment to measure the pitches the Lincoln hurler threw to Tom, then glanced back to the stands.

No sign of Jonas. But he must be there somewhere. Too many people were finding him.

In the bottom of the third, Central now held a 2-0 lead, thanks to Tom scoring on a wild pitch. Soon after that, Matt said he saw Jonas in the third-base bleachers. Each time a player found Jonas for the first time, the team's enthusiasm increased. That, along with finally hitting and fielding well again, had James and his teammates' spirits soaring.

By the sixth inning, Central held a 6-0 lead over Lincoln. It was by now unthinkable to James that they could lose. Everything felt right. But there was no such thing as too many runs, so he focused on his next at-bat, with the bases loaded and two outs.

The Lincoln pitcher, who was the third to take the mound this afternoon, tried to give James a curveball on the first pitch. James recognized it and saw it would not break down but hang around his mid-section. The ball was right in the middle of the strike zone.

His timing was almost perfect on it, and the ball flew out to deep center field. James did not watch it but ran at top speed to first, thinking to get a double. He could hear the cheering of the Central fans as three of his teammates scored, and he continued running to second. As he did so, James saw the ball was still loose in the outfield.

He took no notice of Coach Arim at third base and decided himself to stretch the hit into a triple. He slid in head-first, comfortably ahead of the tag.

Now the cheers seemed ever louder and Coach Arim gave an encouraging shout and patted James on the back. James nodded and smiled at his coach, then looked in the dugout at his teammates. They were all pointing at him and shouting about how well he had hit the ball. Not that it made James stand out at all. He knew they all had played well today. Jubilation mixed with relief was everywhere. The season was not done yet.

James glanced above the dugout to the bleachers. And there he was. Jonas sat in the first row above the dugout. Maggie, Jo, and Martha were all behind him, and James's mother was next to him. Jonas did not clap, but gave James a nod.

James nodded back. It meant more to him than all the cheers of their history-making season. It was not just approval for playing well. James realized that Jonas had forgiven him for the incident involving the van.

He had forgiven them all.

* * *

Pete already knew Central would win this game two hours ago when he first found Jonas behind the third-base dugout. Everything that happened over the last month was building up to their ultimate goal. Jonas's intervening with the team, his lessons and his encouragement were all leading up to this.

Central was going to win this game and then win any remaining games to take the Mid-Atlantic title. They would go to the Armed Services championship series. They would win that, too.

The back of his mind dwelled on his guilt, though. Jonas might be free for the moment, but he could be out on bail. Even if he had been set free for good, Pete had still denied knowing him. Seeing Jonas in the stands would not resolve that. He needed a face-to-face conversation with him.

But for now, winning this game was the most important issue. Central held a 9-0 lead, and three more outs in the bottom of the seventh would finish it. Pete wanted Sam, who had pitched surprisingly well, to make each of the last three outs fly balls to center field.

Actually, it was not surprising Sam had pitched effectively. Lincoln was a good team, so pitching against them could be a challenge. But everyone was on a high right now. Jonas returned and, presumably, they were all off the hook for what had happened to the Puraton van.

The first batter struck out. Two more outs.

Pete could just about visualize it, celebrating a Mid-Atlantic championship on this field. Jonas would be with them, giving them even more wisdom as they prepared for the national tournament. That would be the kind of story baseball fans would tell and retell for a hundred years.

The next batter hit the ball in the air, and Pete reacted. He took a few steps, and a quick shading of his eyes in the noon sun, to get into position and make the catch for the second out. As he threw the ball back to the infield, he saw Jonas sitting behind home plate. This time Jonas was not looking back at him, but he stood and applauded.

So were Pete's parents, and the parents of the other players. The girls stood, along with the fans who Pete saw in the stands throughout the whole summer, and other supporters who started attending when Central began its playoff run.

All those people and all that support were appreciated, but having Jonas's encouragement lifted Pete's spirits.

The last batter hit a ground ball to Little Jimmy at second base, who threw to first for the out. The game was over and the season would continue.

Pete and his teammates did not jump up and down and pile on top of each other as they did when they won the county or Region D. But their shouting was as intense, and high-fives were just as passionate as they had been then. Central celebrated like a team that had been given a second life.

* * *

Lucas scribbled his shorthand of the last quote Coach Deem gave him, then hit stop on the recorder on his phone. "Congratulations, coach," he said. "I guess we will see you again tomorrow."

"I'm just happy to get a win at this tournament," the coach said, wiping his brow. "You can't imagine what this team has put me through in the last few games."

"Is there a celebration or something going on, coach?" Marcus asked. "The boys got out of here quickly."

Lucas looked over to the dugout. All but one Central player was already gone. They had not been interviewing the coach for long after the victory over Lincoln. Usually, the players were all chatting and laughing after a win, taking their time to pack up their equipment.

"Supposedly, a friend of the team has returned," Coach Deem explained.

"Yeah, that's what people are saying," said Tom, the lone player still on the field. "Jonas was here, or so they say. The other guys all said they saw him in the stands during the game. It's one of those things I'll believe when I see it."

"Well, I was gathering some notes about Mr. Davis," Lucas said. "Is he really here?"

"I haven't seen him yet either," Coach Deem said. "But if he is, you can find him by finding where my players are. Jonas has a magnetic effect on them."

"He was arrested in Pennsylvania, and I've never seen him drive," Tom said. He picked up his equipment bag and walked off the field and hopping up into the stands. "There's no way he's here."

Lucas and Marcus both shook hands with Coach Deem, then followed Tom. The three of them walked up the bleachers and back towards the entrance to the stadium. There was a crowd, mostly of people from Central whom Lucas recognized from attending the games this summer. But out past the closest gathering of people, towards the front gate, Lucas saw Jonas surrounded by ten baseball players.

The pair of sportswriters walked past Tom, who seemed to be shocked to a standstill. Lucas pulled out his notepad and flipped to a series of open pages. Whether Jonas had been let go, found not guilty or was out on bail, he hoped some questions were about to be answered.

It seemed to Lucas as if Jonas was wearing all white, except for a few words on his shirt the light was blurring out. But soon Lucas' ears were telling him what he needed to know.

"Is it true? Are you really free?" one ballplayer said. Lucas thought it was James Thun, but other voices called out to Jonas, all asking the same thing.

Jonas waved his arms to calm everyone. Lucas moved to the side of the crowd, close enough to listen and now at an angle where he had a better view. Jonas called out to everyone.

"Yes, I am free. It is true what you all heard. I was arrested and spent three days in jail. But the case was thrown out. I am free." There was a pause, then he added. "And so are all of you."

From the way Jonas said it, Lucas was not sure if "all of you" meant the players or everyone, but the relief coming from the Central players was palatable. He could also hear someone who was not relieved at this turn of events.

"How can you be here?" a burly voice shouted over the crowd. Mr. Antes pushed his way through the other spectators and even some Central players. But he stopped short of Jonas when he got to the front and stared into the mysterious man's eyes. But Mr. Antes found his voice quickly enough. "You smashed up a van belonging to Puraton."

"I'm going to stop you right there," Jonas said. He reached into his back pocket and pulled out papers that were folded together. "First, I did not smash the van at all. But now, it does not matter who did it."

Jonas put the papers in Mr. Antes hands. Flustered, the team sponsor unfolded them and mumbled. But Lucas did not focus on the team sponsor. He noticed there were scars on Jonas's wrists. Had he been hurt during his time away?

Then Mr. Antes's voice got louder and louder, but also took a tone of surprise. "The van is not the property of the Puraton Armed Services team. It doesn't look like the owner is from Puraton or even from Pennsylvania."

"They were borrowing it?" Andy asked.

Interesting, Lucas thought. But he didn't see how that made any difference. Someone had to be guilty of smashing the van, no matter who owned it.

"Take a closer look at the name of the owner," Jonas said.

Mr. Antes looked at the paper again. "Orson Davis. I don't know who Orson Davis is."

"Unfortunately, no, you don't."

"Your father!" Pete Roc shouted. "The van belonged to your father!"

"Exactly," Jonas said. "You never knew it, but Puraton needed a new vehicle. One my father was able to provide."

"So your father was helping other teams while you were helping us?" Andy Roc asked.

"In different ways than I was helping you, but yes. The police knew Orson Davis owned the van after they checked the license plate. But Davis is a common name, so they did not realize we were related, especially since my father's home address is in North Carolina."

"North Carolina?" Maggie asked. "But he was up in Pennsylvania for so many games."

"True, but that distance is no trouble for him. Anyway, it took three days before everything came to light. Of course, my father knew I did not damage the vehicle, and he did not press any charges."

"Not against anyone?" Mr. Antes questioned. "Even if you didn't do it, shouldn't your father get revenge against whoever the vandals were?"

"For my sake, he will not press charges against those who actually did it."

Mr. Antes crumpled the papers and threw them on the ground and stomped away. Some Central fans cheered. Lucas guessed the team would be searching for a new sponsor next year.

"So, what does all this mean, then?" John asked. "Did you come back here to bring us to our ultimate goal?"

"You still do not understand quite what that will involve. Yes, I will bring you all to your ultimate goal. But it will take patience."

There's that word again, Lucas noticed. But he said nothing.

The players and some more fans crowded around Jonas, but he moved through them. Lucas realized he was walking back to where Tom was still standing.

"I, I didn't think you were really back," Tom said. "I'm sorry."

"You believe now because you have seen me," Jonas said. "In time, many will believe who have not seen me."

"But just because you're free, you didn't have to come back to us," Tom answered. "After what we did, you could have stayed away."

"I could have. But why? My love for you brings me back." Jonas put up his hands, palms facing Tom. Lucas could see his arms as well, and saw the scars on both wrists. "I got these marks when I was arrested in your place. The police accidentally cut me with faulty handcuffs. But they have healed, and the scars are not reminders of what you have done wrong. They are reminders that you have been forgiven."

Lucas felt a tear as he wrote that quote. It was only then he could read the words on the front of Jonas's shirt.

"Let me give you life."

Chapter 47

The sun looked the same as yesterday to James's eyes, but everything else about the morning felt different. Central was still playing, and Jonas had returned. Now James knew he would never have to worry about someone accusing him of busting up that van.

Now he was on the field at Firefighter's Park, warming up with his teammates. Even a half-hour before the game, the crowd was already large. James spotted Jonas in the front row of the stands, sitting next to his mother. But it seemed like everyone who had ever come to a Central game before gathered on the one side of the stadium.

Of course, on the other side, it seemed like anyone who ever came to a Puraton game was there. Puraton's backers outnumbered the Central fans, though not by much.

Well, James thought, we have our audience. All those people who came down from Pennsylvania must care about what the team does. Not to mention the newspapers and various online reporters who were there.

The spotlight did not intimidate James, though in some ways it seemed as bright as the sun. Nor was he scared by Corey Newcomer, the Puraton pitcher who had hit several Central players at states.

Jonas was back.

He would take them to their ultimate goal.

* * *

Usually, Pete was calm when he first took the mound for a baseball game. He had taken the game ball and gotten into his windup for the first pitch so many times now, he rarely had any nerves at all. Even key games were routine for him.

Not today, though. Today, Pete's blood pumped through his veins so hard he felt like he had a transfusion. It was like his heart filled up with a mix of supernatural blood and adrenaline.

Some of that rush came from the fact that Central was still in this tournament, beyond the minimum two games. Some of it was that it was an elimination game in which the season could end. A little of it was that Pete wanted to throw a good game after two straight poor showings.

Most of the increased excitement came from having Jonas back. It would be hard to describe to anyone else, save for his teammates, exactly why this was so important. But knowing what Jonas and Jonas's father had done so they would never be punished for their crime, his presence meant more than a relative's.

Pete saw the first Puraton batter dig into the batter's box. This time would be different, Pete knew.

His first pitch was a fastball on the inside corner for a called strike. The second was a curveball that had a perfect break on it. The batter made contact, but weakly tapped it back to Pete. He snagged it without moving off of the mound and threw to first base for the first out.

Against the second batter, Pete threw a fastball, followed by two straight changeups. This batter also made contact with the last of those pitches, but his timing was off, and he pulled the ball foul. James took two steps into foul ground behind the third-base bag and caught the pop-up for the second out.

The third batter was more discerning than the first two and worked the count to two balls and two strikes. Pete shook off the first two signals from Andy and then threw a slider. The pitch broke down late but hard, and the batter swung over it for a strikeout.

Pete hopped off the mound joyously. In the two other games against Puraton, neither he nor the other pitchers had ever retired the side in order. This game would be different indeed.

* * *

James wanted to get to the plate in the bottom of the first inning. Although he had made a play in the field in the top half of the first, he felt the need to make contact with his bat as soon as possible.

There were two outs already when John was batting, but it turned out John would get on base for free. James saw it coming, a low inside pitch with too much velocity for John to get out of the way. This pitch hit John in the thigh, not like what near the head as had happened so often last week. Still, another hit batter from Puraton's Corey Newcomer had the Central bench and fans grumbling.

Trying to put that and his anxiousness aside, James strode up to the plate. He realized he was too eager to swing and told himself to take the first pitch. He also reminded himself to make sure the ball was not coming for his head.

The first pitch flew high, but outside instead of inside. James guessed Newcomer would want to get an easy strike now and looked for the second pitch to be down the middle.

It was not quite in the middle of the plate, but James identified its speed and placement well and took a smooth swing at it. The ball skipped through the left side of the infield, and James ran to first base. He saw John could not get any farther than second base, but getting that first hit of the game reinforced his confidence. It was as good a swing as he had taken in any of the three games against Puraton.

The next batter, Nate, popped up to end the inning, but James knew Central had narrowed the gap between itself and Puraton. Now there were six more innings to get ahead.

* * *

The game was still scoreless in the third inning, but then Pete had some problems. There was no difficulty with his control, as all his pitches were going exactly where he wanted them. But Puraton was now hitting even some of his best offerings.

When Pete had pitched in the state final, Puraton never needed to hit his best pitches because despair had prevented him from throwing them. Now, he was throwing as well as he could remember, but there were runners on second and third base with two outs.

With the count at one ball and one strike, Andy signaled for a low, inside slider. It was a pitch meant to get the batter to swing at an unhittable pitch, or at worst pull the ball foul. Pete nodded, started his stretch, and threw the ball. It reached the plate as Pete intended, slightly inside but at the right height to tempt the batter into swinging, then breaking downward at the last moment.

The batter swung with a cut that looked more like a golfer's motion than a hitter's. He slammed the ball down the left-field line and well over the fence for a three-run home run.

As the Puraton hitter and runners circled the bases, Pete stared out to where the ball sailed over the wall. He did not make any moves to show frustration and oddly did not feel any. Pete felt more confusion than any other emotion. That was a perfect pitch for the situation. While he could say the fences at Firefighter's Field were shallow, that ball would have been a home run in any park Pete had ever seen.

When he turned back to home plate, Andy was there carrying a new ball back out to him. His brother put the ball in Pete's glove and said, "I don't know what to tell you. That pitch was perfect. I thought he would swing right over it."

As Andy walked back to the plate, Pete thought about what he had said. Perfect. Not literally perfect, Pete decided. A pitch that was perfect would never be hit. But it was the best Pete could have thrown.

He realized who was up next. Corey Newcomer was stepping into the batter's box. Pete had already faced him once earlier in the game and got him to fly out to center field. But now, right after the home run, it would be acceptable in most baseball circles to throw a high, inside pitch. The goal was not necessarily to hit the batter, only to intimidate him a little. It was a way pitchers prevented every hitter from digging in and swinging for the fences, by brushing back the batter after a home run.

This unwritten baseball rule would be a legitimate cover for hitting Newcomer with a high fastball now. Pete had a chance to settle the score with him for the batters who had been hit last week, and for John being plunked today.

Pete glanced behind the Central dugout. Jonas was sitting in the first row above it. He said nothing and made no expression beyond a slight smile. There was no need.

Pete nodded toward Andy, started his windup, and threw a low, outside pitch. To Pete's surprise, Newcomer swung at it and hit a soft ground ball to first base. John scooped it up and stepped on the bag for the final out.

Hitting Newcomer in the head might have been a little more satisfying, Pete thought, but I would have regretted it later.

Newcomer walked straight to mound since he was about to pitch, anyway. "Hey, Pete," he called out. "Nice pitch."

Pete nodded in return.

* * *

James was as confused as he was worried that Central's season might come to an end today.

The whole team was playing better than they had the other two times they had played Puraton. Still, they were losing 5-0 in the bottom of the fourth inning. The three-run home run Puraton hit in the third was followed up with two run-scoring singles in the fourth.

John batted to lead off the fourth for Central. This time he did not get hit by a pitch, but he did draw a walk. Many rallies start with a runner on first and no outs, James thought to himself.

James looked to Coach Arim at third base, but he made no special signal. No bunt, steal or hit and run. Just swing at a good pitch, take anything else. The first pitch was a low changeup for a ball. So was the second.

After checking the signals from Coach Arim, which had not changed, James got an idea. He started out to first base, locking eyes with his brother. Then, moving only his eyes, so he did not give anything away to Puraton, he kept switching his look from his brother to second base.

John blinked twice, just like he used to do when they were young boys thinking of ways to pester their mother. The message had been received.

James did not need to see it to know John took off running on the next pitch. That pitch was again low, but this time as a fastball. It was close enough to the strike zone James could take a solid swing at it, and the ball sailed toward right field.

Running to first, James saw the ball go near the fence. It was not high enough to get over, but he heard the ball hit the wall and bounce back to the right fielder. The fielder grabbed it quickly, but James knew he would make it to second base.

As he made his way to a double, he saw the throw from the outfield sail home. John slid into the plate. From James's point of view, it was a bang-bang play which could have been called either way. But the home-plate umpire spread his arms out in a safe signal. It had been risky and against the coaches' wishes, but the silent hit-and-run call between the brothers had worked.

Nate grounded out to the second baseman, but James made it to third base. Then Little Jimmy flew out to center field, and James was able to tag up and score. Finally, James thought, a little success against these guys.

But even with that success, Puraton was still winning 5-2.

* * *

Pete barely understood how he got into this situation. His fastballs had lost none of their velocity, and his breaking balls had lost none of their bite. Still, the first three Puraton batters made contact, and all got singles to load the bases with no outs.

Central was still down three runs. Pete knew whatever chance they had to come back in this game hung on whether he got out of this inning unscathed or not. And it would be him, seeing as Coach Deem was still sitting on the bench as the next batter came to the plate. There would be no pitching change.

Not wanting to walk in a run, Pete threw a pitch on the inside half of the plate, hoping for a first-pitch strike. He got it, though not the way he wanted, as the batter hit a line drive foul on the left side of the field.

The batter had been way out in front of the pitch, though, so Andy signaled for a high fastball which was what Pete was thinking of, anyway. He fired the ball, up around eye level but over the plate. A tempting target that was too high to hit.

It did not occur to Pete until after the ball flew past his head that he had never seen someone with that degree of bat speed.

The ball bounced into center field, and two runners scored. Puraton was winning 7-2 in the top of the fifth and Pete did not know what he should have done differently. He could not find a mistake, not in this inning and not in the whole game.

Now Coach Deem was walking out on to the field. Andy walked to the mound too and rested his hand on Pete's shoulder. His brother did not say anything. There was no reason to. Andy knew that Pete had done his best.

Coach Deem took the ball. "You did all you could, Pete. Sometimes the other team wins even when you don't make a mistake."

After John came in to pitch, and some of his teammates shuffled positions in the field, Pete walked out to center field. Even though a baseball game was never decided until the final out, he understood this game was done. Pete and all his teammates took better swings than they had in either of the state tournament games against Puraton. Pete's pitches crossed the plate where he wanted them at the speed he wanted them.

Puraton was just better.

Pete got to his spot in the outfield and turned back to face the infield.

Puraton really was better. And there was nothing wrong with that.

* * *

Though James got a third hit in his last at-bat in the sixth inning, he took no solace from how his stats would look in the box score.

It was now the bottom of the seventh and Puraton was winning 8-3. John had given up one run to Puraton after relieving Pete on the mound, and Tom had singled in Sam for Central's last score.

Now Phil batted with two outs and no one on base. In theory, James might bat again if Phil, Pete, and John all got on base first. But James knew that would not happen. Corey Newcomer did not dominate them the way he had at the state tournament, but Central never threatened to take the lead against him.

Phil took a couple of pitches, then hit a high fly ball to left field, which an outfielder caught for the final out.

It struck James that, though he was disappointed, he did not have the sickness in his stomach he had after their loss two days ago in the opening game. He felt none of the pain like he had after losing to Puraton at states.

Maybe it was because the game was closer this time. It was not too competitive, but 8-3 was still better than the other losses. It may have been because they did not make any mistakes. There had been no errors, no wild pitches and no mental breakdowns on the base paths.

But James realized there was something else. After the first loss to Puraton, he had worried about Central's reputation when the score appeared on websites and into newspapers. He had been embarrassed to be on the losing side in front of all those eyes, both watching in the crowd and reading across Pennsylvania.

Now, he did not care about that. Given a choice, James would have made Central win. But having done all they could, Puraton still won. And if every baseball fan or even every person in Pennsylvania and Virginia knew Central could not beat Puraton, so be it.

James was happy to be seen as he and as his team truly were.

Chapter 48

It was a dream, the kind where Pete realized he was asleep, merely living out something in his imagination. He was next to Sal, both of them sitting on the mound at Firefighter's Field. They were the only ones in the stadium.

The image of Sal kissed him. "I'm so happy for you," she said, in a voice that seemed to echo. "You had so much success this summer."

"I suppose I did," Pete said, though his own voice seemed distant. "But I think I see success differently now than I did before."

The stadium and field seemed to disappear. All that remained was Sal. "Show me all you have learned," she said, sounding even more ethereal.

Pete startled awake. He remembered the last thing he did before dozing off was call Sal while he and his teammates were in the van coming back home to Central. Sal already knew Central had lost because she had been following the game online. She spoke words of encouragement to Pete though he had already accepted the loss long before packing his bags and checking out of his hotel room.

He suspected Sal was not too disappointed the season was finished. Summer was almost over, which meant they would soon be back in college. They were both looking forward to being together again. Distance did not cool their affection. And while Pete looked forward to rekindling their love for each other, he also wanted that time to talk face to face with Sal. He needed to tell her all he had learned from Jonas.

He glanced out the window and saw a "Welcome to Pennsylvania" sign and the dusk sky. It would still be a couple of hours before they got home.

Pete turned the other way to see if anyone else was still awake. Mrs. Thun drove the van, but his teammates slept. The emotions of the last month had drained all the players.

But Pete did not notice his snoozing teammates. When he turned, he saw Jonas, sitting next to him and alert, with a broad smile. Pete was certain Jonas had not gotten into the van with him. He had assumed Jonas had been in the other van, driven by Coach Arim, when they left Lincoln.

Pete silently added it to the list of things he could not quite explain and smiled in return.

"Pete, do you love me?" Jonas asked softly.

That was not what Pete expected to hear, and he did not know how best to answer.

"Not the way you love Sal, your parents or your brother," Jonas clarified. "But do you love me?"

"Yes, Jonas, I do," Pete answered.

Jonas smiled and nodded. "Take care of my team," he said.

Pete mulled over that. Jonas could not mean the Central team. Pete would never play for them again. He would be too old by next summer. Unless Jonas meant for him to return as an assistant coach.

After a few minutes of silence, Jonas asked again. "Pete, do you love me?"

"Jonas, you know I do."

"Take care of my team."

He's asking again because he knows I'm confused, Pete thought. Perhaps he wants me to repeat his lessons to my college teammates. That would make sense.

"Pete, do you love me?"

"You know I do, Jonas. Why do you keep asking?"

Jonas rested his hand on Pete's shoulder. "Take care of my team. You have spent your life so far going where you want to go and playing where you want to play. But in the future, you will have to go to places you will not choose, and be treated harshly by those who do not understand. Take courage in these times. Even when you do not see me, I will be with you."

Pete finally got it. Jonas's "team" was not another group of baseball players. It was everyone. "None of this was ever about baseball, was it?" Pete asked.

"What I taught could apply to baseball, or to many other areas of your life, or the lives of your teammates and friends," Jonas said. "But you are right. It was never about baseball. It was about honoring my father and loving each other. There is nothing more important than these two things."

"And the perfect sacrifices you told us about, they were about more than sacrifice bunts? You knew you would make the perfect sacrifice for us when we should have been arrested."

"Now you are gaining more understanding. Remember my words and think about them."

Pete nodded. "Am I to tell others what you have told me?"

"Yes. What I have told you at the baseball fields, you will repeat in many new places you will go."

Pete took a deep breath. "And Sal?"

Jonas smiled again. "Your work will start at college, with her and your other friends there. But in time you and your teammates will spread the message throughout your hometown. Then you will go beyond that into other states, and even into the entire world."

"And that is what you and your father want? For us to tell everyone else about you?"

Jonas put up a finger to stop Pete. "Not only to speak, but also to act. The message is hollow if you only talk but take no action along with it. And there is one action you all must take before this summer is done."

There were no more words. Jonas leaned back into his seat and fell asleep. Pete pondered for a moment. What did he mean? Was Jonas too tired now and waiting to explain after he woke?

Pete gazed out the window again, to think about what Jonas had said the rest of his life was to be like.

Telling Sal or a few of his best friends on his college team about Jonas was one thing. He had built up trust with them, and they would likely give him the benefit of the doubt when Pete described some of the phenomena Jonas had caused. But to tell everyone? It might seem too dull to some people, or too unbelievable to others. But Pete could not deny he was no longer the same person he was back in June, and it was because of Jonas.

How could he not tell others?

Back in June, he repeated to himself. Pete realized how he was looking at the season, at himself, at other people, was so different from the beginning of summer. And that was when he remembered. Something had happened then, during the regular season, and he and all his teammates had missed it. Or at least, they had missed how important it was.

He turned his head back to Jonas, who was suddenly awake again. Jonas winked at him.

And Pete was certain what he must do next.

Chapter 49

Though there was noise throughout the day, it surprised Pete to find out that putting up a house was not as loud an event as he had pictured.

You learn something new every day.

He was learning a lot of new things, like the importance of a foundation and how teamwork can build something permanent. And that a house in the middle of construction looked kind of bland.

But there were more important things Pete learned, and among them was how much a simple act of kindness could be appreciated. Not mere words or a brief gesture, but action was needed. He should have made that connection when Jonas carried the equipment bags, but the season needed to end before he understood.

When Pete and his teammates had arrived at the Help for Homes building site, they received stares from the volunteers gathered there. It was clear many people there recognized them, some from the media coverage Central had during its playoff run. Most knew the players because they were the families of three Lavernon baseball players whose homes had burned down in a fire two months ago.

At the time, the only importance of that fire to Pete was it had changed Central's baseball schedule. Neither he nor his teammates had held any ill will to Lavernon's players, but they had no compassion for them either. Now he saw them in a whole new light. After his last conversation with Jonas, Pete got Andy to help him look up any information they could find on the fire. The five displaced families, three involved with Lavernon baseball and two others, were all living in rooms in an inn from the night of the blaze until now. They had been renting the homes that had burned down, so they had no insurance. But they also were having difficulty finding a new place to go. Help For Homes stepped in, but part of the deal to get a place to stay was the families in need helped construct the houses.

Until the Central players showed up, it looked like only the families would be working alongside a handful of professionals. But now, the foreman said, they might finish up the first day of the effort an hour early with the help of the extra hands.

"What about the other days?" James asked the foreman, who was pleased to find out he had eleven strong boys who intended to be there every day of the build.

But even Pete was surprised when a few minutes later, another car pulled up. Martha, Jo, and Maggie came along to help alongside the players. Apparently, Phil told Jo about the team's plan, and the girls decided on their own to join in.

As he carried some wooden planks to one of the structures, it occurred to Pete none of them would be there now if Central had qualified for nationals. That tournament started today and would go on for five more days. There was no doubt in his mind Jonas had seen all that from the beginning.

They all worked throughout the morning, which was warm but not hot. James worked up quite the sweat, though. Along with John, he had been the first of the players to arrive and had to be told several times to slow down. James was not wearing down, even in the heat as the sun rose higher in the sky. He seemed as enthusiastic over making sure the buckets of nails were in the right place as he was for slapping a base hit up the middle of the infield. But what struck Pete as even more significant was, when a photographer from the local newspaper showed up, James stayed out of any shots.

"I think Jonas wants us to help others and tell people about him," James explained to Pete later. "But I don't know if we need to have publicity for ourselves. I've got to put in an effort for others instead of myself."

"It's good to see you putting those muscles to good use," Pete joked. He hardly believed James was the same person he talked to in the early weeks of the baseball season. Maybe he wasn't. All of them, all eleven baseball players were new men, and the three girls were new women.

Seeing his friends work so hard for others was inspiring and helped lift Pete as he started to tire near noon. But all the good done here made the absence of Jules sting all the more. There had been rumors he had left a note back at Central's baseball field, nailed to the press box, saying, "He was innocent." There were also whispers that there was money also held up by the nail. Some people said it was three thousand dollars.

Well, if there was money left at the field, no doubt Mr. Antes scooped it up.

There were much more disturbing rumors. Jules's family had filed a missing persons report. People said there may have been an accident. Others said something deliberate. No one knew for sure, other than that no one had seen Jules since the night they all turned their backs on Jonas.

Pete worried for Jules, but he would not dwell on him now. Today's work helped these families in front of him now. This was not work as much as it was a lesson.

Pete noticed how Maggie and Nate were working together on the same house, the one in the middle. They talked with each other several times. But the affection they had displayed through the summer was gone. There was no touching and no lingering stares. There was no rudeness or scoffing either. Pete could not read their minds, but he hoped they were friends again, the kind of friends they always should have been.

Jo and Phil, however, were inseparable and were laughing so much in each other's company it was hard to believe they were working at all. Of course, they all were working, and that effort did not go unnoticed.

Pete had lost count of how many times someone told him how impressed they were that so many people from another team had come out to help in the build. Sometimes it was one of the Lavernon players, other times it was one of their relatives, and sometimes it was a Help For Homes staffer. Pete tried to shrug it off, but also mentioned Jonas when the chances came up. He had set them all on this path, after all.

At the stroke of noon, the foreman called for a lunch break. The next moment, Pete heard a familiar voice calling out, "I have food for you back over here!"

John did not even turn around before smiling and saying, "It's Jonas."

Pete, who was fortunate in that the road was closed to traffic, ran across it to Jonas. He opened his arms in a big hug which Jonas returned. After the embrace, Pete turned around and called out to anyone who would listen, "This is him! This is the man who got us here."

The Lavernon players and their families came over, as did the Help For Homes workers. Now James took charge, introducing Jonas to each of other volunteers. Jonas gave each person a bag with a sandwich and some fruit in it. It did not surprise Pete when he saw they were fish sandwiches, nor was he surprised when he saw Jonas brought precisely enough for everyone.

The Lavernon families and the professional builders returned to the building site to eat their lunches. The Central players and the girls ate with Jonas.

"These are only the first steps," Jonas told them as they finished their meal. "But you have done well."

"How many steps will there be?" Martha asked. "How many people are we meant to reach out to?"

"To all who hunger, to all who thirst, to all who are lonely, to all who are sick, poor, or have any needs," Jonas answered.

"Just to be clear, that's a fancy way of saying everyone, right?" Nate asked.

Everyone laughed, but Jonas gave a solemn nod. Pete, and no doubt to everyone else there, realized this was a gigantic task they had been given.

"Here, they are starting to listen," Pete said. "But here we have a connection with these people. We don't live far away, and the families we are helping are baseball families. Eventually, we will have to speak to people who see us as complete outsiders."

"And so far, we haven't told them about any of your...I 'm not sure what to call them," James stammered. "But when someone asked me why we are here, I've told them about your guidance. I haven't told them you knew each play or each game before they happened."

Pete nodded. "I've done the same. I don't know how much to tell everyone right away. I'm certain this new life starting in us could only come from you. But how do we express that to other people, especially ones who never got the chance to see you face-to-face?"

"There will be gentle whispers inside you," Jonas said. "My father and I are reaching out to everyone, but everyone will react to your news in different ways. You will be given discernment. You just need time to build experience."

"A lot of people we talk to won't believe it," Tom said. "I mean, I was there when you came back from jail and didn't believe it."

"Many won't accept you healing someone with just a touch, or creating food out of nowhere," Little Jimmy voiced.

"Others will call it some kind of inspirational, but fictitious, story," said Sam.

"Or even that we're a cult," Jo added.

"Even without all that," Pete said, "even if people don't think we're crazy, they may not agree with your teachings. They wouldn't want to forgive people who abandoned them if they were accused of a crime they did not commit. They may not care about you or your father."

Jonas nodded. "Yes, there will be those who speak only evil of you. Some of your friends and even relatives will turn against you. There will be a cost. But, you all know the truth, don't you?"

Silence, as all the faces turned to Jonas and nodded.

"Then do not be afraid for anything you might lose. What you gain in the end will be worth more. And even when you cannot see me, from now on, I will be with you wherever you go."

* * *

Lucas had debated with his editor, and for the rare occasion, won the argument. He still had not approached anyone about writing a story on Jonas, but he knew the Central players would be at the Help for Homes build today. He intended to write a story on that. The editor agreed it was worth a story, but someone from news or features should write it.

Lucas stood firm. He had to do it. The editor relented, confused about why this particular story was so important to him.

So now he was at the building site, and he saw the players and the girls who had followed the team sitting around Jonas. Just as Lucas had hoped. He had been close enough to listen to the discussion they had been having and now got closer as some of the teenagers walked back to work on the homes. He flipped away from his notes on the building project and turned to his papers that had scribblings from the first few times he spoke with Jonas.

Lucas sat down next to Jonas, who was still talking to Pete.

"Can you tell us, will we all be together?" Pete was asking. Then he pointed to John, who was still there with his brother James. "What about him?"

Jonas answered him. "If John were to work in Lavernon or at the end of the world, or if he were to live forever to tell people about me, it makes no difference to you. Just follow me."

"What about me?" Maggie asked before Lucas could speak. "The people who know me think of me as a girl who got caught with a baseball player on the field. I'm sure a bad reputation will spread about me to people I've never met. How could anyone believe I am your messenger?"

Jonas stood up, walked over to Maggie, and kissed her on the forehead. "Like the others, you will have those who criticize you when you speak up for me. But you and Nate will be able to speak as boldly as the others. Maybe more so. Those who are forgiven much, love much. That is how my followers, my father's followers, are to be known. You must be known by how you love."

That seemed to please Maggie, who kissed Jones on the cheek, said her good-bye, and walked back to a frame of a house on the other side of the road. Pete, John, James, and Matt were the only players who remained. There was silence for a moment, so Lucas finally spoke.

"Jonas, I have more questions for you about everything that's happened, and about who your father is."

"I will be happy to tell you anything you want to know," Jonas said, shifting his gaze to Lucas.

"But before I ask those questions, I'm curious about a couple of other things. Not for the story I'm writing, but for me. Do I have a part to play in spreading your message? Or was this only for the younger people who were with you all summer?"

Jonas laughed. "Lucas, the story you are working on was always part of the plan."

Lucas tilted his head as if shifting his ears would change what Jonas said. "You knew I would write a separate story about you before you came to Central?"

"Not only you. Marcus will write one as well. You two should exchange notes. And stop thinking of it as a newspaper story. When you are done, you will each publish your own books about me, and everything that happened this summer."

"Well, he's a professional writer," Matt said, pointing to Lucas. "But we were here with you so long. I even took notes on things you've taught us so I wouldn't forget them. Shouldn't one of us write the story from our point of view?"

"Or, two of us?" John added.

Jonas nodded. "You two don't realize all the talents you have been given yet, apart from baseball. Use them, including your writing abilities, to spread my words. My words cannot be in the hearts of men and women unless they read or hear them first."

Soon after, John and Matt walked away to get back to helping with the building project, and Pete left with them. Lucas heard Pete agreeing to tell them everything he could remember. Lucas would need to talk to as many of the players and others who interacted with Jonas in the weeks ahead. But the man himself was still in front of him, and there were things only Jonas could say.

"You had one more concern," Jonas said.

"I think you already know what it is. Who it is."

"Do you think I'm standing between you and Lydia?"

"I'm not sure. You said I would write this book to help spread your words. But you also said the people who follow you will suffer losses. We could lose loved ones who won't accept the message."

"That is true, and you will face your own trials. Some of the work ahead of you will be difficult, and you will lose the respect of some of your colleagues." Jonas smiled, blinked, and then somehow smiled even more invitingly. "But as for Lydia, she has already accepted my message. You knew that ever since she told you she would pay back four times what she owed."

Jonas put his hands on Lucas's shoulders. "I have already told you that Marcus, like you, will write books about what happened here. But you will also have another book to write, about what will happen in the years ahead. You will travel and will see what my followers do after I am gone. They will go many places to teach others what I have taught them, and you will write the story of their adventures. And while you are on those travels, yes, you will meet Lydia again. When you do, both your patience and hers will have been worth it."

* * *

James waited through the time in which Lucas interviewed Jonas. He knew he could go back to help with the others, but he felt like he should stay here for now. James could sense Jonas had something to tell him.

As Lucas was leaving, James's mother pulled up in her car. She got out and called to him. "Well, I was going to bring you lunch, but I get the idea that's already been taken care of."

"Just a moment, Mrs. Thun," Jonas said. "I need to speak with you for a moment. I was about to invite your son on a short trip. We would fly out in two days after they no longer need the volunteers here. In truth, it's his decision if he wants to come along with me. But he would be more comfortable if he had your blessing."

"Where?" she asked.

"Yes, where Jonas?" James echoed.

"To the place you've been trying to get to all this time. Your ultimate goal."

Epilogue

The sun was coming up on the horizon when Jonas and James stepped out of the taxi and looked at Paradise Stadium.

"It is more impressive in person," James said, half to himself, half to Jonas.

"Most of the stories you've heard about the Armed Services championship series came from people who have never been here," Jonas said. He guided James to one of the entrances. "That's not to say those people were wrong in everything they said, but there's nothing like actually being here."

It had taken a plane flight to North Carolina and a ride in a taxi to get to the stadium before today's triple-header of games began. James was nervous about the trip at first, realizing he had never gone out of state without either his brother or mother there. But with Jonas by his side the whole time, the fear disappeared.

Jonas walked up to an entryway where two security personnel were waiting. Only then did it occur to James he had no ticket or pass into the stadium, but he assumed Jonas did. Instead, Jonas smiled and nodded to two guards. They returned the smile, and Jonas turned back to James and waved for him to enter.

"Don't worry," one guard said. "Whoever comes with Jonas Davis is allowed entry. No questions asked."

That seemed like lax security, but after everything James had seen in the last month, it made as much sense as anything else. But before entering the stadium, Jonas spoke. "These two men were in Lincoln when I returned to you and your teammates. They were supposed to soften the shock for Maggie, Martha, and Jo."

"I don't think they understood us," the second guard said. "But it all worked out. And it's always a pleasure to work with you, Jonas. Whenever you call on any of us, we will be there."

Jonas grabbed James by the hand and led him inside the stadium. The first thing James did was take a moment to look at the field. The ground crew was still working on it to prepare for the first game of the day, but it seemed more wondrous than any other baseball field he had seen. Maybe it was because James knew the national tournament was being played here. Perhaps the grounds crew had done a better job than others had to prepare the field. For whatever reason, he felt no disappointment about not getting to play on it. Instead, James felt gratitude for being allowed to gaze upon the field itself.

The grass was green, but almost a different shade of green than James had ever seen. That did not make much sense, but there it was, a color he recognized yet knew he had not looked at before today. Gazing at it relaxed him.

Jonas put his hand on James's shoulder. "It seems like you're home, doesn't it?"

James nodded. "It seems peaceful."

"It often is here," Jonas said. "And it is exciting when the game happens here. I've noticed many people who have never been here think it's all one or the other. As if it will be quiet during the game, or will be a noisy place from the first second someone walks in the gate. But those who are here understand soon enough."

James looked around some more. The air itself seemed purer somehow, as if he was breathing in freshly fallen snow.

"I know you wanted to be here as one of the teams in the national tournament," Jonas said. "But the truth was, you could not make it here on your own effort. That is why I brought you here."

"Two months ago, that would have wounded my pride," James said. "But I think I understand it now."

Just then, James noticed two people in their uniforms on the field already, even though there was no one else warming up for the early game. Then James realized they were much too old to be in Armed Services baseball. Wait, those were the uniforms of the Philadelphia and Pittsburgh professional teams.

"Jonas, aren't those the same two players we saw with you at states?"

"Yes. There are many people you will meet here. Some came before you, others will come after you. Some you have already heard great stories about, others were known by few people at all. But many will be here over time."

Jonas pointed up to the top row behind home plate. "But the most important reason I've brought you here was to meet him."

He walked up the steps. James followed Jonas, though at first, he could not see who he was leading him toward. Jonas continued talking. "Someday, your brother and each of your teammates will be brought here as well. So will your mother, and all three of the girls who followed your team through the summer. Many others you know will come."

"Couldn't you have brought us all here at once?" James asked.

"I bring individuals to my father, not groups," Jonas replied.

Once they got to the topmost row, Jonas stood aside for a moment and said, "Father, this is James. He is my friend from Central."

The morning sun appeared over the top of the bleachers in the east, casting light behind Jonas's father. James was nearly blinded it. Still, he could not look away. Though he could not make out the man's face due to the light, he could see the man's outfit.

Jonas's father was not wearing casual clothes, nor was he wearing a baseball uniform. He was in a military outfit. Army, if James guessed correctly. The old man who had been watching their games from a distance, of whom James and his teammates had given little thought, was an officer.

"James," Jonas said, continuing the introductions. "This is my father, General Orson Davis."

General. James was paralyzed, somewhat by fear, somewhat by awe, somewhat by reverence. Thoughts of the championship series, the people he would meet here and the beauty of the field all faded away. He was sure he should say something, but no words would come.

No words were necessary. The general spoke with an aged and powerful voice. When the words reached into James's ears, along with his mind and heart, the awe and reverence for the old man remained. The fear was gone.

This was the happiest moment. This was the most fulfilling time of James's life.

"Well done, James," the general said. "Well done."

Made in the USA
Middletown, DE
03 December 2021

54182683R00205